Also by T. Marie Alexander

KINGSTON CITY LIMITS
The Lost and the Scarred
The Saved and the Sorry
The Worthy and the Willful

STANDALONES
Revelations

BETTER THAN REVENGE

NOTHING Sweeter

T. MARIE ALEXANDER

*To those who have been unjustly hurt and crave vengeance.
I hope you know you are not alone and that you will find someone
accepting of all your scars and wanting to live in your crazy.*

Dear Readers,

This book deals with emotionally difficult topics and includes references to rape, incest, sexual blackmail, multiple personality disorder, and depression. Anyone who believes such content may uspet them is encouraged to consider their well-being before reading.

Prologue

Solaris

6 Years Ago

I stare up at the flames and smile.

Innocent isn't a word I would use to describe me. Not anymore. I tried to listen to my mom and let it go. I tried so hard, but somethings can't be forgiven. And what my family did was one of those things. They went too far this time. I let Mom drag me away once without a word. No more. They're going to wish they never crossed me, because now, they have to deal with the monster they created.

My smile grows as the flames engulfing my aunt's house on all sides seem to grow. The firemen scatter like little ants trying to contain it, but my handiwork burns high, coming out of every window and door. The vivid hues of red, orange, and blue paint the sky in a kaleidoscope of colors I only wish to have created sooner.

Dropping the empty gasoline can and matches to the ground, I plop down and cross my legs. The main door to my aunt's house flies opens and a fireman bursts out with a hysterical Loretta in his arms. She scrambles out of his hold and then proceeds to roll on the cobblestone. She's not even on fire. Just a teeny bit singed.

My grin fades away. It's honestly too bad the firemen showed up when they did. I made sure everyone else was out of the house before sneaking in and dousing the place in gasoline. I want the wench to burn. It's the only true way to make sure she suffers as my mom and I have for the last few months. The only real way to ensure they lose it all as well.

My ears perk up at the sound of even more sirens making their way to the scene. I'm not surprised it took the police this long to make it here. My father's estate is massive. They would have to pass the stables, the main property, and then three other guest homes just to get to Loretta's borrowed plot. Taking the empty plastic gasoline can and matches, I rise from the cool stone ground. They are my sign to leave. As much as I want to see this place burn to the ground, I can't give the police any reason to trace this mess back to me. Mom would be devastated, and I can't bear to put even more on her shoulders.

I scarcely make my way down the hill and to the tunnel Lena and I found a few years ago. A loud boom erupts just as another fire truck crests the hill. I grin up at the smoke one more time before removing the shrubbery from the tunnel and climbing down the ladder.

"Good luck salvaging anything, bitch," I mumble as I skip down the tunnel.

One

Solaris

Present

I tilt my head forward as directed. A blinding flash goes off and my body effortlessly flows into the next pose. My morning has been non-stop lights, cameras, and people shouting at me. First, I had to be on set for a last minute reshoot. Then, I had to be here for a photoshoot. I've been up since three this morning, and I'm dying to crawl into bed and sleep the rest of the day. Mom assured me that today would be over around noon; she didn't want me to miss all of my classes. However, that doesn't look like it's going to be the case.

Taylor was late making it to set this morning. The reshoot was only supposed to take two hours since it was a minor scene, but Taylor complained about angle and his good side after being an hour late. That led tome being late to this photoshoot, and I hate when I'm late.

Another flash goes off.

"And that's a wrap!" the photographer yells. "You did great, darling!"

I roll my eyes and walk off set. As much as I love the brand for this campaign, the photographer has been a pain in my butt. He's been calling me darling and honey and touching me since the first meeting. My mom brought it up once with Candice, but that just led to Candice saying it's normal and not to take it to heart. It's been hard to do when he literally groped my ass this morning outside of makeup and mentioned how much I liked it before. The only before was when he tried and I accidentally kneed him in the balls.

I go over to my mom and she looks me over. "You okay, sweetie?"

I nod. "Yeah. Just tired."

"Here." My mom hands me my phone and I immediately look at the time. Eleven thirty-seven in the morning, meaning it's ten thirty-seven back home. There's no way I'm going to make it all the way back to Alabama before noon. I peek up from my phone to my mom. I point at the time. She narrows her eyes at me and shakes her head. I roll my eyes. Her argument is always the same when it comes to trying to get out of class. This is the life I chose. If I couldn't handle the pressure and lack of sleep, I shouldn't have started this in the first place. In my defense, I didn't know I would become Hollywood's new it girl. I auditioned for a small role in a small film to help my mom out. The pay was decent, and I was tired of watching my mom struggle after what my family did to us. I was so, so wrong. Apparently, everyone in the country wanted to watch a film with the fallen heiress. That's what they started calling me after my father died six years ago. Everywhere I turned there was some meme poking fun at mom and me. Not so much anymore. Now, I'm one of Forbes' wealthiest self-made billionaires under twenty. I personally wouldn't call myself that. It was my name, my family's name, that got me my first role to begin with.

"I really need some sleep, Mom, and besides, it's my birthday. Don't I deserve at least one day off from school?" I bat my eyelashes at her, attempting to sway her.

She purses her lips and shakes her head. "What type of mother would I be if I let you skip the rest of classes? This is your last year of high school. You should be enjoying it."

"I should also be getting eight hours of sleep every night, but I don't." I roll my eyes with a groan. "Please, Mom. I won't even make it back until after lunch. Three hours won't hurt. Besides, I've already missed most of the day, and you didn't have a problem with that."

Mom crosses her arms and stares pointedly at me. "Don't sass me, young lady. The only reason you weren't in school today is because of contractual obligations that you forged my signature on. You wanted this brand partnership. You got it. Now deal with the responsibility."

I cross my arms and drop my eyes from her, watching as everyone else hurries around the set. I have no words. I did want this partnership. I'm always getting photographed in their clothes, bringing them in more business, yet I get nothing. Plus, their leggings are really, really comfortable. A partnership with them meant I didn't have to waste my allowance on new leggings.

I'm just about to apologize to my mom when a hand comes down on my shoulder. I turnaround to see Candice, the woman who hired me for this partnership. She smiles and hands my mom some papers before turning back to me.

"You did amazing, and the campaign looks great. Just remember to upload your content for pre-approval."

I nod. It's the same thing every time I work with a brand. There's always some big campaign they put up on times square billboards, but then there are the smaller things like social media. Video and photo content that I'm in charge of. I like it that way. Not going to lie though, part of me misses the days when I could post a photo or video just for fun and not worry about brands pre-approving it. It was honest and genuine. Sure, I could always go back to that, and simply focus on the acting. That's where my heart belongs, but I would be lying if I said the money from these campaigns isn't great. Movies and shows take months of work. These take barely anything. Besides, after losing everything we had when my father died, it feels amazing not having to worry so much now. The fact that it's my own money and not my family's makes it even better. It makes not getting any sleep worth it. This brand, however, has been a little needier since I'm the face of the new loungewear line.

"Some of these dates and times are going to have to be reworked." My mom's eyes flicker across the pages as she slowly turns them. "Sol does have school, and a few of these times interfere with school activities. We discussed this when you called before about the schedule."

"And I'm perfectly aware of that, Mrs. James, but some of these are mandatory. She cannot skip our new branch opening for homecoming. That's a luxury she no longer has, at least for the next six months. If you wanted her to attend those events, you shouldn't have signed the contract."

My mom's eyes flick to me and I lower my head. I take the papers from her hold and survey the schedule. I was aware of the conflicting dates, but I figured my mom had it handled. She handles everything. All I really must do is look pretty and get photographed. Homecoming and the winter solstice ball, though, I kind of really wanted to attend. Taylor might be my cousin's boyfriend and annoying as all hell, but at least he was willing to take me without expecting too much in return. Not one guy at school even bothered to ask me out, and the one I did approach, made a shit joke about bagging me. He received my back in the next breath, invitation rescinded.

I roll my eyes at the absurdity of my life and go back to examining the requirements. My eyes stop at the interview dated for this Saturday.

A *live* interview.

Shaking my head, I give the schedule back to my mom. The live interview is a no-go. I don't want people asking me questions without me knowing what to expect. The last and only time I did a live interview was at the beginning of my career. Reporters wanted to know how it felt to see my mother go from Chanel and Louis Vuitton to working as a waitress and living in a women's shelter for the first three months after everything happened.

It felt horrible and I let every freaking tabloid know it. Headlines read "Fallen Heiress Angry at the World" for a whole three months. I didn't care, but I could see how all the gossip was affecting my mom. She wasn't bringing home as many tips, and we had to ask a church for help more times than I would like once we finally left the shelter. Once I landed the leading role on my show, the church got every cent and more back.

I've avoided doing live interviews since.

"It's okay, Mom." I tune back into the conversation about me. "I didn't want to go to homecoming anyway."

"Sweetie. . ." she sighs.

"No! Really, it's okay. Besides, who would I go with?" I turn to Candice. "I'll be at all the meet and greets, but I can't do the live interview."

"It's already in the campaign schedule. Canceling so close to air date will cost the station as well as us a pretty penny we don't plan to spend. Sorry, but it stays."

"But—"

"No buts, Solaris. Do what you must to be there. I don't care, but you better be at that studio, or we will consider it a breech in the contract."

"Fine."

Candice smiles at my resolve, and I roll my eyes at her. "Awesome! I'll see you both at the interview on Saturday. Try not to be late. Again."

I watch as Candice storms off with way too much pep in her step after threatening me. She goes over to the coffee table and hands the papers to an intern. I roll my eyes at her back again and turn around to my mom. She has her hands held out with two small pills and a bottle of water.

My therapist has been making me take drugs since that day six years ago. It's not a day I like to remember. Mainly because it caused my mom more distress than it did Loretta. Also, I don't exactly remember what happened. Only what the papers reported and what people have whispered around me.

That night I was so angry. All I truly recall is Lena and I talking crap about her mom and drinking a bottle of expensive vodka before passing out. I've had flashes, but nothing substantial.

I glare at the pills in my mom's hand. I honest to God hate them. Mom and the therapist claim they are supposed to help me, but I always feel so drained after them. Like parts of me are being stripped away.

Mom urges me to take the pills.

You really don't have to take them, you know, the little voice inside my head tells me.

Of course I do. Mom wouldn't have it any other way.

"You know these are for your own good," my mom says as I take the pills. "If they didn't help, I wouldn't make you take them."

Popping the cap on the water, I take a swig and swallow down the capsules. "Happy?"

Mom nods. "The jet should be ready. Head back to Mountain Rose and don't skip the rest of school. Lena will be waiting at the airport to pick you up."

"And why do I have to be at school when Lena obviously isn't there?"

My mom's arms cross and her brow raises at my tone. "Lena isn't my child. You are. And if you want to keep all of this," she motions to our surroundings, "you better very well remember that you are the child, and you listen to me."

Biting down on the inside of my cheek, I refrain from reminding her of my birthday today. Technically, I'm no longer a child. I'm eighteen and have every right to get some sleep if I want.

Instead, I nod. "Sorry, Mom."

She let out a sigh. "I'm going to finish up here. Please don't miss the rest of the day."

I nod again and head over to the makeup station where I dropped my belongings upon arrival. Clara, the girl who did my face today, hands me my stuff. I give her a soft smile and head for the elevator. It opens just as I press the button, and I step around whoever is getting off. However, the person decides to move back in my sight. My head snaps up and my eyes widen at the boy in front of me.

Ohmygod, ohmygod, ohmygod! This is, this is, this is! the voice inside my head screams. I rub at my temples and sigh.

"Um, hi. You're blocking my way," I tell him.

"Maybe it's the other way around." He steps forward. "Maybe you're blocking my way."

I glance over my shoulder at all the girly workout clothes and the makeup station and then back at him. "Unless Aiden West is now modeling women's athleisure wear, I don't think I'm in your way."

"I think I'll leave the modeling to Solaris James. Pretty sure you look better in one of my mother's little sports bras than I do." Aiden grins down at me, crossing his arms and giving me a once over.

He knows your name!

"Hmm, well, if you'll excuse me," my cheeks heating under his assessing gaze, "I'm late for school." I step around him and press the button for the bottom floor.

Aiden turns around and blocks the elevator from closing. "School? Why would an A-list actress be in college?"

College?

Oh! He thinks I'm. . .

"This A-list actress is not. I'm in high school," I inform him, not that it's really any of his concern.

His eyes widen slightly before they drop down my body. He smirks. "I would have never guessed."

"Okay then." I step back and avert my eyes away from him, a little turned off by that comment. "Bye."

When the elevator door finally closes, a grin breaks out over my face. Aiden West knows my freaking name. I smile a little to myself as I exit the elevator and then walk out to my car. My driver, Thompson, opens my door and I stop.

"Miss James," he greets me.

"Hi Thompson. You know I can open my own door, right?" I shift my bag and give the elderly man my full attention. Thompson has been my driver here in New York since I started working here, and every time we meet, it's the same thing.

"Yes, but that's what you pay me for." He holds the door open a little wider.

I shake my head. "Technically, my mom pays you to get me to school on days like today. I don't think she would approve of you inflating my ego."

"No, we certainly don't need your head getting too big for your britches."

I giggle and get in the car. "Thank you."

Thompson rounds the car as I pull out my ear pods and phone. I switch to my reading app and start listening to the last few pages of the literature assignment.

By the time we make it to the jet, I've finished the reading and the homework. Thompson comes toa stop on the runway, and before he has time to come open my door, I do it myself. I turn around and look at him with a grin.

"Told you I could open it myself."

"Touché, Miss James. Have a good flight home."

"Will do."

I take the steps two at a time to the plane's entrance. An attendant at the top smiles and takes a step forward as I enter.

"Your mother informed us that you may be tired. We've prepped the flat for you."

A yawn slips from me at her words. "I can definitely use a nap. Thanks."

I head to the back of the plane where the cabin is located and open the door. The bed looks freshly made and there's a canister next to the bed on the small stand. I go over and plop down just as my phone rings. I roll over on the bed and scream into the pillow. That better not be Candice needing more photos. Pulling my phone from my bag, I glance at the unknown number.

Not Candice.

I answer the phone with hesitation. "Hello?"

"Hi, yes," comes a deep masculine voice, "I'm looking for a Solaris James."

I pull the phone away from my ear and stare at the contact. I'm used to getting random calls. It's sort of expected with my chosen field. However, they are usually women calling for brand deals or crazed fans that immediately start screaming when I answer the phone. Never a man that sounds this levelheaded.

"This is she." I pull the phone back to my ear. "Who am I speaking with?"

"Good morning, Miss James. I'm Nelson Stanley with Stanley and Stanley law firm, and I'm contacting you regarding your father's estate."

"Excuse me?" I sit up on the bed, confused. "My father is dead. You are mistaken."

"Yes, Miss James. I am fully aware of your father's state. As I was saying, I am calling regarding his estate. As you may know, there was no will upon his departure. However, one has now become known. Your father left his entire estate to you, which you can collect as of today."

I shake my head at his words. No. He must be mistaken. There was a will. Loretta was put in charge, and she took everything.

"You're wrong. My father had a will," I tell the man.

"Yes, well, that may be true. However, foul play was involved with that one."

"What do you mean?"

The lawyer inhales. "Unfortunately, someone in our camp falsified documents of several clients. Your father being one. His real and rightful will was discovered this week. You were left everything."

My eyes dart around the room as I try to comprehend what he's telling me, but for the life of me, it's not sinking in. I don't understand how a will can go missing or get falsified and it takes six years to discover that. It makes no sense. Besides, I don't need my father's estate anymore. I don't need nor want to be around those kinds of people anymore. If Loretta wanted my father's estate so badly that she had to put my mom and me out, then she can keep it. I'm Solaris-freaking-James after all. One of the wealthiest self-made billionaires under twenty. I don't need my father's freaking estate. I made my own.

"You know what, Mr. Stanley, my plane is taking off. I'll call you back later."

I hang up before he has time to try to convince me I need the estate or that it's rightfully mine. I don't need it. I don't need that family. I came this far on my own. Yanking the comforter back, I climb underneath and bury my face in the pillow.

I don't need that stupid estate or that fucked up family.

Two

Solaris

A knock on the flat door stirs me from my nap. Sitting up with a yawn, I look around the cramped space. The knock comes again, and I slide from underneath the covers and mosey over to the door. I crack it open to see the attendant standing there with a smile on her face.

"Sorry to wake you, Miss James," She bows her head and her cheeks heat a little. "But we've landed."

"It's okay. I needed to be woken up. My mom would kill me if I skipped school to sleep. I'll be right out."

I go to close the door, but the girl stops me. "Actually," she squeaks out and holds up my school-issued uniform. "Your cousin told me to hand you this."

"Thanks," I take the uniform and close the door.

Swiftly, I change from the leggings and sweatshirt. When I reopen the door, Lena is standing with the attendant, eyes glued to her phone like always. I clear my throat and she peeks up from the device. My presence doesn't hold her attention for long.

Lena comes over to me and shoves her phone in my face. "Can you believe that jerk?"

I glance at the image on her screen to see Taylor holding hands with one of our co-stars. The girl's eyes are wide and glossy, and she has a stupid little grin on her face. Clearly starstruck. If she actually knew Taylor, she wouldn't be looking at him like he was God's gift to her.

"How could he do this to me?" Lena whines.

I take the phone from my cousin's hand and exit the internet. "I told you to stop looking at that stuff. You don't know the reason behind this. It could be innocent."

Don't lie to her. She is literally our only friend.

I ignore the voice. It's not lying. It's protecting. Lena is far too fragile for that jerk. She would break if she knew he'd slept with every newbie and intern on set. I can't have her breaking because of that douche.

"Really?" She takes her phone back from me and puts it away. "You don't think he would cheat on me?"

I take hold of her hand and pull her towards the jet's exit. "Lena, you are perfect. You are pretty and smart and so much fun to be around. Any guy would be a major idiot to cheat on you."

And Taylor is an idiot.

I watch as the words sink into Lena. The transformation is astonishing. If I didn't know how much she actually cared about Taylor, I would think this whole little freakout session was an act. The color flows back into her cheeks. Her eyes brighten. And the scowl that was gracing her face a moment ago, promptly turns into a smile. Her blonde hair even gets a tad bit shinier.

She walks ahead of me down the ramp with much more pep in her step. "You're right. I am fire. He wouldn't cheat on me. Now, let's go before we're even more late. Oh!" She stops in her tracks and slowly turns to me, a guilty grin creeping on her face. "We have to make a teeny tiny pit stop before school. It won't even take that long."

I arch a brow at my cousin, not liking the sudden change in her tone. "Where?"

She ignores my question and walks up to an older man in a black suit standing next to a black town car and I frown. Lena might be the only person from my father's side of the family who still talks to me, but she's just as pretentious as the rest of them. Hell, I'm an actress, and the only time I use a chauffeur is when I need a ride to the airport or I'm riding with Lena.

"Why didn't you just drive the BMW?" I ask Lena as the driver opens the back door. She slides inside and I follow after her.

She shrugs again. "This is nothing. You know that."

Doesn't mean we have to flaunt it. We are perfectly capable of driving ourselves to and from school like normal people. There's no need to tell her that though.

"So where are we stopping?" I turn in my seat to face her. "Lunch will be over soon, and I need to go around and get any assignments I need."

Lena bites her lip and looks at me from her long lashes. "Don't hate me, but I sorta forgot my ID at home."

I'm shaking my head before she finishes her sentence. I don't want to go back there. "No."

"I need my ID in order to get in the school," she stresses. "I won't even take that long, and you can stay in the car."

"Lena, I can't go back there. I don't even want to see it."

"Sol, nothing bad is going to happen. You won't see my mom or your brother or anyone. It's been six years. Eventually, you're gonna have to get over it."

"Get over it!" I shriek before lowering my voice. "Your mom literally dragged me from the house, not even twenty-four hours after my dad passed away. They all watched as if we were nothing but yesterday's trash. Do not tell me to get over it."

Her head drops. "You're right. That was wrong of me. I only meant that you can't let that dictate your life forever. I mean, look at you now. You survived. You're literally Solaris-freaking-James. Everyone wants to be you. Your life is so much better. You're not just some bobble-headed heiress like me."

I sit back in the seat and sigh. Maybe she's right. "You're not a bobble-headed heiress."

She scoffs. "Whatever. That's not what the public or my mom thinks."

"Yeah, well, they both suck."

"True. So can I go get my ID?" She pulls out her phone again.

I let out a long exhale. "Sure, but I'm staying in the car, and please don't take forever."

She gives me a salute. "Scout's honor."

I roll my eyes at her and turn around in my seat. I take in a deep breath and let it out. I can do this. I can go back to the estate. It's not like anyone will even know I'm in the car. I don't have to get out. And I don't have to see anyone. I can certainly do this. No one can make me feel inferior, right?

Damn right! Because you are Solaris-freaking-James.

I rub at my temples. *Shut up!*

Don't tell us to shut up. Maybe you should listen to us.

I groan and lean my head against the window.

"You okay?" Lena questions.

I glance over my shoulder at her and give her a thumbs up. "Just a headache."

"Did your mom give you your meds?"

"Yeah, just waiting for them to kick in."

"Shouldn't they be working by now?"

I frown at Lena. "You want me to be a drained, depressed rat?"

Lena's eyes flick away from me. "No. I . . . They help with the . . . headaches, right?"

I stare at my cousin like she's crazy. She, my mom, and my therapist all get freaking weird when it comes to those stupid little pills. They are antidepressants. A lot of people take them. It's not weird.

"Normally," I finally answer. "Will you wake me when we get to school? I'm still a bit tired."

"Sure."

I lean my head against the cool glass.

They aren't going to get rid of us.

I ignore that and close my eyes.

"I'm awake!" I jerk up right at the sound of a door slamming. Voices catch my attention and I turn around. My eyes widen at the tall, blonde woman standing at the steps of the house in a tailored, black pantsuit. I scoot back against the door as spots paint my vision. My breath comes out faster, and I shake my head.

"Miss James, it's okay," someone says. "She can't see you through the tint. Breathe."

I take in a gulp of air. And then another and another.

"That's it. Just breathe. We won't be here long."

I turn around to the driver and take in another breath. "Thanks."

My eyes roam back over to my aunt. She looks the same as she did the day she dragged me from her house. Tall, confident, assured. Also scowling at Lena. I move across the seat to hear what they are saying, but I'm pretty sure I could guess based on the things Lena has told me about her mom.

"I don't know how I birthed such an idiot." Loretta scowls. "He's making a fool of you. And when you look like one, so does this family. End it, or so help me, you will regret it. And get to school."

"Yes, Mother." Lena's voice is soft and submissive, and I hate witnessing her bright demeanor dim at her mother's words.

Lena rushes past her mom and darts into the house.

Loretta's attention moves to the car, and she comes down the stairs. I drop to the floor behind the passenger front seat just as the window comes down.

"Mrs. James?" the driver asks.

"Make sure my daughter gets to that school. We don't need her making an even bigger fool of this family with her partying. I will be calling the school to make sure she's there in thirty minutes. If she is not, you might as well start looking for another job."

"Yes, Ma'am," the driver answers.

I hear the window rise, but I make no move to get up from the car floor. At least she didn't see me. The door next to me opens and Lena slides in. She goes to close the door, but her mother catches hold of it. She doesn't open it wide enough to see me, but I still try to make myself as small as possible.

"Whose belongings are those?" Loretta points to my things.

My eyes flick to the backpack and bag of clothes I left in the seat. I gulp but don't say a word. I can't. In no universe do I want to know what Loretta will do if she spots me. Lena has mentioned in the past that her mom wants her to have nothing to do with me. She's made threats, but as far as I know, nothing has happened. Rather, Lena hasn't told me if something has happened due to her seeing me. I've seen bruises though. Too many times for my liking. If I was a good cousin, I would tell her I'm not worth the torture. But she's my only friend, and I'm too selfish to let her go.

"They belong to a friend," Lena lies. "She left them in the car last night."

"What friend?" her mother presses.

"It's humiliating. Do I really have to explain it?"

Loretta gives a sharp nod.

"I was with Taylor and the girl he was photographed with last night. I didn't know they were screwing. I thought we were friends. She left her stuff in the car last night after I dropped them off at the hotel."

"Can you get any more ignorant? What the hell did you think they were going to do in a hotel room together? Paint each other's nails? Grow up," Loretta berates her.

Loretta slams the door and Lena turns around in the seat. She drags her seat belt on like a robot and I move back over to my side of the car. A tear slides down Lena's face, but she quickly wipes it away.

"You didn't have to lie for me," I tell her. I could have handled Loretta. For Lena, I could have.

She crosses her legs and tilts her body towards the door, giving me her back. "I didn't. No matter what I would have said, she would have still been upset. She always is."

The car pulls off. "You don't have to put up with her. You can come stay with me."

Lena shakes her head with a scoff. "Not all of us are A-list actors. I have nothing if she takes away my inheritance and allowance. I am nothing without my title."

"You can't honestly believe that. You are so much more than shopping and boys and what that woman wants you to be. Are you forgetting that you are the reason I'm even passing half my classes? You're smart. You can be anything you want."

"Yeah, well, I want this conversation to be over." Lena crosses her arms with a huff, effectively shutting down any more talk of this.

With a sigh, I turn away from her. Lena doesn't say anything the entire ride to the school, and when we do make it there, she gets out without a word to me. I glance up front to the clock and my shoulders drop at the time. I literally only have ten minutes to make my rounds to see what I missed this morning. Grabbing my things, I thank the driver and rush up the stairs and through the doors.

The shiny, red halls of Mountain Rose Academy aren't as empty as I was hoping. No, they are filled with girls leaning against their lockers in uniforms like mine whispering about God knows what. A shriek to my right catches my attention and I turn to see Samantha rushing towards me in her itsy bitsy cheer uniform. For the life of me, I don't know why I put up with her. She's just another rich girl using me to make a name for herself. Sam drags me down the hall to my locker. Ignoring her over-excitement, I open my locker and pull out my books for the remainder of the day.

"I didn't think you were going to show up," Sam squeals. "You have to see him. Talk about gorgeous. He's so much hotter in person."

"New student?" I ask her as I put my bag in the locker.

"Seriously?" she chastises. "Where have you been? No, it's not a student. No student could ever compare to his magnificence. The way he talks with so much passion, those navy trousers . . . I've never seen a man's ass look as good in navy trousers as his does." She swoons and I roll my eyes. "The new literature consultant, Lara. He's here for the poetry portion of the class."

I frown at the nickname. She's been calling me that since the first time we hung out. Honestly, I don't even remember it, but I'm sure I've told her Lara is not my name. Actually, I hate it.

The locker to my left slams, and I turn around to see Lena. "You have any idea about this new lit consultant?"

She shakes her head. "I was with you this morning, remember? Haven't seen him either, but everyone is talking about him."

"How are you two this clueless? And about him of all people?" Samantha shrieks. "C'mon!"

Lena and I look at each other and shrug. I have too much on my plate already to worry about every person that comes into this school and to go detective on them.

"He must be hot," Lena mumbles as she loops her arm through mine.

Samantha's eyes widen as she glares at us both. "Don't insult him like that. Hot? No, no, no. No! He is not hot. He is the most spectacular being that has walked these halls in forever. And his voice . . . We all already have a bet to see which one of us can score him first."

Lena leans around me. "Really? That fast? What's it up to?"

"Seventeen thousand three hundred."

"Wow," Lena exclaims. "He's that hot?"

"Hotter, girl. But you should already know that. You guys want to buy in?"

We shake our heads.

"Oh, come on, Lara. If you buy in, just imagine how much the pot will rise."

I shake my head again. "I get sexualized on a daily basis. I'm not going to put some poor man that probably really needs this job through it. Have fun without me."

I turn away from her without another word, unlooping my arm from Lena's, and head to my missed classes. The girls at this school have some nerve. That poor man . . . Jesus . . . They're going to have him wishing he never signed onto this job.

Rolling my eyes, I forget all about the bet and just how hot everyone thinks this new consultant is. With as many professionals the school brings in, they shouldn't even be surprised at this point. I make my way to my first class of the day with Mrs. Cline. She's more than happy to let me turn in my assignment for the day a little late. My second and third-period classes are just as accommodating as my first. They usually are when it comes to my work. And while I should probably feel bad about the special treatment they offer me, I don't. It's not like I don't do my homework. I still do everything.

Exiting Mrs. Haddlebirt's room, I go next door to the lit class I missed. I knock on the door once. Nothing. The rustling of papers has me knocking again. When I still don't get an answer, I push open the door and walk inside.

"Go back the way you came. You were not invited in," the man's voice booms, echoing off the walls, and I freeze at that voice. I know that voice.

I turn to the back of the room where the whiteboard is located. The new consultant caps his marker and turns to me.

I gasp and the books in my hold scatter to the floor. I make no move to pick them up as I take a step back and another and another. I shake my head at the man in front of me. His curly brown hair is cropped close to his head now, but there's no mistaking those piercing green eyes or the cut above his left eye.

"Solaris," he states my name like he's been saying it every day for the last six years, smooth, enchanting, lyrical. "I was wondering if you would show up."

"What the hell are you doing here?" The words fly out of my mouth before I get a chance to stifle them. There's only one reason he's here in this room writing on the whiteboard. "I mean, yeah, what are you doing here?"

He takes a moment to think about his response, his head tilting to the side just a little. It's a tell I use to know very well. One I refuse to still know. I don't care if he's trying to come up with a lie to my question. Silas should not be here. Not in my class, and most certainly not as a consultant at my school.

"I decided it was time to take a break from music and come home," he lies.

I narrow my eyes at him. If there's one thing I know about Silas O'Conner, it's that music is his life. He wouldn't go on hiatus to come advise a bunch of teenagers on poetry. "To be a poetry consultant? At my school?"

He shrugs and leans against his desk. "Well, I do have a degree in literature and creative writing. If I'm not writing music, I might as well put that degree to use. And Mountain Rose Academy is one of the best schools in the state."

I shake my head. "Tell that lie to someone that doesn't know you. Find something else to do with your time."

He straightens from his desk and walks the aisle until he's standing in front of me, the smell of his woodsy cologne doing something to my head. "No. You are here. So, it's time I come back to where I have always belonged."

My eyes widen at his confession and my breath catches in my throat. Twelve-year-old me would have loved to hear those words leave his lips. As much as I wanted him back then, Silas never once crossed a line that was inappropriate with me. And trust I tried to tempt him on multiple occasions. However, eighteen-year-old me is calling BS. I know Silas, and he has never seen me as something to belong to. Just a nuisance he happily got rid of at the first opportunity.

"Please," I beg Silas. "Choose another school. Your presence alone is already causing a ruckus. The girls have a bet on who's going to sleep with you first."

"I'm aware." He takes a step in my direction, eating up the space between us. "They'll all lose."

I drop my head and avert my eyes from him. "Did Lena know you were coming back to Mountain Rose?"

She better not have and didn't tell me.

"No. Why would I have told anyone I was coming back?" Silas crosses his arms and leans against the closest desk.

I shrug and look over his shoulder to the whiteboard. "Is that the homework for tonight?"

Silas peeks over his shoulder at the words on the board. "Yes."

"Is there anything I missed that I should be aware of?" I steer the conversation in the direction it should have gone in at first. Silas being the poetry consultant might have thrown me off for a moment, but that doesn't change the fact that I still need my work. I still need to pass this class in order to graduate in the spring, and him being here isn't going to change that.

Silas gives me his full attention, one of his brows raising. "You would know the answer to that if you were in class."

My eyes bulge and I take another step back, shocked at his tone. "E-excuse me?"

"You heard me. I'm not going to offer you special treatment just because you're Solaris James. If you want that," Silas stands from the desk and steps over my books, "you'll have to work a little bit harder on softening me up, Sol."

My cheeks burn at the insinuation. It's so unlike Silas, and yet . . . I gulp and step straight up to him, removing any space left between us and ignoring the fluttery feeling in my chest. My eyes drop to his crotch. "You look pretty soft to me."

He chuckles. "The navy's obscuring your vision."

Cringing, I take a step back, my cheeks heating even more. I didn't expect Silas to say that. Clearing my throat, I get back on topic. School. Homework. That's what I need to focus on. "I'm not asking for special treatment. I just want to do my work."

Silas' hand twitches at his side, his eyes flickering across my face. "You know, I've followed your career since that first show you had a guest appearance on. So, tell me, what held your attention today? Filming, modeling, or PR? What was more important than being in school?"

I cross my arms. "I had a photoshoot with a brand I'm partnering with, if you must know. I got here as fast as I could."

"You missed a test over the reading the substitute assigned last week. I'm a bit perplexed about how you managed to forget about that since you were in class that day. At least, you signed in on the paper."

My eyes fall to the floor, and I bite my bottom lip. Yeah, I was in class that day, but I was so tired from filming the end of the show that I mostly just slept. It seems I've been more tired than not lately, and I can't even remember if I told Mom to pencil the test in on my schedule or not. She usually doesn't keep up with school stuff. That's on me. But if I have a test or exam, she does make those a priority.

"Can I just take it now?" I ask him, already anticipating a big NO.

"According to the roster, you missed class three days this week. You can't possibly be prepared to take an exam."

I purse my lips and give him a pointed look, tapping my foot against the wooden floor. No, I don't know what to expect, but I'm sure it's over one of the books on the reading list. I did manage to read the entire required list before school started this year, and I'm certain I could score a passing grade.

"Maybe this is a conversation I should be having with my actual literature teacher instead of the poetry consultant. Where's Mr. Stanford?"

Silas' brow jumps at my not so subtle jab. At the end of the day, he's not the teacher and can't tell me if I can or cannot take the test.

Crossing his arms, he tilts his head. "I'm a bit confused how you're even passing if you don't even pay attention when you are here."

"Meaning?"

"The substitute last week should have informed you that Mr. Stanford was going to be out for an extended period and that a new sub would be taking his place for the next couple of months. I.e. me."

Oh . . .

My eyes drop from his.

Well, damn.

"I've read all the required readings. I can pass the test. Besides, we did a lot of discussing of some of the poems when you were in college, remember?"

"I do remember and since I knew you would be in this class, I got permission to change up the readings. The substitute should have given you the new list as well last week."

My jaw clenches and I rub at my brows, a headache starting to blossom from this conversation. "Just let me take the test. Better yet, start acting like all my other teachers."

"You mean, give you special treatment because you're Solaris James?" He shakes his head. "I think not."

"Try it."

"No," he states again.

"Seriously, Silas. Why are you being a dick?"

"That's no way to talk to your teacher." He straightens, towering over me like another worldly giant. He runs his hands up his pants legs and sighs, his shoulders dropping a bit. "I can't let you make up the exam. The rest of the class has already taken it, and anyone could have filled you in on the questions. It wouldn't be fair. I can, however, offer you makeup credit equivalent to the exam."

"Okay, fine. I'll do whatever," I huff out.

"Meet me on Saturday. Have lunch with me."

My head jerks up to him and I gulp. He can't possibly be . . . He isn't asking me out. "Like a date?"

Silas chuckles again. "Your mind would go there, but no. I signed up to volunteer at the local women's shelter and I could use some help."

My heart stops at the mention of the shelter. I haven't thought about it or even been to it since Mom and I left it. And I have no intention of returning to it. "I can't. I have an interview on Saturday."

Silas' right brow ticks and I do my best to hold back a grin. That used to happen when he was on the verge of going off on someone. I've never actually been on that end, but it's still funny that I have the power to make him that annoyed, even six years later.

"You either be at the shelter on Saturday, or I'm dropping you from this class. Decide which is more important: some stupid interview you probably don't even want to do or graduating. I would hate to make you repeat the twelfth grade. Media would have a field day with that."

I step closer to him and jab a finger in his chest. "Listen here, rockstar, I have contracts. You know what that's like. Work around them."

In one swoop, Silas grabs my hand poking him in the chest and swirls me around. My back slams against his chest, the breath getting knocked out of me. Heat rushes to my cheeks at the feel of his hard chest against my back. He drops his head, and I can feel his warm breath against the side of my face, the mint and cinnamon tantalizing, making a low whimper escape me.

"No," is all he replies with.

"Si." His old nickname slips from my lips.

"Hmmm?"

"I'm not twelve anymore." The admission falls from my lips, and he releases me as quickly. "I mean—"

"I know what you mean," he cuts me off. "And I'm all too aware you are not a kid anymore. I literally watched you grow up on screen. I watched it all. It doesn't change anything. Even if you are eighteen today. Did I forget to mention happy birthday?"

My face burns at my childish admission. For so long, I let myself forget about Silas. I forced my mind to separate him from the rest of my family because he's not truly family. He's not blood related. And he was my best friend. I jerk away from him and bend down to finally retrieve my belongings. He bends down as well and helps me. I don't look at him. I can't. It's way too hard after admitting I still have a crush on him. Twelve-year-old me would have made him see we can work now. I'm not a kid. Eighteen-year-old me knows that is not true.

"Sol, look at me," Silas demands.

When I don't pull my face away from the papers and books at my feet, he captures my chin and forces my face up. His thumb runs across the apple of my cheeks, bringing a heat back to them.

"Sol..."

I grab my belongings and jerk up, knocking his hand away from my skin. "Saturday, I'll do my best to be there." I shift on my feet and turn to the open door.

I hear him release a sigh behind me. "Be there at eight o'clock. This is the only chance I'll give you."

Nodding, I jet from the room. My feet make their way to the girls' restroom before they decide to stop walking. Locking the door behind me, I rest my head on it and let out a deep breath. Silas is here. Silas is the new poetry consultant and substitute. And he's even more gorgeous than he was when he watched Loretta drag me from his room six years ago.

15
marc, acuto

Three

Silas

6 Years Ago

Leaning against the cold stone pillar of my father's house, I bring the cigarette to my lips and inhale. I slowly release the fumes and watch the cloud of smoke as a sudden release floods me. While I have never been a big smoker, my father hates the things. He believes only uncivilized humans need the release of nicotine. At the moment, I'll do just about anything to piss him off.

"Babe, you said your dad was picking us up here at five. It's six, and I'm hungry. Can we please just go already?" the girl whines as she wraps her arms around my middle.

I roll my eyes at her irritating voice, shoving her off me. The only reason she's even here is to be a buffer between me and my father. Without her, I would murder the man in ten seconds flat. Pretty sure my manager would get a kick out of cleaning up that mess.

"Didn't I tell you to stop calling me babe? There's nothing going on between us," I remind her for the umpteenth time.

"But you brought me home. To meet your father."

And I'm starting to think that was the worse of the two evils. "No, I brought you home to keep me from doing something I will regret." I let out another puff. "Now, please, stop talking. Your voice is giving me a headache."

Her brows furrow and she flinches back at my words. "You don't mean that."

The front gate creaking open keeps me from responding to her stupidity. I have told her exactly what this is. If she chooses to believe she is anything other than a warm hole for me to sink into while at school and traveling, then that's on her.

A black Audi with deep tinted windows pulls around the circle drive and stops in front of the fountain. My father steps out just as I exhale another puff of smoke. He's dressed in his typical black suit with a white button down undone at the neck. His hair is gelled back and in place, the complete opposite to my "unruly mess" as he so often likes to call it.

My father stops at the bottom of the steps, and I flick the cigarette butt at his feet. His eyes drop to the discarded butt before moving to the chick at my back. He takes the stairs pain-achingly slow before reaching me and straightening his posture even more. He crosses his arms and stares me down. Well, as much as he can. I'm at least a head taller than him, but he's never let me forget for one second who's in charge.

"I told you to come alone." His eyes examine the girl for a second, disregarding her as useless. "This is a family matter."

I shrug. "Yeah, well, I figured it would go smoother with someone between us."

My father ignores me and turns slightly to my guest as he pulls out his phone and types in something. "It's best if you leave. This is a family affair, and I don't need one of his little groupies witnessing it. A car will pick you up at the gate."

"But—"

"Leave," my father cuts her off.

"Yes, Mayor O'Conner." The girl scampers down the steps and around the circle drive. The gates open for her and that's all the attention I spare before turning back around to my father.

I cross my arms and eye my father up and down. "So, what is the meaning of this? I have classes, and my manager booked a gig for Black Roses I had to pull out of."

My father flips the cuffs of his suit jacket. "I've gotten married, and it's time for you to meet your new sister and mother."

My back stiffens and I narrow my eyes at my father. He did not just say what I think he did. My mom has barely been cold a month and he's already remarried? I mean sure, we're talking about William O'Conner. It wasn't like he was around much when Mom was going through treatment for her cancer, but he at least liked to make it look like he was a loving family man. Getting married not even a month after her passing makes him look like the bigot he really is. William O'Conner doesn't like *anyone* to see him as less than perfection.

"I think I heard you wrong. Did you say 'married?'"

He runs his hands down his blazer and grins. "Yes. You might have heard of the family. The James'."

I pull out another cigarette. Just as I'm about to light it, my father yanks it from between my lips and snaps it in half. I shake my head and stand up straight. Inhaling, I take a step away from the bastard. How dare he disrespect my mother like that? She put up with far too much for him to just act like her death was nothing. Like she was nothing.

"Let me get this right," I start. "You called me home to meet a woman you must have had an affair with not even a month after my mom, your wife, died of cancer? You honestly think I give a damn about the whore you're screwing and her snot nose brat?"

My dad's hand reaches out and before I have time to dodge him, he has a hold on my neck. He shoves me back against the stone pillar and squeezes. I attempt to inhale through his hold, but no air reaches my lungs. My vision goes a bit hazy, but he eases up some. As soon as air enters me, he relatches on.

"Listen here, son," he spits the title like it's the last thing he wants to call me. "You are going to go to this dinner. You are going to smile and tell them all about your music and touring and college. You will be the perfect specimen, because if you don't . . ." His hand tightens around my throat.

I reach up and grasp his fingers, but I make no effort to pry them away from my throat. If I do, I know he will only do worse. Only the worse that doesn't leave a bruise on me. No, he would never leave a bruise on me, not like he left on my mother. She could easily cover it up with makeup. Me, not so much. That doesn't mean William O'Conner doesn't know how to leave his mark behind.

His hand relaxes and he drops it from my neck. "Do we have an understanding?"

My teeth clench together, but I nod, refusing to touch my neck. It shows weakness, and I will not show any to this man.

"Good, get in the car, and I'll tell you everything you need to know on the way over there."

Taking the steps two at a time, I do what he says and climb inside his Audi. I glance around for the girl, but she's gone. Good. I don't need some tagalong seeing how the good Mayor O'Conner really treats his blood.

My father gets in the car and pulls away from his house. It's not until we're well past our gated community and headed towards the country club that the name my father gave me hits me like a wrecking ball. James. James as in the fucking wealthiest family in the south. While I wouldn't call my father hard up for money, he's certainly got nothing on the James'. If memory serves me, they own a bunch of real estate across Alabama and all its borders. Most of the hotels I stay at when I do come home, they own. How the hell did my father manage to marry into that family?

"You going to tell me about these people, or do I need to just assume everything online about them is correct?"

"They're very well off," my father states as if that's a surprise. "We'll be having dinner with Loretta, her brother Gregory, and his family. Loretta has an eleven-year-old daughter named Lena. From what I've seen of the girl, she's a handful. She tends to socialize with her cousin Solaris. They're your typical socialites in training. Gregory's wife seems nice. She's biracial and comes from a humble background. Gregory also has a son close in age to you. Cruise. He's eighteen, I believe. He'll be starting college in the fall."

Humble meaning poor. Dad always calls people from a lower income background humble.

I glance out the window at the winding trees. "Is that all I need to know?"

"Lena and her cousin are big into music. They follow your little band. All you need to do is smile and make them happy. Hell, sing if they request it. Just keep them entertained."

"So, the real reason I'm here is to babysit some spoiled brats."

"No. You're here because Loretta thought it would be a good time for us to meet each other's family. If I could decline,

I would. But seeing as you've made a spectacle of yourself, I couldn't very well hide you away."

I scoff at his statement. He would love nothing more than to hide me away like he did my mom. Too bad for him, I chose the one career that doesn't cater to what the great Mayor O'Conner wants.

My father winds down a long paved road that leads to a stonewall with iron gates. He rolls down his window and says his name into an intercom. Moments later the gates slowly open. There's nothing but wide open greenery before me. The once paved road is now cobblestone. As he drives off, I take in the rest of the property. There's a stable not far from the front gate. It's enclosed by a white picket fence. Three horses graze in the field surrounding the stables. I'm not sure what type of horses they are, but they looked well groomed. There's a jet black one with pink ribbons braided into its mane. It probably belongs to one of the brats. The road keeps going for another mile or so.

We pass a few houses before I turn to my father in confusion. "Is one of those not their house? Those look extravagant."

My father scoffs. "Of course not. What do you take the James' for, peasants? Those are a few of the guest houses. This estate holds six guest houses and the main house. We'll be having dinner in the main house. It's where the family likes to entertain."

Six flipping guest houses. Who the hell needs that many guesthouses?

I sit back and cross my arms. My father drives on for what seems like forever before I finally see a huge mansion with a towering fountain in front of it. I thought the mayor's house I grew up in was outrageous. It has nothing on this. Who the hell do these people think they are? The kings and queens of France? There is no reason any normal person needs a home that looks like it was plucked out of seventeenth century Versailles.

My father rounds the fountain and comes to a stop. The doors to the house open and several maids dressed in black knee length dresses with wide white collars and aprons make their way down the steps. A man in a solid black dress suit makes his way down the steps as well and over to my father's side of the car. He opens the door and bows to my father. My mouth literally falls open. I couldn't stop it even if I wanted to. This family is fucking insane.

"Dinner is waiting for you, Mayor O'Conner. And the family's excited to meet your son."

My father steps out of the vehicle and claps the older man on the shoulder. "Is everyone here?"

The butler's face falls for a second before he composes himself again. "We are still waiting on the girls to make an arrival. They had ballet class after school and have yet to make an appearance, but they know Sir Silas O'Conner is here as well and wouldn't want to miss it."

Sir Silas O'Conner?

That's certainly not something anyone has ever called me before. Releasing my seatbelt, I open the door and get out. I glance over the house and exhale. This is going to be a trying evening.

I slam the car door shut, cutting off whatever my father and the butler are conversing about and make my way up the steps of the house. Hell, this place can't even be called a house. It might as well be the Palace of Versailles. It certainly looks like it. One of the maids hops out of line and rushes up to the double doors and types in a code for me. I step inside the place and my mouth drops for the second time today. Not much surprises me seeing as I didn't grow up "humble," but this place certainly does. It's gorgeous. And if it wasn't for the fact that my father literally made me come here, I probably would admit to liking it. Needless to say, I don't. And I certainly don't like the people standing in front of me in this fucking massive foyer.

A woman in a tailored black suit steps forward with a pinched smile on her face. I glare at her in disdain. This can only be Loretta. She looks exactly like someone that would have an affair with a married man while his wife is fighting for her fucking life. She reaches out a hand to me, but I ignore it and her too. I don't give a flying fuck if she is a James. She helped my father commit the ultimate sin against my mom. I want nothing to do with her or this family.

Someone clears their throat behind me, and I look over my shoulder to see my father with a not so pleased expression gracing his face. He tilts his head to Loretta's still outstretched hand. Turning back around, I force a grin just as fake as her face on mine and take her hand.

"You must be Loretta? My father has told me so much about your family." I make it as obvious as I can that he has said absolutely nothing about her, just what her family can offer him.

"Likewise," Loretta says as her smile finally fades, and she drops her hand when she realizes I'm not going to take it. "My daughter and niece are thrilled to have you in our home. They were supposed to have been home but are running a little behind schedule."

"My son is grateful to be here," my father cuts in before I say anything else to this woman. "Why don't we all go to the dining hall and wait for the girls?"

The pair I take to be Loretta's brother and sister-in-law share a look and turn away from us and head farther into the place. My father places a hand on my shoulder and squeezes. He doesn't say anything though. I know well enough what that means. When this dinner is over and he's not around his new wife, I will pay for the disrespect. Maybe I should be the one making him pay for his, but I can't afford it. It would mean the end of everything I care about, and I'm not letting this bastard take one more thing from me.

A tall blond boy about my height is the only one that stays behind. He looks me over and I do the same to him. His hair is gelled back, every hair in place as opposed to mine. He's wearing navy slacks and a blue short sleeve Ralph Lauren polo shirt with a pair of loafers. This guy is the definition of the all-American preppy bastard if I ever did see one.

"So, you're the singer my sister's so crazy about." He steps forward.

I frown at him. "I tend to have that impression on women."

"I wouldn't exactly call her a woman quite yet but getting there." He reaches out a hand to me. "I'm Cruise."

No shit.

We clap hands. "Figured. Why don't you tell the fam I'll be right there. Restroom."

Cruise nods and beacons one of the maids over. The woman's eyes don't rise from the floor or meet Cruise's and that tells me everything I need to know about this guy. "Yes, sir?"

"Show Silas to a restroom and then to the dining hall."

The maid nods. She doesn't raise her head until Cruise has turned and is out of sight.

"You don't have to show me anywhere." I walk past her. "I'm pretty certain I can make my own way."

"But Mr. James told me—"

"Yeah, well, I don't care about the bastard, and I don't need some maid following me around."

The girl drops her head again, and I feel like crap for taking my anger out on her. She's just doing her job. And I don't want for a second to come off like my father or his new pretentious wife.

Running a hand through my hair, I let out an exhale. "Sorry. I shouldn't have said that to you. You're only doing your job. I just really don't like this family."

"They're great." She tries to defend her employers, but her eyes drop when she says it and she bites the corner of her lip. "Well, I mean, most of them are. Gregory and his wife are the sweetest people I know. They paid for me to go to college this year."

That's a surprise. People with this kind of money usually try to keep it to themselves. Then again, it could be a tax write-off.

"And the missing girls?" I ask about my new, ugh, sister and cousin. "What are they like?"

"Like eleven–year-olds?" Her answer comes out more like a question. "They are good kids. When they are not around Loretta. Lena, your um sister, is very smart. And talented. She's taught herself to play the violin and piano without classes or a teacher. She's impressive. Solaris is, well, she's . . ."

"Nothing nice to say about that one?" I lean against the wall, now intrigued. I can only imagine Solaris to be as cultured as the other, but if this girl has nothing nice to say about her, then . . .

"It's not that. She's sweet. It's just that she's a bit emotional. One moment she's quiet and reserved and meek. And then, within a second, she can become prissy and snarky. Almost like she's two different people. It's confusing is all. But she's still a nice kid."

Confusing, right.

I run my hand through my hair a second time before turning from the maid and looking around the place. "Well, um, I guess I'm going to get out of your hair. If my father asks where I am, just tell him you took me to the restroom, and I never came out."

I don't give her time to object to my plan. There's no way I'm having dinner with him, and that woman now that I know he was having an affair while married to my mom with her. No fucking way. I make my way down a hall with portraits upon portraits of this family plastered on the wall. The images start when the house was first built. There are workers in the background and portions of the mansion are still just beams and foundation. A man dressed in an old timey suit stands with a woman straight out of a Jane Austin novel. There's a little boy with them. I walk along the wall of portraits until I get to the current family residing in James' manor. I take in each of the people: Loretta, Gregory, Lena, Cruise, Gregory's wife, and the girl I take to be Solaris. Everyone except Solaris and her mother looks like the typical American family. Well, typical if the American family are blond hair and blue eyes. Gregory's wife has dark hair, golden eyes, and light ebony skin.

Her skin in the photo is much darker than what I'd just seen in the foyer. Nevertheless, she's beautiful with her high cheek bones.

My eyes drop to the little girl beside the woman. She has long curly hair. Unruly hair my father would call it. And a mischievous grin on her sweetheart face. I shake my head. Trouble. This girl is pure, undiluted trouble.

Snickering from behind me pulls my attention away from the family portrait. I turn around and inch over to the door.

"He's cute, and he asked you to the movies," a little girl squeals.

"But he's the maid's son. My mom would never let us be friends."

I turn the knob on the door and peek inside. The two girls from the photo behind me are sitting on the floor in front of a giant bathtub with a bottle of Jack and nail polish. The door squeaks, and the girls' heads snap in my direction. The blonde one squeals and hops up from the floor.

"Oh my God!" She reaches down and pulls the dark haired one up before rushing over to the door and snatching it out of my hold. "Oh my God! You're Silas O'Conner!"

I take a step back from the shrieking girl. "Yeah. And shouldn't you both be in the dining hall instead of drinking Jack by a tub?"

Solaris rolls her eyes. "Shouldn't you be there too?"

I arch a brow at the kid and refrain from smirking at her smart mouth. She's got balls; that's for sure. Crossing my arms, I lean against the door frame. "I don't think you're quite old enough to be talking back, missy."

She crosses her arms and stares me down. "And I think you're too old to be picking on girls in the restroom."

All amusement falls from my face at her remark. Truthfully, I am too old to be standing here. Far too old to be entertained by a couple of kids. I turn to leave the girls—they're not my problem anyway—but am stopped by a hand on my forearm. I glance over my shoulder to see Lena, wide-eyed and shaking her head no.

"She didn't mean that," the girl says. "She's a fan too. I mean, we both follow you. Can I have your autograph?"

I narrow my eyes at her. "My band isn't that well known."

She shrugs. "Not yet. But you are amazing."

"You're not that amazing," Solaris sneers under her breath.

I shake my head at her and give my new sister my full attention. "How about this? You show me how to get the fu—" I rethink my word choice. "I mean, get out of here, and I'll sign whatever you want."

"Deal!" she squeals and finally lets go of my forearm. She squeezes past me and out into the hall. "This way."

I watch her for a second as she skips down the hall before giving the other girl my full attention. She's standing with her hands on her hips and eyes narrowed at me.

"I don't trust you." She shoves a piece of her curly hair from her face.

"And why is that?" I ask her.

"Because."

"Because what?" I lean against the door.

"Because your dad is a bad man."

"If his actions reflect upon me, then I suppose your aunt's actions reflect upon you and Lena. Thus, making you two evil little homewrecking wenches as well."

She drops her hands from her hips and blinks multiple times as if thinking about what I said. "Lena's nothing like her mom. She's nice. And she would be a good sister."

"You didn't include yourself in that statement."

She ignores that and turns around and grabs the alcohol from the floor, along with the nail polish. I walk into the oversized bathroom and take the bottle from her tiny hands.

She pouts. "That's mine."

I glare down at her and shake the bottle that I'm just now realizing hasn't even been opened. But I should have been able to tell that from the lack of alcohol on both of their breaths. And the fact that this stuff would have them out in mere minutes if they had drank it. They are tiny. Far more petite than the preteens I've seen around my gated community.

"And now it's mine." I stuff the bottle in my pants pockets. "Besides, I'm not in the habit of letting kids drink."

She laughs at me. "Do you know who we are? We can do whatever we want. No one's going to stop us."

I squat down to get face level with her. "Yeah, well, I just did, brat."

"Jerk," she hisses and takes a step in my direction. "I'm telling my dad on you."

"You think your dad will be okay with you hiding away in a bathroom with alcohol? You're eleven."

"And you're what?" She looks me up and down. "Fifty?"

I crack a grin at her. "That's your comeback?"

"No." Her eyes search my face as if looking for something. "No."

"Guys!" Lena yells from behind me. "Let's go already."

She must have doubled back when she noticed I wasn't with her.

Solaris glances around me to Lena and then back to me. "How about I keep the alcohol and keep my mouth shut to Gregory, and in exchange, I introduce you to the rest of my band?"

Her eyes go wide the same time squealing from behind me rings out. "All of them?"

I smirk at her. "Which one of my mates do you have a little crush on?"

Her eyes drop from mine and her cheeks heat. "None of them, but Lena likes you, so fine. You have a deal."

"Good, now please get me out of this house before anyone notices."

She nods and rounds me. The girls lead me down the rest of the hall with portraits and to a massive sitting room. Solaris goes over to a plant and moves it aside. Behind it is a small door. She opens it and motions for me to come over.

"Go through here and keep straight. Don't turn off or it will lead to my aunt's place. The tunnel leads to a pool house. You can leave through the back of the property. No one will see. I disabled the cameras earlier."

My brows jump at that. "You sure you're eleven?"

She nods. "I know things. Like that you're really twenty and not fifty. You go to university, and you aren't as bad as your dad. I also know that if you tell anyone about my secret passage, you will end up lip syncing the rest of your shows."

I laugh at her. "I was right. You are an evil little wench."

"Just go," she gestures down the tunnel.

"What about my autograph?" Lena asks as I rush through the door.

"I'll get you one later." I hear Solaris tell her as I make my way through the tunnel.

At least they aren't going to be boring.

Four

Solaris

My car comes to a stop at the gate, and I give the driver a smile as I grab my bag and get out of the car. I wait until the car pulls off to unlock the gate and go inside. As I make it up the short pathway to my townhome, I notice a ton of boxes sitting at the door. I bend down and examine the contents. They are all from the brand I'm working with.

Frowning, I maneuver them aside and enter my credentials into the lock on my door. A year ago, a fan of my show came here and managed to get inside. It was the most terrifying thing I've ever experienced. Mom had a security system put in after that. Mainly because I refused to move to a better gated community. This is what my mother could afford after everything went down with my father's family. This is home.

And it's in the perfect location to my school and downtown. Moving would have meant not getting to go to school with Lena. There was no way I was going to allow that.

Pushing open the door, I grab one of the boxes and bring it inside with me. My mom must still be in New York handling things otherwise the boxes would be inside. I set my bag on the entryway table and turn back for the rest of the boxes. I'm just about to walk off when I notice the picture frame on the table is laid face down. I frown at the placement and pick up the picture. It's the one with my father, mother, and me we took on my birthday the year before my father passed away. Cruise refused to even celebrate with me and stayed at home, which was perfectly fine with me. He ruined every single family outing we had anyway.

I put the frame back where it's supposed to go and head back out. I drag the remaining boxes inside. My phone chimes with a reminder, and I open it to see my schedule for the rest of the day. I groan when I see I must make an appearance at a new restaurant opening in town. I never do events in town for obvious reasons, but the owner of the restaurant talked me into doing it. He wouldn't accept no for an answer. My agent thought it would be a good idea as well. She said that it would make me look like a small town girl from a reputable family. I didn't have the heart to tell her there's nothing reputable about my family. They are a bunch of snakes in designer clothes.

Opening my messages, I send a quick text to Lena.

Me: I have an event in town. Want to come?

Lena replies right away.

Lena: God yes. I'll be over after ballet.

Lena: Can I bring Taylor?

I frown at her question. As much as I love my cousin, if she brings Taylor, it's only going to be the Taylor and Solaris show. I'll have to pretend we're an item. And she'll have to pretend to be okay with it. Even though she says she's fine with this whole publicity thing, I see how she eyes me when he's around. I don't want to deal with that tonight. Especially after I practically told her that he wasn't cheating on her with our co-star.

Lena: Please!!! He's flying into town.

I sigh. I've never been able to tell Lena no. There was no point in me even thinking about her request.

Me: Fine.

Lena: Yay. See you after class.

With a yawn, I put my phone away and head upstairs to my room. The event doesn't start until eight. That gives me three hours of sleep. And I desperately need some sleep. Kicking off my shoes, I climb on the bed. As soon as my head hits the pillow, my phone rings and I groan. The freaking universe just can't give me a break today. Are a few hours of rest so much to ask?

I pull my phone from my blazer pocket and look at the number. It's the same number that man called me from this morning. The lawyer. I hit the ignore button and toss my phone to the foot of the bed. I have no time to talk to some man about an estate I want nothing to do with. If the freaking will was lost to begin with that means someone didn't want it found. And if someone didn't want it found, I don't want to be the one in the way of them getting that property. The phone rings again, and I bury my head underneath my pillow. Nope, I'm getting some sleep.

My phone rings again, followed by someone banging on the door. I pull the pillow tighter around my head and ignore it. The banging comes again, followed by someone shouting my name. I moan into my bed and try to ignore it again. People really need to let me just be for five minutes. That's all I'm asking. Five minutes for a right that every other person on the planet has. The ringing comes again and I turn over. Slowly, I crack my eyes open only to be surrounded by pitch darkness. The only light in my room is coming from the screen on my phone lighting up.

Setting up, I reach down and pluck my phone from where I threw it earlier. Lena's name is flashing across my screen. Why the heck is she calling me so soon?

"Solaris-freaking-James!" someone yells. "Open the door before I knock it down!"

Suddenly, my eyes widen as I finally take in Lena's name on my phone and the banging at the door. Crap. I overslept. I never oversleep. Then again, Mom is usually home to make sure I keep to my schedule. Crawling out of bed, I rush out of my room and downstairs. I yank the door open to see a red face, fuming Lena with Taylor right behind her. Lena shoves into the house, but Taylor is a little more reluctant to come inside. When he finally does, I shut the door and turn around to them with a yawn on my breath. I do my best to keep it in. I've slept. I shouldn't still be tired.

"Sorry," I mumble.

Lena pouts, hands on her hips, and stares me up and down. "What are you wearing? Why aren't you dressed?"

I ignore her question seeing as the dried drool on my cheek should speak for itself. Instead, I take in what she and Taylor are wearing. Lena is in a skin tight red dress with her hair pulled up into a sleek ponytail. She has on her highest black stilettos. Taylor is in a black suit with a silk white button down underneath. It's undone at the neck as per usual. I move past them and rush to my room.

"What time is it?" I call back to them. "How late am I?"

Lena's right on my tail as I rush into my room and over to my closet. I flip through all the dresses until I land on a cute pink midi-length lace number. I'm just about to pull it from the hanger when Lena reaches around me and takes the black mini with the cut outs. It still has a tag on it.

"Ugh, we're going out. You are not dressing like we're having tea with the queen. Wear the black one," Lena tells me.

Since I don't have time to argue with her, I take the dress and rush into the bathroom, making a quick effort to put it on. I don't bother with a full face of makeup. Just lip gloss and a little eye shadow. I fluff my curly hair, wishing I could throw it up into a sleek pony like Lena, and go back to my room. Lena is already holding out a pair of heels for me and a clutch.

"I took the liberty of getting us a ride," Taylor says, and it's the first thing he's said since coming inside. "Although it would be a lot easier for us to get a decent ride if you lived somewhere less . . . inviting."

I frown at him as I finish strapping on my shoes. "My house is fine, Taylor."

"It's not even a house. Why must you insist on living in the poorest part of town? It's not a good look on us. Everyone knows you have the money to live wherever you want. Why do you insist on embarrassing all of us with this place?"

Rolling my eyes, I ignore him and take the clutch from Lena's hold. It's not the poorest part of town. I'm just not living in a freaking gated community with a bunch of country club snobs. There's nothing wrong with this area.

"Alright. I'm ready," I announce to no one in particular. "Let'sgo."

"About time," Taylor mumbles.

Lena cuts him a glare and head out of my room. I follow after them. Once we make it to the vehicle, we all climb in the back with Taylor in between us. He lays a hand over my thigh and drapes his other arm around Lena's shoulders. I toss his hand off me. We might have to pretend in public, but in private he has no reason to touch me.

"Don't be like that," he says to me. "Tonight is meant to be fun."

"Tonight is meant to be work," I correct him.

"Doesn't mean we can't have some fun. Like that one night when we—"

"Don't be silly," Lena blurts. "You know that was a one-time thing."

"Doesn't have to be," Taylor mumbles and rests his hand back on my leg, squeezing it.

I bite down on my bottom lip to keep from saying anything. That night should never have happened. We were all drunk and horny. The next day, we all regretted that night. At least Lena and I did, and we vowed never to drink so much that a threesome sounded like fun again.

But I can't outright scold Taylor for wanting that. As much as I hate this publicity thing, I'm not going to lie and say I don't benefit from it as well. Before Taylor, I was only a troublesome heiress. People knew me from my show of course, but they knew me better as the riches to rags heiress. He gave them a reason to see me as something other. I'm not going to do anything to make them think I'm still the same girl that came onto the scene all those years ago. Including yucking Taylor's yum.

I sit in silence as we make our way downtown to the little restaurant. At least tonight should be easy. A quiet dinner with friends. All I really must do is snap a few images of me at the place for social media and then I can leave. And hopefully the food is actually good.

When the car comes to a stop, I finally look up and acknowledge my surroundings. My heart stops when I spot the multiple paparazzi with cameras hanging outside the restaurant. I whip my head to Taylor, but he's already shaking his head at me.

"It wasn't me," he defends himself, but he's the only person I can think of that would call them. Lena would never do that to me. "Besides, what's the big deal, huh? You should be used to it by now. It's part of the business."

I scowl at him.

You would have to be soulless and lifeless to get used to them. I don't care how long I've been doing this, I will never get used to these people treating me like an object. Like I'm less than a person simply for the path I've chosen to follow. It's inhumane and rather rude. Maybe Taylor likes the attention, but I've had enough bad headlines to last a lifetime.

Sighing, I get out of the vehicle. My body braces as the reporters rush over. The driver jumps out of the front, but he's instantly pushed out of the way. Cameras go off and I blink back at all the flashes. I breathe in once, then twice. I can handle this.

I can handle it better.

I ignore that voice inside my head. I've been hearing it all too much recently, and I can't let myself go down that path. The last time I listened, I blacked out for days and then was blamed for something I didn't do. I got put on those stupid pills which I'm certain is what's making me so tired today.

Putting my on-screen smile on, I give the cameras a wave. Taylor and Lena get out of the car, and Taylor beams at the attention. He steps in front of me and I'm relieved. That's until the photographers start hurling questions at us.

"Solaris, what's next now that your show is over?" one throws at me.

Another hurls, "Why don't you two show us why you're American's sweethearts?"

I scowl at the reporter and walk off. My hand is grabbed and from the silky smooth skin and heaviness of it, I know it's Taylor. He spins me back to him, and my chest slams against his. Before I have much of a chance to pull back, his mouth descends on mine in a slobbery kiss. I hear my cousin gasp and then the clicking of her heels. More cameras go off. My heart stops beating. I shove Taylor back and I race after Lena.

"Solaris!" I hear.

"Solaris!" another yells.

"Solaris!" Taylor bellows, and I ignore the bastard as well.

Lena goes inside the restaurant, and I pick up my pace. "Will you stop for one second?"

She comes to a complete stop at my words and turn to face me. Her face is red, eyes a darkened blue. She's pissed which is rarely the case with Lena. She glances around us at all the people and shakes her head. Her eyes flicker around the intimate room before pointing to a hall. She turns and I go after her.

Lena comes to a stop when we're out of hearing distance and scowls at me. "How could you?"

"I didn't," I defend myself. "You know I didn't."

She crosses her arms, eyes watery and lip trembling. "Have you been kissing my boyfriend this entire time?"

"Ew. Lena, you're talking about Taylor. Double ew."

Lena shifts on her feet and glances past me to the occupants of the restaurant. She lets out a sigh. "Just tell me, Solaris. I'm a big girl now. I can handle the truth. Has he really been . . .?"

My shoulders drop when I realize this isn't about me or that kiss. It's about the fact that she knows he's not who she thought. And I can't lie to her again.

I nod. "I'm sorry."

"How long?"

"The entire time."

If at all possible, her face gets even redder. "Why didn't you tell me? You're my best friend! Why would you let me walk around making a fool of myself?"

"Because you love him, Lena." I pull her farther down the hall. "I didn't want to be the one to make you hurt. And I knew you would eventually see the truth."

Lena grabs a strand of her hair and twirls it tightly around her hand. Straightening her posture, she steels herself. "Yeah, well, it does hurt, and you should have told me."

"I'm really sorry."

She swats my apology away. "It doesn't matter. Let's just go back out there and do whatever you need to. I will deal with that lying, cheating, bastard afterwards."

I smile at her. "What do you have in mind?"

"He's still afraid of spiders," is all she says before prancing back down the hall. I follow her and go over to where she's posing fora photo. I stop next to her and throw an arm around her shoulder. A camera goes off and it's the most comfortable I've felt in front of a reporter's camera in a while. Clapping behind us has me turning around.

"Solaris and Lena James! Come, come!" a man in a chef uniform announces and motions for us to follow him.

He leads us to a round table with a bouquet of black roses and candles in the center. Fitting for the moody atmosphere of the cozy eatery. I take a seat snd so does Lena. Moments later, Taylor joins us as if nothing happened. He shoves his hair away from his face and scoots his chair closer to Lena.

She shoves him away just as a waiter comes over with three glasses of water.

"Oh my God, kill me now!" Lena says abruptly and I sit up straight in my chair.

My fingers start tapping on my glass. "What?"

Lena points behind me and I turn around. I gasp, shaking my head as I see Loretta standing at the front of the place in a one shoulder, effortless satin black dress that flows over her lean body. She's smiling at the cameras as if it's next nature. The worst part, Silas is on her arm.

I jerk around to Lena. "What is she doing here?"

Lena shrugs and I can tell from her pale face that she didn't expect to see her mother here anymore than I did. She glances down at the red dress she's wearing and then over to Taylor and gulp. I turn around to look at my aunt again just as her roaming eyes decide to land on my table. Loretta eyes widen then narrows on me. I gulp and turn back around in my chair.

This can't be happening.

I've managed to evade everyone in my family since that awful day, and now I'm seeing them everywhere. Taking my glass of water, I guzzle it down. Taylor grabs my hand, and I snarl at him.

"You're going to break that glass if you keep tapping it so hard." He motions to my fingers on the glass.

My eyes snap to my fingers around the glass, and I force my hands to still, taking in a deep breath.

I can handle this.
Loretta is no one.
Abso-fucking-lutely no one.

Five

Solaris

I cross my arms and arch an eyebrow, fixing Loretta with a steely gaze as she scrutinizes me. Her eyes narrow, but I stand my ground. The air between us crackles with tension, even with a room full of people dividing us. When I refuse to falter under her piercing glare, her lips curl into a displeased frown.

"Waiter!" I call and finally give her my back. A young man in a pair of black slacks and a white button down comes over to the table immediately. "Bring a bottle of your most expensive red wine to the table."

His eyes widen, and I can practically see the nervousness dripping from his pores before he acknowledges my request. "But you're underage."

I rest my chin in my palm, curling a finger to beckon the waiter closer. As he leans down, the fresh scent of spearmint on his breath wafts over me. My hand lands lightly on his forearm, and I gaze up at him through my lashes, a playful smile dancing on my lips.

"I'm pretty sure we can work around that."

He gulps, opens his mouth, and then gulps again. "Of course, Miss—"

"You will be doing no such thing." My fingers stop stroking the man's arm as a smooth voice hits my ears.

I glance over my shoulder and grin up at the intruder. "Well, if it isn't Silas O'Conner, ladies and gentlemen."

"Dude, you're Silas O'Conner!" Taylor announces and I roll my eyes.

Silas glances across the table at Taylor, and I can pinpoint the exact moment he decides Taylor is nothing more than a nuisance. Loretta struts over and rests a hand on Silas' arm. I arch an eyebrow at him, but he barely acknowledges me. Loretta, noticing my reaction, leans in and plants a kiss on his cheek. I recoil in disgust.

"Gross," Lena mumbles and her mother's eyes leap across the table at her.

"What are you all doing here?" Loretta questions us, but I can tell it's more so for her daughter. My aunt couldn't care less about me.

Attempting to regain her attention and pull it away from Lena, I rise from my chair, crossing my arms as I do so. "I could ask you the same question, Aunt Loretta."

"You little—" she cuts off as a camera flash in our direction. We all turn to see who decided to forfeit their life tonight and come face-to-face with the slimiest reporter of them all, Brandon Black. If I'm being honest, he's not slimy, just honest, but his honesty has caused more drama than a reality TV show. It's also usually aimed at me.

"Almost the whole James' clan together under one roof," he says lowering his camera. "This must be the event of the century."

Loretta's hand instantly falls away from Silas. Because yeah, getting caught being cozy with your stepson isn't ideal for someone like her. Ugh, I roll my eyes again at the thought and glance around the venue. The waiter is long gone, and I highly doubt he's bringing me my wine. Whatever.

"Brandon Black," I put on my best grin for him and step forward. "It's good to see you. It's been a while."

He gives me his classic flirty grin before his eyes shift to someone over my shoulder, dilating a little. I turn around to see who's caught his attention and frown when I see Lena. No way he needs to focus on my cousin. I want her nowhere near someone like him.

"Solaris James," his eyes flick back to me. "I must say, you're looking good."

I bat his compliment away. "Don't I always? What brings you here tonight."

"Surely he's here for the grand opening," Loretta throws in her two cents.

"Actually," Brandon corrects her, "I heard Solaris was going to be making an appearance. She doesn't normally do appearances. Thought I could get a statement since your show is coming to a close. However, the entire family in one place is much more interesting. When was the last time that happened? Gregory's funeral?"

My grin falters, and I take a step back. Brandon knows fully well we weren't there. Loretta had banned Mom and me from my father's ceremony. We weren't even listed as family in the obituary. The only reason I have a copy is because Lena gave me hers at school afterward.

Loretta steps aside Silas and tosses an arm around my shoulders. I instantly shrug her off. No chance, bitch. Brandon's eyes light up at the interaction. But no. Just no. My life might be entertainment for the masses, but I do have my limits. And my mess is my limit.

"It was a coincidence," I say before Loretta can make up some BS to fit her agenda. "I was invited. I showed. And now I'm leaving." I turn to Silas. "Don't have too much fun."

I turn back to my table and grab my clutch. Lena's already made her escape. I head towards the back of the restaurant. There's no way I'm going through the front with all those cameras. Lena's already at the door with a whiskey glass in her hand. She's pale and has a faraway look in her eyes. I've only ever seen her look like this once.

"Lena?" She glances at me over the rim of her glass. "Are you alright?"

She barks out a laugh and tosses the rest of her drink back. "My mom is going to kill me for being here tonight."

"Where did she think you were going to be tonight?" I lean against the wall and wait for her answer. I already know what she's going to say. It's been the same answer for almost six years.

"Anywhere would have been better than being with you," she tells me. "My mom really hates you, and I don't understand it. You're family."

I shake my head. As much as I would like to tell my dear cousin that Loretta loathes me for something I can't control, for being the "black sheep" of the family, I don't think Lena is ready to hear that our family may be a little bit partial to the white side of life. Moreso, Lena just wouldn't understand. I didn't either until I heard the words Loretta said to my mom the day she threw us out. Words no twelve-year-old should ever have had to witness.

Lena shakes her head. "You know what? It doesn't matter. You're my cousin and my best friend. She can deal. And since I'm already going to die, let's just get out of here and really party. I hear the club on Broadway has the best drinks and the hottest guys."

Grinning, I let her change the subject. I didn't really want to hash out the whole problem anyway.

"So where are we headed now?" Taylor strolls between us and drapes his arms over our shoulders. "That was awkward as hell back there, huh, babe?"

Lena and I look at each other before knocking Taylor's arms from our bodies.

"Actually," I give him a pointed look. "*We* aren't going anywhere. This whole fake relationship is done. And you're done with my cousin. Go use someone else."

Taylor bursts into laughter, but when he sees we haven't joined in, his eyes flicker across my face and his grin evaporates. As he's finally put it together, his features shift into a scowl. He takes a menacing step towards me, but I don't back down. If I know anything about this boy, it's that he's not going to do anything to harm his money maker. Touching me would ensure that face is wrecked.

"No," Taylor tells me. "We have a contract. And you're sticking to it."

I arch a brow at him and purse my lips. "If you're going to behold me to this contract then I'm entitled to do the same. That contract explicitly states that while we are 'together' you can be seen with no other partner in a romantic nature. You've been photographed with our co-star multiple times. Not counting the endless wannabe models. Now, I could sue you for breach of that contract since there is proof everywhere. Or you could just walk away and forget you know me and my cousin."

Taylor opens his mouth to refute my claims, but there really is nothing he can say. I'm right. He knows I'm right and anything else would just make him look pathetic and weak.

"Y-you can't—" he stutters out.

"I-I-I very well can." I shoo him away.

Taylor takes another step in my direction and Lena tenses behind me. Taylor's hand rises swiftly, and I flinch back out of self-preservation, but his palm never lands. Taylor is hauled backwards. My eyes snap to the man behind him and my cheeks heat. Silas tosses him up against a wall, causing a mirror to fall and shatter. I grimace at the loud sound but quickly search behind the men to see if anyone noticed. The only person present is Brandon Black with his camera. He snaps a few photos, and Silas must notice. He instantly drops Taylor and move over to us, effectively putting himself in between us and the douche.

"S-Silas, man, it wasn't what it looked like," Taylor stammers out as he gets to his feet. "We were just talking business."

"Yeah, well, now you're talking to me." Silas voice is deep and dark, threatening, and it makes my stomach flutter. "You even think about laying a hand on Solaris or my sister, your acting career will be over."

Taylor runs his hands down his suit jacket and glances around Silas to us. His eyes don't linger too long. Instead, he scoffs at all of us and walks away, which is probably the best thing he can do right now. I've seen Silas get pissed off. And Taylor couldn't handle him. That doesn't change the fact that I didn't need Silas to butt in. I could have handled it. I have been handling assholes like him for almost five years now.

"Let's go." Lena tugs on my arm. "I really don't want to be here."

She shoves open the door and I follow after her. When I don't hear the door slam behind me, I turn around to see Silas standing in the doorway.

"Where do you think you're going?" he asks.

"A club," Lena tells him. "You should come with us. You could use a breather too after that. And we owe you."

I glare at her over my shoulder. We do not owe him. "We do not need a has-been rockstar telling us what to do all night."

The door shuts and I jerk back around to Silas. "You know what, I think I will tag along. Someone has to keep you both in line."

I cross my arms and purse my lips at him. "And you think that's going to be you, Mr. Rockstar? Don't you have test to grade since you're a teacher and all now?"

"Solaris," Lena chastises. "Be nice."

Silas comes over to us and smirks down at me. "First, I'm a rockstar and now I'm a teacher. Which one is it, Sol?"

I narrow my eyes on him.

He drapes an arm over my shoulders. "Besides, I have to make sure you actually come to my class tomorrow. Who else can I count on to be a buffer between me and all those desperate girls trying to bang a rockstar?"

"All the more reason to quit." I roll my eyes and give Lena my full attention. "You did order an uber or something, right?"

Lena gives me a pointed look and points up head to the discreet black vehicle with tint just as dark. "Do I look like an amateur? Just because I don't have Brandon Black showing up places to interview me doesn't mean I don't have my fair share of followers. Not to mention, he's back in town."

She points to Silas, and I roll my eyes again. He's not that big of a deal. Sure, he's done two worldwide tours, won a Grammy, and snagged a few CMA awards, but that doesn't mean much to me. As we approach the end of the alley, we come to a halt and peek around the corner. All the reporters are still clustered at the front of the restaurant, their attention fixed elsewhere. None of them are even glancing in our direction. We dart to our waiting car and slide into the backseat just as one of the reporters turns to look around. Fortunately for us, we're inside before he can get a clear view.

"Your life always this exciting now?" Silas nudges me and I peek over at him.

"Uh, yeah," Lena answers for me. "But you probably know all about that, don't you?"

He shrugs. "Touring wasn't as exciting as you might think. It gets old pretty fast, especially with bandmates like mine. One reason I'm back in town and subbing for now."

"And you just had to choose our school?" I mumble.

He glances down at me and quirks an eyebrow. "I'm starting to think you don't want me around."

"Why would I?"

"Because you love him," Lena blurts out, her words a little slurred from the whiskey, and I freeze. Silas whole body goes just as taut next to mine. "I mean, c'mon, Solaris. You asked about him all the time when everything first went down. You—"

I elbow her in the ribs to keep her from talking. God, I forgot she gets talkative when she drinks. Silas doesn't need to know anything about what happened afterwards. He hasn't earned that yet. And he's certainly not going to earn it tonight. Lena turns to look at me and she must see just how much I want her to shut up. She mouths 'sorry' and I nod.

None of us say a word until the car comes to a stop outside of the club. I glance out the window to see how long the line is and sigh in relief when it's not that long. Then again, it's early and most people probably aren't out partying on a Thursday night. Silas opens the door, allowing us to slide out, and close the door. We head up to the entrance manned by a giant of a man dressed in black cargo pants and a plain black T-shirt.

Lena pulls out her ID and I do the same. Correction, fake ID. We got them made a while ago. It was our only way to see each other for a while after my mom and I were kicked out of the manor.

The man nods. "Ms. James. Ms. James. Mr. O'Conner."

Silas steps forward and bumps fists with the security. "Good to see you again, Adams. You manning this place now?"

Adams shrug. "Gotta keep food on the table and a roof over my head. You performing?"

Silas shakes his head. "Nah, not tonight. I'm out with family."

Family? Really?

Lena isn't really his freaking sister.

And I'm certainly not his anything.

"Go on in. The VIP is open tonight, and I'll let Lawerance know y'all are here."

Silas tilts his head in appreciation at the man. "Thanks."

Rolling my eyes, I step inside. The energy in the club is electric, pulsating through the air and around the small, vibrant crowd. I grin, feeling the beat take hold of me, and I begin to sway in time with the music. Glancing over at Lena, I can see the infectious energy affecting her too. She's moving with her arms raised high, eyes closed, lost in the rhythm. The neon lights cast a colorful glow on her porcelain skin, making her look every bit the goddess her mother refuses to acknowledge.

My movements come to a halt when a large hand comes down on the exposed part of my back, and I glance over my shoulder to see Silas. Heat rushes to my cheeks as I take him in. The small cut above his left eye. His perfect lips that aren't too plump but plump enough. And those amazing green eyes. He has a little stubble lining his strong jaw that I'm itching to touch, but I refrain.

Silas leans down and mutters something in my ear, but I can't hear him over the music. When I show no sign of understanding, he takes my jaw in his palm and turns my head away from him and to the very clear VIP lounge. It's the only seated area raised above the dance floor and blocked off by a bright red rope.

Silas' hands leave my hips and something inside me deflates. I know I shouldn't react like that to him, but I do. I can't help it. And the fact that I couldn't act on it even if I wanted to, makes the want that much worse. It would be a PR nightmare trying to cover up that situationship. Because that's the only thing it could ever be. Not that it would ever happen. Silas is damn near a decade older than me, a teacher, and technically family. It would ruin us both.

"C'mon!" Lena bumps my hip as she dances her way down the few stairs and through the swarm of gyrating bodies. Lena heads straight towards the bar and I follow after her. I take a second to see if Silas followed, but nope. He went over to VIP.

The song changes and Lena lets out a loud screech. "I love this song!"

I nod, because yeah, I know. She sings along to it every single time it comes on. I haven't had the heart to tell her it's a bad song. If it makes her happy, then I'm happy.

"Let's get drinks and then find me a new boy. That'll show Taylor," she says that last part loud enough to catch a few eyes.

I chuckle. Should have known the moment she decided to let Taylor go, she would be on the prowl for her next conquest. That's just the type of person Lena is. She's in one hundred percent if she chooses to be, but the moment anyone pisses her off or she decides you are unworthy, she is on to the next.

We head to the bar, but the bartender is already getting drinks for someone else. Turning my attention back to the crowd, I tune back into the music as I survey the people.

"What about him?" I say to Lena as my eyes lock on an older man leaning against the back wall like he doesn't have a care in the world while some chick grinds up on him. "He might be good for a hookup. To get over Taylor."

"Who?" Lena shouts. "That guy?"

She points to the man who's caught my attention. I don't know why I find him attractive, but I do. He looks like he has his shit together.

"You've got to be joking. He looks old enough to be our dad. Next, please."

I shrug. "I'm going to introduce myself if you're not inter-ested."

"What about our drinks?"

"Have mine sent to VIP," I shout over my shoulder as I make my way across the dance floor to the man.

The girl grinding on him must see the way I'm looking at him because she scowls at me. I pay her no mind. If he's truly not interested, then he won't notice me. But if he does notice me, then I just saved her the rejection. Because she does honestly look into him.

Grinning up at him, I come to a stop at his side. My body begins to move and just as I thought, he turns to me fully.

"Seriously?" the girl cries out, but I don't think either of us really care.

The man gives me a once over and then pushes off the wall. Without even a question, he grabs my hips, turns me around, and pulls me back against him. I gasp at his roughness, but something inside me comes to life. A gentle purr leaves me at the feel of his hands on my body. He shoves one of his legs between mine and starts rocking with me. I gasp at the friction.

"What's your name, doll?" he whispers in my ear.

The fact that he doesn't recognize me, makes me like this man even more. Then again, he's not necessarily my target audience.

"You can call me Sol," I purr out.

"I think I like do—"

Emtpiness replaces the man's leg in between mine, and I turn around to see Silas, who's rearing back to punch him. The crowd around us falls silent, and I hear a few whispers of Silas' name. He must hear them too, because his fist stops short of making contact. Instead, he grabs my forearm and yanks me toward the entrance of the club. I struggle against his grip, but his hold only tightens, his anger and frustration palpable.

"Let me go, Silas!" I shout at him.

When we reach the exit, he does exactly that and shoves me out the door. There's a line of people now, and I know the moment they recognize me. My name leaves all their mouths. A few of them scream for Silas, but unless you're into country pop, he's an unknown. Silas doesn't seem too bothered by the scene he's causing. He grabs hold of me again and pulls me over to a waiting cab. A flash goes off and I groan at it. Great. Just fucking great. Now, Mom is going to have to deal with this.

Wrenching open the door, Silas shoves me inside and follows. He gives the cab driver the manor's address and doesn't say anything else until we're pulling up outside the gate to the estate. Silas rolls down a window and puts a number into a keypad. That's new. The gate opens and the driver drives down the long pathway that leads to one of the guest houses.

Silas drags me out of the cab without a word and up the steps to the house I'm guessing he's living in during his stay. He shoves me inside, hard, and I slam against the table in the foyer.

"Fucking hell, Silas!" I scream.

He slams the front door behind him and charges toward me, eyes blazing with fury. Grabbing my arm, he drags me up the stairs with relentless force. When I can't keep up with his pace, he bends down and effortlessly tosses me over his shoulder. My face flushes with a mix of indignation and a thrill at his caveman-like possessiveness, even though I know he has no right to do this.

Without hesitation, he barges through one door after another until we reach the bathroom. My eyes widen and my pulse quickens as I see him turn on the shower. Before I can protest, he hurls me inside, and the freezing cold water crashes down on me. I scream and scramble away from the icy stream, shivering. Silas stands there, arms crossed, glaring at me with a mix of anger and frustration, his presence both infuriating and intoxicating.

Glaring at him, I ask, "What the hell was that for?"

"You looked like you needed to cool down."

"You left Lena," I huff out, as I turn the water off and crawl out of the shower. I deliberately shake my hair out and get him wet.

"She knows her way back."

"Screw you!" I shout at him. "You had no right!"

"No right? Really. Was I meant to watch as a grown ass man took advantage of you? Is this what you've become? Some desperate child grinding on a man's knee in public? Grow up, Sol."

I point at myself. "Don't call me that. And if I do need approval from men, it's your fault. You were the one that didn't protect me. You are the one that stood by and watched as guards three times my size dragged me from your room. You are the one that I—"

"Shut up!" he cuts me off and my eyes widen at his tone. "I had no fucking choice but to let all that happen. And I would do it a thousand times over. It got you out of this house. It got you to safety."

I shake my head at him. "Safety? I was perfectly safe. This was our home, and you didn't even try to help us."

He steps forward and grabs both of my shoulders. He doesn't squeeze or anything, but the fury is evident enough. And God help me, I kind of like it.

"You don't have to pretend with me." His voice calms and I search his face in confusion. "I knew what was happening."

I gulp and shake my head again. "No. You just abandoned me. Like everyone else."

Silas lets go of me and leans against the double vanity. "I didn't abandon you. Just because you didn't see me, doesn't mean I wasn't there. I saw everything."

Shivering, I lean against the opposite wall. "Yeah, well, shadows have never been a help to anyone."

He sighs and drops his head. "Look, it's been a long night. You obviously don't want to talk about everything, including what happened to you, and I don't want to beat around the bush. So unless we're talking about all the shit that went down inside of James Manor, this conversation is over."

I cross my arms and shrug. "Fine by me. I'm a little tired anyway."

Silas goes over to a cabinet and pulls out a towel. He tosses it to me and points to the room behind me. "Make yourself comfortable and I'll . . . um, I'll . . ."

He runs a hand over his face and walks away from me. I hear the door to the room open and close before I slump against the wall. What does he mean the crap that happened at the manor? Nothing happened at the manor. Life was great until my dad died. Shaking my head, I go to the bedroom. Climbing on, a whiff of sage and cardamom hits my nostrils. It smells like him. Like Silas.

I roll over and inhale more of his scent like a little creeper. Slumping into his pillow, I groan.

Things are about to get freaking complicated with him back in town.

Six

Solaris

"**L**et me go!" I scream, jolting awake. My breaths come fast and ragged as I clutch the blanket to my chest, trying to calm my racing heart. It was just a nightmare. No one touched me. No one touched me. No one touched me. I frown, my fingers instinctively going to my neck. A cold chill runs up my arms, and I pull the blanket even tighter around me. I lay back down, but a hint of cardamom mixed with something almost floral hits my nose. My body goes rigid. I know that scent. I know the person it belongs to would never hurt me. Yet, my body trembles uncontrollably.

Swallowing hard, I pull the blanket away and glance down at myself. I frown at the sleep shorts and tank top I'm wearing. I don't remember changing into these clothes. I don't remember coming home or anything after leaving the restaurant. My eyes scan the bed, widening as I realize this isn't my cream bedding.

I throw the covers back and leap out of the bed. A bed that's not mine. Panic surges through me, and I turn frantically, taking in the unfamiliar room. None of this stuff is mine. This is not my room. Oh, God. What happened last night? And where the hell is Silas? I know his scent like the back of my hand. He was here. He had to be here.

Calm down, the voice inside my head tells me. And for a moment I do just that. I breathe in and out, trying to get the racing of my heart under control, but it doesn't work.

I search the room for my belongings and rush over to where they are folded neatly on a brown leather chair. Cocking my head to the side, I stare at the chair. I know that chair too. I turn around and take in the room again. I know this room too. It's Silas'. Well, the room he used to occupy before everything happened. With that knowledge, I manage to finally calm myself. I probably drank too much last night after the whole Loretta run in. Silas must have brought me back here. Why he would bring me to the manor is beyond me, but this is better than waking up at some random house. Well, maybe. . .

I go to grab my clothes when I notice a yellow sticky note placed on top of them. Taking the note, I read across Silas' sleek strokes.

Had to go to work. Don't miss my class again. Take the exit by the pool so Loretta doesn't see you. We need to talk.

I run my finger across his words and try to think about what we might have to talk about. Truth be told, there's a ton we need to discuss. None I actually want to talk about. Silas doesn't get to come back and pick up where we left off like nothing happened. Everything happened. He became Silas O'Conner, while Mom and I were rebuilding our lives. He was nowhere to be seen. No where when I actually needed him. Now, I'm Solaris James. I don't need him.

Not to mention, he's parading around with Loretta on his arm. Ew. Of all the women he could be with, he chooses his father's wife. The she-devil in designer shoes and a terrible spray tan. Something's not right there. He couldn't stand her before. He saw how she treated me. And not just me, but the staff too. Everyone. The old Silas would never have even entertained the idea of being with that woman.

Scoffing, I grab my clothes and head into the small bathroom off his closet. I come to a stop at the sight of the sparkling marble clawfoot tub with gold hardware. I'd forgotten just how extravagant these people are. Even this pool house must be worth a million bucks. Trying to ignore my opulent surroundings, I slip back into last night's dress and attempt to finger-detangle the nest that has formed in my curls. I huff in frustration as the tangles seem to worsen. With none of my things here, this is the best it's going to get.

I go back out to the bedroom and immediately spot my phone on a charger beside the bed. A small grin stretches across my lips. At least Silas thought to put the phone on a charger. Picking it up, my eyes are drawn to the time. School hasn't started yet, and I really don't need to be late or absent any more this week. Especially not after missing most of yesterday.

Mom's messages catch my eye, and I wince. God, she's going to kill me. I've had late nights before, but I've never stayed out all night, and I've always responded to her messages. Opening the text, I release a breath. She's still in New York, handling business. I quickly type a reply, letting her know I stayed at a friend's place and fell asleep, just so she doesn't worry. There's no immediate response, which likely means she's asleep in her hotel room.

Searching the room one more time, I let out an exhale. I stayed on the property and didn't freak out. That's a step forward. Although, this is Silas' space and I've always been comfortable in Silas' corner of the world. Anyway, I'm taking it as a win.

My phone pings just as the clock switches to 7:15 am.

> **Silas:** You have 30 minutes to get to school. You better be awake.

My eyebrows shoot up in surprise at seeing his name. He still has the same number as when I was a kid. I never imagined that, after his music career skyrocketed, he would keep it. I had to change mine when weirdos and superfans started harassing me. Although shocking he managed to keep it in his line of work, there's a comforting thought in knowing I could have reached him anytime I needed to.

Solaris: How'd you get my number?

Silas: I have my ways. Now get going before you run into Loretta. She leaves around 8 every morning.

My eyes flick to the corner of my phone screen. 7:16 am. I have time. Not a lot, but I'm not late and I shouldn't run into her.

Solaris: I'm on my way. And for future reference, don't undress me without my permission.

Silas: I had your permission. Remember, you once told me that I could do anything to you, and you'd be happy.

Solaris: I was eleven. That doesn't count, perv.

Instead of another message coming through, my phone vibrates in my hand. Silas' name flashes across my screen along with a photo of us from my twelfth birthday. I slide the answer button over and bring the phone to my ear.

"Don't ever fucking call me that," he hisses into the phone.

I pull the phone away from my ear and gape at his crude tone. It wasn't the playful tone of the past. Or the serious one he seems so keen on using now.

"Do you hear me?" Silas' muffled voice comes through the receiver. "Solaris?"

I bring the phone back to my ear. "Sorry. It was just a joke."

"It wasn't funny. After everything you've gone through, the last thing I want you to think of me as is that."

My brows lower in confusion as I make my way out the pool house. I have no idea what he's referring to. But he keeps saying things like that.

"I would never actually think of you that way, Silas. I know you're not like that."

"Good," he exhales. "I would never hurt you. Not like that. Not in a way you wouldn't want."

"So, what you are saying is that you would hurt me in a way I would want?"

Silas lets out a chuckle. "You would take that away from this conversation."

"What else was I supposed to take away?"

"Nothing. Get to school." The call ends.

I roll my eyes at his dramatics. Maybe he should have been the actor instead of me. His mood surely switches like one. Before pocketing my phone, I shoot a quick message to Lena letting her know to bring an extra uniform to school. There's no way I have time to go home, dress, and make it to school on time. Nope, I'll just have to dress in the girls' restroom.

Making my way around the pool house, I come to a stop at the edge of the pristine pool. I smile at the sparkling blue waters. So much time was spent in this pool the summer before everything went down. Silas thought it was a crime for me to be the only one in my family not to know how to swim, so he made teaching me his top priority. He took Lena and me to the mall, and we picked out so many bathing suits. Silas even sat down while we gave him a fashion show of all the swimwear. Biting down on my lip, I cock my head to the side. Now that I'm thinking about it, maybe it was a little inappropriate for a twenty-year-old man to be watching eleven-year-old girls parade around in what's essentially underwear. He was family so . . . And it didn't mean anything.

I pull my phone from my pocket and check the time again. 7:27 am. I glance swiftly around for signs of anyone that may report me to Loretta. When I see no one, I bend down and remove my heels. A little dip won't hurt. I ease to the pebbled ground and dangle my feet over the edge. A light moan leaves my lips as the cooling waters engulf my legs. This feels so good. It's been ages since I've been in a pool. Closing my eyes, I lean back against the pebbles and relax for a minute. I can't remember the last time I was just able to relax.

The clacking of her shoes catches my attention just before her shadow engulfs me. I jerk up from the stone ground and look up at my aunt. She doesn't give me time to stand.

Instead, she reaches down and grabs my forearms, yanking me up with a painful grip. I wince as her nails dig into my skin and shove her away. Her eyes narrow into sharp slits, and I glare back at her, matching her intensity.

Loretta's eyes blaze with fury as she steps closer. "What the hell are you doing on my property, girl?"

I cross my arms, meeting her glare head-on. "This isn't your property; it belonged to my father. And I was invited."

"Invited?" She straightens and glances around, suspicion etched on her face. "No one would be dumb enough to invite the likes of you here. Were you with Silas?"

I stay silent, refusing to rat him out.

Loretta takes a menacing step toward me. "Stay. Away. From. Him."

I wrap my arms around myself, trying to keep from trembling in front of this snake. "Maybe you should take your own advice. You're the one married to his father. Doesn't look too good when you go from the father to the son."

A ringing fills my ears, and the sharp sting on my cheek registers just after the sound of Loretta's slap. My hand flies to my face as I take a tentative step back, almost stumbling. Steadying myself, I glance down at the edge of the pool.

"And one more thing . . ." she begins.

My head snaps up just as Loretta lunges, gripping my neck with her talon-like fingers. A yelp escapes me as her other hand joins, both squeezing hard. I gasp for air, trying to shove her away as she tightens her hold, her grimace morphs into a twisted grin. My struggles weaken, and my body starts to shake. My clutch falls to the ground as Loretta forces me down. Small, ragged breaths escape me as my vision blurs and my head starts to spin.

"And one more thing, I know my brother's will has been rediscovered. If you're a smart girl, which you obviously are not since you are on my property right now, you will ignore anyone who tries to contact you. We don't need for things to get even uglier, do we?"

She lets go of my neck and I gasp in air. I blink back the dots from my vision and do my best not to let the tears and fear show. Loretta pats my cheek and smiles.

"Do we have an understanding, girl?" Loretta rises from her crouched position above me.

I nod and grab my purse. I scooch away from her as fast as I can.

Loretta wipes her hands down the front of her Versace suit as if touching me somehow sullied her. "You should get going now. There's a car waiting for you."

She doesn't have to tell me twice. I scurry to my feet and just run. With adrenaline pumping through my veins, my feet pound through the lush green foliage and then onto the pebbled pavement. I don't pay attention to where I'm headed; I just keep running in the direction I know the gate is. A thin layer of sweat coats the nape of my neck and my breathing becomes even more haggard, but that still doesn't stop me. With burning calves, I dart by the first guest house. Then the second and the third. My heart picks up and I push myself to run even faster as the gate comes into sight. A small cry of relief leaves me at the sight of it.

Almost there.

Almost off these forsaken lands.

The gates open and the moment they are wide enough, a bright red Ferrari 812 GTS comes darting through. I throw myself off the pathway and against the white picket fence that encloses the horses. The car comes to a halt in front of me and I gulp. The door flies open and out pops a head full of suave blond hair and a torso covered in a pink polo. I gulp again as Cruise steps around his car and looks me over.

"Well, if it isn't my little sister," he coos.

Standing up straighter, I flick my hair back and cross my arms. "Get lost, Cruise."

He steps closer to me and moves a piece of my hair aside."Long time no see. How I've missed you."

I slap his hand away from me. I go to shove him, but he grabs my arm and pulls me flush against his body. His arm drops around my waist and secures me there. I squirm against his hold but instantly stop when I feel something harden against my side.

"You've grown up really nice." His head drops and he places a kiss along my neck. The arm holding me against him drops, and I let out a shriek as he grips my backside.

"My friends have missed this sweet little body of yours as well."

My brow ticks at his words, and I shove him hard. He takes a step back laughing.

"You're fucking disgusting!" I yell at him. "For Christ's sake, we're related."

He shrugs. "Never stopped anyone in this family before. Besides, I told you the night you set the fire what I would do to you if you came back. And today must be my lucky day."

I have no clue what he means. That fire everyone seems to think I set—I didn't.

Cruise charges at me, and I sidestep just in time. He whirls around, nearly slamming into the gate, and yanks me down with him. We land hard against the foot of the fence, and in an instant, Cruise flips us over so he's hovering above me. He slams my hands above my head, pinning me in place. Grinning, he moves my captured wrists into one hand. I squirm backward, desperate to get away, but he's bigger and stronger. Nothing I do works.

With one hand free, Cruise yanks at the hem of my dress. I cry out, pulling on my wrist.

"Stop, Cruise! I'm your sister, for goodness sake!"

He pushes aside my underwear, and I shake my head in disbelief. His finger trails up and down my most intimate area, and my body freezes. His eyes flick up to mine as he plunges his finger into me. A small cry escapes my lips, and I turn my face away, tears stinging my eyes.

Leaning down, Cruise kisses up my neck to my ear. "Doesn't it feel just like old times?"

I shake my head vehemently. "I don't know what you're talking about."

"Hmmm . . ." My brother leans in closer, practically crushing me under his weight, and forces my face toward him. "You must not be too opposed to familial fucking if the way you're dressed is any sign. Isn't this the same dress you wore last night? And you haven't been back here in how many years? Yet, our cousin shows up and here you are, running off the estate grounds in the same dress paparazzi photographed you in last night."

Another cry escapes me as he jabs his finger into me harder, each stab more brutal than the last. Over and over and over, the pain intensifies, until a frustrated growl leaves his lips.

"Get fucking wet!" he shouts, his voice a venomous snarl. "Or else I'll invite some people over here who will gladly take you dry. Doesn't bother me either way."

A shiver of pure terror runs up my spine at his threat. I turn to look at him, my eyes pleading. "Please, Cruise."

He sits back on his legs, lifting me with him and loosening his grip on my legs, a smirk curling his lips. Seizing the opportunity, I wrench a leg free and drive my foot into his crotch. His hold on my wrist instantly releases as he doubles over onto the grass, groaning in pain.

"Fucking cunt!" he bellows.

I scramble to my feet, urgency propelling me into the running car he abandoned. I back out quickly, my heart pounding as I swerve around and floor it through the gate. A black town car parked at the edge catches my eye, and I assume it was meant for me. I drive recklessly, weaving in and out of the morning traffic, until I finally reach the academy.

I glance at the clock and frown at the time. 8:01 am. I'm late. And as much as I hate being late, I don't really care right now.

Taking the keys out of the ignition, I walk numbly into the school. My steps are heavy, each one echoing with the weight of my memories. I head to the bathroom on the first floor, where I find Lena pacing outside. The moment she hears me, she turns around. Her eyes widen, and the uniform in her hands falls to the floor. Her hand flies to her mouth, a small gasp escaping her lips.

My body starts to tremble, and my knees go weak. I collapse to the floor, bringing my knees to my chest as tears stream down my face. Lena's voice sounds distant, like she's a thousand miles away. "I'm going to get Silas."

That's the last thing I hear before glimpses of last night's dream flash through my mind, and I scream.

15
B
6
marc. acuto

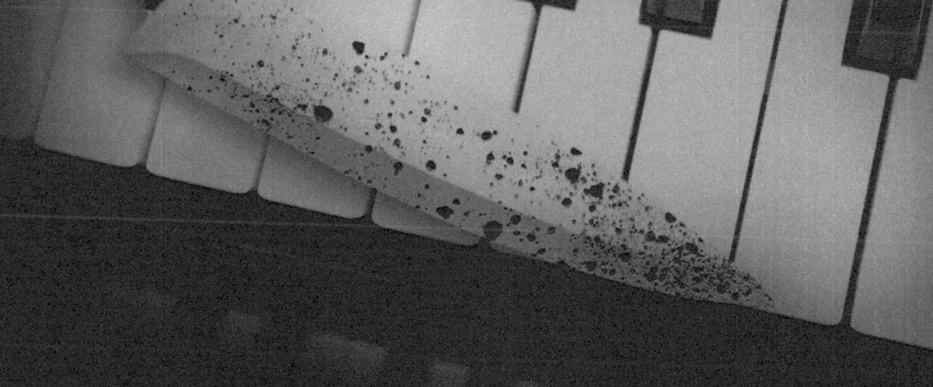

Seven

Silas

I pluck the strings of my guitar, humming the notes softly as I fine-tune each one. The lesson plan Mr. Stanford left behind says we're writing our first poem today. And what better way to give life to poetry than by weaving it into music? At least, that's always been my approach. Sure, I came back for Sol, but I also took this job hoping the muse would find me again. The label's been hounding me to write our new album for a year now, but my creativity's been a barren desert. Truth is, the closer we got to Sol's eighteenth birthday, the less I cared about the album—a fact my bandmates haven't been too happy about. But I couldn't stay in Nashville pretending everything was fine when I knew shit was about to hit the fan.

Then there's Loretta, summoning me back the moment she heard Gregory's rightful will had surfaced. She's convinced I can keep Sol in check. I have no idea where she got that notion—Sol's a firecracker, and she's going to blaze her own trail with or without me around.

With a sigh, I strum the guitar again, the familiar weight of the gold pick grounding me. Just as I'm about to lose myself in the melody, the door flies open with a bang, crashing into the wall. I jump from my seat, the pick slipping from my fingers as Lena bursts into the room, her chest heaving, eyes wide with panic. She jabs a finger toward the hallway, words caught in her breathless gasps. I stoop to retrieve the pick, clasping it tightly before tucking it back under the stiff collar of this damned button-down the school makes us faculty wear.

"What's wrong?" I set the guitar on the desk and stride toward her, worry gnawing at my gut.

"Solaris." Lena's voice trembles as she points toward the door. "She needs help."

A cold dread seizes me, and my breath catches. Without another word, I bolt from the room, my heart pounding as I follow the surge of students crowding the hallway. I try to push through the sea of bodies, butt heir phones are up, blocking my path.

"Move!" I roar, but they barely flinch, more interested in whatever they're filming than in getting out of my way. I catch a glimpse of a screen, but there's too much chaos to see what's happening.

Suddenly, a scream cuts through the chatter—a sound so raw and piercing that it freezes the air around me. Solaris. My blood runs cold, and instinct takes over. I shove past the students, no longer caring about anything except reaching her.

I skid to a halt at the entrance to the girls' bathroom. There, in the center of the tiled floor, Solaris sits, rocking back and forth, her eyes vacant, lost in some distant place. Her fingernails dig into her arms, leaving trails of blood where she's scratched herself raw. Tears streak her face, mingling with the dirt that stains her dress and tangles in her curls.

A voice mutters behind me, "Must be drugs."

My hands clench into fists, rage bubbling up.

"Shut the fuck up!" Lena's voice snaps, followed by the sharp sound of a slap.

"What the hell happened to her?" I demand, though I'm not sure who I'm asking.

Lena steps up beside me, her voice trembling. "I—I don't know. She texted me for a—"

Sol's scream cuts her off. "Let me go! Get off me!"

She thrashes wildly, and I lunge forward, dropping to the cold tiles. "Sol!" I grab her before she can hurt herself, pulling her into my arms. I rock her gently, shushing her, trying to soothe whatever nightmare she's trapped in. But she's sobbing, twisting in my hold, repeating, "Please, please, please," over and over again.

Suddenly, she jerks back, her hand flying up, nails raking across my face.

"Dammit!" I hiss, pinning her hands down just as a camera flash goes off. My head snaps toward the crowd of students, and I glare at them, my voice a low, dangerous growl. "Get the fuck to homeroom!" Lena crouches beside me, worry etched across her face. "We need to snap her out of this."

"She needs her meds," Lena mumbles, almost to herself. "She needs her meds."

Meds? My mind races. What kind of medication is she on for this?

"I'm sorry, Cruise." Sol's voice is broken, choked with tears. "I'm sorry. I'll do it. I'll be a good girl."

Cruise?

My blood turns to ice at the mention of her brother. That bastard. Whatever he did, it's clear his actions are haunting her now. This is more than a breakdown; it's a memory tearing her apart.

He's fucking dead.

"What medicine?" I demand, lifting my gaze to Lena while trying to ignore the cameras behind her. "She wasn't on anything when I left."

Lena shakes her head, frustration tightening her expression. "I'll explain later—when we're not surrounded by idiots filming this. I'll go get them."

She hurries off, and I refocus on Solaris, adjusting her in my arms as she continues to plead, her voice small and broken. "Come on, Sol. I need you to snap out of this. You're here, at school. No one's going to hurt you. I'm right here. Please, Sol."

She whimpers into my chest, her body trembling against mine. I hold her tighter, rocking her gently, desperate for her to find her way back. Whatever Cruise did, whatever hell he put her through—she's stronger than it. Stronger than her past. I need her to remember that. I can't lose her to the shadows of her memories, not when I've just come home.

"Come on, Sol," I whisper, pressing a kiss into her tangled hair. "I'm right here."

"I got them!" Lena's voice cuts through the tension as she shoves through the crowd and drops to her knees beside me, fumbling with a small pill bottle. "Here."

I take the blue pills and the water from her, my hands steady despite the turmoil inside. "Hold her jaw open."

Lena nods, her movements quick and sure, just as Solaris bolts upright with a gasp. I pull her back down, pinning her gently while Lena grips her jaw, prying it open. Solaris thrashes, but I manage to keep her still long enough to pour the water and slip the pills into her mouth. She coughs, sputtering around the liquid, but I tilt her head back, forcing her to swallow.

"Come on," I murmur, my voice low and coaxing. "I need you to swallow." Her throat works, and for a moment, I hope that somewhere in the chaos of her mind, she hears me, knows I'm here for her. When her coughing subsides and her body relaxes slightly, so does mine. I wipe the sweat from her brow, smoothing her hair back from her face.

I turn to Lena, urgency tightening my chest. "How long does it take for these to work?"

"Not long," she says, her voice edged with worry. "They upped her dosage a few months ago. She should pass out within ten minutes."

I snatch the bottle from Lena's hand, needing to know what I've just given Solaris. My eyes narrow as I read the label—Diazepam. A glance at the dosage makes my gut twist. A hundred milligrams. That's a hefty dose, way too strong for something this addictive. But as Sol starts to calm in my arms, her frantic trembling easing, I push aside my concerns. It's working, and that's all that matters for now. Questions can wait, but there's no way she should be on something like this.

I scoop Sol into my arms and rise from the cold bathroom floor, her weight light and fragile against me. "I'm taking her home."

Lena stands as well, determination hardening her expression. "I'm coming with you."

The crowd of gawking students still hasn't dispersed, blocking our path. Frustration surges, and I shove through them, only to come face to face with the headmaster. His gaze flickers from Sol to me, a mixture of concern and authority tightening his features. "You can't take her. An ambulance is on the way. Staff can't remove students from the premises."

"Try to stop me." The words leave my mouth as a low growl, my eyes locking with his in a silent challenge. Without waiting for a response, I brush past him, Lena right behind me.

"Silas!" he calls after us, but I don't break stride. My focus is on getting Solaris out of here, away from the prying eyes and chaos. We make it outside, and I head straight for the faculty parking lot. Lena hurries ahead to open the car door, and I carefully lower Sol into the backseat. Her head lolls to the side, her breathing shallow but steady. Gently, I brush her hair from her face, loving the feel of the strands soft beneath my fingers.

She'll be okay. She has to be.

"I'll follow you," Lena says, her tone resolute.

I nod sharply, acknowledging her before sliding into the driver's seat. My fingers jab at the screen, navigating to Elizabeth's contact. As the phone rings, my grip on the steering wheel tightens, tension coiling in my chest.

The call barely connects before Elizabeth answers, her voice strained. "Silas . . . What's wrong with my daughter?"

I grit my teeth, bypassing her question. "Why the hell is she on such a high dose of diazepam?"

A heavy sigh echoes through the line. "You had to sedate her?"

The light ahead turns red, and I slow the car, casting a worried glance over my shoulder at Solaris, still unconscious in the back seat. "I didn't have a choice. We found her in the girls' restroom, rocking and screaming. What's going on, Elizabeth?"

"Nothing," she replies, the word too quick, too defensive. "It's just a precaution."

"Precaution?" I scoff, disbelief tightening my voice. "You don't put someone on that kind of medication unless there's a damn good reason. Tell me what's really going on."

Silence stretches for a moment, thick with unspoken truths. "You don't have the right to ask about her medical history, Silas. Just get her home. I'll catch the next flight out of New York."

Before I can push further, the line goes dead. My jaw clenches as frustration boils inside me. She's right—I don't have the right to demand answers. But this is Sol. She knows what her daughter means to me.

In the back seat, Solaris stirs but doesn't wake. I exhale slowly, turning down her street and pulling up in front of the red brick townhouse. Lena's already out of her car, rushing up the steps before I even open my door. I move quickly, circling to the back to lift Sol from the seat, her limp form light in my arms. By the time I reach the steps, Lena's got the door open, worry etched into every line of her face.

We step inside, the door closing behind us with a quiet thud.

Inside, I take a moment to absorb the atmosphere. The townhouse feels warm and lived-in, the complete opposite to the cold opulence of the James manor where Solaris grew up. Photographs from different stages of her life line the walls, capturing moments of laughter and triumph. Shelves are filled with awards, mementos of her hard-earned success. This is the life I always hoped she would find—simple, authentic, hers.

"This way." Lena darts up the stairs, and I follow, my gaze lingering on the homely touches around me.

The door creaks open, and I stride past Lena into Solaris' bedroom, laying her gently on the plush bed. As soon as she touches the soft sheets, she curls into a ball, her body trembling with unspoken fears. I reach out, brushing a curl from her face, letting the silky strands slip through my fingers. The sight of her like this, fragile and haunted, twists a knife in my chest.

"Cruise . . ." she murmurs, her voice barely audible in her sleep. The name sends a bolt of rage through me, my jaw tightening until it aches.

"You only came back for her, didn't you?" Lena's voice pulls me from my thoughts. I turn to face her, seeing the hurt in her eyes, the pain I didn't intend to cause. "You didn't even tell me you were coming home."

Her gaze drops to the floor, and guilt hits me hard. I cross the room in two strides, pulling her into a tight hug.

"You know that's not true," I say, holding her close. "You're my sister, Lena. I care about you just as much as I care about Solaris."

She pulls back, her blue eyes filled with sadness. "But you didn't come back for me. You left me with Mom while you traveled the world." Her eyes flick to Solaris, curled up on the bed. "Everyone's always here for her."

"Don't think like that." I tilt her chin up, forcing her to meet my gaze. "I'm here for you too. If you ever needed anything, all you had to do was call. I would've dropped everything and came back for you."

Lena searches my face, as if trying to believe me. She then moves to the bed, her gaze settling on Solaris' still form.

"Do you love her?" Lena's question catches me off guard. I jerk my eyes back to her, stunned. "I ask because Solaris has been in love with you since before your father even married into our family. And after everything happened—when she lost you—she didn't handle it well. If she hadn't landed that first acting role, I don't think she'd still be here."

Her words hit me like a punch to the gut. My brow furrows as I cross my arms, trying to process what she's saying. "What happened?"

"She and her mom were living in a shelter for a few months afterward."

"I know," I murmur, already aware of that dark chapter in her life.

Lena bites her lip, hesitating before continuing. "After she set the fire at my mom's house, they put her in therapy. Her mom thought it would help, but it didn't. Things got worse. She started blacking out, losing time. And when she blacked out . . . she wasn't herself. It got so bad, she spiraled and tried to kill herself. If you look closely enough, the scars are there, on her inner thigh."

A cold wave of horror washes over me. My eyes snap to Solaris, still trembling in her sleep. I start to reach for the hem of her dress, then stop, disgusted with myself. I'm not about to invade her privacy like that. If she ever feels comfortable enough to tell me, I'll listen. But right now, I need to get out of here. I can't stand here knowing what I know and not do something about it.

"Can you stay with her for a few hours?" I ask Lena, my voice rougher than I intend.

"Where are you going?"

"To pay Cruise a visit. Whatever set her off today, he's behind it. He needs to answer for that."

Lena nods, concern shadowing her features. "Don't hurt him too badly."

"Sure," I mutter, already halfway out the door, my mind focused on the confrontation ahead.

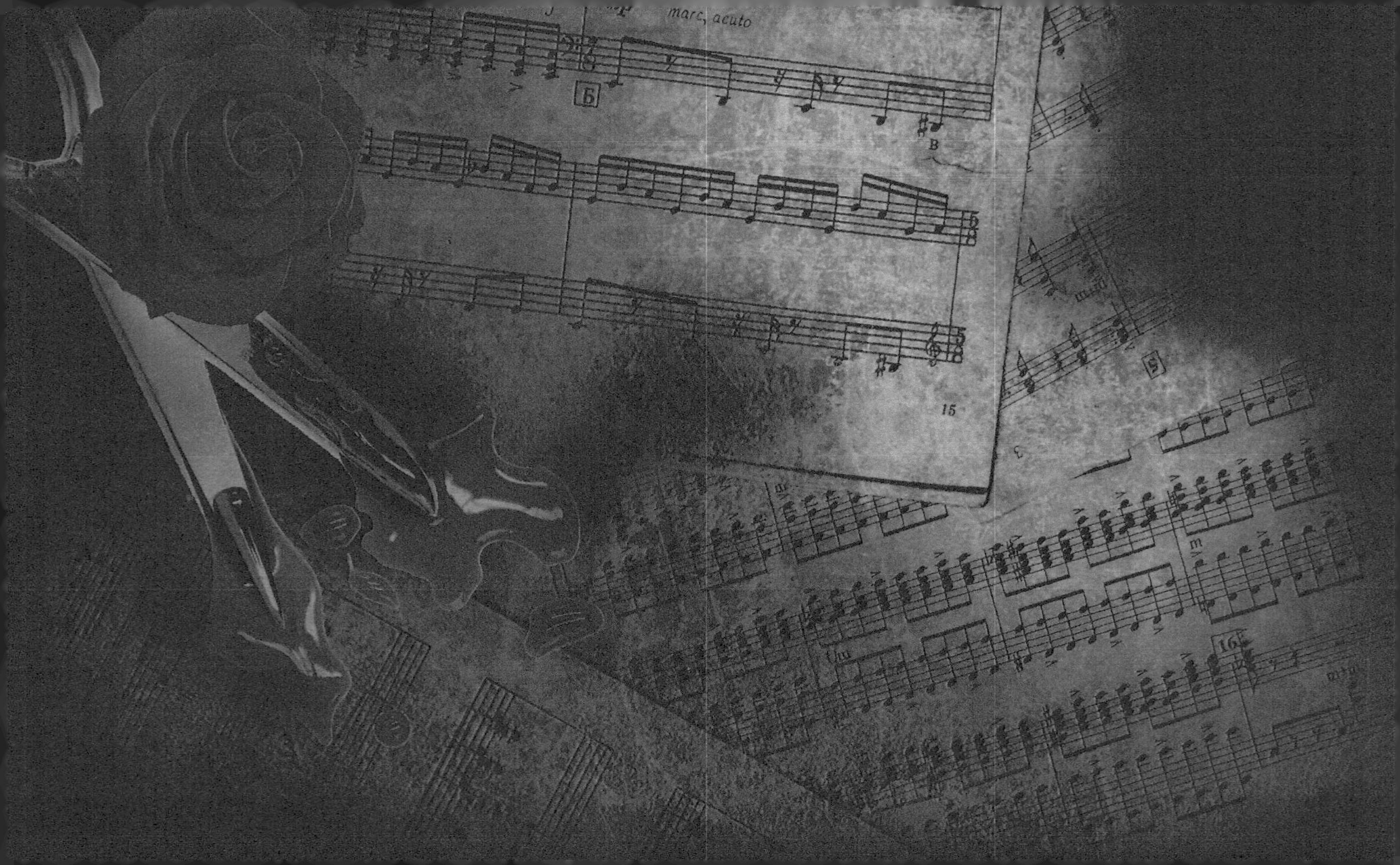
marc, acuto
Б
В
15
16

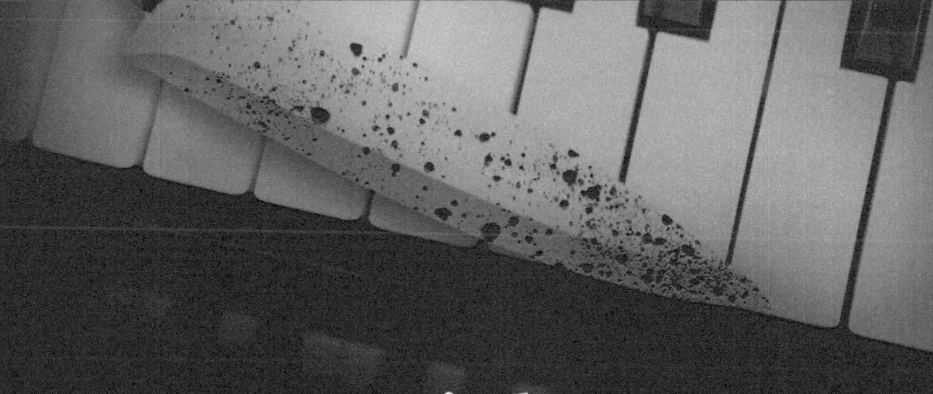

Eight

Silas

Six years ago

Tyson pulls the car to a stop right outside the main house, and I groan at the thought of stepping inside these walls. Ever since my father chewed me out for skipping that horrid dinner where he introduced me to Loretta, he's been making me stay at this manor. Says it's good for the image. Claims that if I mess with his image, he'll do the same to mine. If it were just me he was threatening, I'd deal. But bad publicity could ruin my career and my band. The guys are truly the only thing I care about right now, and I will do anything to prevent William O'Conner from screwing with that.

Even live in this house with Loretta and smile like I'm loving it.

"Don't forget. The meeting is at 10 sharp. This is our shot, man," Tyson reminds me for the umpteenth time in the last thirty minutes.

Our manager finally got us a meeting with one of the top executives in the music world. Luckily, he's staying in town at one of the James' hotels in between a layover to New York. He graciously agreed to meet us and listen to our demo.

"I know. I won't be late," I repeat again. "I'll be there."

"I'm just saying," He turns in the driver's seat to look at me, "you've been late to a lot of stuff lately. We've had to cancel three shows in the last month alone."

I comb my fingers through my shaggy hair and sigh. He has a point. Things haven't been going well since my father forced me to move in here. I've had to watch my back constantly and bend over backwards to please him. But tomorrow is different. Tomorrow is everything we've been working towards since we started this band five years ago. There's no way in hell I'm going to let him ruin this. It's my shot. My time. I can feel it, and I'm not relinquishing that for my father.

"I will be there," I tell Tyson more sternly. "You can count on that."

"Also, leave the girls at home," he stresses.

I frown at that. Lena and Solaris have been glued to my side since the day I got here. More Lena than Solaris. She seems really into music. I think it's a way for her to escape her mother. Since the school year ended, Lena's been wanting to be anywhere but at that manor. I get it. I do, but my mates have been having a problem with two preteen girls hanging around. No matter what their last names are.

"I wouldn't bring them to a meeting."

Tyson's hands flex around the stirring wheel. "Yeah, I know. Things are just weird with them around. Maybe cut back on it all together. I mean hell, they're adorable and all, but hot chicks aren't digging the look."

I nod at him. Lena's not going to like it, but my band-mates come first. Besides, I'm sure she and Solaris can find something to do. Solaris doesn't even seem interested half the time. She sits in a corner with a book in her hand, reading throughout the shows and rehearsals. She's been nothing like the gutsy kid I first met who called me a jerk. Now, she's quiet and reserved, just like the maid said. It makes no sense. I think I've seen her show that spirit maybe twice since then, and I've been living here for a month now.

"Alright then, I'll see you in the morning. Turn on your alarm and don't forget, 10 sharp."

I open the car door and get out without acknowledging him again. I'm not going to be late. He drives off and I don't make a move until his taillights disappear past the golden gate. Turning away from the main entrance, I make my way around the manor and down the path that leads to the pool house. I've been using Solaris' little passageway since she showed it to me. Even though I practically have to crawl through the tunnel, it's better than getting bitched at for coming in late after rehearsals. I swear part of my father must still think I'm some punk kid. He certainly treats me like one.

Bending down, I remove the prop I put in place to keep the pool house door from locking when I left earlier and go inside. I immediately go over to the basket of towels and move it aside. I pull my phone out in order to light the passage and head into the tunnel.

It takes me a good twenty minutes to make it down the tunnel and to the other door that leads to the sitting room. I'm just about to push through when I hear voices coming from inside. Glancing at the clock on my phone, I take in the time. It's a little after midnight. Usually, everyone in this house is in bed by ten.

The voices come again, and I push the door ajar a little just to see who I have to face. My father and Cruise are standing off to the side of the room with whiskey glasses in their hands. I frown at them. I can't stand fucking Cruise. He's literally the poster boy for rich, privileged jerks.

My father takes a drink of his whiskey. "And you're sure?"

Cruise tilts his head to the side as if asking my father if he's for real. "Of course. No one has had any complaints. And she hasn't said a word since this started five years ago. If you want her, you know the terms."

My father licks his lips and straightens. "And you're certain Solaris isn't going to cause problems for me. I don't care how delectable she might be, if she can't keep her trap shut—"

"From what I can tell, she doesn't remember," Cruise states. "She'll be the easiest fuck of your life. That I can promise."

My breath catches as I finally piece together what they're discussing. My stomach churns, and I recoil into the tunnel. They can't be . . . There's no way they're talking about what I think they are. I run a hand over my head and down my face. No. I must have heard it wrong. My father is a cruel man, but he's not . . . He can't be . . . My mother would have warned me if he was doing shady shit like this. And Cruise . . . How can he even talk about his sister like that? Sure, they aren't full-blooded siblings, but they are still blood related. My hands ball into fists at the mere thought of someone hurting that girl. Because that's what she is. A little girl. A kid.

God, I'm going to be sick.

When I hear laughter coming from inside the room, I crack open the door again. The whiskey glass William was drinking from moments ago is empty and in its place is a roll of bills. My father hands the cash to Cruise who's beaming like a schoolboy that just got his dick wet for the first time. A snarl leaves me at the sight of the money in Cruise's hand. Both of their eyes snap over towards the hidden passage, but the tree has the crack well hidden. When they don't see anything, they go back to their conversation. My father pours himself another glass and takes a sip.

"She'll be in her room at ten thirty tomorrow night. I'll disable the lock. Just go inside," Cruise tells William.

My father grins. "And she doesn't remember any of the encounters? I can do whatever I want?"

"My other clients tell me that she puts up a fight at first but after a minute or so, it's like she blacks out."

"You don't know firsthand?" my father asks.

Cruise scowls at him. "I don't need to see what you sick fucks do to her, as long as she's well-prepared for what I need. The only rule I have is to use a condom. No one comes in my sister."

My father loosens his tie before saying, "I suppose not. Wise. If you don't see it, you can deny it."

Cruise mutters something else, his voice low and indistinct, before turning on his heel and striding away. My father casts a final, sweeping glance around the room, as if checking for hidden threats, before following Cruise out. Once I'm certain neither of those bastards is coming back, I stumble out of the tunnel, my breath ragged and uneven. My hands claw at the artificial plant beside me, desperately trying to anchor myself. My entire body trembles from the gravity of the conversation I've just overheard. The realization of what's been happening is a gut-wrenching shock. This can't be real. Surely, the girl's father must be oblivious to this. Surely, if he knew, he would put a stop to it immediately.

I force myself to stop shaking, gritting my teeth as I steady my breathing. The urgency of the situation propels me forward. I can't let this happen. I can't allow William to follow through with his plans tomorrow. I sprint toward the entrance of the sitting room, my footsteps echoing down the hall as I dart toward the left wing of the mansion. Gregory has secured this part of the house for himself and Elizabeth. If I can reach him, I have no doubt he will intervene and prevent this nightmare from unfolding.

I round the corner only to come to a complete halt when I find my bastard of a father leaning against the banister with his whiskey glass still in hand. He looks me up and down, a sneer on his aging face as if I'm the one that has done something wrong. As if I'm the one who just paid to molest a fucking kid.

"I thought I heard something in there." He descends the stairs with deliberate slowness, his eyes narrowing. "What did you hear?"

"Nothing," I lie, my voice steady.

He circles me like a predator, his steps measured and purposeful. Once. Then twice. "Let's keep it that way," he says, a dark undertone in his voice.

I force my hands behind my back, clenching them into fists to steady my nerves. "What makes you think you'll ever get away with all the shit you do?" The defiant words are out before I can stop them.

My father pauses, his eyes scanning me from head to toe with a cold, calculating gaze. "If you're smart," he sneers, "you'll act like you didn't hear a thing. You have plenty riding on keeping me pleased."

"I don't need you," I shoot back, trying to keep the tremor out of my voice.

He laughs, a harsh, mocking sound that echoes in the hall. He steps closer, invading my space, his breath hot against my face. "Oh, but you do. You have a meeting with some hotshot music executive tomorrow, right? Your little band is counting on you. It would be a shame if that meeting went up in smoke."

I study his face, searching for any sign of weakness. His smirk widens, a self-satisfied gleam in his eye. A realization dawns on me; he knows. He's behind the meeting. He must be. I never discuss my career with him, yet here he is, using it as leverage. The truth is a knife twisting in my gut. My father, the puppeteer, pulling strings I didn't even know were attached.

"How?" I demand, my voice sharp.

He smirks, a cruel glint in his eyes. "You honestly think it's a coincidence that you just happen to get a meeting with a man staying at one of my hotels? Don't be stupid, Silas."

It's not even his hotel, but I bite my tongue, knowing it's not the point. "Why?" The question tumbles out, my voice barely a whisper.

His smile widens, turning into something dark and menacing. The sight chills me to my core. This man—this monster—has no limits. How can I share blood with someone so devoid of humanity? How could my mother have loved a creature like this? My stomach churns, threatening to expel its contents, but I manage to keep it down.

"You're my son. That's reason enough," he replies, as if that twisted logic makes any sense.

I shake my head, disbelief coursing through me. He's never done anything out of paternal instinct; there's always a sinister motive. "William O'Conner doesn't have a paternal bone in his body. So, what's the real truth?"

He takes a leisurely sip of his drink, swirling the amber liquid with a nonchalant sigh. "The truth? You have the potential to wield influence on a grander stage. If you're determined to pursue this path, I might as well leverage it to my advantage."

A surge of anger flares within me. "I will never let you use my bandmates," I hiss, each word laced with defiance.

His grin vanishes, replaced by a cold, hard expression. "You have no choice. Haven't you realized that yet? I own you. Just as I owned your mother. And just as I will own everything the James family has. This is my town."

I glare at him with defiance. "You're delusional if you think Loretta isn't playing a game of her own. I've seen the way she looks at you, and let me tell you, Dad, it's far from hearts and flowers."

My father halts his pacing, eyes narrowing with cold fury. In an instant, the crystal whiskey glass flies through the air, smashing into the side of my face. The impact sends me reeling, stumbling back into the giant round table in the middle of the foyer. Before I can regain my footing, his hand clamps around my throat, shoving me against the table's edge. William's grip tightens, cutting off my air, and I claw desperately at his hand, gasping for breath.

"Listen here, son. Fall. In. Line," he growls, each word dripping with venom. "I've tolerated your little rebellion for far too long, but I'm done. If I have to make you disappear like your mother, I will. And stay away from Solaris. I don't share my toys, especially not with the likes of you."

A low, primal growl escapes my lips, rage surging through me. I won't let him hurt her. I won't let this bastard hurt any child.

He releases me, and I collapse to the floor, gasping for air. Grabbing me by the collar of my now-soaked shirt, he hurls me toward the foot of the stairs. "Go clean yourself up and get to bed. You've got to make a good first impression in the morning."

I lie there, chest heaving, the weight of his threats pressing down on me. But as I stagger to my feet, one thought crystallizes in my mind: I will protect Solaris, no matter the cost.

My father walks away, leaving me sprawled on the floor. When his footsteps finally fade against the hardwood, I tentatively bring a hand to my face. A sharp pain flares through the right side, and I bite back a cry. I refuse to show weakness—not to him, not to anyone.

Forcing myself upright, I grip the banister and painstakingly make my way up to the second floor, where my room is. August can't come soon enough; at least then, I'll be back on campus, away from my father and this twisted family.

But even as the thought crosses my mind, I know it's unfair to lump everyone in this manor together. Gregory and his wife have been kind, and Lena and Solaris are wonderful. It's just my father, Loretta, and Cruise who are the real problem.

It takes me a grueling ten minutes to ascend the stairs. Each movement sends fresh waves of pain through my head, as if shards of glass are embedded in my skin. Finally, I reach my room and push the door open, only to hear a gasp. My head snaps up, and I wince at the pain.

Solaris stands by my bed, wearing a pair of night shorts and a tank top. She rushes over, her eyes darting over my injuries with concern. Even through my blurred vision, I can see the worry etched on her face.

"What happened?" she questions, her voice soft and sweet.

I ignore her question, still in shock seeing her in my room. "What are you doing here?"

She shakes her head and grabs my hand, pulling me over to the bed. She searches my face one more time before darting off to the adjoining bathroom. I hear the water running and her rummaging through cabinets for a good five minutes before she darts back over to me. She lays a pair of tweezers, a bottle of peroxide, a bowl of water, and two towels on the bed. I go to arch a brow at her, but even that's painful. The last time I saw that bowl, it had noodles in it. That was three days ago. Hopefully, she did more than pour out the noodles and fill the bowl with water.

"What happened?" she asks again. "Did you get into a fight?"

She takes the tweezers and I jerk back. "Do you know what you're doing?"

"No," she states and moves forward with the tweezers anyway.

My whole body tenses as Solaris gently plucks the first piece of glass from my face. She drops it into the bowl of water and immediately goes in for a second shard. I watch her closely, mesmerized by her calmness. Not once does she flinch at the sight of blood or the jagged pieces of glass.

When she sets the tweezers down and picks up a towel and peroxide, I intercept her hand, taking the items from her. She frowns but remains silent. Uncapping the brown bottle, I soak the towel with the antiseptic and press it against the left side of my face, hissing at the sting. For the first time, Solaris cracks a small grin. She takes the cloth from me, carefully dabbing at the individual cuts.

"Are you going to tell me what happened, Si?" she asks, her voice soft. She drops the towel on the bed and then sits down on the floor in front of me.

I slide down beside her, leaning against the bed frame. "Are you going to tell me how and why you're in my room?"

Her eyes drop, and she pulls her knees up, resting her chin on them. "I got scared," she admits with a shrug.

"Of what?" I ask, leaning in closer. "Did you have a nightmare, kiddo?"

"No." She shakes her head defensively. "Someone tried to get into my room."

"What?" I jerk up, alarmed. Her eyes widen, and she scoots back slightly. "What do you mean?"

"I was texting Lena, and then I heard something," she explains, her voice trembling slightly. "At first, I thought it was just my imagination. It tends to run wild sometimes. But then they started pulling on the door."

A chill runs down my spine as my mind immediately goes to my father. Surely, he wouldn't be that desperate. But then, who am I kidding? He'll do whatever it takes to get what he wants.

"When was this?" I ask, trying to keep my voice steady.

"About fifteen minutes before you came up here," she replies.

I feel a slight relief. It couldn't have been my father; he was with Cruise. "You decided to come to me with this? Why not go to your dad?"

Solaris bites down on her bottom lip, tapping her fingers against her knee. She blinks several times before finally answering. "He and my mom are out of town. They left earlier tonight after he got a call about one of the hotels in Florida."

Her words hit me like a punch to the gut. I lean back, rubbing a hand over my face. She's alone in that house aside from Cruise and vulnerable to whatever he might be cooking up. The gravity of the situation sinks in, making my protective instincts surge.

"What about telling your aunt?" I suggest, trying to think of someone who could help. "You know, someone who's family."

Solaris scoffs, crossing her arms. "Oh, please, that woman's a bitch."

The sudden venom in her voice startles me. My brows shoot up at the unexpected shift. One minute she's a scared, sweet kid, and now . . . her eyes flash with a mixture of anger and disdain, so different to the vulnerable girl who was just trembling at the thought of an intruder.

"You okay?"

The corner of her mouth tilts up and she rises to her knees. "Do I not look okay?"

"Umm . . ." I ease back a little.

What the hell?

She steps closer, her eyes locking onto mine. "I'm fine, but I'll be even better if you let me stay here tonight. I don't want to go back to that room."

No. No. No. Definitely not a good idea. Especially after what just happened.

"That's not a good idea," I stammer, swallowing hard as she bats her lashes at me. I scramble to my feet, trying to put some distance between us.

Reaching for the bowl of bloody water on the bed, I feel her hand stop me, resting gently on mine. I freeze, staring at her small, delicate fingers for longer than I should. No. Just no. I'm not my father. I won't look at a kid like that, no matter how much she's trying to be close right now.

"You need to leave," I say, my voice firmer than I feel.

Her eyes narrow, and a sly smirk plays on her lips as she steps in even closer. "Remember when I told you I know things?"

I nod, searching her face. My gaze shifts to her hand tapping a rhythm against her leg. She doesn't seem aware of it, but I recognize the beat instantly. It's from one of my songs. One I thought she barely noticed when I brought her and Lena to rehearsal.

"Yeah, well, I know lots of things," she says, her voice laced with a cryptic edge. "So let me stay."

The tapping quickens, and her eyes flicker past me. I turn around to see what caught her attention, but there's only a window there. I turn back to her just as her brows furrow, confusion evident. She bites her lip and looks back at me.

"You okay?" I ask, concerned.

She nods, her eyes darting to the bowl of water and then back to me. She tucks a curl behind her ear, her cheeks flushing. "Did we get all the glass?"

I'm caught off guard by the sudden shift in her demeanor. "Are you sure you're alright, Solaris?"

She nods again, this time with a forced smile, and grabs the bowl. "I'll get this cleaned up."

Before I can process the rapid changes in her behavior, she gathers everything from the bed and rushes to the bathroom, closing the door behind her. The absence of running water makes me uneasy. I turn to the dresser with the mirror and inspect my reflection, trying to make sense of what just happened. There's a gash above my brow still oozing blood, but at least my face doesn't look too bad.

Confusion and worry gnaw at me as I try to piece together Solaris' erratic actions. Surely, it isn't just me trying to rationalize her little crush. She was acting strange.

When the bathroom door opens again, I turn to see Solaris standing in the doorway, her gaze fixed on the floor. Relief washes over me; at least she's not looking at me like she did earlier. The sheepish expression on her face is a welcome change from the unsettling one she wore moments ago.

She walks over to me, still not meeting my eyes. "Please don't make me go back to that room."

I know the right thing to do is to tell her she should go. I know it as surely as I know every note to every song I've ever written. But the tears glistening on her lashes choke my words. Not only that, I just overheard a conversation about her being molested. It feels wrong to send her back, especially after she said someone tried to get into her room. Cruise made it clear that my father wasn't the first person to pay for her. It could've been another one of his clients. I can't send her back if there's a risk she'll get hurt even worse.

"Okay," I relent. "You can stay. But only until your parents get back. Then you need to tell them what happened tonight."

She finally lifts her head to look at me and nods, giving me a shy smile before yawning. I check the time on my phone; it's just after one.

I gesture toward the bed. "Go get some sleep. It's late."

She glances at the bed and then back at me. "Where are you going to sleep?"

I look at the king-sized bed, then back at her. "I'll take the floor. Don't worry."

She shakes her head before I even finish speaking. "It's a big bed, Si. We can share. I share all the time with Lena during sleepovers. It's no big deal."

Wrong. It's a huge deal. A grown man should never share a bed with a child. The mere idea of it is sickening. Disgusting.

"Please," she adds, her voice small and pleading. "I don't really want to be alone."

I glance at the bed again, and even as I hear myself saying it, I know I'm making a mistake. "Fine."

Her face lights up, and she quickly climbs onto the bed, patting the space beside her. Reluctantly, I turn off the lamp and join her.

"Thank you," she whispers, rolling over to face away from me.

I lie there in silence, listening to her breathing as it slows and steadies, indicating she's asleep. My mind races, trying to process everything I learned tonight and the fact that I am sleeping in a bed with a kid. A little girl. A child who I just learned has been assaulted for the past five years.

God, someone strike me down now.

Nine

I roll over, trying to escape the oppressive warmth enveloping me. The heat follows, and with a groggy sigh, I turn onto my back and slowly open my eyes. As I rub the sleep away, my vision clears to reveal messy brown curls and a chiseled jaw beside me. A squeak escapes as I jerk upright, hand clapping over my mouth to stifle the sound. Panic surges as I glance around, taking in the surroundings.

We're in my room.

A gasp slips out as the events of the day crash down on me—Loretta, Cruise, and a stranger.

Oh God . . .

My body trembles uncontrollably, a low whine building in my throat as memories flood back, each one more horrifying than the last. I shake my head, trying to dispel the images, just as Silas stirs beside me.

"Sol?" he murmurs, my name a soft exhale mingled with a yawn.

I don't respond, too consumed by the horror replaying in my mind. He shifts behind me, turning me gently to face him. I stare at the cream comforter, unable to meet his eyes, the weight of the revelations crushing me.

Then, it clicks—his words, his actions. He knew. Silas knew what was happening to me.

"You knew." The words choke out of me, raw and accusatory. "You knew and you let it happen."

Silas shakes his head, confusion creasing his brow. "What happened yesterday?"

"Yesterday?" My voice rises, shrill and panicked. "It's Saturday?"

He nods, pushing a stray curl away from his face. "You had a panic attack. You were screaming for help. Lena and I brought you back here. She called your mother, and Elizabeth is coming home today."

I stumble out of bed, colliding with the wall, my breath hitching. "Cruise, he . . ."

Silas jumps up and circles the bed, pulling me into his chest. His arms wrap around me, strong and comforting, like they used to. "Don't worry about your brother. I'll handle him." His voice, edged with cold resolve, sends a shiver through me.

I glance up, meeting his intense green eyes. For a moment, they search my face before he pulls me closer, rubbing soothing circles on my back.

"He let people . . ." I struggle, the words catching in my throat.

"Say it," Silas urges, his voice firm yet gentle. "Admit what you went through."

A violent shiver courses through me as flashes of men pawing at my body sear my mind. My fists clench against Silas' crumpled shirt, the reality of it all too much to bear. "Cruise let people a-assault me. He sold me."

Silas continues to trace calming patterns on my back as the confession spills out, each word a jagged piece of my broken past. How could I have forgotten something so monstrous? How could my own brother, someone meant to protect me, have orchestrated such horror? My thoughts spiral, wondering how many knew—how many turned a blind eye because it was Cruise, the golden boy, giving the orders.

Oh God . . .

I break away from Silas and rush to the bathroom, collapsing against the toilet as dry heaves wrack my body. Nothing comes up, only a strangled sob escaping as I stare at the dirt caking my hands. I need to wash it all away, every last bit of filth clinging to my skin. On unsteady legs, I yank at the skimpy dress, desperate to shed the remnants of yesterday.

Silas steps in behind me, silently helping as I struggle with the fabric. He pulls the dress over my head, and I stand there, bare and vulnerable, feeling like I'm shedding layers of guilt and shame with each discarded piece of clothing.

"Sol, are you alright?"

I shake my head. "No, but I will be."

Silas looks at me with concern. "I hate to leave, but I need to go to the women's shelter. You can come with me if you want. It might help distract you from everything."

I turn away from him, my voice trembling with anger. "Why didn't you stop it?"

He exhales deeply, leaning against the double vanity. "I did everything I could once I found out. Do you remember the first night you came to my room? When you said someone was at your bedroom door?"

I nod, hugging myself tightly. "That's the night I learned the truth. My father had paid Cruise for you, and he didn't like that I overheard their conversation."

"What?" My face flushes with anger and shame, my body shaking. "No! I didn't sleep with your father."

Silas places his hands on my shoulders, eyes locking with mine. "You didn't sleep with any of them. They preyed on an eleven-year-old child. You were innocent."

I want to believe him, but the memory of that night lingers. Yes, I was frightened initially, but once I reached Silas' room, my fear dissipated. I had harbored feelings for him for some time, and that night, after tending to his face, I attempted to convey those emotions. I longed to remain by his side. An innocent girl wouldn't have acted so boldly.

"No, I wasn't innocent," I murmur, catching a glimpse of my reflection in the mirror. I sigh deeply. "That night I came to your room, I desired you, and I shouldn't have even understood what that meant."

"Even so, you're still a child," Silas replies, his eyes searching my face. He exhales heavily. "No one should have ever laid a hand on you."

A heavy silence falls between us, his meaning crystal clear. To him, I'm just a child—that's all I'll ever be. Perhaps that's a blessing, considering what I've just remembered. Yet, something about his statement unsettles me. Despite the six years lost, I still care for him deeply. And even after recent revelations, a part of me yearns for him to reciprocate my feelings.

My head drops in defeat. It's a futile hope. Why would Silas O'Conner, country pop sensation, want someone so ir-revocably tainted? Because that's what I am—what Silas has known me to be since the night I tried to convince him that my presence in his bed was something harmless. He could never truly want someone who has been so thoroughly used and couldn't even remember it.

As I turn away, Silas grasps my arm gently. "Hey, what's that look for? I don't want to leave if you might do something rash."

I shake my head, avoiding his gaze. "I just need a shower."

He rests his chin atop my head, nodding slightly. "Alright. I'll be at the shelter until noon, but I'm coming straight back afterward, okay?"

"What time is it now?" I ask, reaching to turn on the water.

"A little after seven."

I test the water, adjusting it to scalding before unhooking my bra. I hear Silas inhale sharply and shift uncomfortably. I tense at his reaction to me. He can't possibly be attracted to this body, not knowing what it has gone through. No one would be. But maybe, just maybe . . . smirking to myself, I turn to face him. His eyes widen momentarily as they rake over me, taking in every part of me. As is shocked though, he abruptly turns and strides towards the door. He pauses in the doorway, his back to me.

"Don't do that," he admonishes. "Don't try to gloss over what happened just because I'm here and you have a mis-guided infatuation."

"Misguided?" I scoff, a bitter laugh escaping my lips. I close the distance between us, wrapping my arms around his waist and pressing my chest against his back. The warmth of his body seeps through the thin fabric of his button down, igniting a spark within me and causing my pussy to weep. "It's not misguided or mistaken or any of those things. I'd much rather focus on us than dwell on Cruise and his . . . exploits."

Silas shakes his head, his muscles tensing beneath my touch as he extricates himself from my embrace. "No," he says, his voice firm. "I won't be like them. I refuse to take advantage of you. You should be grateful for that."

"I'm offering myself to you," I insist, my voice barely above a whisper. "That's not the same."

As a matter of fact, I wish he would touch me. I wish he would erase the memories flooding my brain right now. Maybe then, with his touch, I wouldn't feel so dirty. So tarnished.

"It is when you're just now—"

A piercing scream cuts through the air, drowning out the sound of running water and silencing Silas mid-sentence. I inhale sharply, my heart leaping into my throat as I bend down to retrieve my dress. Silas bolts from the bathroom, his footsteps thundering down the hallway just as a deafening gunshot echoes through the house.

I freeze, my body rigid with fear. The sound of Silas' feet pounding down the stairs reverberates in my head, each step like a hammer against my skull. Then, an eerie silence descends, broken only by the quiet hiss of the water.

Shaking myself from my paralysis, I hurries to don the dress. The only person who would have a key to this place is my mother. She would be the only woman entering this town house who could possibly make such a sound. Swallowing hard, I ease my way out of the bathroom, my bare feet silent against the cold floor. I take a deep breath, steeling myself before approaching the stairs.

I look down.

And scream.

Silas' head whips towards me, his eyes wide with alarm ."Go back to your room," he commands, his voice strained.

Ignoring his words, I rush down the stairs, my legs nearly giving way beneath me as I drop to the floor beside Silas and my mother's motionless form. Blood pools around us, a crimson tide seeping into the pristine carpet. My eyes fix on the gaping wound on the right side of her head. I shake my head, not believing what I'm seeing. Who would do this? Why would someone do this? My mom is a sweet woman. She wouldn't harm a freaking fly, nevertheless do something to deserve this.

"Call the police," Silas instructs, cradling my mother's head in his lap. When I remain frozen, my gaze locked on her lifeless face, he raises his voice. "Solaris, phone!"

With trembling hands, I pull myself up from the floor, my legs unsteady as I climb the stairs. I find my phone where I left it, lying abandoned on the floor. Grasping it tightly, I dial 911, my heart pounding in my ears as I wait for someone to answer. When the call connects, I bypass all pleasantries, my voice raw and urgent.

"T-there's been a murder," I stammer, forcing the words past the lump in my throat. "Come right now." I recite our address, the familiar numbers feeling foreign on my tongue, before ending the call and rushing back downstairs.

Silas paces, his clothes stained with blood, and I gasp at the sight. For the first time since the gunshot, the scene registers in horrifying clarity. Blood splatters the open front door, a macabre contrast to my mother's lifeless, shocked expression. Her fingers clutch a piece of paper, her last grip on the world. My heart races, pounding in my chest like a war drum, as the reality of the crowd gathering outside the house sinks in.

A violent tremor overtakes my body, and I collapse to my knees, crawling towards my mother's body. I pry the paper from her rigid fingers, desperate for answers.

"No!" Silas shouts. "Don't touch anything!"

But it's too late. I unfold the parchment, my hands shaking, and read the chilling message meant for me:

This is your final warning. Stay away from the estate.

A red haze clouds my vision, and I crush the letter in my fist. They did this. All because of the damn will, something I never wanted. Rage boils inside me, threatening to erupt. I grind my teeth to keep from screaming. They are going to pay for this. I don't care what it takes. I don't care who I have to hurt. They will all suffer.

A dull ache blooms in my chest, and I press my hand against it, trying to calm the storm within. The sound of sirens grows louder, and Silas reaches down to pull me to my feet. I wrench myself free from his grasp and glare at him, my eyes burning with accusation. He's one of them. If he can casually dine with the worst of them, he's complicit.

He's no better. He stood by while they hurt me. He stood by while Loretta had me dragged from his room like trash.

He may not have inflicted the pain directly, but he enabled it. Silas made me feel safe, made me believe I mattered in a mansion that despised me. He pretended to care. But let's be real—you don't let the kind of horrors that happened to me happen to people you care about. You just don't.

But they'll see.

They will all see.

They will all feel my pain.

They say there's nothing sweeter than revenge. Well, my "family" is about to find out just how sweet it can be.

"Ma'am," a voice finally breaks through the chaos. "We need to secure the scene. Paramedics are on the way."

I look around, disoriented, and see the sea of police uniforms. Numbly, I comply, stepping aside as Silas grasps my arm, guiding me to the edge of the hall. A camera flash catches my eye, but I ignore it, knowing the media vultures have already begun to circle.

"Solaris," Silas murmurs, pressing his forehead against mine. I don't pull away. "Tell me you're okay."

"I'm okay," I lie, my voice steady. He doesn't need to know I'm being torn apart inside. He doesn't need to know that he's on my list too. He doesn't need to know that, at the first opportunity, I will dismantle every member of that family. He doesn't need to know that his fate is sealed, just like the rest of them.

"You don't look okay," he whispers, concern etched in his voice. "You're kind of scaring me."

I offer a small, cold smile but say nothing.

He should be scared.

They all should be scared.

Another officer catches my attention. She's young and petite, looking almost too delicate for this grim scene. "Ma'am, I need you both to step outside so we can tape off the area."

"But my mom . . . You have to get her to the hospital." The words tumble out of me, nonsensical. She's gone. She doesn't need a hospital. I know that. A hospital can't bring her back. Nothing can bring her back. My grip tightens around the crumpled letter in my hand. No, nothing will bring her back. But something can avenge her—and me.

The officer's voice is gentle yet firm. "I'm sorry, but your mother is dead." She lays a hand on my arm, her touch meant to comfort. "I truly am sorry, but please, step outside."

I nod, numbly stepping out the door into the harsh, flashing lights. The cacophony of camera shutters and shouting voices is overwhelming, like a physical assault.

"Solaris James!" a voice shouts above the din. "Is that your mother's corpse?"

"Did you kill your mother?" another one yells, the accusation piercing through the noise.

I turn, blinded by another flash directly in my face.

"Does this have anything to do with drugs?"

Drugs?

"Shut up," I mutter, but my voice is barely audible amidst the frenzy.

"Solaris!"

"Solaris!"

"Solaris James!"

"Shut up!" I scream, my voice cracking as I collapse to the ground, the weight of everything crushing down on me. This isn't real. This can't be happening. A sob escapes me, raw and involuntary. The questions and accusations continue to rain down, each one sharper than the last. My vision blurs, and a relentless pounding throbs in my head.

I need them to leave. I need to be alone. I need air. I need a shower. I need my mom . . .

Hot tears stream down my face as a strong grip pulls me away from the crowd. A door opens and closes, muffling the chaos but not stopping the flashes or the pounding in my head. I curl up on the seat, burying my face in my knees, trying to shut it all out.

"Sol," Silas gently lifts my head from my knees, but I jerk back, recoiling from his touch. "I know this is difficult, but a lot is about to happen. I need you present, and I need you okay."

"I'm fine," I lie, my voice hollow. "Completely fine."

He shakes his head, not believing me. "No, you're not, but I need you to pretend to be."

I nod, barely hearing his words. "How long is this going to take?"

He shrugs, a look of helplessness crossing his face. "As long as it takes for them to question us."

"I have an interview at noon," I say, not caring about it but desperate for any excuse to get away from him, from this nightmare.

Silas' expression tightens with concern, but he reluctantly nods. He moves to open the door, then hesitates, looking at me intently, likely gauging how well I'm holding it together. He edges closer, and my body stiffens. Noticing, he keeps a respectful distance, conscious of the eyes of the media and the police outside.

"Look, I know this is hard. And I know you may feel like you have no one right now. I did when my mom died—"

"My mom didn't die," I cut him off, my voice cold and resolute. "She was murdered. She was murdered, and they are all going to pay."

Silas reaches over, his hand resting on mine. "Sol, revenge won't solve anything. Besides, you don't even know who did this."

I turn to face him, the crumpled note tight in my grip. "Yes, I do. They think they can scare me away from what's rightfully mine. They think they can let me be a-assaulted and walk away unpunished. They're dead wrong."

Silas takes the note, his eyes narrowing as he reads it, lips pressed into a thin line. "We need to turn this over to the authorities."

I shake my head, defiant. "No. This is my family we're dealing with." And you, too. "Do you really believe the cops will make them pay? They won't touch them. But I will."

He pulls his hand away, a flicker of something—fear?uncertainty?—crossing his face. "You need to think about what you're saying. You're grieving—"

"No!" My voice rises, sharper than I intended. "I'm not grieving, and I know exactly what I'm saying. Since it's you, I'm giving you a choice: them or me. Make no mistake, if you choose them, I'll take you down with the rest."

"What about Lena?" he asks, eyebrows furrowing in concern.

"What about her?"

"Are you lumping her in with the rest of your family, like you just did with me?"

"No, of course not. I'd never harm her." A camera flash catches my eye, and I glance back to see Brandon Black arriving on the scene. Ignoring him, I turn back to Silas and lower my voice. "But you, Silas, you've already betrayed me once. You left me. You let Cruise do that to me."

"I—" he starts, but I cut him off, raising a hand.

"You could have called the police. You could have told my dad. You could have done more than just get me out of the house. You didn't, and I blame you for that. But I'm giving you a choice now."

Silas' shoulders slump slightly, a resigned look in his eyes. "You're right. But you're wrong if you think I would ever choose them over you. I've always put you first, even when it was the wrong thing to do. If helping you get your revenge will bring you peace, then I'm with you. All in."

I tilt my head, eyes wide with a mix of surprise and skepticism. After seeing him with Loretta, I didn't think he'd actually choose me. This could spiral out of control quickly, and he has more at stake than I do.

"Really?" I ask, searching his face for any hint of deception.

"Yeah," he affirms, his voice steady. "It's always been you and me. You know this. However, we're doing this my way, or not at all."

A slow grin spreads across my face. "Fine. But I want them to suffer before they die."

Silas leans back against the cloth interior of the car. "Between the two of us, that shouldn't be a problem."

The car door opens, and the female cop from earlier slides in. She adjusts her mirror, catching my gaze in its reflection. "You must be famous or something, kid. These reporters are relentless."

I shrug, indifferent. She's probably not a fan of my show, but everyone in Mountain Rose knows my family. Even if Loretta kicked me off the estate, she can't change the fact that I'm a James. And this cop can't pretend to not know who Silas O'Conner is. His father was the freaking mayor up until last year.

The cop starts the car. "I'm taking you both to the precinct for statements. After that, you'll be free to go."

I give her a polite smile. "Free to go." Free to start enacting my revenge.

Ten

I run my fingers through my straightened hair, staring out the window at the line of sleek town cars parked in front of my aunt's home. After being released from questioning, I finally contacted the lawyer handling my father's will. I informed him of the recent events and expressed my intention to take over the estate. Mr. Stanley suggested I move in while he prepared the necessary paperwork and my letter of inheritance. Silas had boldly agreed, insisting it would be best for me to be on the property as well. I reluctantly complied, and ever since, I've been confined to this room—grudgingly offered by Loretta, who didn't want me setting foot in the main manor.

And now, on the day of my mother's funeral, I have to face a parade of hypocrites. I have to plaster on a smile for the press and act like I'm holding it together, while inside, I'm losing my freaking mind.

The door to my room creaks open, and I glance over my shoulder to see Silas enter. He's dressed in a sharply tailored Louis Vuitton suit. I scoff at the sight, turning my attention back to the cars outside. The Silas I knew would never have worn something so formal, preferring his black tees, jeans, and boots. The only time I'd seen him dress up was for his 21st birthday, and even then, it had been reluctantly.

Silas crosses the room in a few quick strides, stopping behind me. This is the first time he's come to see me since everything happened. I've seen him around, mostly with Loretta, who undoubtedly placed me in this house to keep us apart. She clearly wasn't pleased when she saw the photo Brandon Black published of us walking out of the police station last week.

My hands twitch at my sides as his scent envelops me, warm and familiar like a heavy blanket. The heat from his body radiates like a sauna, and despite the part of me that wants to lean into him, the more rational part resists. This situation is his fault. He insisted I stay in this house with that woman, instead of finding a place where my mother's blood didn't stain the carpets. He claimed we could better investigate her murder from inside the compound.

But where has Silas been?

Trailing Loretta like a devoted lapdog.

Silas' hands land on my shoulders, but I keep my gaze fixed ahead. "You haven't answered any of my messages or calls," he says.

I shrug off his hands and scoff. "I figured you were too busy working and fucking Loretta. Didn't want to intrude on your precious time."

"It's not like that," he defends.

"Whatever," I mutter, shrugging again.

He pulls me away from the window, out of sight from anyone who might glance up, and shoves me against the wall. My eyes widen in surprise. The last time I saw Silas like this was before the club, back when I was a kid. He was always so angry and brooding—never with me, of course—but there was something captivating about it.

"I said it's not like that," he growls, his voice low and intense. Heat rises in my cheeks. "Believe what you want about why I let you go all those years ago, but don't for one second think I would be with that woman if I didn't have to."

I gulp and look away, fighting the urge to do something reckless, like kiss him. "So you are? With her, I mean?"

He grabs my chin and forces me to meet his eyes. Silas bends slightly, bringing us closer. "Not in the way that matters," he murmurs, his breath tickling my cheeks and making me weak.

His words twist something in my chest, my brows scrunching in confusion, but I refuse to let it show. That could mean two completely different things depending on who you ask. Should I take that to mean they aren't having sex? Part of me wants to believe that may be the case, but at the end of the day, he came back to Mountain Rose for Loretta, not for me. He's here because she ordered him to be.

"But you are sleeping with her?" My voice lowers, fear of the answer chasing away some of the confidence I had in asking.

Silas' hand falls from my chin, the absence of his flesh against mine killing something inside me. He straightens and runs a hand through his hair, turning to the window to avoid my gaze. "We're not talking about my sex life."

I scoff, feeling a bitter laugh rise in my throat. "So you can force me to admit what Cruise did, but you can't answer one simple question?"

He glances over his shoulder at me and scowls, his voice cold. "One question that no student of mine should be asking."

I stomp over to him, my anger replacing the scorching heat from a second ago. "But you're not a real teacher, Silas, are you? Because teachers don't throw their students over their shoulders and drag them back to their place, do they? You're just a substitute, and soon you won't even be that."

His brows furrow and his eyes darken, the vibrant emerald turning nearly black. I instinctively step back, but he closes the distance with a single step, bringing us back to where we started. I swallow hard, taking him in once more. The crush

I had on him as a child has only intensified over the years. Seeing him up close, the longing for him hits me even harder. I hate that the suit he's wearing hides the sleeve of tattoos he got when he first signed with the record label.

I bite the inside of my cheek and search his face, finding that the hardness from a moment ago has faded. Taking a risk, I gently grasp his left hand and push up the sleeve of his blazer and dress shirt. My heart flutters at the sight of the cluster of stars surrounded by a variety of poisonous flowers inked on his skin. He told me once that my name meant star, which I had already known. My father always called me his shining star. So, when he got this, I knew it was for me, even with him denying it the whole time. I was Silas' bright light amongst a sea of vipers.

"I missed you," I finally admit. "I went to as many concerts as I could, but I never had the courage to talk to you. I want us to go back to how things were. Can't we have that?"

Silas pulls his arm from my grasp and turns away with a sigh. "No."

I go and sit on the bed. "Why not?"

He moves to the window and leans against the frame, shaking his head before speaking. "Because it was inappropriate then, and it would be a scandal now. You're not the bratty little girl who crawled into my bed because you were scared. And I'm not going to be the man who ignores the stars in your eyes anymore. Going back is impossible, Sol."

I hop off the bed and approach him, taking his hand and pulling him away from the window. "It doesn't have to be. I'm finally eighteen. We could leave, and go wherever we want. Travel and actually see the places we go. You don't have to stay with Loretta."

For a moment, time stands still. Silas just stares at me, his gaze flickering across my face. I take a step into him, my hand landing on his chest, and he lets me. His arm circles my lower back, his thumb rubbing circles through the thin silk of my black dress. The look in his eyes strips me bare, and I can't seem to pull my gaze away from the intense emerald of his. He licks his bottom lip, and a whimper catches in my throat.

"And what about your revenge?" His question catches me off guard, pulling my thoughts back to the here and now and away from the idea of us running away. "Are you willing to give that up so easily?"

I bite my lip and step out of his hold. As much as I care for Silas, my family still needs to pay. They need to plead and beg like my mother and I had to. Cruise needs to know what it feels like to be so utterly violated, and then to lose it all. And Loretta—she has to face justice for what she did.

"That's what I thought," Silas says, pulling me back from my thoughts of revenge. "I'll make you a deal, Sol."

I arch an eyebrow. "What kind of deal?"

"Let's finish what we started. If we both make it through this alive and not incarcerated, then it'll be you and me all the way."

My eyes widen at his offer. I never imagined Silas would say something like this. I know how much he doesn't want to be seen like those men Cruise paid to take advantage of me. And though my heart urges me to agree, I can't. Not to him. It would be as bad as buying into that stupid bet at school. I don't want him to feel pressured into a situation he wouldn't choose for himself. I don't want him to hate me if things go wrong. As much as his abandonment hurt me, I can't do the same to him.

I shake my head. "No."

He tilts his head, frowning.

"You made it very clear we were never going to happen," I continue. "You said you didn't want to be like all the others. And I don't want to put you in a situation where you'd regret everything later."

Silas' lips part and close without uttering a word. He grabs hold of me and pulls me flush against his chest, closing the distance between us. Before I can react, his mouth slams to mine. A whimper leaves me, caught off guard by the sudden shift. His lips are firm and bruising like he's punishing me for even questioning his resolve. My hands slide up his chest and wrap around his neck, drawing him closer. His hand trails up my back and threads in my hair. A flood of heat pulses through my body, and I dig my nails into the collar of his blazer. Oh, how I wish to feel his skin. His flesh against mine. Silas breaks the kiss and tugs my head back by my hair, leaving me breathless and confused while still plastered against him. I don't want him to stop.

"Last week, you would've been right," Silas says, his fingers tightening in my hair. "Last week, I wouldn't have considered making a deal like this. But last week is not this week, and this week, I realized how wrong I was about myself. I've been avoiding you, pretending I'm different from those men who hurt you. But the truth is, I'm not. The only difference is that I played with your emotions instead of that sweet little cunt I've been dying to taste since you walked into my classroom."

I search his face, looking for the truth in his words. I don't know how Silas can for one second think he is like the others. He cared for me. He was there when no one else in this family seemed to care about me. I loved him. He didn't take something I didn't willingly give him. Because the truth is, I was his before he even stepped foot in James manor that first day. I was his the first moment I heard him sing and listened to the haunting melodies that meshed so perfectly with how I was feeling but unable to speak.

A mix of emotions swirls inside me, my center becoming hot and slick as we continue staring at each other.

"Nothing to say?" he asks, his voice low.

I shake my head. "You're not like them."

He leans down and presses another kiss upon my lips. "You're right. I'm worse. I made an eleven-year-old girl fall in love with me. I made a child trust me, only for me to now do this."

"Do wha—"

My question is abruptly silenced with the slam of Silas' lips back on mine. His arms wrap around me again, cupping my butt and hiking me up him. My legs automatically lock behind his back.

"God, you're way too light," he mumbles against my lips as I slam into him.

Slowly, Silas walks a couple of steps to the bed, and I grab hold of his shoulders for support. He pushes me backwards and moves over me. Light from my windows stream through, making his emerald eyes dazzling, hypnotizing. Completely and utterly tantalizing. Silas' thumb strokes my cheek so softly as he gazes back at me. I swear that simple touch feels as if he's everywhere. I bite down on my lip to keep from shivering beneath him.

His mouth descends on mine again, and a gasp escapes me a sour lips fully meet. I instinctively lift myself toward him, but he firmly presses me back down. Breaking the kiss, he shakes his head, then grabs a handful of my hair. He tugs my head back and trails kisses down my neck, his breath hot against my skin.

"Si!" My body tenses at how similar this position is to how Cruise had me, and I start to panic.

"I know," he whispers in my ear. "I saw the surveillance footage at the gate. But I want you to remember my hands on you like this." His free hand skates up my side, grazing the outside of my breast through my dress, and up to my neck.

"Because you now belong to me. This body," he pulls my hair tighter and tightens his hold around my neck, "is mine. Not his. Get him and all the other men out your fucking head. I'm the only one allowed to occupy that space."

A moan leaves me, letting Silas know I like everything he's saying. God, I like it too much. I press my thighs together to help subdue the ache building in me. While I'm not completely innocent in this department, I can't remember a time I was this hot. This needy for a guy.

Silas leans forward and our tongues collide, heat flaring between us. He pries open my thighs with his knee and presses his erection into me. My eyes fly open at the feel of his length through his trousers. He's big. Just from the feel of him against me, I can tell that much. As he presses harder into me, my body melts into him and my eyes roll shut. This man definitely knows what he's doing.

His mouth leaves mine and a low whine leaves my throat. Silas presses his lips into my neck, removing his hand to shove aside the neckline of my dress to cup my breast. His finger tugs at the stiff peak and I cry out at the same time he bites down on my neck. He blows on the bite and my cheeks heat.

Oh. My. God.

Something shifts inside me, a feeling heating my blood. Desires forcing their way to the surface. I thread my fingers into his hair and move his head to my breast. As much as the bite on my neck felt amazing, I want to feel his mouth there. Silas grins into my skin and obliges. His hand squeezes my boob just as his mouth encompasses it, his tongue tracing my nipple. I arch up from the bed and attempt to close my legs again, but Silas keeps them wide open. Gripping the duvet to ground myself, low mewls leave me. His erection grows even harder at my center, and I love it. Love that I can make him do that just from a simple sound.

He groans, biting at my nipple and rocking himself into me harder. My stomach flutters at the sound, and it's the sexiest thing I have ever heard. And I want to hear it again.

If only there weren't so many layers between us.

"Silas . . ." I moan out, a whispered prayer on my lips for more.

"Solaris," he growls, shoving the cup of my bra down and attacking my other breast. I yelp at the bite of pain, but then he instantly licks it away.

"Oh, yes. Just like that," I utter, my hips rolling into him.

Silas' mouth leaves my chest, my peaks hardening even more from the warm absence. He peers down at me, licking his lips. "You like that. A little pain with your pleasure."

My cheeks heat in embarrassment. In all honestly, I don't know what I like. I've only had consensual sex with two people. The first time we were both fumbling around like newbies. And I was too drunk to even remember the threesome with Taylor. Only that the next day I felt like crap and never wanted to do it again. I can't deny, though, that I like the bite of pain or the way he licked it away. It was hot. Like really, really hot.

"Good to know." He smirks down at me.

"Please don't stop. I want . . . I want you. . ." I trail off, not knowing how exactly to tell him I want more. So much more of him.

Silas' hand skims down my side and under my dress, his eyes never leaving me. He runs a knuckle against my covered core, and I throw my head back in pleasure, mewing again. He chuckles and repeats his actions. My legs tremble as wetness floods my center.

"You're so wet, Sol," he whispers. "Look at me."

I open my eyes and meet his gaze.

"Tell me you like this."

I nod, too afraid to use words.

"You want me to continue?" he asks as he shoves aside my panties and runs a finger through my slickness.

"Yes!" I shriek out as he inserts a finger. "More. Good. So much more."

"Good. 'Cause I'm about to eat you up."

My brows crinkle in confusion for a second and then widen when I get his meaning. No one, and I do mean no one that I can recall, has ever gone down on me. A warm sensation fills my lower stomach, and I'm on the verge of telling him he can do whatever he wants to me when the door to the room slams open. Silas stiffens above me and his finger stops its perusal of my pussy. My heart stops, and I squeeze my eyes shut.

This cannot behappening right now.

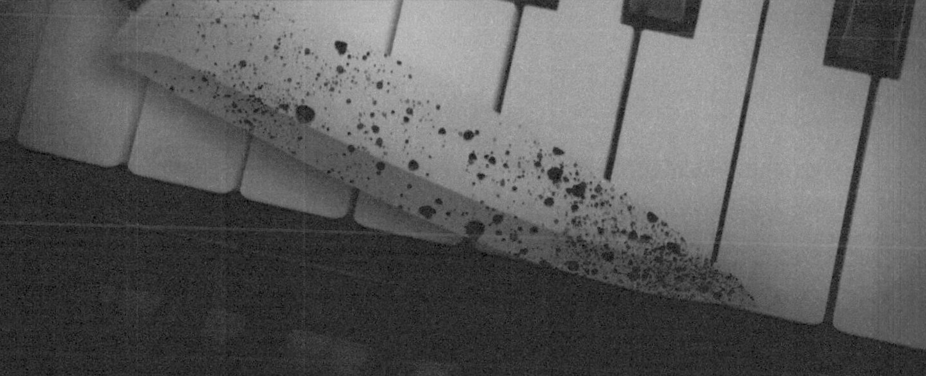

Eleven

Silas

"**W**ell, well, well," Loretta's voice cuts through the tension. "You give them an inch, and they take a mile. I told you to come get her."

I inhale deeply, closing my eyes to keep from showing any type of emotion towards this situation. Slowly, I pull my fingers from Solaris, the squelching of her arousal doing nothing to tamper my own. Not wanting to waste any part of her, I bring my fingers up to my mouth and suck them clean. She gasps below me, but I don't open my eyes just yet to see her. I know when I do, hers will fill with confusion and now is not the time to explain why I must do what I must do.

Once I've allowed myself to enjoy her taste, I square my shoulders and open my eyes. Solaris' brows dip and her sweet lips that were momentarily o'ed in pleasure, turn down, her doe eyes searching me for understanding. And while I would love to offer her an explanation, I can't with Loretta here.

Solaris shakes her head at me, silently pleading.

I bite the inside of my jaw to keep from saying the words I so desperately want to utter to her. To keep from telling her I'm sorry. Truthfully, I'm not sorry. This was going way too fast. She just remembered what her brother did to her. She just lost her mother. She's grieving for Christ's sake. And while I have wanted this since she walked into that classroom a week ago, I don't want to break her even more. And that's what would have happened if we weren't interrupted. She wouldn't have told me to stop, and I wouldn't have stopped.

A throat clears behind me, Loretta reminding me she's here as if I need the reminder. I step away from Solaris and over to Loretta. She wraps her arm around my waist, and I do everything in my power to stay still, to not jerk away from her. Sol sits up and turns to face her aunt, the hurt and anger warring on her face.

"Considering we're about to lay one of my problems to rest, I'll let this little incident slide." Loretta releases me and steps around to Sol, her voice icy. "But know this, child: you will not win this battle. I am the head of the James estate now, and you are nothing more than an inconvenience I'm putting up with for the sake of my image. And like every inconvenience, you will fall in line." The 'or else' is clear, even without explicitly stating it. "Now, right yourself, and let's go before I cancel this farce and have the whore cremated."

Solaris glares her aunt down and for a moment I think I might have to step in, to calm her, but then the fight fades from her eyes, just like it used to all the time when she was a child. Her shoulders drop and she stands from the bed, eyes not meeting mine as she combs her fingers through her straight hair. I hate it straight. I love the energy of her bouncy curls. This looks too put together. Too conformed. Too much like a James.

Without another word, Loretta turns, looping her arm through mine, and walks from the room.

"You'll pay for your defiance," she utters low enough for only me to hear.

I scoff. "There's not much you can do to me anymore."

"Oh really?" she questions as we make our way down the stairs of her home. "You're not the only one back in town, you know. Cruise is home."

My teeth grind together at her not so subtle threat. Cruise was probably back at the manor the moment the clock struck twelve. The moment Solaris came of age to him. For a moment, I thought California would hold his attention. As I've kept track of Solaris over the last six years, I've also kept tabs on Cruise. Just to make sure he didn't go near her. But he always seemed content partying it up with others. Hooking up with Hollywood starlets and the occasional model. Not once in six years did he go near Solaris. Not even when she was in California filming her TV show.

As we come to a stop in front of the family car, the door opens, and Cruise pokes his head out, grinning. He looks past us, and I follow his gaze to Solaris. My heart skips a beat as I see exactly what he sees. Her slender curves wrapped in silk that looks too much like a robe, waiting for someone to pull the little knot loose and reveal her to the world. God, I shouldn't even be thinking that. She's been eighteen for only a week. If I can see her like this now, did her age ever really matter? Was I ever any better than the men that preyed upon her?

"You're late, sister." Cruise exits the car, along with Lena and my father.

Solaris comes to a halt at the sight of her brother and before she can back pedal, I free myself from Loretta and grab hold of her wrist. She can't run. If she wants revenge like she says she does, then she needs to stand up to them. They can't see her as weak, and I'm not going to let them perceive her as such. Mainly because she's not. She's a survivor and one of the strongest people I know. If they think she's still the same eleven-year-old girl, they are going to treat her as such.

Solaris' fingers flex in my hold and she looks up to me. She licks her bottom lip, gulps, and nods ever so gently. She pulls her wrist free of me and steps to her brother. Before anyone knows what she's doing, a sharp loud sound rings out. Cruise's back hits the car. Lena shrieks and grabs for Sol. I take a step forward, but Loretta pins me with a stare. Cruise rubs the spot where Solaris slapped him.

"That was for last week." She pushes past him and gets into the car. My dick hardens at her actions, and I can't keep the grin off my face. That's my girl.

Cruise's gaze follows her and there's also a grin on his face. He turns and gets in the car as well, followed by my father and Lena. Loretta looks me over for a second and frowns. She steps up to me and fixes my tie.

"Behave, darling," she tells me.

"As long as he keeps his hands off her, we have no problem."

"Solaris belongs to him. Not you. Remember? Now that she's of age, he can do what he pleases." Her eyes drop to my crotch, and I curse myself for the reaction to Sol. Loretta palms my length through my trousers, and I hiss out as her claws dig in. "Get yourself under control."

Loretta turns away and gets in the vehicle. Taking a deep breath and fixing myself, I do the same and slide in by the door. My eyes immediately land on my father sitting on the opposite side of the vehicle, his hand on Lena's knee. She's smiling and conversing with him like it's nothing. Like he's her father and not a slimy old man who gets a kick out of torturing people to make up for his own really shortcomings.

"Lena," her name comes out all too abruptly, but I don't want her anywhere near my father. "Why don't we change seats?"

Her brow scrunches in confusion. "Oh, I was just telling William about the autumn ballet. Representatives from Julliard are going to be there, but if we need to—"

"Yes," I cut her off and she frowns.

She gets up from her seat and moves beside Loretta, forcing herself as close to the door as possible. While she might hate her mom, at least I know Loretta won't try anything like my father. I take her seat, and my father crosses his arms.

"Good to have you home, son," he says with a choking cough.

Since I arrived back in Mountain Rose a week and a half ago, I've avoided running into him. It helps that he's in horrid shape and Loretta has him locked in a room somewhere. Cancer, I found out two years ago. Bet he's loving his justice; serves him right.

"Working on a new album, I heard." He attempts to make small talk.

I turn slightly to him and whisper. "Let's not do this. You and I both know you couldn't care less about my music, and I can't care less about you."

His eyes narrow and I honestly don't care.

"That was mean." My eyes snap to Lena, her arms crossed and narrowed at me as if I insulted her.

Ignoring her naive statement, I lean my head back against the rest. As much as Lena means to me, the girl has been guarded from what people are really like. Mean? No, what's "mean" is beating your wife and son every day just to prove to yourself you are not weak. Mean is marrying into a family just so you don't lose a political campaign. And if my father can't handle a few choice words, then maybe he shouldn't be so mean.

From my peripheral, a blurry motion catches my attention, and I glance over to see Cruise's hand come down on Solaris' thigh, stilling her fidgety fingers. He leans closer in and whispers something. Her eyes widen and her whole body goes taut. My hands ball into fists at the sight of him so close to her. Too close. Breathing the same air as her so freely as if he has the right.

"—I can't wait to fully claim my prize." I manage to hear him tell her. While I can't hear everything he's saying to her, anything he has to say can't be good.

Solaris sends her elbow into his gut at whatever he says, eliciting a low grunt that echoes off the interior walls. She mutters something to him, but it's only meant for his ears. Cruise chuckles before leaning in and placing a swift peck upon her cheek, a satisfied smirk on his smug pretty boy face.

"Solaris," I call, my voice tense. "Why don't you come over here by the door?"

Loretta's gaze snaps up from her phone, and she searches between us all as the car goes over a bump in the road. Her eyes settle on the hand Cruise has resting on Sol's upper thigh and grins more to herself than anyone else.

"She's perfectly fine with her brother," Loretta interjects, her tone dismissive.

"It's her mother's funeral. She should be the first one out. It would look awfully suspicious if she isn't," I counter, locking eyes with Loretta. "We wouldn't want the press asking even more questions, now would we?"

Loretta groans but shifts slightly. I reach out a hand to Sol and she grasps it, allowing me to pull her away from Cruise and Loretta. "Thank you," she mouths, crossing over to me and settling into the seat. I turn my hand palm up and without thinking, she slides her delicate hand into mine. Right where it belongs. I smile to myself and meet both Cruise's and Loretta's gaze. They aren't pleased. I squeeze Sol's fingers, and she leans her head against my shoulder. The rest of the ride to the gravesite is tense and silent.

I don't care.

They both need to get used to the idea of me and Sol.

For far too long, I've let Cruise believe he was actually going to have her. And for far too long, I've allowed Loretta all the power. That's over now. I'm done being controlled by them. I'm not letting them hurt my girl any longer.

As we arrive, Solaris leans forward and looks out the window. I do the same and frown at the crowd of police officers and photographers gathered. I expected some media presence—this is Solaris after all— but not this overwhelming number. Who would even leak the burial site?

Sol glances over her shoulder at me, confusion written on her doll-like face. "Why are there so many cameras?"

I shrug but Loretta answers with a cold smile. "If I have to bury that woman next to my brother, you can bet I'm getting something out of it. If it wouldn't make this family look worse than it already does, I would have thrown her in a ditch and given her a pauper's grave."

"Maybe it's you who deserves a pauper's grave," Sol snaps. "You're the one borrowing space, after all."

"Sol," I hiss at her, voice sharp. "Get out of the car. Now."

She turns away from her aunt and obeys me. Today, right now, is not the time for them to go at each other. The press would have a field day seeing niece and aunt fighting at a funeral. I can already see the headlines now, and that is not something we need PR fixing when it can be avoided.

As soon as the door swings open, Solaris gets out and I follow right behind. A barrage of flashes erupts, and the blinding strobe lights make me want to retreat back into the car. This is no way to send someone off. Elizabeth deserves so much more than this spectacle. Sol smooths down her simple black dress, lifts her chin with a measure of dignity, and steps into the cemetery. I run my hand through my hair and walk in as well.

The cemetery is sprawling, with rows of graves stretching out in endless lines. The air is heavy with the scent of fresh earth and wilting flowers. The grounds are a sea of muted colors, dying flowers at the base of moss-covered tombstones.

Even the green of the grass seems to be dull amongst the glossy black attire of the mourners.

The "family" follows behind me, along with a dismal procession of people I don't recognize. I bet not even Sol knows them. They're all draped in black, their faces painted with feigned sorrow, false tears glistening on their cheeks. They're all impostors, pretending to share in the grief they don't feel.

We all take our spots around the pristine white and gold casket. The priest begins the service with a prayer, but his words are nearly drowned out by the relentless clicking of cameras and the shuffling of feet. I try to concentrate on the ritual, but the constant noise is overwhelming. I glance back at the line of police officers struggling to maintain order, but their efforts are futile. The crowd presses in, invading the sacred space with their intrusive curiosity.

Solaris' head snaps up as her name is screamed out. She glances around at all the people. Digging her nails into her thighs, she jerks back around to the priest. Her jaw tenses and I wish I could do something about all the people. About the press using this as some story to make a quick buck. But unfortunately, they come with the territory. They come with being one of the big four families, along with her title of America's sweetheart. I try to ground myself against the invasion of my private grief.

Sol's head drops as the crowd gets louder. She takes a deep breath before letting it out. She mutters something so low to herself before glancing over her shoulders once more.

A nearby camera goes off as the priest's prayer finally draws to a close. Solaris pivots to face the scene at our backs and I tilt my head in concern. My fingers graze hers to get her attention, but she jerks her hand away as she backs away from the grave.

She darts through the throng of onlookers, and I go to follow, but Loretta shakes her head at me.

"Let her go," she mutters for only the family to hear.

I bite down on the inside of my jaw. "This is her mother's funeral. Someone needs to show that they care. To have a little bit of decorum."

Her voice lowers even more, her gaze icy and angry. "You follow after her, you will regret it."

"I already regret so much. What's one more thing?"

"Solaris!" A photographer's voice pierces through the cacophony of shuffling feet. "Why are you leaving?"

I shove my way through the crowd and dart to Sol. She's just about to grab the door to our car when I yank her back. She whirls around to face me, her face a cluster of frustration. Her feelings all too clear on her face. An open book if there ever was one.

"Where are you going?" I demand.

"I'm getting away from this charade," she retorts, crossing her arms defiantly.

"If you walk away from your mother's burial, it will be talked about," I warn her, as though she's unaware.

"I'm leaving regardless," she tells me. "I have planning to do. My time is better spent on that than enduring this sham."

I straighten at the subtle mention of her revenge and cast a glance over my shoulder at the cluster of reporters before focusing back on her. "I heard what Cruise said in the car, and I want to make something very clear—to you, to him, to Loretta, and to the world."

She raises an eyebrow in curiosity.

Leaning closer, I speak with a fierce intensity. "You. Are. Mine. You are not some prize to be claimed."

I grip the back of her head, holding it steady as my lips descend to hers for the third time in one day. The flash of cameras pop around us, the photographers' shouts blending into the backdrop of chaos. Solaris' lips curve upward under the kiss, and I love that she likes this. Likes the defiance and public spectacle.

Pulling away, I rest my forehead against hers. "There. Now everyone will have something more interesting to talk about."

She chuckles softly. "What about your job? The academy won't keep you on when the photos leak."

I shrug nonchalantly. "I'm Silas O'Conner, baby. I couldn't care less about that job. It served its purpose—it brought me to you."

She glances over my shoulder at our family, and I rotate to see them as well. They're all watching the exchange. Lena's eyes are wide with amusement, her grin evident as she bounces slightly. Loretta's face is a mask of stern disapproval, but her anger is inconsequential to me. My gaze shifts to Cruise, who wears his usual smug grin as if this changes nothing for him.

Solaris looks up at me. "Cruise goes first. See you back at the estate."

She doesn't elaborate and I don't need her too. She climbs into the car, instructing the driver to head back to the property. I watch as the car pulls off and vanishes from sight.

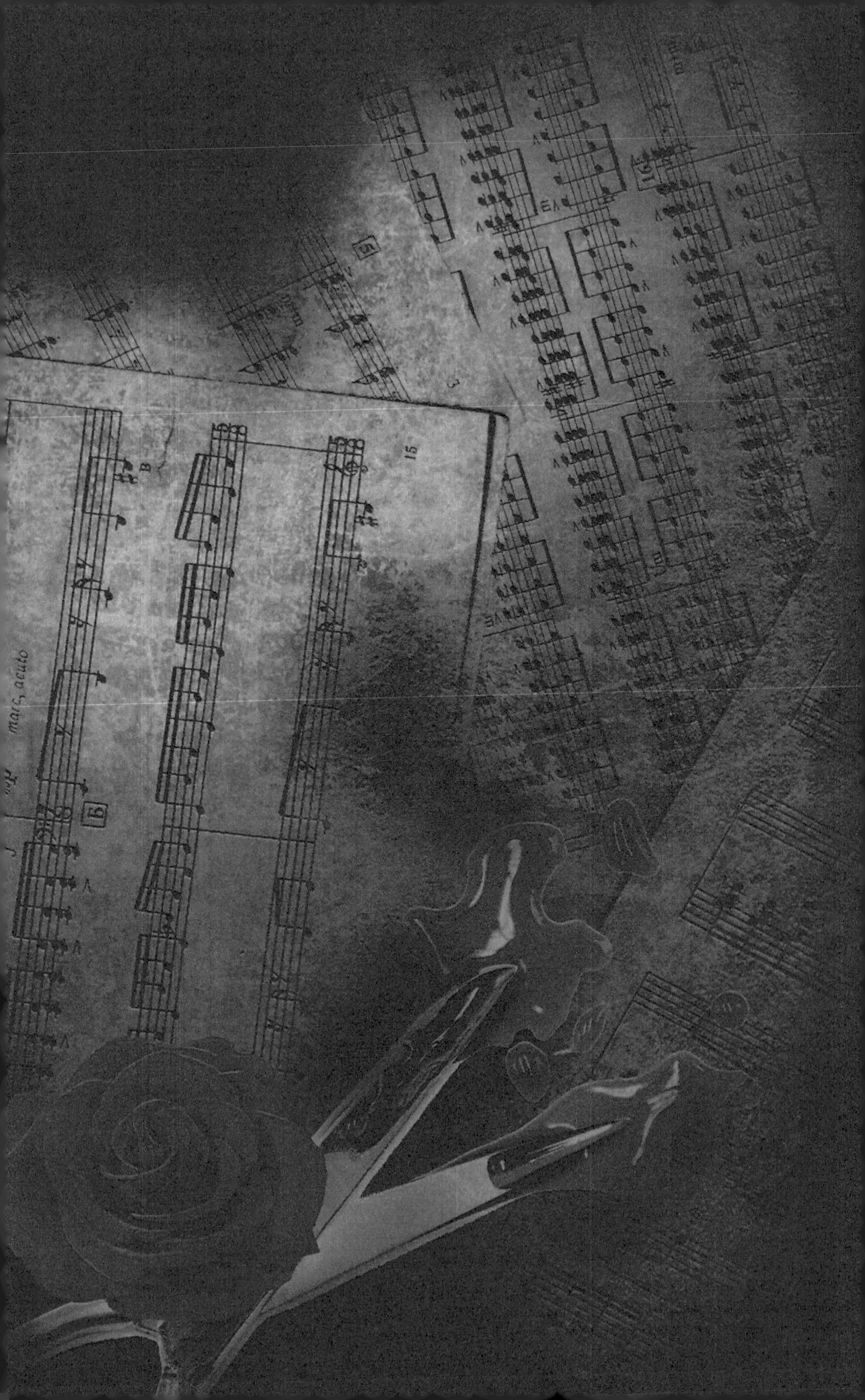

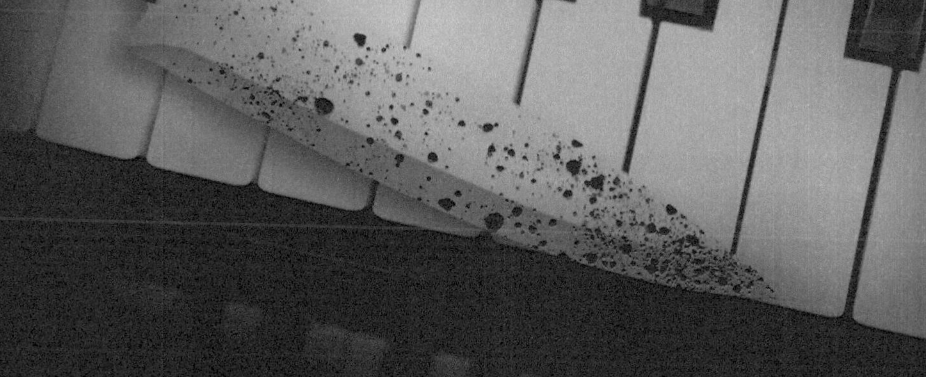

Twelve

Silas

Six years ago

The cab glides to a halt in front of the sprawling mansion, and the driver lets out a low whistle that echoes off the towering columns and grand staircase. The estate sprawls before me, its numerous balconies adorned with intricate ironwork, all overlooking elegantly manicured fountains and lush gardens. I've only set foot in the main manor once, when I was first introduced, and the opulence I see now is overwhelming. It's hard to fathom why three people need so much space.

"Your family must be quite something," the driver remarks, his voice laden with awe.

I disregard his comment, quickly settling the fare on the screen and handing him a generous tip. Grabbing my overnight bag, I step out of the cab and watch as it rolls back toward the gate. With a deep breath, I ascend the grand staircase. Solaris had mentioned she would be at the main house today, as her father is expected to return from his mysterious business trip. I can't fathom being away from my child for so long without knowing what's happening on my property.

The dark thoughts from my last visit to this estate creep into my mind, and I clench my fists. The whole situation is unsettling. I doubt my father has laid a hand on Solaris yet, but the fact that others have, and her father remains oblivious, is beyond troubling. I've only known Solaris for a few months, but even I can sense that something is amiss. During my forced summer stay, Solaris practically lived in my room, and I couldn't turn her away, not with the shady dealings of Cruise and that little black book hanging over us.

I exhale deeply, pushing away those thoughts. Today isn't for dwelling on such dark matters. It's Solaris' twelfth birthday, and I'm finally taking her to the studio—a promise she and Lena have been eager for. My record label has been pressuring me for new material, so this serves a dual purpose. It also offers Solaris a break from the mansion, which has been oppressive since school started in August. With Cruise away for his freshman year, I hoped things might have settled.

I shake my head, pushing these thoughts aside as I pull out my phone and locate the text from Solaris with the code for the main door. Unlike the other cottages on the estate, which are manned by butlers and maids, Gregory prefers a more personal touch.

Entering the code, the lock's light turns green, and I push open the heavy door. Inside, I am greeted by an opulent foyer with soaring ceilings and lavish decor. The grandeur is almost overwhelming. I stand momentarily, surveying the scene: the left staircase curves up gracefully, while the right staircase mirrors its elegance. I'm unsure which leads to Solaris' wing, but it's staggering that a twelve-year-old has an entire wing of this mansion to herself—well, technically, as her brother is away.

Choosing the left staircase, I make my way up the seemingly endless steps to a long corridor. Like at Loretta's, the walls are lined with portraits of past family members, their faces eerily similar. There's an unsettling uniformity—blond hair, blue eyes, pale skin, and unnervingly perfect teeth. The only exceptions are Solaris and her mother, standing out distinctly in the sea of clones.

A soft giggle drifts through the corridor, pulling my attention. I follow the sound, turning down a hallway, and then come to an abrupt halt, stunned by what I see. I back up as quietly as I came, struggling to process the scene. Unable to comprehend, I cautiously peek around the corner, my mouth dropping open.

There, in the open hallway, Loretta and Gregory are entangled against a chaise lounge. Loretta's head is thrown back in pleasure, her back arched as she moans, "Harder." Gregory's hands grip her thigh, delivering a sharp smack that echoes off the walls. "Lay there and be quiet," he orders, his voice a harsh whisper.

Loretta nods, compliant, as Gregory thrusts deeper. I jerk my head away, my mind reeling. What the hell did I just witness? I shake my head, retracing my steps down the hall, the family portraits seemingly glaring at me with silent judgment. I stop in front of a photo of Gregory, his wife, Cruise, and Solaris, my eyes shifting to another of Loretta and Lena. Notably, there is no husband in Loretta's photo. As I scan the rows of portraits, a pattern emerges: whenever a daughter appears, there is no husband by her side, yet always a child. The male heirs, however, are accompanied by wives—some with brunette hair, others with red—yet none of the offspring bear the features of these women.

No. This can't be right.

My eyes dart back and forth between the images of Lena and Solaris. Lena, with her blonde hair and blue eyes, fits the family's mold perfectly. Solaris, more exotic with her multiracial heritage, still shares some features—the same mouth shape, the same eye shape, the same face structure. My gaze shifts to Gregory, and suddenly, everything clicks into place. Gregory is Lena's father. Lena and Solaris are more than just cousins.

What the hell did my father marry us into?

I gaze up at Solaris' mother in the photograph, my heart heavy with sympathy. The woman's smile is radiant, her eyes brimming with a love so evident that it's almost painful to see. Does she know the truth? Of course not. She's too infatuated with Gregory to suspect a thing. The realization twists inside me like a knife. Until now, I wouldn't have suspected anything either—not without witnessing the scene I just stumbled upon.

Shaking off the unsettling thoughts, I make my way back down the grand staircase and cross over to the other wing of the house. The opulence of the mansion feels cold and suffocating as I walk down the long, silent hallway, knocking on each door. I receive no response until, finally, a door creaks open. Solaris stands there, eyes red and swollen, tears streaking her cheeks. The sight of her tears pierces my heart, and I drop to my knees in front of her.

"Are you okay?" I ask, gently wiping away her tears. "Did someone hurt you?"

She shakes her head. "I didn't think you were coming. Everyone else forgot about me."

My chest tightens. "I will always come when you need me. I didn't forget you." I reach into my overnight bag and pull out the gift I brought for her. "Happy Birthday, Sol."

She unwraps the present, revealing a doll. Her expression falls, and my own smile falters. I was assured this was the most popular toy for girls her age.

"You do know I'm twelve and not eight, right?" she asks, a hint of irritation in her voice.

"Is there a difference?" I reply, feeling awkward.

"Yes," she says with fierce conviction, then adds, "but thank you."

I offer her a small grin and stand up, slinging my bag over my shoulder. "I was thinking we could finally go to the studio. You mentioned you wanted to go. We could bring Lena too."

Her eyes brighten momentarily, but the spark quickly fades. She shakes her head, her shoulders slumping. "I can't. My dad told me not to leave this room until my mother gets home."

I scoff inwardly. Right, because he's too busy indulging himself with his sister in the hallway. Heaven forbid his daughter sees and tells her mother.

"Where is your mom?" I ask, suspecting that her absence is the reason for the unchecked behavior in the house.

"I don't know. I heard them arguing last night about my grandmother, and then Mom left."

Elizabeth's mother, then.

"Mom wanted to bring her here since we have all this space, and Dad said something weird about bringing in more outsiders. I don't know, but I can't leave."

I nod. "Alright, kiddo. We'll stay here. Do you have a keyboard?"

She nods. "Yes, and Lena has a ton of instruments here too. I think there's a guitar, but I'm not sure."

"Show me."

Solaris steps out of her room, closing the door behind her, and leads me down another series of hallways. The maze of corridors seems endless until we arrive at a set of French-style glass doors. My eyebrows rise at the sight of a white grand piano dominating the large, sunlit room. The back wall behind the piano is lined with an impressive array of instruments: a keyboard, violin, drums, cymbals, and more. Solaris walks in, heading to the wall, and picks up an acoustic guitar from the end of the lineup. She turns to me, holding the instrument carefully.

"This is incredible," I say, taking in the sight of the music room. The space, filled with potential and creativity, feels like a hidden sanctuary within the cold, vast mansion. It's a small comfort in a place that harbors so many dark secrets.

"Will this do?" Solaris asks, handing me the guitar.

I take the instrument from her, examining its fine craftsmanship. "Has this room been here the whole time I've been staying with Loretta?"

She nods. "Yes. My father wanted me to learn to play that," she points to the grand piano, "but everything else belongs to Lena. Her mother doesn't like the noise, so she keeps them here."

"Do you know how to play?" I gesture towards the piano.

She frowns slightly. "Not well."

"Let me be the judge of that."

Solaris hesitates, glancing at me before making her way to the piano. She sits on the bench, straightening her back as she positions her fingers on the keys. The moment she begins to play, I'm taken aback. Her fingers glide over the keys with a natural grace, coaxing out a melody that flows effortlessly. The rhythm of her body sways in sync with the music, her playing far beyond what her modesty suggested. It's mesmerizing. The complexity and emotion in her improvised piece are breathtaking, belying her young age. I can't believe she downplayed her talent.

As the last notes fade, I move to sit beside her on the bench. "That was incredible. What song was that?"

She shrugs nonchalantly. "It wasn't a song. You said to just play, so I did. I don't read music; I just play whatever sounds good to me."

"Are you serious, Solaris? You just made that up?"

She shrugs again, avoiding my eyes.

"Can you play it again? I want to try something."

She nods and starts playing once more. I position the guitar and begin strumming along with her. The blend of the piano and guitar creates a synergy that's nothing short of magical. We continue, lost in the music, until the improvised piece comes to a natural conclusion. When I finally pull my fingers from the strings, I can't suppress the grin spreading across my face. I turn to her, and she meets my gaze, the earlier sparkle back in her eyes. It warms me deeply, and I silently vow never to let that light fade from her again.

"We sounded amazing," I tell her.

"Really?" She looks down, uncertain. "It's not what you usually play."

"Different isn't always bad. This was incredible."

She beams, her posture straightening with newfound confidence.

"Can I use this? The band would love it."

She's nodding eagerly before I finish the question. "You can use whatever you want."

"How about we write the lyrics together?" I suggest, fingers gently strumming the guitar.

"That's more Lena's thing than mine. I'm terrible with words. You write them, and I'll just play it again."

I nod, pulling out my phone to record. "Let me capture the music, and then I'll work on the lyrics. Are you okay with playing it a few more times?"

She nods again. I hit record, and we begin anew, refining the piece with each take. We tweak notes here and there to better complement the guitar, which is my main instrument. Time slips away as we work, the sun setting unnoticed beyond the windows. By the time I have a rough outline of the song, Solaris is slumped over the keys, fast asleep. I glance at my phone—it's already nine at night. We've been at this for hours.

Gently, I place my notebook back in my bag and return the guitar to its spot. I carefully lift Solaris, cradling her in my arms, and head towards her room. As I approach her door, I stop short. Gregory stands there, as if about to knock. He looks from his daughter in my arms to me, his expression unreadable.

"Lay her in bed. I need to talk to you," Gregory says, his tone calm but firm. There's no hint of impatience, just an unsettling air of control.

I nod and carry Solaris inside, gently placing her on the pink duvet. I smooth back her curls and press a soft kiss to her forehead. Her eyes flutter open, and she gives me a sleepy smile.

"Did you finish the song?" she asks, trying to sit up.

I ease her back down. "Yes, we did. Now, go back to sleep."

She shakes her head, a hint of worry in her eyes. "Please don't go."

I glance over my shoulder at Gregory, who stands just outside the door, watching us with an inscrutable expression. He doesn't seem impatient, more like a predator patiently observing its prey.

"I'll be right back," I assure her, my voice low. "I just need to talk to your dad."

She nods reluctantly, her gaze following me as I leave the room. I close the door gently behind me, then straighten my posture, bracing myself for whatever Gregory has to say. The tension between us is palpable, like the charged air before a storm.

"You wanted to talk?" I ask, my voice steady.

He crosses his arms, glancing at the closed door before turning his attention back to me. "You two seem close."

The statement hangs in the air, and I resist the urge to respond. The truth is glaring: if he were a good father, I wouldn't need to be here. Solaris wouldn't need someone else to protect her from the twisted secrets lurking within these walls. A good father would know his son's sick games and protect his daughter.

"I'm glad she has you," Gregory continues, his voice carrying a hint of genuine appreciation. He moves to lean against the wall, his posture relaxed but his eyes serious. "I know you saw Loretta and me today. My security cameras caught you, and I want to explain."

I raise my hands in a defensive gesture, shaking my head. "No need. I don't want to know."

But Gregory persists, his tone insistent. "You need to understand. This family has . . . traditions, things that have been happening long before we left England. Contracts that involve the three other families."

"Look, really, you don't need to—" I try to cut him off, but he interrupts, more forcefully this time.

"I do," he asserts. "The men in this family take wives for appearances. If a daughter is born, she belongs to the eldest brother. It's how we've been raised, to secure the line. But when I met Solaris' mother, things changed. Still, I have a duty to Loretta. It's all she knows, and I can't hurt my sister. I also can't let the other families think we are weakening."

His words twist my stomach. There's a sick logic in his explanation, a perverse sense of duty wrapped in centuries-old traditions. "Loretta is married to my father," I retort, barely keeping the disgust from my voice. "She doesn't need you."

"Loretta married your father to spite me for marrying Elizabeth," Gregory says, a bitter smile playing on his lips. "She always promised she'd find a way to make me pay, and she did. But that doesn't change the fact that, all my life, Loretta has been mine."

His twisted confession hangs heavy in the air. I can feel the weight of their history pressing down, an oppressive force that has shaped and distorted them all. My chest tightens with disgust, and it takes everything in me not to barf at this family's perversions. It's a reality I never wanted to glimpse, and one I wish I could erase.

I slump against the door, exhaling a long breath. This is too much. "Why are you telling me all this? I'm not really a part of this family."

"I'm telling you because you seem close to Solaris. When the time came for Cruise to choose between Lena and Solaris, he chose her. He claimed her, and I don't want my daughter to go through this."

"Lena is your daughter too," I point out.

He nods. "But she wasn't claimed, and Cruise cannot reclaim. She's safe—an outcast, but safe. Solaris is not. I need you to get her away from this when the time comes. Can you do that?"

I stare at him for a long moment, gauging the sincerity in his eyes. I haven't known Gregory long enough to trust him completely, but he doesn't need to ask. I'd do anything for Solaris and Lena; they're just kids trapped in a nightmare they never chose. Innocent and undeserving of the horrors lurking in this family. I nod, and Gregory visibly relaxes.

"Thank you," he says, turning to leave. He pauses, glancing back. "One more thing—can you forget what you saw? Please, don't bring it up. It would destroy Elizabeth, and I love her. If I could stop what's happening with Loretta, I would. But this is the family I was born into. It's either this or hand Loretta over to one of the other families and allow them to control the James fortune. I cannot forsake my blood like that."

I tilt my head. "Not even for the woman you claim to love?"

Gregory sighs, a deep weariness settling in his eyes. "I cherish them both in different ways. Turning my back on one means denying a part of myself."

I can't say I fully understand, but for Solaris, Lena, and Elizabeth's sake, I agree to keep his secret. They don't deserve the fallout from this twisted legacy. If my silence can spare them, I'll bear it.

As Gregory walks away, I frown at his retreating figure. He came all this way to talk about what I saw, yet he couldn't even wish his daughter a happy birthday. With a sigh, I return to Solaris' room. She's sitting up in bed, knees drawn to her chest, her eyes searching my face.

"What was that about?" she asks, suspicion in her voice.

I grab my bag. "Nothing. He wanted me to wish you a happy birthday."

"Oh."

Pointing towards the door, I add, "I should probably head to Loretta's and check on Lena."

Solaris shakes her head. "Stay with me. Just for tonight."

"That's not a good idea, and you know it."

She shrugs, her fingers tapping restlessly on the blanket. "Don't care. It's my birthday until midnight, and I want you to stay. Sing to me."

"Sing to you? Haven't we done enough of that today?"

"I don't care what we do. Just stay."

Her delicate face, framed by big, pleading eyes, is impossible to refuse. I know this is a terrible idea, one that'll come back to haunt me, but a part of me needs her as much as she needs me.

Solaris must see my resignation because she climbs under the duvet and looks at me expectantly. Against my better judgment, I lie down beside her. She smiles, pressing a quick kiss to my cheek.

"See?" she whispers. "Nothing happened."

Wrong.

A million things just happened, and she has no idea.

Thirteen

Solaris

As we step off the plane at JFK, Silas and I make a beeline for the nearest cab, heading straight to the Carlyle. We had to fly out right after school for a makeup live interview that Candice had rescheduled. The journey felt interminable with two layovers, but Candice insisted it was the best she could do given my schedule. It feels more like payback for missing the first interview. She made it clear this one was non-negotiable. Silas decided to come along, claiming he needed to talk without Loretta around. Ever since he kissed me at my mom's burial, Loretta hasn't left us alone. After tomorrow, she'll have bigger things to worry about than that kiss.

The cab stops, and Silas leaps out, popping open the umbrella before heading to the trunk for our luggage. A couple of quick taps on the trunk get the driver's attention, and it opens. Normally, I'd fly here in my jet and have Thompson pick me up, but I was unprepared, and the jet wasn't ready. Plus, I didn't want to inconvenience Thompson on such short notice.

Silas hands our luggage to the doorman, who loads it onto a cart. He then opens my door and holds out the umbrella as I step out of the cab, and we hurry inside the hotel. Being seen entering a New York hotel together won't be great for our image. The gossip columns are already speculating about our relationship, questioning if Silas groomed me. Staying together in a hotel will only fuel those rumors.

At the front desk, I address the clerk. "There should be a reservation for Emily Wolfe, a superior two-bedroom suite, booked through Candice Nelson."

The clerk types into her computer, her brow furrowing as she glances between Silas and me. "Yes, I see the reservation." She hands me the key card and the necessary information. "Enjoy your stay, Ms. James."

I nod and don't correct her on the name. For all intents and purposes, I am Emily Wolfe today. There should be no Solaris James staying at this hotel. Letting it go though, Silas and I head up to our suite. We drop our bags near the sofa and move toward the bedroom. If I need to be on set by eight in the morning, I need sleep. But when we reach the suite, we both stop short, staring at the single bed. I could've sworn I requested two beds.

Silas breaks the silence. "I can take the sofa," he says, already turning back towards the living area.

I grab his forearm, halting him. It's just a bed, and we've shared one plenty of times before. "You don't have to."

His eyes darken with a mix of emotions as his gaze skates over me. "If I get in that bed, you won't be sleeping, and we won't be talking."

The insinuation in his tone and the heat in his gaze make me gulp, heat rushing to my core at the mere thought of us. In that bed. Not sleeping nor talking. After leaving the funeral on Saturday and going back to the manor, I was still so achy and aroused from that toe curling kiss. I tried everything to lessen the urge Silas had built and nothing worked. Staring into those deep irises now, all those unsatiated feelings slam into me. I bite down on my bottom lip and glance back at the bed.

Ever since I returned to the manor, I've struggled with memories of unwanted touches, none of them from the one person I wish they were from. Despite sleeping in the same bed for months, Silas never crossed a line, even when I wanted him to. Now, in this private, luxurious hotel room, I have the chance to choose him freely, without Loretta's interference. I really do need sleep, to be refreshed and looking my best for the brand I have to represent in the morning. But isn't that what makeup is for? And besides, who knows when we're going to be this alone again?

"Are you still sleeping with Loretta?" the question spills out, my cheeks flushing with heat.

Please say no.

Please say no.

Please say no.

Silas gently tilts my chin up, locking eyes with me. "I haven't been with Loretta since the day you walked into that classroom and restarted my heart."

My eyes widen at his confession, and fireworks explode in my stomach, my heart racing wildly. His thumb grazes my bottom lip, his eyes darkening even more with intensity. Our mouths crash together, and I can't help but revel in the instant pleasure his kiss brings. His lips are warm and soft, yet insistent as if we're sharing our last chance at this moment.

Silas' hands grip the collar of my blazer, swiftly pushing it off my shoulders. Still in my school uniform, I wish I'd had time to change. We have too many layers between us. He walks me backward until my legs hit the bed frame. As I unbutton my shirt, I keep my eyes locked on him, feeling his gaze never waver. Climbing onto the bed, I watch as he presses himself between my parted thighs. A low whimper escapes me at the sensation of his firm body against my still-covered core.

"This is your last chance to stop me," he warns, his voice a low growl.

I gulp, then lift the hem of my skirt an inch higher. "I'm ready."

Silas grips my knees and pulls me to the edge of the bed. I frown in confusion as he drops to his knees before me.

"What—"

"Quiet," he interrupts. "I missed dinner on the plane. It's time for me to eat."

Realization dawns, and I lower myself onto the bed, anticipation coursing through me. This is new territory; I have no memories of anyone doing this for me. I grip the duvet, preparing for the sensation of his mouth on me. Down there. But when I don't feel anything, I glance down, wondering what's holding him back.

"You need to relax," he instructs, gently pulling my skirt down my legs.

"I am," I protest, though my voice betrays my tension.

"You're tense," he says, his tone softening.

I exhale slowly, trying to let go of my nerves and be present in the moment. I want this. I want this with him more than anything I have wanted in such a long time. And I don't want him questioning that just because of my past. It is irrelevant at this moment. I will make it irrelevant. I exhale again.

Let me take over.

No, I respond automatically to the voice. *He is mine.*

Party pooper.

"That's my good girl," Silas praises, his voice soothing, and I melt even more under his reassurance and gentle touch.

He takes his time, painstakingly slow, as he eases my underwear down my legs next. The cool air hits my bare skin, and instinctively, I close my legs.

"Nuh-uh, baby girl. Open those gorgeous legs for me." Silas' voice is low and coaxing.

I bite my lip, heat flushing my cheeks as I obey. A shiver runs through me, my arousal already evident as I feel myself getting wet from his voice alone. He hasn't even touched me yet. Silas groans, drawing my gaze to him. He peers up at me, his fingers trailing along my inner thigh. Our eyes lock as his finger traces the outside of my lips, teasing my entrance.

"Oh God," I breathe, my head falling back against the expensive comforter. This is pure torture.

"You're so beautiful like this," he murmurs more so to himself. "So wet, glistening. You're already dripping for me."

"Mhmm."

His finger slips inside with ease, and he sets a teasing rhythm. Rolling my hips into his hand to force his finger deeper, I groan and silently beg for more. My body has never felt like this. So alive. So on the verge of exploding. While I've gotten off before—or so I thought at the time—this is all new and I want him more. Harder. Deeper. God, I don't know. Just more.

"You want more?"

My body arches toward him, my pussy weeping for him. "Mhmm."

"Use your words."

"Yes. More. So much more." I writhe under his touch.

He adds another finger, then his mouth is on me, licking up my slit. A gasp escapes me, my body arching into the sudden flood of pleasure. His fingers quicken, and I feel his tongue lapping up every drop. I grab at his hair, pulling him closer, desperate for more of this feeling. More of this easily addicting high. Silas hums against me, his mouth relentless, sending waves of ecstasy through me.

"Please," I moan, my voice breathy and desperate.

His only response is pushing his tongue inside, never removing his fingers. My entire body tingles and I feel myself getting wetter. How that's possible, I'm not even sure, but God . . .

I whimper, my back arching off the bed as an orgasm begins to rise. "More."

"More what?" His tone is demanding.

"Fuck me, please, Silas!" I cry out, closing my eyes against the embarrassment.

"Not until you come," he commands, his fingers and tongue working in perfect rhythm.

His tongue stops but his fingers continue to pump. I feel his teeth around the little ball of nerves at my core, and then a sharp twinge as he bites down. I yelp out, but my body tightens, pleasure coiling tighter and tighter until it snaps, sending me over the edge in a burst of pinpricks and heat.

"Silas!" I scream, the pleasure so intense I could cry.

His mouth returns to licking and sucking at my center, swallowing every drop of my pleasure. My eyes flutter closed, and I moan softly, completely spent. As the orgasm subsides, I open my eyes to see Silas peering at me with glee. Like he's the cat that got the cream. I suppose he is.

Licking his lips, Silas stands between my thighs and pulls his shirt over his head. My eyes widen at his toned physique. I knew he was fit; he must be in order to perform night after night on stage. But damn . . . He looks so much better than my imagination conjured up.

"You still want to continue?" he asks, popping the button on his jeans.

I nod, too breathless to speak.

"Words," he demands as he pulls his cock free.

Sitting up, my fingers inch towards him, wanting to touch him. He's big. Like too big. I felt him before but actually seeing him is something else entirely. I haven't had sex since my attempt with my costar a couple of years ago and then that terrible night with Taylor. Both times were awkward. Silas might not fit.

"Yes. I want you to fuck me, Silas O'Conner. I want you to erase everyone else's touch and replace them with yours."

He cups my cheek in his hand, his eyes dark and tender. "That, I can do."

Silas crawls on the bed, easing me back, and settles between my legs. He runs his cock against my core and we both groan in unison. I go to reach for him, to give him as much pleasure as he offered me, but he grips my wrist and pins it above my head. I smirk at him and go for his cock with my free hand. He stops stroking himself momentarily and grabs that wrist too. He pins it with this other hand, both my wrists bound in one. I pull against his restraint and his hand tightens around mine. I bite my lip at the pressure, pleasure rushing right to my center. Never have I imagined I would like the idea of being restrained. Not after everything that happened to me. But I do. Does that make me sick?

He grabs himself again with his free hand and goes back to slowly running the head of his cock over my vagina. I watch enthralled as he does that a few times, completely coating himself in me. A vibration rattles in his chest, and I can literally see him breaking down. Losing his control. He leans down and kisses me hard, this kiss brutal and urgent. He slides his dick up and down on me one more time and pushes in.

I flinch and then my whole body stills. Silas doesn't move, waiting to see how I respond. By no means am I a virgin, but this intrusion still burns. Silas kisses the side of my neck, and my body relaxes into him, accepting him. I finally roll my hips against him, urging him onward. His hand around my wrists tightens as he pulls out and then slams right back in.

This time he isn't gentle. His thrust is so hard I swear I feel him in my uterus. It burns for a second but then fades away, leaving only pleasure behind and me urging for more as I meet his thrust.

"God, Sol . . . You feel so fucking amazing," he pants against my neck. "Like you were made for me."

Silas releases my aching wrists, his head falling to my chest. My hands instantly wind around his waist. His mouth finds a peaked nipple and he bites down. Hard. I groan out, my mind becoming a hazy mess from the pleasure coursing through me. My nails dig into his back as we rock, his mouth not leaving my breast. His other hand tweaks my right nipple, and I moan out loud. God, I hope there's no one else on this floor.

Silas groans when he pulls away, releasing my nipple with a pop. "Fuck, yes."

He withdraws from me and flips me over on my stomach. Before I have time to miss him, he pushes back into me, the weight of his body a warm welcome against my back. He grips my chin and turns my face around, so I'm forced to look at him over my shoulder. His mouth slams to mine, his tongue dipping in as his dick dives deeper, harder into me. This position feels different. Like there's more pressure and I love it.

Silas smirks and turns my face around. "Open those eyes and watch us."

I hadn't realized they'd closed, but I obey anyway. I open my eyes and in front of me—us—is a mirror. I take us in and for the first time ever, I notice just how much bigger than me Silas is. Our bodies glisten, and he looks completely enraptured in the moment. My breath catches in my throat as I watch him move. My inner walls clench around him and he moans.

"My little voyeur. You like watching," he mumbles.

"How can you tell?" I ask, my eyes rolling shut once more at the feel of his hand running over the globes of my backside.

"You just clenched around me so hard."

I swallow. "Are you okay?"

His hand swats my ass, and I yelp. "Eyes open. And yes. Feels so damn good."

Silas begins pounding into me harder, faster, my breath coming out in haggard huffs. I do everything I can to keep my eyes open and on us. His are and it's the most erotic thing ever. Silas wraps an arm around me and hauls me to my knees. My fingers dig into the duvet at his relentless pace. He grips my hips, holding me steady. Every time he surges back in, he hits my clit, and it feels amazing. Another orgasm begins to rise. My toes tingling and curling. Heat climbs up my spine and I moan out.

"Yesss." The orgasm rips through me and my hips tremble against him. Darkness encompasses me as a wave of bliss overtakes me, stars painting my vision. I shudder from the onslaught of pleasure. Sex has never felt like this. Not when I'm by myself. Not from any memory. And certainly not from the one and only boyfriend I had two years ago. This here is everything, and I don't want Silas to ever stop.

"I can feel you milking me." He grunts as he rams through my pleasure, bringing me even higher. My arms feel like Jell-O and I collapse under him. Silas doesn't stop though. He moves like lightning, his hands pinning me in place. I don't know why. I'm not going anywhere. I couldn't even if I wanted to.

I don't want to.

His movements become jerky and a strangled sound leaves him. He pushes into me one more time and then I feel warm fluid shoot into me. My core clenches and I moan. Silas collapses on me, breaths coming out in heavy pants. He moves my hair aside and kisses my nape, his nose nuzzling me like a cat.

"God, Sol, that was spectacular. Wish I could stay buried in you all night."

I want to tell him he can. I want to tell him that he can do anything he wants, but words don't leave my lips. I'm too spent and honestly, all I want to do is close my eyes and sleep.

After Silas has had a moment to calm himself, he pulls out and rises. I roll over and wince at the burn I hadn't noticed until now.

Silas' brows dip as he examines me. "Are you okay?"

I nod. "It's just been a while."

"Yeah, I know. That prickly face punk who thought he had the right to touch you."

"Hey!" I swat at him. "He was my boyfriend."

"He didn't deserve that gift."

"And you do?" I arch a brow at him.

He picks me up from the bed and moves the covering aside. "No, but at least I will put in the work. At least I know what a treasure you are. I will never take you for granted."

Silas lowers me underneath the duvet and then crawls in. I want to tell him we need to bathe. To clean the sweat and cum from our bodies, but if I'm being honest, I like him in me.

Silas' fingers trace a lazy pattern along my arm as he pulls me across his bare chest, a content grin lingering on my face. Even though this wasn't my first time, it feels like it was—like his touch is the only one that has ever mattered. Rising slightly, I meet his warm, languid gaze and give him a quick peck. Blush creeps over my cheeks as I roll away and bury my face in a pillow, loving the way his cum feels seeping from my core.

He pulls me back over to him, raising an eyebrow playfully, and shifts to lie me back where I belong. Silas places a gentle peck on my head and I bite my lip, resisting the urge to ask to go again. It's too soon, and we've already stayed up far too late.

"Talk to me, Sol," he murmurs. "I need to know."

Snuggling into the crook of his arm, I tell him, "I'm great. That was amazing."

"Are you in any pain?" His concern is evident, even as he brushes a strand of hair from my face.

I shake my head, unable to put into words the mix of joy and giddiness I feel. I'm the luckiest girl in the world right now and nothing can bring me down from this high. I wonder if that bet is still going around at school, now that Silas technically no longer works there.

Silas lifts himself onto one elbow, scrutinizing my expression. "What's that look for? What are you thinking?"

"That I won the bet," I confess, a sly smile tugging at my lips.

He chuckles, pulling me closer. "Really? You always knew you'd win. There was never any competition."

Loretta's shadow briefly crosses my mind, but I quickly push it away. Silas hasn't told me what was going on there, but I know he was with her for a reason, not by choice. And since he's been back in my life, she's no longer a factor. He said so.

Silas shifts, gesturing to our intertwined forms. "Now that we're both satisfied, can we discuss what I needed to talk about before . . . this?"

"Sure," I reply with a mischievous grin. "We can talk about whatever you want."

He arches a brow, settling back against the pillows. "I'll remember that you're more agreeable when you've been properly fucked."

I blush, giving him a playful shove. "Shut up."

His laugh sends a pleasant shiver through me, and I snuggle deeper into his embrace. Silas pulls the thick, black duvet up over us, cocooning us in warmth.

"You mentioned at your mom's funeral that Cruise is our first target," he begins, his voice serious. "I've been planning. There are three things he cares about: his lavish lifestyle, sex, and how others perceive him. We can't touch his lifestyle since he's a trust fund baby like you."

"Hey, you're one to talk," I interject, teasing. "Your dad was the mayor of Mountain Rose."

"Being mayor is nothing compared to the James real estate empire, baby girl. I'm a pauper next to you."

I roll my eyes, knowing full well that Silas has carved his own path, becoming a sensation in country pop. There are probably more little girls with posters of him on their walls than there are of me. He doesn't need the James name.

"As I was saying," he continues, a smile playing at his lips, "we can't do much about his trust fund. But we can ruin his reputation and his sex life. Knock him off his pedestal."

I turn in his arms, my head resting on his chest. The idea seems too small, too insignificant compared to what I want. They threw me out like trash, abused me, killed my mother, and then mocked her memory for publicity. I don't just want to take away a trust fund or a house—I want to destroy them all. Maybe I haven't been clear enough with Silas.

He tilts my chin up, his eyes searching mine. "Are you even listening to me?"

"Mhmm. What did you say?"

Silas shifts underneath me, pulling me closer. "Cruise keeps a little black book with all the names of people who paid for you. It's his leverage. If we get that book, we have him and everyone in it."

I jerk upright, the revelation hitting me like a bolt. I hadn't considered the men who actually violated me, focusing solely on Cruise. But this book—it changes everything. It gives me names. I can ruin them all. They'll finally pay.

"Are you sure he has it?" I ask, still processing the implications.

Silas nods, his face serious. "I saw my father put his name in that book. Cruise insists everyone provides leverage. I'm not sure what else is in there, but it's definitely more than just names."

I rise to my knees, facing him. "We need that book. It's the holy grail. With it, we can finally take him down."

He pulls me back down to the bed. "The problem is getting it. I don't want you near him alone, and he wouldn't trust me in his space."

"You know," I yawn, glancing at the clock, "he would let me in. He wouldn't think twice about it."

Silas' tone hardens. "No. You're staying far away from him. Do you hear me?"

"Sure," I mumble, another yawn overtaking me. "But we need that book. The only other person who could get close is Lena, and I don't want to involve her."

"Would she do it?" he asks, a hint of concern in his voice.

"Of course," I reply, stifling another yawn.

Silas reaches over, switching off the lamp. He settles back down, pulling me into his arms. He kisses my forehead, then my lips—a chaste, tender kiss that stirs the embers of earlier. I lean in for more, but he pulls back, his hand tangled in my hair.

"Be a good girl. You need sleep for your interview later."

I roll over, giving him my back, and he chuckles, the sound rumbling through me.

"As much as I hate the idea, we might have to involve Lena," he says, his voice thoughtful. "She's the only one who never abandoned you. She's trustworthy."

"I know," I mumble, the weight of sleep pulling me under. "I trust her with my life."

Silas wraps an arm around my waist, his warmth soothing. "Get some sleep, baby girl. We'll finish this conversation later."

Before he finishes speaking, my eyes close, and the darkness of sleep envelops me.

Fourteen

My eyes flutter open as the morning sun streams through the expansive windows of the luxury suite at The Carlyle, casting a warm glow over the plush furnishings and elegant decor. Rolling over, the coolness against my back draws my attention to the empty space beside me. I frown at Silas' absence. After what we did last night, it would have been amazing to wake up with him. Rising from the bed, my mind races with the weight of the day ahead. Today is going to be bad. I don't know how I know, but I do.

I dress meticulously in the outfit Candice had delivered to the hotel yesterday before we arrived–a matching hot pink leggings and sports bra set with plain white shoes that don't take away from the outfit. Behind me, I hear the door open and Silas comes in with two silver trays on a cart. He frowns seeing me standing there and already awake.

"I had hoped to bring you breakfast in bed," he states and places the trays on the end of the bed. I give him a small grin and sit at the foot of the bed. At least he wasn't feeling bad about last night and running away. He has a habit of being hot and cold. We sit in quiet and enjoy our breakfast, punctuated by the distant hum of the city in full throttle outside. Neither one of us says much.

"We should probably head down so you're not late," Silas says when I'm doing nothing but moving the food around on the plate. "I know how you hate being late."

I glance up at him and nod. His eyes search my face and I'm not sure what he sees there, but apparently, he doesn't like it. He gets up from his side of the bed and comes around to me, pulling me up.

"Are you regretting what we did?"

I'm shaking my head before words can even leave me. "Of course not. Last night was the best night ever. Why would you even think that?"

He lifts my chin. "You seem off this morning."

I sigh. "It's this interview. I have a bad feeling. Candice said she gave them a list of questions not to ask, but the last time I did a live interview, the interviewer didn't care. I just don't like live interviews."

"I'll be there this time. Don't worry," he assures me. It doesn't help, but I offer him a reassuring smile anyway.

Downstairs, a sleek town car awaits outside, its polished exterior gleaming under the morning sunlight. Thompson gives me a grin as we approach. I throw my arms around the old man's center, hugging him.

"I'm sorry to hear about your mom, Ms. James." He rubs my back and pulls away. "Let's get you to the studio.

He opens the door and Silas and I step into its cool interior, the leather seats embracing us in luxurious comfort. The ride to the studio is a mix of quiet anticipation and nervous energy. On my part more so than Silas. He tries to make conversation, but I pay him no mind, choosing instead to watch the cityscape blur by through the tinted windows and losing myself to thoughts of the interview.

As we come to a stop, Silas' hand finds mine, offering a reassuring squeeze. I lean into his touch, drawing strength from his unwavering support.

"I'll wait for you in the corridor. If you need me, you know where to find me," Silas says gently, his voice a reassuring anchor amidst the uncertainty. How I so wish I could back out of this interview. Hell, the whole contract at this point. My mind isn't on it. My heart isn't in it anymore. I don't even know if I can do this without my mom. She made it possible.

I nod and come back to the now, gratitude flickering in my eyes as I squeeze Silas' hand even tighter. "Thanks for coming with me," I murmur, my voice tinged with both vulnerability and resolve.

Getting out of the car, we head inside the building and up to the fifth floor where the interview is filmed. I'm greeted with forced smiles by the studio assistants—a harsh difference from the warmth I had grown accustomed to from the executives on my show. The atmosphere crackles with tension as the assistant outfits me with a mic, and I make my way to the interview set. I glance over my shoulder at Silas one more time and he gives me an encouraging smile.

I can do this.

I can do this.

Damn right you can, the voice inside my head announces. *You're Solaris-freaking-James!*

The interviewer, a seasoned journalist with a reputation for incisive questioning, welcomes me with a smile that doesn't reach her eyes. The pleasantries exchanged feel superficial, a facade barely concealing the underlying tension.

The interview begins innocuously enough, with questions centered around my hit television show now drawing to a close. The woman then moves into my unique style and how that has led to this partnership. I navigate the questions with practiced ease, my responses a blend of diplomacy and genuine passion for my craft just like my publicist taught me when I was thirteen.

Suddenly though, the studio audience grows quiet, and the tone of the interview changes. The interviewer shuffles her note cards, sets them down, and angles her body more towards me. The sudden shift is like a heat wave over the entire studio and the beaming camera lights don't make the tension any better.

"You've had your share of personal tragedies recently," the woman begins, her voice tinged with a calculating edge. "Most notably, the untimely death of your mother, may she rest in peace. Can you elaborate on the circumstances surrounding her passing?"

My composure falters for a fraction of a second, a fleeting vulnerability betraying my practiced facade. I take a deep breath, steeling myself against the invasive inquiry. This is one question that Candice was supposed to make sure was on my do not ask list. Anything about my mom or Silas is meant to be off limits.

"My mother's death was a profound loss," I reply evenly, my voice steady despite the turmoil churning within me. "It's a private matter, and I ask for respect and sensitivity during this difficult time."

The woman sits forward in her chair, crossing her legs and resting her elbow against her knees as if waiting for some juicy gossip. I can see the persistence in her eyes. She's not going to give up. Then again, that's why she's so popular. She gets answers.

"Rumors have been circulating regarding your involvement in your mother's death," she presses on, her voice lowering to a whisper that carries far too much weight. "Some suggest you may have had a part in it since you and your boyfriend were the only ones present at the time of the murder. How do you respond to such allegations?"

My jaw clenches, my hands balling into fists at my sides. The accusations strike a nerve—a primal instinct to defend my mother's memory and my own integrity. But I can't let these people see just how much it hurts. Just how much those accusations tear me up inside. Releasing my fists, I run my sweaty palms down the front of my leggings. Good thing these things have great moisture wicking capabilities.

"I will not dignify those baseless accusations with a response," I tell her, my voice taut with restrained fury. "My mother's death was a tragedy, and any insinuation otherwise is not only false but deeply disrespectful."

The interviewer's facade cracks a bit, a flicker of unease betraying her composed demeanor. She presses on nevertheless, undeterred by my obvious discomfort.

"But the public has a right to know," she insists, her tone laced with skepticism. "You being welcomed back into the James' good graces coinciding with such a convenient tragedy—it raises eyebrows."

A surge of anger rises within me—a potent mix of indignation and frustration. Without another word, I push back from the table, my chair scraping loudly against the floor. The room seems to tilt on its axis, the walls closing in around me. All I see is red.

End her. End her. End her, the voice in me chants and I have to force it back into submission. This woman is not my enemy.

She's only doing a job she is paid to do. That doesn't mean I have to take this after giving her my do not ask list.

"I will not sit here and be subjected to this," I declare, my voice trembling with contained rage. "This interview is over."

Silas, sensing the storm brewing, stands abruptly in the corridor, as I stomp back his way. He reaches for me, but I storm right past him. My strides purposeful and unyielding as I flee the suffocating confines of the studio.

"Solaris, wait," Silas calls after me, his voice filled with urgency and concern.

But I don't stop. I march through the corridors with determined steps, my mind a whirlwind of emotions. I need air—space to breathe, away from the suffocating weight of scrutiny and suspicion.

Outside, the city buzzes with oblivious activity. Thompson rushes to open the car door and I jump inside, the cool interior offering a brief respite from the searing heat of my emotions. Why would anyone ask that? Do people really think I would kill my own mother? Especially to get back in good with the very people who stole my fucking life.

My car doesn't stop again until we're back at the Carlyle. I rush past all the people and head to my suite. The heavy door of the room slams shut behind me, reverberating through the suite like a thunderclap. My breath comes in ragged gasps, my chest heaving with a mix of fury and anguish. The opulent surroundings that once offered solace now feels stifling, suffocating. I pace the length of my room, adrenaline coursing through my veins and rage boiling my blood. I lean against the window, watching the people rushing in the distance as a way to calm me.

It doesn't work.

I jerk away from the window and pace across the floor.

"Fuck," I scream into the luxurious void.

Without a second thought, I unleash my pent-up rage on the room. The vase of fresh flowers on the side table is the first casualty, crashing to the floor in a burst of shattered glass and scattered petals. Books fly off the shelves, their pages fluttering like wounded birds in the air. The plush cushions of the couch are flung aside, their softness offering no comfort amid the turmoil of my emotions.

My hands tremble as I continue my sweep through the room, a tempest of fury and grief. Objects become projectiles—shattering a framed photograph on the wall. I rip the duvet from the bed, clawing at the thick threads. It does not shred. Spotting a pair of black scissors on the nightstand, I grab them and begin again. Nothing is left untouched in my reckless abandon, the neatness of the suite giving way to chaos under my frenzied assault.

But as the room lay in disarray, a sudden wave of exhaustion washes over me. The adrenaline that was fueling my rage ebbs away, leaving me feeling hollow and spent. I sink to my knees amidst the wreckage, hands shaking as I drop the scissors.

I bury my face in my palms as the tears stream down my cheeks, my body trembling with the weight of everything I have been enduring—the loss of my mother, being back at the estate, the relentless scrutiny of the public eye, the cruel insinuations that tarnishes my grief. The facade of strength I have been wearing so bravely shatters and a soul-eating sob leaves me.

"I miss you, Mom," I whisper hoarsely into the silence of the room. "I wish you were here. I don't know how to do this without you."

The enormity of my grief crashes over me like a tidal wave, overwhelming and relentless. Memories of my mother flood my mind—the sound of her laughter echoing through sunlit afternoons, the warmth of her embrace after a long day of filming, and the unwavering support that had always been my anchor after my dad died.

Then, footsteps approach—a tentative presence entering the room. Silas' concerned face appears in my blurred vision, his eyes widening at the sight before him—the suite in shambles, and me, broken and vulnerable among the wreckage.

"Solaris," he breathes, crossing the room in swift strides. He kneels beside me, gathering my trembling form into his arms. "It's okay, Sol. I'm here."

I cling to him desperately, my tears soaking into the fabric of his shirt. I tremble with the release of emotions long held in check, the weight of my grief finally finding a voice in my cries.

"I'm sorry," I manage to choke out between sobs, my voice raw with pain. "I'm so sorry."

Silas holds me close, his own tears mingling with mine. He presses a gentle kiss to my forehead, his touch a soothing balm against the storm still brewing in me.

"You don't have to apologize. There's nothing to be sorry for," Silas whispers, his voice a gentle comfort. "I'm here for you. Always."

We stay like this for what feels like an eternity, wrapped in each other's embrace among the ruins of the room. Outside, the city continues its relentless rhythm, oblivious to the instability within the walls of The Carlyle. In this moment though, all that matters is the solace I have in Silas' arms. As the tears come to a stop, replaced by a quiet calm, I know that no matter what challenges lie ahead, I will have Silas to face them with me.

He rises to his feet and brings me up with him. He wipes at the remaining tears lingering on my lashes and pulls me into a hug. Pulling back, he searches the room again, taking in the disarray. "We should probably clean this place up before security gets here and we're banned for life. This is kind of my new favorite hotel."

"Agreed."

Fifteen

Solaris

The jet engines roar as we taxi down the runway at JFK Airport, leaving behind the skyline of New York City. I stare out of the window, the events at The Carlyle replaying in my mind like a relentless film reel, each scene etched with pain and humiliation. I can't believe I did that. I can't believe I let Silas see me like that. Lord knows what Brandon Black will write about me once this gets out. I'm under no impression the staff will keep quiet. Not with the broken photos and shredded comforter. The worst was done in that hotel room, and I can't believe it was me.

Beside me, Silas sits in somber silence. He held me through the darkest hour today, his touch a soothing shield against the storm that raged within me. Now, as the plane soars through the clouds towards Alabama, he watches me with concern etched into his features. Hopefully, he doesn't ask me to explain. He didn't at the hotel, but then again, we were trying to get the place as clean as we could before security came. They never came and he never questioned.

"Are you okay?" Silas finally expresses his concern, his voice a gentle breeze cutting through the turbulence of my thoughts.

I sigh, tearing my gaze away from the window to meet his eyes. "I don't know," I admit hoarsely. "Everything just . . . unraveled back there. I didn't mean to destroy that room."

Silas reaches for my hand, his fingers intertwining with mine in a gesture of solidarity. "You don't have to talk about it if you don't want to," he assures me. "But I'm here if you do."

The warmth of his words eases some of the tension coiled within me. I lean my head against the headrest, closing my eyes briefly to shut out the memories that threaten to overwhelm me. "I just kept hearing this voice in my head, egging me on. Wanting to destroy. It's as if I was someone else for a moment. As if I was just a passenger in my own body, watching it all play out and helpless to do anything about it. But it was me, Silas. I did that."

Silas' thumb caresses the back of my hand, and he brings it up to his mouth, placing a petal soft kiss upon it. "We all lose it sometimes. You've been bottling your feelings since your mom, and you haven't had a chance to really grieve her. The interviewer went too far. No one truly believes you killed your mother."

I don't respond to him. I don't know what people believe I did or didn't do. However, there must be enough talk for that woman to completely disregard my do not ask list. Leaning my head against the cooling glass, I watch as the plane cruises through the sky. Time seems suspended in a fragile cocoon of silence between us—a sanctuary amidst the chaos that will await us when we make it back to the estate.

The descent into Birmingham-Shuttlesworth International Airport is smooth, the Alabama landscape unfolding beneath us like a patchwork quilt of green fields and winding rivers. My heart sinks at the familiar sight before me, a measure of discomfort blossoming deep within my chest, reminding me of what's waiting in Mountain Rose. My family will have found out that I'm the sole heir to James' fortune today. I knew it was coming, which is one reason I left school yesterday and went directly to New York. I didn't want more threats. I didn't want to hide in my room. I didn't want Loretta stealing Silas away as a way to punish me. I wanted a day of peace and luxury, not that it happened with all the layovers.

Silas releases his hold on my hand and grabs our luggage. He tugs out a baseball cap and a pair of dark lensed sunglasses, putting them on as if that's going to hide him. I roll my eyes at the ridiculous disguise. Like me, there's not a place on this planet where he can go unseen. I honestly don't know why he's even trying.

We disembark from the private jet, stepping onto the tarmac where the Alabama sun bathes us in its beaming heat. The air is thick with humidity, a glaring contrast to the cool crispness of New York City. We make our way through the airport terminal, the clickity-clack of our footsteps echoing in the cavernous space. Silas keeps a protective distance, sensing the fragility of my resolve as we navigate the bustling crowd. I swear if one person stops me and asks for an autograph or worse, asks about my mom, I'm going to flip. His presence is a shield against the prying eyes that seem to follow us, their curiosity palpable in the air. Even with him in the stupid cap.

"Do you even like baseball?" I murmur to him as we make our way outside.

"Not the point of it." He grins at me as we come to a stop in front of a black SUV awaiting us. The driver, a stoic figure in a dark suit, holds open the door with a respectful nod. Silas ushers me inside.

The drive to Mountain Rose is a blur of familiar landmarks—the towering pines that line the winding roads, the quaint storefronts that dot the main street, and finally, the looming gold and stone gates that mark the entrance to the James estate.

My childhood home looms ahead, an immense mansion nestled among rolling hills and manicured gardens. While the sight of this place would have had me quaking in my heels weeks before, it doesn't tonight. Instead, I can't help the grin spreading across my face as we make our way up the cobblestone path to the main mansion. I own it all now.

The grin gracing my face spreads even wider as the car comes to a stop, revealing my family waiting—the very representation of simmering tension and unspoken truths. My heart hastens as we get out of the car and we come face-to-face with them. Cruise's expression is guarded and unreadable. His usual cocky nature is nowhere to be seen. He actually looks quite a bit like our father right now. Lena is beaming with joy. She already knows she has nothing to worry about. And Loretta, the animosity seeping from her pores can sink a thousand ships.

Silas tenses next to me and his hand falls from my hold. I turn to search his face only to see him glaring off in the distance. My eyes track to the figure holding his attention, a frail and sickly man that appears to be on death's door. This is the first time I've seen Mayor O'Conner since my mom's funeral. No one has even mentioned him, and I certainly didn't want to ask about the man. I knew all I needed to from the silence on Silas' part and the fact that he was creepy as hell on the drive to the gravesite.

"Solaris," Cruise greets, his voice tinged with a hint of skepticism. "Silas."

Silas maintains his composure with a respectful nod, unfazed by the palpable unease in the air. "Cruise, Loretta, Father," he acknowledges, his gaze never once venturing back to me.

I eye each member of my family, my hands clasped tightly in front of me, waiting for one of them to say something about the events that have unfolded.

"Where have you been?" Cruise steps forward, his tone a mixture of curiosity and reproach. "We've been waiting."

"I had . . . things to take care of," I reply carefully, choosing my words with deliberate precision. He doesn't need to know anything about my life or the things I do. "I apologize for any inconvenience."

Liar. The voice in my head rears its ugly head again.

Loretta steps forward then, shoving Cruise out of the way."We saw your televised interview in New York," she says. "It's truly a shame those reporters are so inconsiderate?"

I swallow hard, giving her a tight smile and ignoring her remark. "It was difficult," my eyes narrow on her. "But I'm fine. The *real* people who killed my mother will get what's coming to them soon enough."

Silas' father let out a guttural, rasping cough that slices through the heavy tension, commanding everyone's attention. As he struggles to regain composure, we fall silent, all eyes instinctively drawn to the frail figure that seems to shrink further in his weariness. When he finally steadies himself, his gaze fixes on me with an intensity that opposes his weakened state.

"Your father would have wanted us to unite during this trying time," he declares, his voice carrying a surprising strength. "Not to stand here on these steps, on the verge of brawling over mere objects and money."

A choked laugh escapes me at his assumption. While he might have married into this cluster fuck of a family for prestige and privilege, not all of us care about those things. Besides, from the look of him, he couldn't brawl even if he wanted. I honestly don't even know why he's out here when he should be lying in a bed somewhere waiting on the reaper to send him to hell.

I cross my arms tightly over my chest and glare at him with irritation blazing in my eyes. How dare he presume to know what my father would have wanted? The few times he bothered to be around Dad, he was too busy kissing up to Loretta to give a damn about the man who funded this whole lifestyle.

Silas' hand finds mine once more, finally proving to our family that we're a united front. He glances at me briefly, his eyes filled with unspoken understanding and unwavering loyalty.

"We should continue this inside," Lena interjects.

All eyes turn to her, and she responds with a nonchalant shrug. The group begins to disperse, heading toward the entrance, except for Loretta, Silas, and me. Silas raises an eyebrow in my direction, silently questioning my hesitation. This needs to happen.

"Go," I tell him, my voice firm but calm. "I'll be right there."

He searches my face but reluctantly goes inside the sprawling manor. I watch as Silas disappears, and I take a deep breath, steeling myself for the inevitable confrontation with Loretta. With everyone else inside, her stoic facade cracks. She crosses her arms tightly over her crisp, tailored button-down, her face a mask of fury. Her eyes blaze with a mix of anger and resentment, her lips curled into a sneer.

"Do you really think you can waltz in here and take everything?" she hisses, her voice dripping with venom as she takes a menacing step toward me. "Do you think a measly piece of paper is really going to change how things have been for generations?"

I go to take a step back but remember I'm standing on narrow stairs. "Loretta, I never asked for any of this. Maybe this is your karma for discarding me like yesterday's trash all those years ago."

"Don't play the victim with me!" she shrieks, her hand reaching out to grab my arm. "You've always had a way of landing on your feet. Actress. Model. Youngest billionaire under twenty. You just couldn't seem to stay in your place. Out of sight. Out of mind."

"Well, you see, dear aunt, I was raised by a James. And apparently, none of us take too kindly to being out of sight. Out of mind. If so, you wouldn't have felt the need to make yourself known."

"You're not a James." She hisses at me, her grip tightens and nails digging into my arm.

I wince at the pressure and the memory of that fateful day when she tossed me out on the street resurfaces vividly. The cold, the hunger, and the fear that had consumed me as a child slams into me with the weight of a wrecking ball. That year spent watching my mother struggle to provide for us had hardened me, but standing here now, I feel a surge of vulnerability I haven't felt since before landing my first acting role. And I absolutely loathe that it's this woman who's bringing forth that feeling.

"You're pathetic," Loretta spits, her face inches from mine now. "You've always been a thorn in my side, and now you think you can just come back and take what's mine?"

"This estate was never yours, Loretta," I say, my voice steady despite my tumult of emotions. "It was my father's, and now it's mine. You can't change that."

Her eyes narrow, her expression twisting into one of pure malice. "You ungrateful little brat."

With a sudden, violent motion, she shoves me with surprising force. I stumble backward, my feet slipping on the edge of the step. Time seems to slow as I flail, desperately trying to regain my balance. The world tilts, and I fall, tumbling down the stone steps in a blur of pain and confusion.

I land hard on the cobblestones below, the impact jarring my bones and knocking the wind out of me. I lie there for a moment, staring up at the bright Alabama sky, my vision blurring with tears of shock. Every part of my body aches, the physical pain mingling with the emotional wounds that have been ripped open anew today.

Loretta stands at the top of the stairs, looking down at me with cold satisfaction. "Remember this, Solaris. You may own this estate, but you'll never be welcome here. Not ever."

With that, she turns and disappears into the house, letting the door slam with a jarring thud behind her. The sound echoes in my ears, a harsh reminder of the rejection I had faced so many years ago.

I try to sit up, wincing at the sharp pain in my side. I take a few shallow breaths, but the effort is too much; my vision swims and darkens at the edges. The world around me begins to fade as my strength ebbs away.

As consciousness slips from my grasp, I feel a mixture of despair and determination. This estate represents more than what I lost; it's a symbol of everything I have endured and everything I am determined to reclaim. I can't let this family win, not after everything I have gone through. They will pay, and claiming this estate is the first step.

Another sharp pain ricochets through me and I succumb to the darkness, my body lying still on the cold stones.

I wake to the sterile smell of antiseptic and the rhythmic beeping of machines. My head throbs, a dull pain reminding me of the recent altercation. Slowly, I open my eyes, blinking against the harsh hospital lights.

Lena sits by my bedside, her eyes red and puffy from crying. She clutches a tissue in one hand, her shoulders shaking with silent sobs. When she notices I'm awake, she wipes her tears hastily and forces a weak smile.

"You're awake," she says, her voice thick with emotion. "I'm so sorry for what happened. I can't believe my mother did that to you."

I take a deep breath, wincing at the slight pain in my ribs. "It's not your fault, Lena. You don't need to apologize for her actions."

Lena shakes her head, fresh tears spilling down her cheeks. "I do. She's my mother, and I feel responsible. I never should have suggested we go inside. I just didn't want anyone to overhear. I'm so sorry."

"Don't worry about it," I say softly, reaching out to squeeze her hand. "So, how bad is it? What's broken?"

Lena's eyes dip. "Nothing. You were lucky. There are only a few bruises, and you have a concussion. The doctor said the pain should go away within a few days."

I slump back against the hospital bed and let out a sigh. A shot of pain shoots through me, and I wince.

"Do you need a doctor?" Lena goes to press the nurse call button, but I shake my head. I'll be fine.

She sits back down and a moment of silence stretches between us before Lena speaks again, her voice hesitant. "So, what are you going to do, Sol? With the estate, I mean. And with everyone else? Do you plan to take over the businesses as well?"

I look up at the ceiling and let out a sigh. To be honest, I haven't given much thought beyond acquiring it. I've been focused on proving that the empire is mine and that Loretta is nothing without it. I never considered the practical aspects of taking over my family's empire. I have little knowledge about real estate and the hospitality industry, so I'm not suited to run it. However, that doesn't mean I'm leaving Loretta in charge. I would rather see the entire empire fall apart than give Loretta the satisfaction of thinking that I can't handle it.

"I don't know yet, Lena," I tell her honestly. "But I promise you, you're safe. Your trust fund is safe. I would never take that from you. I just . . . I need to figure things out."

Before Lena can respond, the door to the room opens and I glance that way to see Silas walk in, holding a familiar cup. He smiles when he sees me awake, and the sight of my favorite iced coffee order brings a small measure of comfort.

"Thought you might need this," he says, handing me the cup. "How are you feeling?"

"Like I got hit by a truck," I reply with a wry smile, taking the coffee from his hand and wetting my dry throat.

Silas pulls up a chair next to Lena, his expression serious. "Care to tell me how a simple conversation turned into a hospital visit?"

I roll my eyes at his stupid question. "My aunt's a bitch and couldn't handle losing."

A snort leaves Lena. "That's an understatement."

Silas' lips twitch in response. "How about we focus on getting you out of here and back home, aye?"

"Yes, please," I tell him.

As much as I hate being at the manor, I hate hospitals and doctors even more. Besides, I can't do anything from a hospital bed.

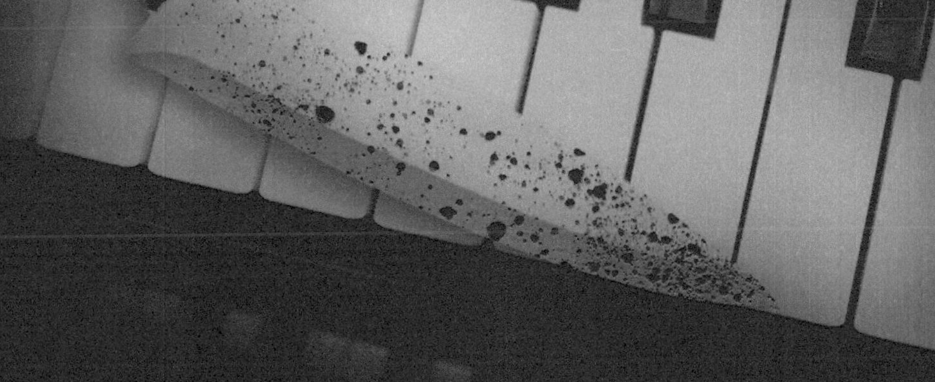

Sixteen

Silas

Six years ago

The sun dips below the horizon, casting long, golden shadows across the sprawling grounds of the James family estate. I glare at the ridiculous knot at my neck as I adjusting my tie in front of a large, ornate mirror, trying to suppress the irritation bubbling inside me. The masquerade ball downstairs is an extravagant affair, filled with influential people from the country music world. My father invited them all here to celebrate my 21st birthday and my band's recent success. Or at least that's how he stated it on the invite to them. I know the truth though. This party is just another way my father is showing me how much control he has over me, my life, and my career.

A soft knock on the door pulls me from my thoughts. "Come in," I call, expecting one of the servants. Instead, it's Solaris peeking in with a shy smile.

"Hi," she says, stepping into the room. She's wearing a simple, elegant pink dress that accentuates her youthful innocence, but on her, it looks perfect.

"Hey," I greet her, a genuine smile spreading across my face. "What's up?"

She hesitates for a moment, then holds out a small velvet pouch. "I wanted to give you your birthday present early. Before all the craziness starts."

I take the pouch, curiosity piqued. "You didn't have to get me anything."

"I wanted to," she insists, her eyes bright with excitement. "You spent the whole night with me on my birthday, so . . . Open it."

I pull the drawstring and tip the contents into my palm. A gold guitar pick slides out, catching the light. Our initials are etched into it—S and S, intertwined in a delicate script. It's beautiful, thoughtful, and more than I could have asked for.

"Solaris, this is incredible. Weighty," I say, genuinely touched. "Thank you."

She beams, her cheeks flushing with pleasure. "I'm glad you like it. I wasn't really sure what to get you, but I know your band means a lot to you."

I smile at her as my fingers glide across the surface of the metal. No one has gotten me anything this thoughtful before. The facet that it's coming from Sol causes my heart to swell. Solaris is one of the only bright spots in this otherwise bleak family. She makes me smile. Hell, dare I say even happy. But that's a cause for concern. She's getting attached to me in a way that's starting to feel . . . complicated. I've noticed the way she looks at me, the way she seeks me out. It's innocent, but still, I can't shake the feeling that I need to put some distance between us. For her sake and mine.

"Come here," I say, pulling her into a gentle hug and contradicting my own thoughts. Her arms wrap around me tightly, and I can feel the rapid beat of her heart thumping against me. The connection between us is undeniable, and for a moment, I just hold her, savoring the warmth and comfort she brings. But then, a wave of guilt washes over me. This isn't right. She's only twelve, and I'm a grown man. In no universe should I be holding her like this.

I pull back, needing to establish some boundaries. "We should get ready for the party," I say, trying to keep my tone light. "It's going to be a long night."

Her smile falters slightly and her eyes dip, disappointed. While I hate doing this to her, the gift is too much. It's the type of thing a girl give her crush and I can't have Solaris thinking we might be anything than what we are. Friends. Only friends.

"Okay then." Her gaze drop to the carpeted floor in an attempt to keep me from seeing her hurt, but I do. "I'll see you downstairs."

As she leaves the room, I slip the guitar pick into my pocket, feeling its weight against my leg. It's a reminder of the bond I share with Solaris, but also of the need to tread carefully. I can't let things get out of hand. Not with her.

I sit down on the edge of my bed, running a hand through my hair. The emotions swirling inside me are a tangled mess. I deeply care about Solaris, but the intensity of those feelings are starting to worries me. The lines between us need to stay clear. She's a child for goodness' sake, and I don't want to be another man that misuses my authority to take advantage of her. I don't think that's what it is. The relationship we share doesn't feel sordid, yet I know I would never allow anyone to be this close to my daughter if I had one her age. I also can't deny the pull I feel towards her, my desire to protect her, to be the one she turns to.

I shake my head, trying to clear my thoughts. This isn't the time to dwell on such things. I need to focus on the party, on playing my part at this absurd event my father has orchestrated. Letting out a guttural groan, I get up from the bed and leave the room.

By the time I make it downstairs, the grand ballroom of the James family estate is a sight to behold, transformed into a glittering wonderland for the masquerade ball. Crystal chandeliers cast shimmering light across the room, reflecting off the opulent masks worn by the guests. I stand near the entrance, greeting a steady stream of attendees. My birthday coincides with Halloween, and my father spared no expense to celebrate both occasions.

The event is more than just a birthday party though. My band, Black Roses, has just cracked the top 100 on the Billboard charts with our hit song Solaris helped me write. Everyone fell in love with the song the moment I let them hear it. My team spared no time getting this song out as our first official single. We laid down the tracks and recorded it all within a week. It's been playing on every station, and people even recognized me on the street a few times. The past month has been a whirlwind, and if I'm being honest, I'm only holding it together because of Solaris and her nightly phone calls. This all seem like it happened too fast and I'm terrified of the part my father had to play in it.

I glance around at the extravagance and all the people and let out a sigh as I finally descend the staircase to the sprawling ballroom full of people in shimmering gowns of gold, red, and black. I can't help but feel it's all overkill. I would have preferred something simpler, more intimate. But this isn't about what I want; it's about what this family think will maintain our image. For the life of me, I didn't think I would be worrying much more about my image until I started selling out stadiums.

As the night progresses, I make my rounds, chatting with guests and accepting their congratulations. I wear a sleek black suit and a matching mask that covers the upper half of my face, giving me an air of mystery that only adds to my allure. At least that's what my manager told me. My other band members, around here somewhere, are dressed in similar fashion to me. In case any photos leak from the event, my team wanted us all to look on brand.

"Silas, my boy!" booms a familiar voice I've been avoiding all night. I turn with a grimace to see my father approaching with a broad smile that doesn't reach his eyes. He's in a tailored tuxedo, his dark elf mask equally as grandiose as the rest of the evening. "Happy birthday, Son."

I force a smile, knowing that's what's expected of me tonight. "Thanks, Dad."

"Quite the party, isn't it?" He gestures around the room, his tone dripping with self-satisfaction.

"Yeah," I say, my voice flat. "A bit much, don't you think?"

His eyes narrow slightly, catching the undercurrent of my remark. "Nonsense. This is a celebration worthy of your achievements. You should be grateful. It's not every day that a small band reaches your heights so swiftly."

"I would've preferred something simpler. Maybe just the band and a few friends."

He chuckles, a low, humorless sound. "That's precisely why I organized it, Silas. Left to your own devices, you'd squander opportunities to make valuable connections. You think too small."

"And you think everything has to be a spectacle," I retort, unable to keep the bitterness out of my voice.

My father's smile tightens, eyes narrowing on me. He claps me on the shoulder with a grip that feels more like a warning than a gesture of pride. "Keep it up, son. You're doing great."

As he moves on to mingle with other guests, I feel a hand on my arm. I turn to see Loretta standing behind me. She's dressed in a silver gown, her mask adorned with intricate crystal detailing that makes her blue eyes stand out against all the pale material. If I didn't loathe this woman so much, I would even call her stunning tonight. Nevertheless, I know the skeletons in her closet, and nothing could make me see this woman for anything other than the vile fae she's posing as tonight.

"Silas, darling," she purrs, her voice low and sultry. "Can we talk for a moment?"

"Of course," I reply through a knot of unease in my stomach.

Loretta leads me away from the throng of guests, down a quiet corridor, and into a secluded alcove. Once we're alone, she turns to me, her expression shifting from pleasant to something more predatory. My walls instantly go up.

"Silas," she says, stepping closer and running a pointy finger nail up my suit jacket. "You're looking very handsome tonight."

"Thanks, Loretta," I reply, trying to keep my tone neutral and stepping away from her touch. "What did you want to talk about?"

Her eyes roam over my face, and her hand goes back to my chest. "You know, I've always admired you. You're quite a fine young man if I do say so myself."

Cocking my head to the side, I narrow my eyes on her. "Loretta, what is this about?"

She leans into me, her breath hot against my ear. "Don't be coy, Silas. You know what I want."

I pull back, my jaw tightening. Of course I know what she wants. This entire month, she's made her sudden interest in me known. Showing up in my room in lingerie. Cooking me breakfast. Or rather having breakfast cooked for me. Making flirty little remarks whenever my father isn't around. Yeah, her wants are clear at this point.

"No," I tell her. "I'm not interested."

She jerks back at my rejection and narrows her eyes on me. "Why not? You're on your way up, and I can make even bigger things happen for you."

"Even so, my answer is still no," I say firmly. "I will not be a part of whatever this fucked up family has going on."

Loretta's expression darkens and she straightens to her full height. "What are you talking about?"

"I know about your affair with Gregory," I say quietly. "And I'm not going to be part of whatever generational trauma this family has going on. I'm not into the whole incest thing."

Her face twists with rage. "You don't—"

"Save it, Loretta," I interrupt. "Gregory's told me all about this family's traditions."

She glares at me, her chest heaving with anger and her pale skin turning a cherry red. "You'll regret this. I promise you that. No one rejects me."

With that, she storms out of the alcove, her heels clicking angrily against the marble floor. I take a deep breath, trying to calm myself. That was wild. Then again, Gregory hasn't been around since his confession outside of Solaris' room, and I can't figure out Loretta's situation with my father. They don't seem to be screwing, and they are hardly spotted together.

"Well, that was quite a spectacle," comes a voice from the shadows. I turn to see my father emerging from the darkness, his expression grim.

"Dad," I begin, but he holds up a hand.

"I heard everything," he says quietly. "And let me make one thing clear, Silas. You need to keep Loretta happy. No matter what."

I feel a cold chill run down my spine. "What are you saying?"

He steps closer, his voice low and menacing. "Loretta is important to this family. You will do whatever it takes to keep her content. Do you understand?"

I stare at him in disbelief. "Even if it means compromising my integrity?"

"Especially if it means that," he replies, his eyes hard. "This family comes first, Silas. Always."

I clench my fists, anger boiling inside me. "No. I will not play whatever twisted game you have going on with this family."

"And why not?" my father asks. "You, abstaining from gorgeous women throwing themselves at you, wouldn't have something to do with a browned-haired little girl that's off limits, would it?"

Biting down on the inside of my jaw, I reframe from answering such a ridiculous question.

"You think I haven't noticed the lack of females you associate with now? Matter of fact, you haven't been seen with any girl since the moment you set foot on this property five months ago."

"I hate you," I say through gritted teeth, not wanting him to realize just how spot on he truly is. I haven't been with anyone since the very first day here. "I hate everything about you."

He merely shrugs. "You'll get over it. Just keep Loretta happy, or it won't be you that hurts. It's already such a shame what's happening to that sweet little girl. I would hate for it to get worse."

My hands ball into fist at his threat. He turns from me without a second thought, and I watch as he walks away, leaving me alone in the alcove. The weight of his words settles heavily on my shoulders, and I realize that my life is about to become much more complicated. No one is laying another finger on Solaris. If it's the last thing I do, I will get her out of this family. I will set her free from this nightmare.

Returning to the party, I plaster a smile on my face and rejoin the festivities. The masquerade is in full swing, and I scan the crowd, looking for a familiar face. My heart sinks when I spot Solaris wandering through the ballroom with her shady brother trailing behind her. If he is following her, then there's only one thing he wants, and I will not let that happen on my watch.

I make my way toward them, hoping to intercept before anything happens. Solaris looks up and spots me, her face lighting up with a grin. But before I can reach her, Cruise steps in front of her, blocking my path.

"Silas," crossing his arms. "Enjoying the party? My family went all out on you."

"Go away, Cruise," I say, my tone cold. "I need to talk to Solaris."

He smirks but steps aside, enough for her to look between the two of us in confusion. "What exactly do you need to speak with my sister about?"

I glare at him, reaching around and taking hold of Solaris by the arm. Gently, I lead her away from her brother and to the other side of the room where more kids her age are hanging out. She looks at them and then back at me.

"If I wanted to be at the kids table, I wouldn't have left," she tells me with a huff, pursing her mouth as if that's going to make me listen.

"Are you okay?" I ask, keeping my voice low. "Did Cruise touch you?"

She shakes her head, looking up at me with wide confused eyes through her white sequin kitten mask. "No. Cruise just wanted—"

"Stay away from him," I interrupt. "He's trouble."

Her face scrunches up in confusion, and she looks away from me and back at him standing near the bar. "I know. But he's my brother. Cruise wouldn't hurt me."

She doesn't know how wrong she is. Cruise would do just about anything to get what he wants. I know his pretty boy type. And while I might not understand his motives behind pimping out his sister, I know enough to keep her away from him.

"I know he's your brother," I say softly, squeezing her hand. "Just be careful, okay? I don't trust him, and I don't like the way he looks at you."

She nods again, and I feel a pang of guilt. I want to protect her, but I can't always be here. And with everything else going on, it's hard to know who to trust. Maybe I should confront her father when he's back in town. Just because Cruise claimed her, doesn't mean he gets to do this to her. If her father knew in detail what I know, maybe he would put a stop to it.

"Stay here with the other kids," I tell her. "And don't wander around this party by yourself. Matter of fact, just hang out with Lena and draw or do whatever kids your age do."

She narrows her eyes at me. "Lena couldn't come tonight, and I don't appreciate you treating me like a kid. I'm not a kid."

I ignore her statement. "Just be a good girl and stay put."

Leaving her with the other kids, I continue my facade for the night. As it wears on, I find myself constantly scanning the crowd, keeping an eye on Solaris while trying to navigate the treacherous waters of family politics. The masquerade is supposed to be a celebration, but for me, it feels more like a battlefield. And as the clock ticks toward midnight, I can't shake the feeling that this is only the beginning of the chaos to come.

Seventeen

Solaris

It's been a few days since the incident with Loretta, and I'm back in my old childhood bedroom. Not once did I think I'd be living here again. The familiar surroundings bring a strange mix of comfort and unease. Every corner of this room holds memories, both sweet and bitter. The wallpaper, the canopy bed, the shelves filled with childhood mementos—it all feels like a time capsule of a life that was abruptly taken from me. I sit by the window, staring out at the sprawling gardens, lost in thought when a knock on the door pulls me back to the present.

"Come in," I call, my energy still a little depleted from the hospital stay.

My lock beeps, signaling my code was input, and Lena bursts into the room with her usual vigor, a small package in her hands. "Look what just arrived!" she sing-songs, her eyes sparkling with excitement.

I turn to her, trying to muster a smile. Honestly, today has just been a bit blah. Silas was supposed to come over, but something came up with Black Roses. I've just been sitting here, surrounded by all this stuff that no longer feels like mine, and trying to figure out how I can make Loretta suffer for her little stunt on the steps. Apparently, I'm too nice. That's what the voice in my head says anyway since I keep vetoing everything it wants to do.

Actually, I called you a pushover.

Go back into hiding! I shout at her and give Lena my attention.

"What is it?" I ask her, trying to find any identifying marks on the black box in her hands as I go over to her.

She hops onto my bed. "It's for Silas' masquerade party. Open it!"

Curiosity piqued, I carefully tear open the packaging to reveal a beautiful half-face black lace bunny mask. The lacy ears are elegant, and the strings of crystals cascade down around the mouth, catching the light and shimmering like tiny stars, are beautiful.

"Lena, this is gorgeous," I breathe, running my fingers over the delicate lace.

"I knew you'd love it," she says, grinning. "I got myself a mask too." She pulls out a simple gold eye mask adorned with lace and jewels from her bag. She places the mask against her eyes and poses. "What do you think?"

"It's perfect for you," I tell her, genuinely impressed. "Your taste is unmatched. I would have picked up something from the local costume shop."

Lena's grin widens and she leaps up from the bed with way too much pep in her step. "Thanks! Now get up. I figured it's been a while since we spent any real time together. How about we go shopping for gowns to match our masks? You know, have some fun and take our minds off the whole inheritance BS and the things Brandon Black is saying."

I jerk my head to her a bit confused. "What is he saying now?"

Lena pats my question away, and I get up from the bed and prance across the room to where my phone lay on the charger. I immediately pull up Brandon's column and read the latest on me.

"What the hell?" I shriek. "He can't say that! Did Silas try to get this retracted?"

Lena shrugs. "Silas isn't even in Mountain Rose right now. He had some urgent meeting with his records executives about his hiatus."

I arch a brow at her, completely interested. "Go on."

"We talked last night when he got off his plane. Apparently, the band is supposed to be working on a new album, but they can't without their lead singer. Silas mentioned going in and laying down some tracks on a new song. I wonder if it's about you."

I roll my eyes at the suggestion. He wouldn't. It's far too soon for that. "When will he be back?"

"Before his party on Friday." Lena cocks her head to the side and raises an eyebrow in a questioning manner. "He didn't tell you any of this? With the way he's been touching you and making googly eyes at you, I just figured—"

"He probably did mention it," I cut her off. "But I've been so drugged out on these pain meds, I just maybe forgot."

"Hmm … Anyway, you, me, shopping, Rodeo Drive. What do you say?"

I hesitate for a moment. The thought of going to California where paparazzi run wild feels daunting. Having more reporters taking photos and talking about me is not on my wish list right now, but Lena's enthusiasm is infectious. We do need dresses though, and while Mountain Rose may have many things, luxury shopping is not one of them.

"Okay. Let's do it." I find myself nodding along to her. "I could use a day with it being just us."

"Yay!" she exclaims, pulling me into a hug. "We'll take the jet and be back before anyone even knows we're missing. Maybe we can even stop by the studio in Nashville and check on Silas. Nashville isn't that far from here, right?"

I shrug, not wanting to tell her that it's only a measly four hours from us. She doesn't need to know that I practically stalked him right after her mother threw me out. Besides, Silas didn't even tell me he was leaving; I'm not going to chase him to Nashville.

A few hours later, we're soaring above the clouds and sipping on cheap champagne, chatting about everything and nothing. The plush seats and the gentle hum of the engines are a welcome departure from James Manor. Lena leans over the armrest, her excitement palpable.

"But seriously though . . ." She takes a sip of her drink. "You have to tell me. Everybody at school is wanting to know since you've been MIA recently."

My cheeks heat at the thought of Silas and me. "Do we really need to talk about my sex life with your brother?"

"So there is one?" she urges.

"Lena!" I giggle. "I am not going to tell you if we have been together. One, ew! Two, I never bought into that stupid bet. And three, why does it even matter?"

"Because I told you when Taylor and I had sex for the first time. If you can't tell me, then who are you going to confide in?"

She has a point, but I'm still not telling her that Silas and I have been together. I don't know. It's just weird. While I know there is no actual familial relation between us, our relationship still feels like something people will disapprove of. Right now, I just want to keep this for myself. The world doesn't need to know everything we do.

"Remember when we used to play dress-up in your mom's old gowns?" Lena changes the topic, sensing I'm done with that conversation.

I laugh and take a sip of my own champagne. "Yeah, and we'd pretend to go to the balls and charity functions everyone tried to keep us from."

Lena giggles. "Those were the days. Do you ever miss when our parents seemed to be a little decent?"

I frown, her questioning bringing up thoughts of my mom. My parents were never as awful as Loretta. Yes, my dad was away a lot, but that was his job, and I was used to it. Sometimes, my mom would go with him, but not once when they were away on their business trips did they not call me to wish me a good night or to check up on me. At least my mom always did. My parents were the best I could have asked for in this life we live. I learned a long time ago there are sacrifices that come with being rich and powerful. My father was certainly that.

With a sigh, I murmur to Lena, "Those were the best of days."

Lena keeps going on and on, talking about everything and nothing. It sit back and watch the clouds pass. A few hours later, we descend into Los Angeles, and find a town car already waiting for us. Lena must have already assumed I would agree to this little excursion in order to have a car booked and ready. Then again, she knows I never really tell her no.

The bustling street of Rodeo Drive is exhilarating. The shops are filled with the latest fashions, and there's people everywhere. No one here pays any attention to who we are, and I love it. We're all on equal footing here. I mean, you must be somebody to afford to shop on Rodeo Drive.

We dive into the first store with gusto. Store after store Lena drags me in search of the perfect dress. In one of the boutiques, Lena tries to get me into a black sheer mini dress that looks more like fish netting than an actual dress. I turn her down, but she buys the dress anyway.

We find ourselves in three more stores before Lena holds up a stunning emerald green gown. "This would look amazing on you."

I take the dress from her and turn to the mirror, holding the dress up to my body. It's beautiful and elegant with slits going all the way up each thigh. The crushed velvet feels luxurious, and I can't get over how perfectly the color matches Silas' eyes.

"I love it," I say, feeling a spark of excitement.

"Yeah, and Silas won't be able to keep his hands off you." I roll my eyes at her.

That didn't even cross my mind.

Liar, the voice in my head says to me again.

"It doesn't look cute and innocent like a bunny mask does though," I state in regard to the mask she picked out.

She bats my concerns away. "Who cares? You are going to look freaking stunning, and no one is going to care about the mask."

Lena continues to peruse the store until she finds a gorgeous gold dress that complements her mask perfectly. We head to the fitting rooms to try them on. As I step out in the emerald gown, Lena's eyes widen. I'm pretty sure my face is just as in awe as hers.

"We look like total movie stars." She beams at me. "Let's see the guys try to keep their hands off us Friday night."

I roll my eyes at her, but I agree; we look badass. There will be no hiding in these dresses. Not from Silas and certainly not from Loretta. And for the first time, I'm fine with that. Maybe it's time that everyone sees that I'm not a little girl anymore.

Changing back into our civilian clothes, we're head to make our purchases when we hear a familiar voice. "Lena?"

We both halt and groan in exasperation as we turn to see Taylor standing there with a beautiful girl on his arm. I cringe when I recognize her. Kassi. One of the actresses that guest starred on our show.

Kassi gives us a smug smile. "Solaris, Lena. What a surprise to see you here."

"Likewise," I say, forcing a polite smile. "How have you been?"

"Oh, you know, just living the dream," she replies, her eyes flicking to Taylor with a possessive gleam. "Taylor and I have been having a wonderful time."

Taylor's eyes flicker between Lena and me, a hint of nervousness in his gaze. "Yeah, it's been great," he says, his arm tightening around Kassi's waist as if to emphasize his point. "I heard about the masquerade party coming up this week. Unfortunately, we won't be attending."

Lena's expression remains cool, unbothered by Taylor's attempt to provoke her. "It's a private event," she says smoothly. "Exclusive guest list."

Kassi's smile falters slightly. "Yeah, well, we should get going. So many shops to visit."

"Of course," I say, eager to end the awkward encounter. "Enjoy your day."

As they walk away, Kassi's displeasure becomes evident. She pulls away from Taylor, muttering something under her breath. Taylor glances back at us, a flicker of regret in his eyes before he turns away.

I turn to Lena with concern. "Are you okay?"

He needs to die, die, die. I shake off the voice and focus on my cousin.

She takes a deep breath and nods. "Yeah, I'm fine. That was just . . . unexpected. Who would have thought we'd run into Taylor in Rodeo Drive?"

I squeeze her hand. "Let's get our dresses and go have some fun. We're not going to let the likes of him ruin our day."

She smiles, though it doesn't quite reach her eyes. "You're right."

We make our purchase and pretend the encounter never happened as we continue to shop hop, collecting more than the dresses we intended to buy. We make our way to a cozy little café and order lattes. The café has a warm, inviting ambiance, with soft jazz music playing in the background. We sit by a window, watching the world go by as we decompress from our excessive shopping.

"I'm sorry you had to see him," I tell her, stirring my drink absently.

Since running into him and Cassandra, Lena's mood has been on a downward slope. Her energy isn't its normally bubbly self and her overall presence has dulled. I hate that I allowed her to fall for that dirtbag only for him to break her heart. I should have told her when I first saw him flirting with interns and extras on set that he wasn't right for her.

"Don't be," she replies and attempts a cheerier tone. "I'm just glad we got to spend the day together. Between hospital stays, photoshoots, and Silas, it's like we don't see each other anymore. I kinda missed my bestie."

"I'm sorry," I tell her with my whole heart. "I know things have been hectic."

She shrugs, her eyes softening. "Don't worry about me. Today is meant for you. You've been through so much, Solaris. I want to make sure you're okay."

I reach across the table and take her hand. "I am. I have a feeling things are going to be changing soon."

She squeezes my hand back and cocks her head to the side, her expression serious. "What are you planning?"

Grinning, I shake my head at her. She doesn't need to know. "Nothing too scandalous."

Lena drops my hand, crosses her arms, and gives me a pointed look, like she knows I have something more salacious planned for this family. "Anything I can assist with, dear cousin?"

I hesitate, biting my lip. There is something, something I've been meaning to ask her. If I bring her into this and things go wrong, I will never forgive myself. Lena is the one person in my family that I don't want to see suffer. And while she may dislike her mother, I can't see her being okay with all the things I want to do to them.

"I can see it on your face," she calls me out. "What is it?"

"There is something. It has to do with Cruise."

Lena's eyes narrow slightly. "What?"

"He has this little black book," I begin, keeping my voice low. "It's full of names, contacts, people he's been dealing with. I need to get my hands on it."

Lena looks intrigued. "Dealing? As in drugs? Why would he need to do that?"

I shake my head at her. "No. Think of it as . . . sex trafficking? I'm not sure how to describe it."

"Are you serious?" she shrieks.

"Shhh," I hush her. "Not too loud."

"I can't believe this. Why would he need to do something like that? Why do you need the book?"

I sit back in my chair and take a sip of the latte, making sure no one is watching us. "It could have information that might help me understand what he's been up to, maybe even something that could protect us."

Lena nods, her expression determined. "Okay. I'll help you look for it. Do you have any idea where he might keep it?"

"Probably somewhere in his room or his study," I reply. "You'll have to be careful. Cruise can be dangerous."

"Of course," Lena says. "I'll get you the book."

I smile. "Thanks. I don't know what I'd do without you."

"Hey, we're family," she says, her eyes glistening. "We lookout for each other. Always and forever, remember?"

"Always and forever." I repeat.

We spend the rest of the afternoon browsing more shops, trying on shoes and accessories, and laughing like we used to do. For a while, it feels like we're just two ordinary girls enjoying a day out. As the sunsets, we head back to the jet with our purchases. I lean back in my seat, feeling a sense of contentment I haven't felt in a long time.

"Today was fun," Lena says, her head resting on my shoulder. "We should do this more often."

"Definitely," I agree, smiling. "Thanks for dragging me out of the house."

"Anytime," she replies, closing her eyes. "We're going to look phenomenal at Silas' party."

I close my eyes too, the gentle hum of the jet lulling me into a peaceful state.

It's not long before the jet touches down on the tarmac, and we're in yet another town car heading back to the manor. It's dark by the time we arrive, and all the lights are out.

"I'm going to stash these in my room and then be back over here," Lena says, gesturing to her bags. "Meet you in the kitchen for a snack?"

"Sure," I reply, forcing a smile. "I'll see you in a bit."

I watch the car disappear with her down the path to her home before turning and jogging the grand staircase to my room. I drop the bags on the floor and glance around at the cavernous room. My eyes go to the window seat, and I frown. My mom used to braid my curls back every night before I went to sleep. My lips tremble and I press them together in order to hold back the onslaught of memories. I need to get out, to breathe, to think. My apartment isn't far from here, and all my things are still there anyway. It's where I've built my life, away from the shadow of this family.

I slip out of the manor into the cool night air. I pull out my phone and send a quick text to Lena, letting her know I'll be back. After today, I don't want her worrying about me. I begin walking and don't stop until I recognize familiar streets and the gate to my building. I come to a stop when I notice the small memorial someone set up outside it. There're pictures of my mom and me from over the years. Flowers and a stuffed bear. A tear drops from my eyes. I would have expected something like this for me, but my mom was a relative stranger to the world. She wasn't in the spotlight, and yet they did this. Another tear falls and I open the gate and go inside.

As I walk into my apartment, it's like stepping into another world. The cozy living room, the photos on the wall, the simple, modern furniture—it's all so different from the grandeur of the manor. I go over to the couch and collapse down, staring at the ceiling. I close my eyes, replaying the day's events in my mind. For a moment, I wonder if I can let go of my vendetta. Today with Lena was almost normal, almost happy. What if I could have more days like that? What if I could just let go of my need for revenge and live in the moment?

But then I the hatred in Loretta's eyes, the cold satisfaction as she watched me fall, slams into the forefront of my mind. I remember the years of pain, the betrayal, the injustice. And then I remember Cruise. He nor Loretta would allow me to live a peaceful life. Not as long as I am the sole heir to the James estate. They made that perfectly clear when one of them killed or had my mom killed. I sit up, taking a deep breath. I can't run from this. I can't be the girl I was today. I can't let this injustice go.

A knock at the door startles me from my thoughts and my head snaps to it. No one knew I was coming here. No one should be knocking on that door. Cautiously, I get up and slowly make my way over to the door. Peeking through the peep hole, I see Silas standing there with two cups of iced coffee in his hands.

I frown at his presence and opens the door. "I thought you were in Nashville."

He steps over the threshold of my apartment, causing me to take a step back towards the stairs. "I was. But then I noticed you in California and drove back here immediately. I almost hopped on a plane."

I arch a brow at him. "You just happened to notice I was in California?"

He pulls his phone from his pocket. "There's a tracker on yours."

"You put a tracker on my phone?"

He doesn't acknowledge that. Instead, he hands me one of the cups. "Thought you could use this."

I take the coffee, a small smile tugging at my lips at the sweet caramel taste. I go back into the living room and sit down. He follows me. For a moment, we sit in silence, sipping our drinks.

"I've been thinking," I say finally, breaking the silence. "About what it would be like if I was a normal girl. If I wasn't a James and if I just let my need for revenge go. Would I be happier?"

Silas looks at me, his expression serious. "Solaris, you will always be a James. And while I don't agree with your idea of revenge, I do believe something needs to change within your family. I believe you're the only person willing to make that change."

I let his words sink in before nodding. "You believe we can get justice for me . . . without the need to get rid of them."

He nods. "I do. You don't need to become like them."

Yes, you do.

I meet his gaze and sag a bit under its weight. While I want to believe there might be another way, the voice in my head is right. The only way to beat them is to join them.

Silas smiles, a genuine warmth in his eyes. "How about we get out of here? I don't think being here is good for you."

I arch a brow at him but take his hand and nod anyways. "Sure."

I don't tell him this is the only place that gives me clarity.

Eighteen

Solaris

I weave through the guests, the elaborate masks and vibrant costumes creating a kaleidoscope of colors around me. Dressed in leggings and an oversized T-shirt, I'm the one that doesn't belong. The grand manor feels even larger tonight, every room bustling with laughter and music. But amid the festivities, I feel the unsettling absence of Silas. He's nowhere to be found, and it's been that way since last Saturday when he found me at my old apartment.

Up until now, I didn't think too much about him not being here. I know what our lives are like. Being on the go is part of what it takes to make it in the entertainment business. However, this doesn't feel work related. And while I don't want to jump to conclusions, I can't help but think he's starting to avoid me.

Determined, I make my way through the crowded ballroom, getting a few puzzled looks as I do. I should be dressed and in my gown by now, making nice with all the fake people flaunting their fake jewelry. Yet, I'm here looking for a man that clearly doesn't want to be found. I told myself I wouldn't do this. I wouldn't chase after him, but unfortunately, I can't seem to follow my own rules.

I head toward the left wing of the house, my footsteps echoing in the silent corridor. The dressing room that used to belong to my father was set up early this morning for him to dress in. That way he wouldn't have to haul his suit from Loretta's place and risk messing it up. I also, kind of, sort of like the idea of him getting comfortable here. At my house. Instead of at Loretta's.

The door creaks open, and I step inside. The scent of old leather and musk hits me, bringing a wave of nostalgia. I suck in a deep breath and glance around for Silas' suite, but the black tuxedo that was brought over is gone. The room is empty.

With a heavy sigh, I leave the dressing room and head to the kitchen. The employees are busy preparing hors d'oeuvres, their hands deftly arranging platters of delicate pastries and canapés.

"Excuse me," I say, catching the attention of one of the girls. "Have you seen Silas around?"

She shakes her head, a polite smile on her face. "No, Miss James. I haven't seen him tonight."

Disappointed, I thank her and turn away. My frustration grows as I push through the crowd once more and finally make my way over to the room Lena is occupying for the night. I find her adjusting her gold eye mask in front of the mirror. Her dress shimmering with the sparkle of a thousand stars, a perfect match for her mask.

"Lena, have you seen Silas?" I ask, trying to keep the worry out of my voice.

She glances at me in the mirror, her eyes widening at my appearance. She turns and glowers at my outfit. "What, Are. You. Wearing? Where's your dress?"

"In my room," I roll my eyes at here. There are more important things besides my dress. "Have you seen him? I ordered him a matching tie to my dress and thought it would be nice to walk in with him. I looked everywhere."

Lena sighs, walking over to me. "You worry way too much about him."

I cross my arms. "Coming from the girl who cried over every photo of Taylor with another girl."

"Touché." She shrugs. "But you know Silas. He'll show up. He's probably just caught up in something. You know his bandmates are here. He's probably just hanging out with them."

I don't mention he was supposed to be with them all week recording their next album. He could pull himself away for one night.

With reluctance, I go back to my room and slip into the emerald green gown. The fabric feels like a second skin, luxurious and comforting. I put on the intricate bunny mask Lena bought for me, the lace and crystals making me look much more sultry than I feel right now. I take a deep breath, trying to steady my nerves, and head downstairs alone.

Masks of every shape and color fill the room, laughter and music mingling in the air. I search the spacious ballroom, thinking maybe I missed Silas somewhere among the throng of people earlier. I mean, this is his party, and he didn't know about the tie. Technology, he had no reason to wait for me to join him. However, the only person that catches my eye is the one person I don't care to even see.

Brandon Black.

He's the only guest without a mask, his camera slung around his neck. His eyes meet mine as if he can feel me watching him. Grinning, he saunters through the crowd and makes his way over to me.

"Solaris James!" He comes to a stop, his voice cutting through the noise. "You're looking gorgeous tonight. Is your equally gorgeous cousin going to join the festivities?"

I force a smile and ignore his question about Lena. Surely, he's not referring to Silas. "Brandon, I wasn't aware you were on the invite list."

He smirks, his eyes gleaming. "You know me. I have my ways. So, tell me, how does it feel to be back in the James manor after all these years? I can't imagine you missed the happenings within these walls."

I raise a brow at him, not quite understanding what he's getting at. No one knows about the things that went on here. To me. He couldn't know unless he knew someone that did it or . . . he was here.

Before I can comment, the lights dim, and a hush falls over the crowd. My head snaps around, heart racing, and I look up to finally see Silas. My heart stops at the sight of him at the top of the staircase. With Loretta. While they're not overly close or locked in an embrace, they look all too comfortable next to each other. And that alone causes something to break within me. Silas' eyes search me out as if he can feel what this is doing to me. That should be me up there. When he finally meets my glare, his brows pull together, the crease deep and all too evident even from my spot aways from him. I see the apology, the sorrow in his gaze. It's as if he's silently begging for forgiveness, for understanding. But I don't understand this. I don't understand why he's been distancing himself from me only to turn to her. To show up at his birthday party with her. To share his spotlight with her.

Did I do something wrong?

Don't be silly, the voice in my head says. *We should get rid of him too. Or at the very least make him suffer for this discretion.*

Shut up. Shut up. SHUT UP!

You know what, you're right. We can't get rid of him. He's too yummy.

My heart twists painfully as I watch them descend the staircase. Loretta looks stunning in a sleek, black gown that clings to her in all the right places, her mask an intricate design of lace and jewels. She exudes confidence and elegance. I jerk my eyes away from her and glance down at my own dress. My mouth dries at the sight of it. I might as well be a toddler playing dress up in my mother's gowns again. I don't look like her. I don't look anywhere near as classy, sexy as my aunt. Jealousy and insecurity gnaw at me. How can I compete with that?

Anger boils within me, and I barely hear Brandon's next question. Without a word, I turn and walk away, ignoring the murmurs of the crowd. I need to get out of here. As I make my way through the manor, I don't notice the figure trailing me until it's too late.

Mayor O'Conner steps into my path just as I reach my room, his eyes cold and calculating. His eyes drop to my cleavage, and he wets his lips. My stomach churns at the sight of this frail, pathetic excuse of a man checking me out. He inputs the code to my room door, and I quirk a brow at him. Not many people have the code to enter my room. But then I frown when I remember that he's one of the men in Cruise's book. Of course Cruise gave that out to the people he was letting in here. William gestures for me to enter my own room and I hesitate. Anything could happen.

Yup, anything.

"Solaris," he says, his voice dripping with false warmth. "You are a hard one to get a hold to."

I step into the doorway of my room, blocking his entry. "Now is not a good time."

He steps into me, grabbing my arm in his fragile grip and pushes me inside. I don't bother to fight him. Mainly because I want to know what this man actually thinks he can do to me. He's dying for crying out loud. And I'm the picture perfect image of health. William wouldn't stand a chance if I fought back.

"I'm owed a debt, and I'm finally coming to collect," he says as he closes my bedroom door, his voice low and menacing. He undresses me with his eyes once again. "My son is a fool. You look so stunning tonight. Anyone can see you're twice the beauty of my wife."

My jaw clenches at the mention of Silas with Loretta. William takes that moment to reach for me, as if I would go to him willingly. He takes hold of my neck, drawing me in, and it's so much like how Silas does it that something within me snaps. Rage and years of pent-up pain explode inside me. Without thinking, I punch him, the impact sending him sprawling to the floor. His cane clatters away, and he struggles to get up.

Kill. Kill. Kill, the voice in my head chants. *Make him pay. Make them all PAY!*

This time, I don't bother trying to fight the voice.

I agree.

It's time for William to die.

I kick his cane aside then kick him in the ribs. He holds u pa hand to stop me, but I don't stop. He didn't stop for one second to think about paying for me. He didn't even stop tonight before following me up from the party. My heeled foot slams into his side again. He chokes out a sob, and I drop to the floor beside him, snarling my frustration at the man. My hand slams into his face over and over and over, the sensation of my fists connecting with his flesh a twisted mix of satisfaction and horror. He deserves this. They all do.

Mayor O'Conner tries to shield himself, but my fury is relentless. Each punch is a release of the anger that has festered within me for years. Each punch mimicking the thrust, thrust, thrust I had to endure from men just like him. He might not have gotten his chance, but he would have been just another one of them.

"Please," he pleads, but his pleas for mercy fall on deaf ears as I continue to pummel him, my vision clouded with rage.

No one ever cared about my pleas.

Blood splatters my dress, and my knuckles throb with each impact. But I can't stop. The feel of his body breaking beneath my blows is the most gratifying thing I've felt in a long time.

O'Conner's face is a mess of blood and bruises, his breathing ragged and labored. I sit back on my haunches, panting, my chest heaving with exertion. The sight of him brings a grin to my face. But it's not enough. The anger still burns within me. I raise my fist again, ready to strike, ready to see the life fade from his eyes.

But then the door bursts open. Silas stands in the doorway, his eyes wide with shock and disbelief. The sight of him, the horror on his face, snaps me out of my frenzy and I lower my fist.

I scoot away from Silas' father, my hands trembling, blood smeared on my knuckles. I wish I could tell him that I'm sorry or that I feel an inkling of guilt for what just happened, but then I would have to lie to Silas. And that's one thing I'm not going to do. Not with something like this.

Silas takes a step forward, his voice shaking. "Solaris, what have you done?"

My breath comes in ragged gasps as I try to process the scene before me. Mayor O'Conner lies crumpled on the floor. I look down at my hands, the evidence of my rage clear on my skin. I wipe the blood on my dress and stay silent.

"Please," Mayor O'Conner pleads again. "Please, son."

Silas looks from me to his father and then back to me. His face is a mask of confusion as I wait to see what he's going to do. There're really only two options here: he can save Mayor O'Conner and throw me to the wolves, or he can choose me.

Silas closes my bedroom door with ease and steps to me, tilting my chin up. He stares down at me, and I can see the struggle in his eyes, the battle between doing what is right and joining me on the dark side.

Gliding his hand up the side of my neck and to my face, Silas cups my cheek. He runs his thumb across my cheek bone. His finger comes away tinged with red. I gulp as he places the pad of his thumb into his mouth and sucks.

"Find me something sharp," he demands, squatting down towards his father.

"What do you mean?"

Silas glances over his shoulder at me. "Solaris, they might have stolen your virtue, but I will be the one to save your soul."

"I don't understand."

Silas rises from his father's still side and glances around the room. He goes over to the vanity in the corner and opens a drawer. Pulling out a pair of golden shears, Silas comes back over to me. He gives me a quick look over before dropping back to the floor. Before I have time to realize what's going on, the sharp ends of the scissors come down hard, blood splattering across Silas' face. His father doesn't even make a sound. He pulls the scissors loose, and his hands hover above his dad's still form for a moment, trembling from the onslaught of emotions he must be feeling.

But then, the scissors come down again and again and again. Silas' breaths come out in ragged huffs as he finally stops stabbing his father. He tosses the shears to the side, his hands just as bloody if not more than mine.

Twenty-seven times. That's how many I managed to count. That's how many times he stabbed his father. A crime of passion they would call it. But to me, it's justice.

He stands and comes over to me. "He got blood on your dress."

My breath hitches and my heart picks up speed. "How dare he?"

His eyes lock onto mine, burning with an intensity that sends a thrill through me. Before I can react, Silas grabs me by the nape of my neck, hauling me close with a sudden, almost primal force. Our bodies collide, the shock of it sending a gasp from my lips.

"Silas," I whisper, trying to mask the blend of defiance and desire in my voice.

He doesn't answer. Instead, he tilts my head up, his grip firm yet tender, and his lips crash onto mine. The kiss is fierce, full of the raw passion and unspoken emotions that have been simmering between us. My knees go weak, but he holds me steady, his arm wrapping tightly around my waist and pulling me even closer.

I press my hands against his chest, feeling the rapid beat of his heart beneath my palms, mirroring my own frantic pulse. Silas deepens the kiss, his tongue exploring my mouth with a hunger that leaves me even more breathless than I already am.

We stagger backward, moving as one until we hit the wall. He presses me against it, his body a solid weight against mine.

The pressure is intoxicating, sending shivers down my spine. I arch into him, my nails digging into his shoulders.

In a whirlwind of movement, we tumbled to the floor, landing not so gracefully next to Silas' father's corpse. Our formalwear becoming casualties of our heated struggle. His jacket is the first to go, flung aside without a second thought. He tears my dress at the seam as I move, the delicate fabric no match for our fervor. I barely notice, too consumed by the sensation of his lips, his hands, the overwhelming presence of him.

His hands roam over my body, tracing every curve and line. He breaks the kiss, trailing his lips down my neck, and I can't suppress the moan that escapes me. I respond in kind, my fingers fumbling to undo the buttons of his shirt, desperate to feel his skin against mine.

Our breaths come out in jagged gasps. Formalities and decorum lay forgotten as we roll on the floor, lost in each other and covering ourselves in even more blood. Silas pulls back just enough to look into my eyes, his expression fierce and filled with unspoken emotion.

"Solaris," he murmurs, his voice rough with passion.

I meet his gaze, feeling a mix of vulnerability and longing."Silas," I breathe, my hands cupping his face as I pull him down for another searing kiss.

"No," he murmurs. "I'm done kissing you. I want to ravish you in the blood of our enemies. Right here. Right now. Tell me I can."

My breath catches in my throat and all I can do is nod. He can do whatever he wants as long as he never stops looking at me like I'm his. Like no one else in the world matters.

"You can."

With a growl, Silas tears off the remainder of my dress, leaving me in the little thong I had on underneath. His eyes rake over me in a frenzy as he grabs the underwear and yanks it off. He spreads my legs wide and before I have to time adjust to his frantic actions, he thrusts inside. I cry out at his rough treatment. I can't believe he just did that. No foreplay. No extra lubrication. No nothing. It doesn't matter that I am already ready, wanting. Something more would have been great.

He continues his attack on my pussy, holding me still against the floor as he does. His eyes stray from me once to his father. When they return to me his pupils are entirely dark. His hands are bruising at my hips, and I shake my head at him.

"Silas, calm down, please," I mutter through the hurt.

"You can handle this," he speaks. "Tell me you can handle me."

I stare up at him, not saying anything. He doesn't stop. And if I'm being honest, I don't want him to. This is what Silas looks like coping. I know he's not trying to hurt me; he just killed his father and this is what he needs. So instead of showing the hurt, I simply nod. I can be this for him. I can handle all of him. The good. The bad. And whatever this is.

Silas pushes into me again and again before I feel a rush of warmth coating my insides. He grunts, his pacing slowing as his cock twitches and jerks inside me. He comes with a sign, his forehead falling to mine. Breaths coming out in heavy puffs.

"I'm sorry," he apologizes. "Tell me I didn't hurt you."

I run my fingers through his hair, my breath equally as frantic as his. "You didn't hurt me. I kind of liked it."

He's quiet for a moment. The air is heavy with the scent of blood and the raw energy of our shared violence and fucking. Silas pulls out of me and stands, guiding me up with him, his eyes dark and intense and mirroring the chaos that just unfolded. His finger dip down to my still aching pussy, and push inside. I moan as he scoops his semen out of me and bring his finger back up between us. It's tinged pink, and I don't know if the blood is from his hand or me.

"I might have tore you a bit. My apologizes." He lifts his cum covered finger to my lips. "Taste us."

I obey and suck the cum from his finger. A burst of salt and iron fill my mouth and I groan around his fingers, heat flooding my core. God, why is this so hot?

"And Solaris," he says softly, almost tenderly as he pulls his finger from between my finger with a pop. "Don't ever let me be this rough you again. You're not some groupie."

My eyes drop to the floor. "It wasn't that bad. I can handle that."

He pulls me close and places a gentle kiss at my temple. "You shouldn't have to. Now, I need you to go wash the blood off. As much as I loved ravishing you in it, I don't want to keep watching you wear my father's blood like a second skin."

I blink, still coming down from the adrenaline high. Looking down, I see the dark stains on my skin. The realization hits me like a punch to the gut.

"We just killed your father," I murmur, my voice trembling.

"I know," Silas replies quietly. "And I would do it a thousand times over if it meant not putting that burden on you. I meant what I said, Sol. They're not taking anything else from you. And that includes your soul. It's fucking belongs to me. Have since I walked in on you in that bathroom."

My breath catches in my throat and my stomach flutters at his words. "Are you okay, though? I mean . . ." I point to his father laying there, eyes wide and shocked. "He was your father."

"He was a piece of shit that was already dying. I put him out of his misery."

My eyes lower to the body. I don't think that's a healthy way for Silas to cope with that, but what do I know about coping? I listen to a voice inside my head that tells me to kill.

"But—"

Silas sighs, effectively cutting me off and running a hand through his dishevel hair. "Right now, we need to clean up and get rid of any evidence."

I shake my head, trying to make sense of it all. "Silas, how are we supposed to clean this all up? There's blood everywhere and . . . the body . . ."

He places a hand on my shoulders, his touch grounding me and calming the panic rising. "I will handle this, but I need you to trust me and go wash his blood off your skin. I can't concentrate with any part of that man touching you. Now go wash it off."

I swallow hard, my mind racing. "What about," I gesture at him covered in just as much blood, "you?"

Silas' grip tightens slightly, his eyes boring into mine."I know people. Professional people, Solaris. They'll take care of everything. But we don't have much time. Please, just do this for me."

I take a deep breath, nodding. "Okay. I'll go wash up. But I want to know more about these people afterwards. And we still need to talk about Loretta."

He leans in, pressing a soft kiss to my forehead. "We will have that discussion. Now go."

Reluctantly, I make my way to the bathroom, my legs feeling like they might give out at any moment. I turn on the faucet, watching the water flow for a second before plunging my hands under the stream. The water runs red as I scrub, the reality of the blood on my skin hitting me hard. This wasn't just some unfortunate accident. This was a murder, and we did it. I put Silas in a position to kill his own father.

I glance at my reflection in the mirror, my eyes wide and filled with fear. The pounding of my heart becomes deafening. If I can do something like this, truly do it and not just talk about it, what does that make me? Does that make me just as vile as the creatures that broke me? I know technically Silas offered the final blow, but he only did it for me. In no other world can I imagine my literature loving, guitar playing Silas doing something so gruesome.

After what feels like an eternity of scrubbing my hands, I get into the shower and stay there until the water runs clear. I dry off, taking a moment to steady my breath before stepping back into the main room. Silas is already at work, stripping the bed and wiping down surfaces with a calm efficiency that both reassures and terrifies me.

"How do you know what to do?" I ask him, my curiosity piqued.

He glances up and shrugs. "Are you forgetting I'm in a band? It's not the first time I've had to strip a room clean of debauchery."

Debauchery, yes. I can picture that, but this . . . this is not that kind of debauchery.

I tighten my hold on the towel. "What do we do now?"

"Now," he says, his voice steady, "we wait for the cleaners to arrive. And we make sure there's no trace of anything left behind."

I move to help him, determined to do whatever it takes to get through this. "Silas."

He looks up at me, halting when he sees my face.

"He was your father."

His expression darkens, and for a moment, I think he might not comment. But then he sighs, a weary sound that seems to come from deep within. "He threatened you, Solaris. Maybe not tonight, but he did all those years ago when he put his name in your brother's book. You want revenge, this is what it looks like. Can you handle this?"

Yes!

I cringe at how true that is, a chill runs down my spine. "But you . . ."

"Would do it again in a heartbeat," he says simply. "Should have done it when I first found out what was happening to you. That's a mistake I will not make again."

I swallow hard at his words.

Yet, there's still one more thing I need to know. "Loretta? What was that?"

Silas stops scrubbing surfaces and stands to face me. "That was Loretta putting on a show for you. She knew I had been in Nashville for a week, and she wanted to see you squirm. I had no choice."

"What does she have on you?" I question him. "She must have something in order for you to obey her like this."

"It doesn't matter. Let's just finish this so I can take a shower."

Reluctantly, I nod at his evasiveness.

Sooner or later, he's going to have to tell me the truth.

Nineteen

Solaris

The final bell rings, signaling the end of chemistry class. I gather my books and notes, shoving them into my bag with a mechanical efficiency. My mind has been elsewhere all weekend, replaying the events of Silas' party and the blood that seems to linger on my skin, even after washing it away. The hallway is a blur of students, chatter, and laughter as I make my way to the cafeteria, my phone vibrating with a text notification.

Lena: Found the little black book. In the cafeteria.

My heart skips a beat. Finally. I quicken my pace, pushing through the throngs of students. The cafeteria is its usual cacophony of noise and activity, but I have no intention of staying. I scan the room until I spot Lena, her eyes meeting mine with a mix of urgency and concern.

She gets up from her seat with Samantha and the other cheerleaders and rush over to me. We both know this conversation can't happen here. The stakes are too high, and the information too sensitive. Without a word, we hurry down the hall and make our way to the basement.

The basement of Mountain Rose Academy is dreadfully less modern than the rest of the school. While the upper floors gleam with modern renovations and polished surfaces, the basement is dark, musty, and forgotten. The air is thick with the scent of mildew, and the walls are lined with old pipes and peeling paint. Once thing for sure, I wouldn't want to be caught down here after dark. We find an empty room near the end of the hall. Lena glances around nervously before closing the door behind us.

"No cameras, no nosy ears," she utters, her voice low.

I take a deep breath, trying to steady my racing heart. "What did you find?"

Lena pulls a small, worn leather book from her bag, holding it up like it's a ticking time bomb. "The little black book you requested."

I reach for it, but she pulls it back slightly, her eyes locking onto mine. "Before I give this to you, I need to know what's going on. I looked through it, and . . . it's all very disturbing. You need to tell me what this is and how you even know it exists. Because this," she shakes the book, "is not what you said in California."

I hesitate, but the truth is, Lena deserves to know. She is risking a lot by helping me, and she needs the full truth. "Cruise," I begin, my voice trembling slightly, "used to sell me. He would have men assault me. Silas informed me about the book because his father's name is in it as well. This book is leverage, Lena. It's proof of what they did to me. It's a way to bring them all down."

Her eyes narrow on me. "Is this why we haven't seen my stepfather since Silas' party?"

I bite down on my lip, uncertain if I should tell her about what happened on Friday. The right thing to do would be to tell her every little thing, but I just can't bring myself to involve her that much. If she knows about Silas and I getting rid of William, then she's implicated if this whole mess comes back to bite me in the butt. It's bad enough that Silas is involved. I never wanted him to be. Not in this compacity.

So instead, I lie. "I have no clue where your stepfather is. Last time I saw him, he was standing near the bar with a glass of whiskey in his hand."

"Oh," Lena says, almost solemnly, but then her eyes jump tome again. "Lie all you want. I don't care about that. I want to know why you never told me any of this. I could have at least been there for you."

I shrug. "Honestly, I didn't remember. The day here in the hall is when I started remembering. I had spent the night with

Silas after the club incident and ran into Cruise. Everything came back all at once and then my mom . . ."

"Oh my god," she whispers. "I'm so sorry."

I shake my head. "It's not your fault. But now you see why I need this book. It's the only way to make them pay for what they did."

Lena looks at me with a mix of sympathy and determination. "I'll do whatever it takes to help you. These people deserve to be exposed."

I take the book from her, my hands trembling. "Thank you, Lena. That means more to me than you could ever know."

She nods. "So, what's the plan?"

I opened the book, flipping through the pages filled with names, dates, money amounts, and photos of men in compromising positions. My stomach churns at the sheer number of dates. I knew all this happened to me. But I didn't know how frequently. I scan the photos again. Luckily for me, I'm not really in the photos. Maybe a hand here. A foot there. But nothing that would distinguish the person with these men as being me.

"First, we need to make copies of everything," I tell her. "We can't risk losing the original. Then, we need to start figuring out who these men are and how to use this information against them."

Lena frowns. "This is going to be dangerous, Solaris. These are powerful people. If they find out what we're doing . . ."

"I know," I say, my voice firm. "But they can't hurt me any more than they already have. And I won't let them get away with this. Not this time."

"In that case," Lena takes the book back. "You handle your brother, and I'll handle these people. They'll expect retribution from you, but no one will see me coming. You don't need to have this on you if it gets back to someone."

"So, you're going to help?" I question her. "Just like that?"

My cousin gives me a pointed look. "You should have come tome sooner like I said. Many of these people were probably at Silas' party. We could have done some damage."

I can feel the color draining from my face at the thought. I would hope none of the people in the book would show their faces around me after what they did, but Lena's probably right. People with our lifestyle usually stick together. And if they had the nerve to go to Cruise before, they've probably gone to him time and time again for something. I've probably talked to someone who did it.

My mind instantly goes to Brandon Black and his weird comment at the party. "Hand me that book for a second."

Lena gives it to me, and I instantly start flipping through pages, searching for the reporter. When he's not among the people listed, I let out a long breath. Okay, that's good. He was simply speculating at the party. That or he knows something.

I hand Lena the book, and we spend the rest of our lunch hour making plans and poring over the contents of the book.

Each page is a new revelation, a new piece of the puzzle that could bring down the monsters who have haunted my past. Lena takes photos with her phone, ensuring we have digital copies of everything.

As we work, the reality of what we are undertaking begins to sink in. If we attempt this, it must work, or I'm screwed. Cruise got in with some powerful people. Like really powerful. Lawyers. Film directors. There's even a freaking senator named in the book. I cross my arms and sit back in my chair, fear starting to seep in for the first time since I started this whole revenge agenda. If these people wanted to make me disappear, they could.

If anyone of these people wanted to kill my mom, they could have.

Suddenly, I'm not so sure Loretta or Cruise had anything to do with my mother's death. Anyone who didn't want me finding out the truth and going back to the James' estate could have done it.

"Lena?" Her name comes off my lips with a tremble. "Can I ask you something?"

She pulls her eyes away from the book with a nod. "Anything."

"Do you think your mom and my brother are capable of murder?"

You are, the voice in my head tells me. *And they're your family.*

She lets out a long breath, sitting a little straighter. Her eyes flicker across my face, and I can see the gears turning in her brain. "Honestly, Cruise, no. But my mom . . . my mom wouldn't get her hands dirty. She would hire someone though if she was sure it couldn't be traced back to her. Then again, we all would, wouldn't we?"

I quirk a brow at her. "Even you?"

She smirks at me and flips her blonde hair over her shoulder. "What makes you think I haven't already?"

"Have you?"

She burst into laughter. "No, silly! I'm just saying. You have to expect the unexpected. Do you think Cruise or my mom killed yours?"

I nod, confirming my original beliefs. "I did, but I'm unsure now. Anybody who didn't want me going back to the estate and remembering those things that happened could have done it. The note—"

"Note?" Lena's eyes widen, her left brow twitching. "What note?"

"Did I not mention that?"

"Solaris!"

"My mom was clutching a piece of paper when Silas and I found her. It said 'this is your final warning and stay away from the estate'."

Her eyes drop back down to the book. "We really need to start having girls' night again, because you've been through some juicy drama."

I roll my eyes at her.

We stay hunched over the book for another few minutes. When we finally emerge from the basement, the halls are clear and everyone's back in their rightful classes. Lena and I make plans to meet again tomorrow after she's had time to really investigate all the people and come up with a plan.

The next day at school, the atmosphere is thick with anticipation. Lena and I exchange knowing glances between classes. She texted me last night saying she had a plan but that I might not like it. She wouldn't give me any more details than that. Since then, I've been anxious, giddy mess. That could be the three large coffees I had earlier, but I don't think so.

When the final bell rings, I make my way to our agreed-upon meeting spot: an old, abandoned storage shed on the outskirts of the school grounds. We both agreed that would be better than hanging out in the basement. Just in case we didn't make it out of the school on time and they locked us in. Neither one of us want to be locked in the basement, especially not this close to the founder's day festival.

Lena is already here when I arrive, the screen of her phone illuminating her pale face. She looks up as I approach, her expression serious.

"I did some research last night," she says, her voice low. "Some of the names in the book... they're big players. Politicians, businessmen, even a few celebrities."

I nod, not surprised in the least. "We need to be careful. If they find out we're onto them, they'll come after us."

"Agreed," Lena says, her eyes glinting with determination. "But we also need to start thinking about how to use this information, which is why I think we should bring in someone else. Someone who has the eyes and ears we don't."

A chuckle leaves me. "Are you forgetting we have both of those things? We're James'."

"Yeah, I know," she says with an eye roll. "But people think of us as the airheaded heiress and the TV star. No one actually takes us seriously."

I frown at the truth in her words. Us against politicians, a senator, is a joke. "Who is this person you want to bring in?"

Lena's eyes fall from mine and she grabs the book like it's a security blanket. I yank it out of her hold and away from her.

"Who?" I repeat.

"Ugh! Brandon Black," she shouts.

"No. Hell no!"

"Sol, just listen—" she starts.

"No."

"Everyone reads his column," she continues.

"No."

"He's at every social event. And people actually listen to him. That's why he's so popular."

"No, Lena. That man literally wrote an article about me setting your mom's house on fire. When I was twelve!"

Lena cocks her head to the side. "You did set that fire."

"I don't remember doing it."

She shrugs. "Doesn't mean you didn't. Besides, you just proved my point. His column has such an impact that you are still bent out of shape over a six-year-old article. We need his help. He can leak the information. Say he got it from an anonymous source."

I sigh, running a hand through my curls and reluctant to admit she has a point. There is a reason he's everywhere. And just because I happened to be his first article, doesn't mean he isn't good at his job. "You're right."

Lena nods and continues, "I also think we need allies.

"Allies?"

"If these men did this to you, then they've probably done it to other girls. Cruise is just one person providing a service. If we can find other victims—"

"I'm not a victim," I cut her off, not liking that word. "I survived what they did to me and I'm still here."

Lena holds up her hand in defense. "Fine. If we can find other survivors, maybe they'll be willing to help. We can build a network, share the risk. The only downside is that you will have to put yourself out there. Make yourself relatable. No one is going to step forward if you can't step forward and say what has been done to you."

"I can't," I tell her, my eyes dropping to the floor. I can only be so strong and saying all this out loud . . . for the public to hear. . . I'm not ready. Besides, I don't need even more people looking at me. Not after what Silas and I did. Not when I know William won't be the last.

Lena nods in understanding, a small, sad smile gracing her face. She squeezes my hand. "That's okay. I understand you are still processing everything. We don't have to do that. Brandon's column could be enough, if you agree."

"Fine." I reluctantly give in to her idea. "We'll meet with him and tell him what we found. But I have stipulations."

"Of course. Should I set up a meeting with him?"

My face scrunches together at her statement. "And you just happen to have him on speed dial?"

A blush creeps into her cheeks. "I . . . I may have gone out with him after the restaurant fiasco with Taylor."

My eyes widen at that. "I thought you weren't into older men."

"He's not that much older!" she defends her actions. "He's literally younger than Silas. I just don't like men that are old enough to be my father. Just because I have no clue who knocked up my mom doesn't mean I have a daddy complex."

"Okay, okay," I tell her. "What was the date like?"

A tint paints her whole face, and a silly little grin pulls at the corner of her mouth. "At first, I thought it was going to be all about you. He only ever seemed interested in you in the past. But he didn't ask. He actually didn't even question me about our family. It was . . . nice."

I wiggle my brows at her. "Oooh, you have a new man."

Lena shakes her head. "No. Absolutely not."

"Why?" I demand. "If the date was nice and he has you blushing like this—"

"Because he hasn't asked me out again," she states, crossing her arms and rolling her eyes. "He thinks I'm too young for him. Said some stupid crap about me not being ready for what he's into. Yada, yada, yada."

I cock my head to the side. "Hmmm, guess we'll just have to show him at this meeting that you're not as young as you look."

Lena frowns and shakes her head at the idea. "How about you let me handle my love life? You don't see me butting in with you and my brother."

"Okay, okay," I relent. "Let's just get this meeting setup and then we'll worry about getting you another date with Brandon."

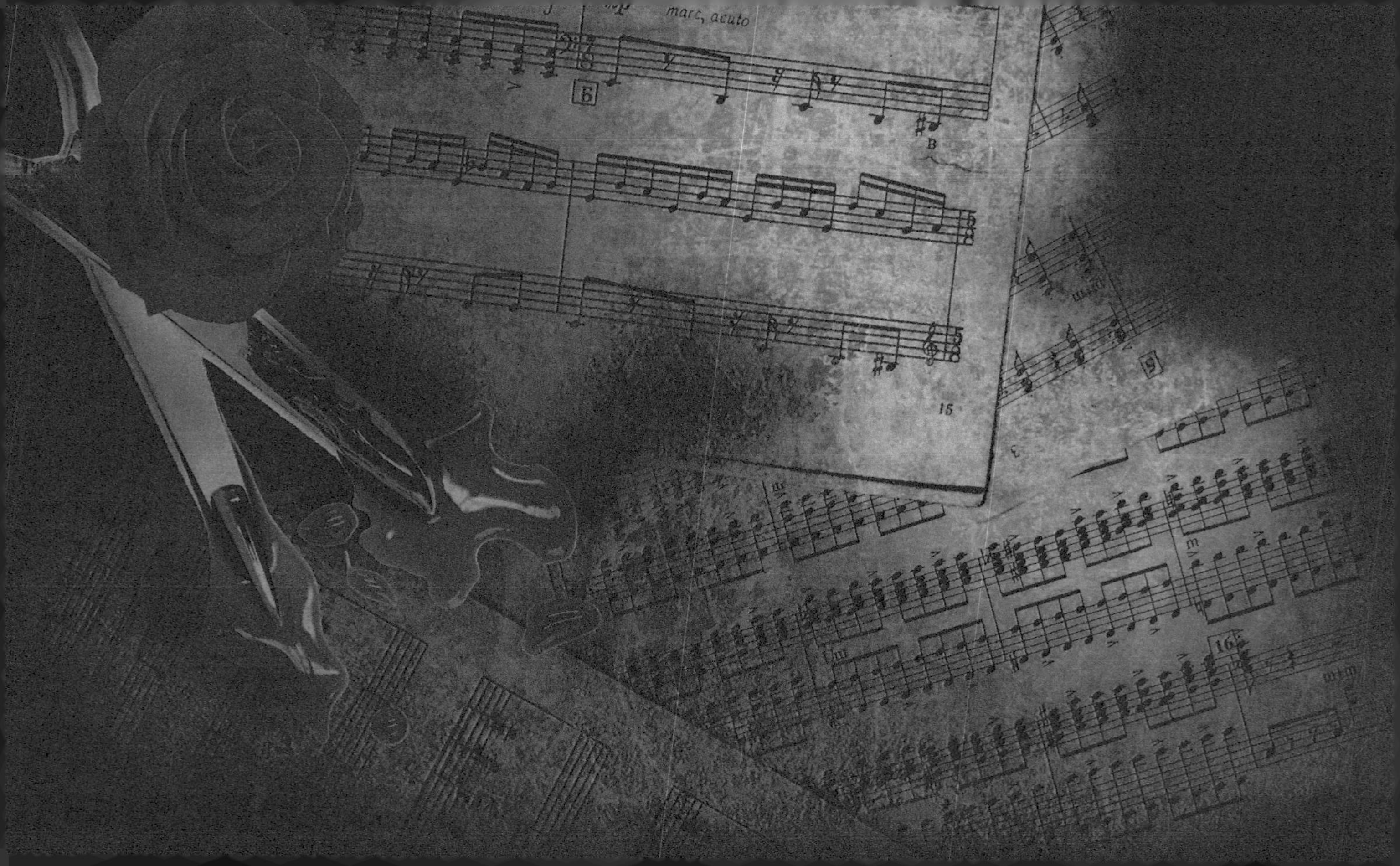
marc, acuto
15
16

Twenty

Silas

Six years ago

The clock on the wall ticks past midnight, but I can't sleep. Since the masquerade party, I've been staying here at the pool house. I just have this feeling that something is going to happen. With Cruise being back, anything is possible, and I'm not going to give him a chance to hurt Solaris. Especially since he's been snooping around her a lot these last few days.

I pull my phone from the side table and check my messages for the umpteenth time in two hours. Solaris was messaging me about some crazy crap that was going on at her school, and some knuckled-headed boy that's supposed to be escorting her for the Mountain Rose founder's day festival, but she hasn't answered my last message.

She always responds.

Getting out of bed, I go over to my closet and pull out a pair of sweatpants and a shirt. Dressing as quickly as possible, I sneak out of the pool house and walk down the stone path to the main James' manor. Something is wrong. I can feel it. And while I know it's not my responsibility to care nearly as much as I do, I can't help it. I can't help the pull I feel towards her or the fact that I want to protect her. Maybe it's a her thing or maybe it's a me thing; I don't know. I do know that since she gave me that guitar pick with our initials engraved on the front, my protective nature has worsened to the point that I don't even want to leave this house of horrors.

I have no clue how I'm supposed to handle going on tour at the beginning of the year to promote our new single.

Ascending the flight of stairs, each step echoes with a foreboding that settles in my gut. I input Solaris' code into the house and go inside. I tread to her wing of the house, which just so happens to be Cruise's wing as well. Someone really should have put him somewhere else. Hell, gave him his own house on the estate like they did with me. Anything would be better than him literally having a room right down the hall from Solaris.

As I reach the second floor, Solaris' door catches my eye. It's slightly ajar, and the faint rustling sounds from within send my heart racing. Quickening my pace, I reach the door just in time to see some man sneaking out, his hand zipping up his fly. Fury ignites within me; I don't think—I just act.

"You sick bastard!" I roar, my fist flying at the man with a rage I can't control.

The satisfying crunch of bone beneath my knuckles does little to quell my anger. I shove him against the wall and punch him again and again.

"Get the fuck off me, you psycho!" He shoves me back, managing to slip from beneath my ravenous hold. "I'll sue you for this! Assault and battery, you hear me?"

I laugh in the face of his threat. He can't sue me. Suing would mean admitting why the hell I did this. And I know for sure he's not going to tell a room full of people he was sneaking out of a 12-year-old's room at midnight. But if he wants to sue, he should sue. Sue and then maybe this mess would be over with.

"I will end you!" he yells at me again just as the door to Cruise's room yanks open.

Cruise surveys the altercation and then walks out. "What's going on here? Why are you in my house, Silas?"

"I want my money back, man!" the imbecile states. "You said no one would know about this."

I snarl at Cruise as he simply retreats into his room and then comes back. He shoves some money at the man. "Leave."

The guy doesn't need to be told more than once. He stuffs the money in his back pocket and bolts. I go over to Cruise. "What the hell?"

"You're trespassing," he states calmly. "I have the right to shoot you."

Grabbing Cruise by the collar of his V-neck T-shirt, I slam him into the wall. "She's your fucking sister."

Cruise laughs as if something I said is funny. He then cocks his head to the side, his eyes going to Solaris' door and then back to me. "Why are you really angry right now? Is it because you would rather be the one fucking my adorable little sister?"

"Shut the fuck up."

"Everyone sees the way you trail behind her like some pet she has on a leash."

"I said shut up!" I shout at him.

"If you want a piece, all you have to do is pay the piper. Then you can have her. Her tight little pussy is quite nice. Or so I've been told."

I snarl at him. My hand falls from him as if been burned. "She's a child."

"And yet, you didn't say no."

"No," I tell him straight forward. "I don't want her like that."

Cruise chuckles again, smoothing down the wrinkles in his shirt. "Yes, you do. You're just too uptight and righteous to take what you want."

My fist flies into his jaw without a second thought.

He chuckles again and spits blood at my feet. "No, you just want to groom her and then fuck her when she's at the right age. I see you, Silas O'Conner. You don't fool me. But news flash cousin, we are the elite. Rules do not apply to us."

I take a step away from Cruise as if I can undo what he just said. I don't want Sol like that. Not once have I even considered something more than protecting her. That doesn't mean Cruise's words don't hit their intended mark. Especially since I know she has a crush. She wouldn't have given me a guitar pick with our names on it if she didn't.

"Look, man," Cruise states. "You can have her now. I won't even charge you since we're family. Because if you wait until she's eighteen and grown and filled out in all the right places, you won't get her at all. She's mine. I chose her long before you came into the picture. And when she turns eighteen, it'll be me she's fucking. My babies she pops out of that soft little cunt. Right now, I'm just getting her ready for me. My tastes are very distinct, and I need her trained to take me right away. So what do you say?"

I shove him back. "This whole family is fucking disgusting."

"You're a part of this family, cousin. Or are you forgetting that?"

I shake my head at the insinuation. Married into this family doesn't count. Even if in the future, Sol and I got together, it wouldn't be what they are all doing. We're not blood related. We're not related at all.

"Go back to your little pool house and get some sleep, Silas," Cruise commands. "Think about my offer. It won't last for long."

He goes back into his room, the door slamming in my face. I slump against the wall, cursing at myself. I failed. I was too late to save her this time. Even with me being in town and on the same forsaken land as her, I can't protect her like I want. I should have come running the moment she didn't respond. What happened to her tonight is my fault. I knew something was off.

Clapping cuts through my mental tirade and I turn to see Loretta standing next to the stairs in an ivory silk nightie and robe.

"That was interesting," Loretta's voice cuts through the air like a blade, cold and sharp.

Her presence brings me back to reality, but the sight of her calculating eyes only causes the frustration in my veins to rush to the surface once more.

"What do you want?" I demand.

She struts over to me. Standing at least a head shorter than me without her heels, I'm able to sneer down at her. She places her soft, overly manicured hands against my chest. "I want what I've been wanting since the moment you stepped foot into my house. And now I have all the means of getting it."

I shove her hands away from me. "I did nothing wrong here."

"You've assaulted a guest. You broke into our home. Also assaulted my nephew. I'm sure I can come up with so much more."

"Your guest was—"

"I know exactly what goes on in this house," Loretta cuts me off, her head jerking back towards Solaris' door. "She and her homewrecking mother aren't a part of us. Gregory should have left her in that dank little cabin in the woods."

I tense at her words. Not much is spoken about Solaris' mother's background. All I really know is that she was middle class and married into this family at a young age.

"Who hurt you so badly that you turned into such a cruel woman?" I ask my stepmother.

She cocks her head to the side as if truly trying to think of who hurt her. "I'm not hurt. I just don't like when people try to take what's mine."

"You think I'm yours?"

She crosses her arms, pushing her breasts up, the top of them peeking through the thin lacy frill. "I made you mine the moment I married your father. That girl cannot and will not have you."

I scowl at her. "I am not my father. And I am not yours."

"You will do as I say, Silas," she says softly, her voice dripping with malice. "Or I will ensure that Solaris suffers far worse than anything you can imagine. You think Cruise is bad.

I practically raised that boy. I'm a thousand times worse. So, if you want to keep her safe, I'd advise you to jump on the band wagon and obey."

My fists clenches, knuckles white. Loretta's grin grows as she takes one of my fists in her hold. She unclenches my hand and intertwines our fingers. I inwardly cringe at the sight. She walks past me, towing me down the hall behind her. We bypass the music room and continue until we're standing outside of a small kitchen.

Loretta leads me by my hand to a stainless steel island. Leaving me, she goes to the big industrial fridge, opens it, and pulls out something. She comes back to me and hops on the metal island. I give her a quizzical look, not too certain what the point of this is.

But then she raises the hem of her gown and exposes her bare self to me. There's still fresh cum on her mound, and I pull my eyes away. I can only guess as to who she's been with already since she is in Gregory's house.

A squirting sound captures my attention, and I glance back to see what Loretta is doing. My eyes widen at her rubbing chocolate sauce into herself, mixing it with the cum on her skin. My lip curls as my nose wrinkles at the sight. A wave of nausea hits my stomach, and a sour tang coats my mouth. I do everything in my ability to keep my barf back. My eyes search for the door we entered, a compulsion to flee overtaking me.

I need to get away from this woman.

Before I can make a move, she grabs hold of my neck, her pointy claws digging in and pulling my face to hers. Loretta's lips descend upon mine and I jerk away from her. With a smirk, she leans back against the metal table and spreads her legs wide.

"You know what I want," she tells me, her voice dripping with malice. "Lick. It. Up."

"And if I say no?" I ask her, slowly inching away from the woman.

Loretta sits up, grabs a knife from the block, and before I know what's happening, she brings the blade down her left arm and through the thin material of her robe, blood bubbling to the surface and running down her slim arm.

"If you say no," she places the knife down on the cold table, "you will be carted off this property in cuffs and then I'll tell Cruise to have your little Solaris gangraped while I watch and record it for you."

My body freezes in place, and my eyes widen at her threat. She wouldn't. At the end of the day, Solaris is still her niece. They're still family. She wouldn't really do any of that just to have control over me, right? I mean, I'm a nobody in comparison to this family.

"W-why?" My voice comes out shaky and I swallow.

"Because," she states with a shrug, and my eyes catch on the blood pooling around her hand on the table. "Why shouldn't I take what I want when I'm already denied my rights? If Gregory can have playthings, so can I. And I choose you. Besides, your father just isn't cutting it."

I scowl at her statement, and her brow twitches, amusement playing at her features. She points at her exposed pussy and the chocolate sauce on her. When I don't make a move, she arches a brow. Would this woman really force me to do this? Would she really hurt Solaris the way she claims? I mean, Solaris is Lena's best friend. It would hurt her daughter too.

"Lena would hurt too if you hurt Solaris."

She cackles. "You think I give one damn about my daughter? Cruise chose Solaris. Not Lena. Meaning Lena will not inherit a damn dime of this place. She only gets the small piece that every daughter gets now."

Christ.

She points again to herself. "Start licking, Silas."

If she can talk so ill-hearted about her own child, then I know for sure she wouldn't give two damns about Sol. Squeezing my eyes shut, I try to come to terms with what's about to happen. What this woman is about to make me do.

"You won't harm Solaris?" I stall.

She shakes her head. "Your precious Solaris will be unharmed until you disobey."

Hatred for this woman blooms like a fire in my chest as I meet her gaze. But if it means keeping Sol a little safer, I can't reject her. My eyes squeeze tighter as I lower myself closer to her. My mind goes numb, and I empty all thoughts of Solaris from my head. If I'm going to do this, I can't feel. I can't see her face in my head. I need to be numb.

The first swipe of my tongue against Loretta's folds has tears welling up in my eyes. I force them back. This woman doesn't get them. The second swipe, my skin tightens and a slight pain blossoms in my chest. In my throat. At the third swipe, blackness encompasses my mind, and I grab the discarded knife.

"Yessss," Loretta moans. "Give me more."

I pull my tongue away from her center and wait until she notices the absence. She lifts up on her elbows, a grimace gracing her cold face.

"Did I tell you to stop?"

My lips pull up in a smirk as I spin the knife between my fingers. Loretta's eyes jump to it, but she's not scared. Not like I want her to be.

Her brow ticks again and she crosses her arms over her small chest. "And what do you plan to do with that?"

I don't answer her. Instead, I shove the hilt of the knife into her cunt, blood pooling in the palm of my hand as I grip the blade. Loretta eyes roll back, and she collapse against the table. As much as I wish it was the other end fucking her, I will not go to prison for this woman. For this family. I won't allow them to win. If Loretta wants me, she gets what I give her.

I fuck her with the hilt of the knife for what seems like forever before she finally comes, stilling in a satiated bliss on the table. The knife falls from my hold at the sight of her, and this time I don't hold back my vomit. I heave all over the kitchen floor, hating myself for what she just made me do.

Loretta sits up and scoffs at the vomit. "Don't be disgusting. This wasn't that bad."

Wiping my mouth with the back of my hand, I scowl at her. "Speak for yourself. I got no pleasure."

She shrugs. "That's your own doing. You could have gotten all the pleasure you wanted."

"From you? Doubt it," I tell her.

She shrugs. "As long as you do as I say, you can hate me, fuck me with a knife, do whatever you want. Because at the end of the day, I still own you." She hops down from the island and looks at the cut on her arm. "I better go get this taken care of. Good night, darling."

I watch as she goes before darting out to find a spare bathroom. I need her scent off me. I need to cleanse myself of that beast. I stay in the shower, scrubbing and scrubbing, until my skin turns red and there's prickles of blood on my arms. I take a deep breath. Once and then twice, calming myself before I go back to Solaris' room to check on her. I don't want her to see me like this. I don't want her to question why I look so disheveled when it's her who needs to be taken care of.

Getting out of the shower, I put the clothes back on, hating the lingering smell of her on them. I'll burn them in the morning. I return to Solaris' room only to find her asleep on top her mattress, her small form curled into a ball. The sight of her missing pajama bottoms causes an ache to bloom in my chest. The rage from earlier comes back ten folds, but I hold it down. Cruise will pay for this.

Silently, I search her room for some shorts and dress her. She rolls over, opens her eyes slightly before closing them, and going right back to sleep. My fists clench at my side. My poor, poor Solaris.

My eyes widen at calling her mine, my hands trembling at the realization of that simple word. I pull myself away from the bed and march over to the reading chair she keeps in the corner.

No.

She's not mine.

She's a child.

A child I'm protecting from her fucked up family.

But not mine.

Not like that.

I stare at the clock on her wall, barely able to make out the time. I'll stay until the sun rises, and then I have to get out of here. Away from her to clear my head. Then, I will come back. Do what I must to in order to keep her safe from them . . . and from me.

Twenty-One

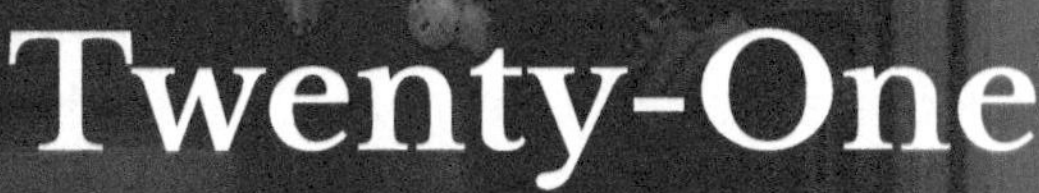

Solaris

The door to my room opens and I shift to see the intruder. Silas walks in, dressed in jeans, a fitted turtleneck, and a leather jacket. He strides over to my bed and glances at the textbook in front of me before climbing on and resting against the headboard. I lean back and look at him, a grin spreading across his handsome face.

"Can I help you with something?" I ask, crawling up the bed to him.

Silas pulls me into his lap, and I wrap my legs around him. He leans forward and gives me a swift peck, sweet and sincere.

"Maybe I just wanted to see you," he locks his arms around my waist, fingers tracing my lower back in a circular motion. "Maybe I want to take you out on a proper date."

I wrap my arms around his neck, grinning at the prospect of a date with Silas. While we used to do plenty of things together, none of those could be called a date. Mainly since I was twelve and he was twenty-one and it would have been inappropriate. Also, Silas just isn't that man.

"And where would you take me?" I ask, my voice playful.

He smirks, a mischievous glint in his eyes. "How about a trip to Nashville?"

"Nashville?" I echo, surprised. "You want to take me to your studio?"

"How about we hop on a jet and see what's there?" he asks back, his grin widening. "I thought we could spend the day together. We haven't just had you and me time. There's always something crazy happening and today, I just want to spend it making you happy. I might even play you a song."

I roll my eyes at him. "Oh geez!" I feign excitement. "Silas O'Conner is going to sing to me!"

He swats at my back side. "Don't act like you and Lena weren't my biggest fans as kids."

"Keyword. Kids." I smirk. "I don't know if you've noticed, but I'm not such a kid anymore."

Silas grips the back of my head and pulls me close. He kisses me once. Then twice. "Yeah, well, I can still bend you over my knee and spank that ass."

My cheeks heat at his words. "You never did that when I was a kid. But I don't think I'm opposed"

He nips at my bottom lip. "Get your head out of the gutter."

"Kind of hard when," my hips move on their own accord at the very present length of him, "you're not out of it yourself."

Silas swats at my back side again. "Behave. Now, what do you say? Nashville?"

I stare at him, the thrill of adventure and the promise of intimacy making my heart race. "You really want to do that? Spend the day with me?"

"Why wouldn't I want to spend the day with you?" he questions, brushing a strand of hair behind my ear. "It's about time I took you on a real date. And I need to make up for my birthday fiasco. I saw the disappointment on your face and I never want to be the one that put it there."

I nod, excitement bubbling up inside me. "Okay, let's do it."

Silas' smile deepens, and his lips press against mine again, this time lingering a little longer. He pulls me flush against him and my fingers curl into the knit of his turtleneck. His lips are warm, soft. Almost too gentle. They part just enough for my tongue to slip inside, but has a swiftly as the kiss begin, Silas pulls away, leaving me wanton.

My head drops to his chest in frustration, causing him to chuckle in response. "Pack a bag. We'll leave in an hour."

"You can't just interrupt my studying and then leave me like this." I grumble.

He full on laughs at my expense. "Didn't anyone ever tell you delayed gratification is the best kind of gratification?"

I roll my eyes at him. He moves me aside and rise from the bed. I watch as he exits the room, giddiness overtaking me. The idea of spending an entire day with Silas, away from Mountain Rose and the James name, feels like a dream. I quickly gather my things, my mind already racing with possibilities.

An hour later, I meet Silas outside. He's waiting with a small duffel bag slung over his shoulder next to a bright yellow car. It look at odds with the early November atmosphere, bringing a bit of luster to the overwise muted vibes. his eyes lighting up when he sees me. "Ready?"

"Ready," I reply, my heart pounding with excitement.

Silas opens the door for me and he slips in on the driver's side. The drive is short, and soon we're boarding the band's jet. The interior is luxurious, with plush leather seats and all the amenities one could imagine. I settle into a seat by the window, watching as Silas speaks to the pilot.

Once we're airborne, he joins me, settling into the seat beside mine. "Comfortable?" he asks, his hand finding mine.

"Very," I reply, squeezing his hand. "But my jet is better."

He shakes his head at me. "We can't all be America's sweetheart, now, can we?"

"Sounds like someone's jealous," I tease, before turning serious. "This is amazing though."

He smiles, leaning in to kiss my cheek. "Wait until we get to Nashville. I think you'll like it even more."

I don't say anything to that. Instead, I simply sit back in my seat and relax.

The flight to Nashville is smooth. Silas and I spend most of it talking and laughing. The tension that usually hangs over us is lifted, replaced by a light-hearted, almost giddy feeling.

"So, tell me more about what we're doing. All I know is that you record your albums here," I say, leaning back in my seat and turning to face him.

Silas grins, his eyes sparkling with excitement. "I actually have a house here. Bought it about three years into my contract. It's a bit different from the manor. More modern, with all the latest tech. I've got a recording studio, a home theater, and a kitchen that's actually fun to cook in."

"Sounds impressive," I reply, raising an eyebrow. "Is this where you've been the last three years?"

"When I wasn't on tour or traveling, yeah."

"I'm guessing you and the band wrote that last album there too?" I ask.

"For the most part," he admits. "It's where I can escape and just be myself, you know? No expectations, no pressure."

I nod, understanding more than he realizes. "It must be nice to have a place like that."

"It is," he says softly, his hand finding mine again. "And I can't wait to share it with you."

We spend the rest of the flight talking about everything and nothing, our conversation flowing easily. Silas tells me stories about his time on the road with the band. In return, I share stories of filming onset and what my costars were like.

As we begin our descent into Nashville, Silas looks at me with a tender smile. "I want this day to be special for you, Solaris."

"I don't need a special day," I reply. "Thanks, though."

He leans in, kissing me softly. "You deserve all the special days."

I roll my eyes at his cheesiness, but I can't say I don't like it.

The jet touches down smoothly, and soon we're on our way to Silas' home. The drive through Nashville is a blur of excitement and anticipation. When we finally pull up to his house, I'm struck by how different it is from the manor. It's sleek, a modern marvel of architecture. Glass and steel blend seamlessly with natural wood, creating a space that feels both luxurious and inviting. As we step inside, I'm immediately struck by the high ceilings and open floor plan. The living room is spacious, with floor-to-ceiling windows that offer a stunning view of the city.

"Wow," I breathe, taking it all in. "This place is incredible."

Silas smiles, clearly pleased by my reaction. "I'm glad you approve. Come on, I'll give you the grand tour."

He leads me through the house, showing me the state-of-the-art recording studio, the cozy home theater, and finally, the kitchen. It's a chef's dream, with sleek stainless steel appliances, a large island, and plenty of counter space.

"This is where the magic happens," Silas says with a grin, gesturing to the kitchen.

I laugh, feeling completely at ease. "I can't wait to see you in action. I'm really hoping you don't burn anything or cut off a finger. You kind of need those."

"Well, you're in luck," he replies, rolling up his sleeves. "Tonight, I'm cooking for you."

I watch as he moves around the kitchen with practiced ease, gathering ingredients and setting up his workspace. There's something incredibly attractive about seeing him in this domestic setting, so different from the polished rock star image he usually projects.

As he starts to cook, I sit at the island, sipping a glass of wine, and watching him work. "You know," I say, swirling the wine in my glass, "I never pegged you for a chef."

Silas chuckles, glancing up at me. "There's a lot you don't know about me, Solaris."

"I'm beginning to see that," I reply, a smile tugging at my lips.

He cooks with a confidence and skill that surprises me, preparing what looks to be a delicious meal. The kitchen fills with a mouthwatering aroma, and I can't help but smile. This . . . this is what we should be like all the time. Worry free and content.

Once dinner is ready, we sit down at the island to eat. The food is delicious, and the conversation is easy and relaxed. Our conversation picks up where it left off on the jet, discussing our favorite shows and things to do when we're not working, or in my case, in school.

When both our plates are clear, I take them to the sink. I don't bother trying to wash them or load them in the dishwasher since I've never done dishes a day in my life. Instead, I gently place them in the sink and return to Silas. He arches a brow at me and then glance at the pile of dishes I just left there. I shrug. Me trying would seem like I'm trying too hard, and there's no need for that.

"We're going to have to fix that." He says as the picks up his acoustic guitar, a mischievous glint in his eye.

I cross my arms. "If you wanted a domestic little housewife, you chose the wrong girl."

"I don't know." He strums a note. "I think I can domesticate you."

I snort at his assumption.

"I know I've been a bit flakey lately," he changes the subject, strumming a few chords, "but I really have been here working. I wrote what I think will be our top single for the upcoming album. Want to hear it?"

"Of course," I reply, leaning forward in anticipation.

He begins to play, the soft, melodic notes filling the room. His voice is smooth and rich, and the song he sings is beautiful and haunting. As I listen, I feel a deep sense of connection to him, a bond that goes beyond words. He wrote a song about us. Well, him missing me and waiting a lifetime to see me again.

When he finishes, I feel tears in my eyes. "Silas, you wrote a song about me?"

He sets the guitar aside. "I've written hundreds songs about you. Do you liked it."

I wrap my arms around him, pulling him close. "I more than liked it."

Silas' hands find my waist. "Is that so?"

I nod, and he lifts me onto the kitchen island, his lips capturing mine, and I melt into him. His hands roam up my back, sending shivers down my spine. My fingers make their way into his hair, tugging him closer and losing myself in the moment. The kitchen seems to fade away, and everywhere Silas touches seems to come to life even through the layers of clothes. God, I wish I would have worn something less bulky than a sweater.

We kiss deeply, hungrily, the intensity of our desire taking over. Silas' hands slide under my sweater, caressing my skin, and I shiver with pleasure.

We break apart for a moment, both breathing heavily. Silas' eyes are dark with desire, and he gazes at me with a mixture of tenderness and hunger. "Sol."

"Silas." I tug him back to me by the front of his turtle neck, our lips meeting again in a fervent kiss. Talking has no place in this moment. All I need is for him to keep kissing me and his hands on my skin. Words can wait.

Silas slides me forward on the island as our kissing grows more urgent. He presses his center into mine and a soft whimper escapes me at the hardness pressing into my center. His lips trail down my neck, leaving a trail of fire in their wake. He reaches for the hem of the sweater and tugs it over my head, leaving me sitting on the island in nothing but my bra and a pair of leggings. He steps away from me, eyes deepening as he takes in my half-naked form.

"You're beautiful."

Heat rushes to my cheeks at his compliment. "And you're overdressed."

Smirking, he hauls his turtleneck over his head as he makes his way back between my thighs.

Silas captures my lips one more time, his eyes searching mine. "Are you sure you're okay with this? I know last time wasn't the best, and I don't want to push you into anything."

Push. Take. Devour.

My heart pounding in my chest, I nod, agreeing with the voice. "I'm more than okay with whatever you want to do with me. I was okay last time too."

Silas' brow—the one with the cut—ticks likes that the best news he's had all day. He leans in to kiss me again, his lips moving against mine with a blend of passion and gentleness. His hands are firm but tender as they move to the waistband of my leggings. Lifting me slightly, he slides the fleece-lined fabric down my legs, tracing the contours of my curves as he does. I kick off my shoes and they hit the floor with a loud thud, the leggings following soon after them, leaving me completely bare to Silas.

Hooking his hands under my knees, he pulls me to the edge of the island. My legs wrap around his waist as he picks me up and walks out of the kitchen.

"As much as I would love to have a second course, I want you in my bed."

A giggle leaves me as he takes the steps two at a time. "I've been in your bed plenty of times."

He grunts and smacks my butt. "I wasn't fucking you then. Nor was I planning to. Now, I'm going to ravish you."

Silas kicks open the door to his room and goes inside, straight to the bed. He tosses me down onto the lush comforter and a soft moan leaves me at the coolness of the silk. Silas crawls over me, a hand skimming up my side and over my right breast. His mouth lowers to my peaked nipple, and I arch into his touch, my fingers sliding back into his curly hair, pulling him closer.

"So responsive." He nips at me. "Only for me."

He nips at me again, and my eyes roll shut, unable to say anything through the sheer pleasure coursing through me. One of Silas' hands move down my body, inching towards my sex. He shifts and then a finger dives into me. My head spins, and I gasp out, sparks flying behind my eyes. His mouth leaves my chest, and my eyes pop open, my head shaking at the sudden loss of him.

Silas' eyes lock onto mine, his expression filled with a mix of lust and hunger. "So wet for me. I'm going to fuck you now."

I bite down on my bottom lip and press my legs wider, inviting him to do whatever he wants.

He smirks down at me, his finger still thrusting inside of me. "Let me show you how much I care."

With that, he leans down and kisses me again. He pushes inside me slowly. Too slow, and I groan out in frustration.

"I am not going to break, Silas," I tell him. "Fuck me like you mean it. Fuck me like a groupie."

He rolls us over so I'm straddling him. "Your wish is my command, baby."

He thrusts up into me hard, and I have to grab his shoulders to steady myself. He chuckles and does it again, his hands skating up the side of my hips and around to my backside. He spreads my cheeks as I move above him. My eyes widen as his finger circles the one area I know no one has taken. I shake my head at him, and he smirks. Like hell anyone will go back there. That is an exit only zone and not even Silas O'Conner is going to enter.

"You said to fuck you like a groupie," he grunts out. "One day, when you're ready, I will."

He flips us over again, so that he's back on top and picks up the speed. I lose myself in the rhythm of our bodies moving together, the sensation of him filling me is a heady mixture of pleasure and contentment. This right here is the best drug in the world and I'm surely an addict.

My orgasm comes fast and quick and so does his. His room becomes our private world, and we stay engrossed in each other's bodies for hours. He takes me in his shower and then again on the vanity counter. Each touch, each kiss, is a declaration of our feelings, a way to express what words cannot.

By the time we're done making love for the fourth time, we're both too spent to move. Silas stays buried to the hilt in me, and I don't want him to pull out. I love the fullness of him. Breathless and flushed, Silas pulls my back to his chest as his finger traces lazy circles on my stomach.

"How many kids to you want?" he asks out of nowhere.

"Kids?" I glance at him over my shoulder. "You do remember that I'm just now eighteen, right? I haven't thought about it."

He lifts a brow at me. "You're a girl. You all think about that stuff. So give me an answer. I'm not going to go running scared."

I think about his question and think about my life. Truthfully, I used to think about me and Silas all the time as a kid, back before everything happened. Back before the world became such a dark place. While I'm not an only child, Cruise always seemed other to me. He was the big brother that was never around and when he was, things always ended badly. Of course, now I know why, but back then I thought it was an age thing. That he was too cool to care about me. And I desperately longed for someone other than just Lena.

"Maybe four," I tell Silas. "But they would need to be close in age."

"So you would want to get pregnant back to back to back?"

"This is hypothetical."

"Sure," he says and finally pulls out of me.

I miss the fullness as soon as it's gone, but I don't tell him that. Instead, I turn over and smile up at him. "Best date ever."

His thumb caresses my chin. "Really?"

I kiss his chest and nod. "What's not to like about getting fucked on every surface in the man I love's room?"

"Love?"

My cheeks heat at the fact he caught on to that. Then again, he writes music for a living. I shouldn't be surprised that words are his jam. So instead of trying to cover up the word, I nod. Silas' arms wrap around my back and pulls my naked body flush against his. He kisses me again, and my toes curl into the bed.

"I love you, too," he confesses and it's the first time he's used those three little words.

After a few more tender moments, we gather ourselves, and walk hand in hand back to the kitchen where my clothes lie. I dress in silence before turning back to him. The night is still young, and I don't really want to head back to Mountain

Rose quite yet. It's nice being here with him. With no one lurking around the corner.

"What now?" I ask him.

Silas pulls me to him. "That's up to you. My plan is to stay the night, maybe show you a few of my favorite places around the city tomorrow, and then head back so you don't miss school on Monday."

I tilt my head to the side. "Can we just walk around Nashville without a bodyguard? I know we do in Mountain Rose, but everyone knows us there."

"You probably shouldn't walk around anywhere without a bodyguard, but I don't want to think about another man spending every waking minute guarding your body. The whole idea makes me want to tie you to my bed and never let you leave the house."

I roll my eyes at him. "Okay then. It's settled." I take his hand in mine and raise it, spinning around. "Show me how Silas O'Conner has spent the last three years in Nashville."

He grapples me around the waist and spins us around. "With pleasure."

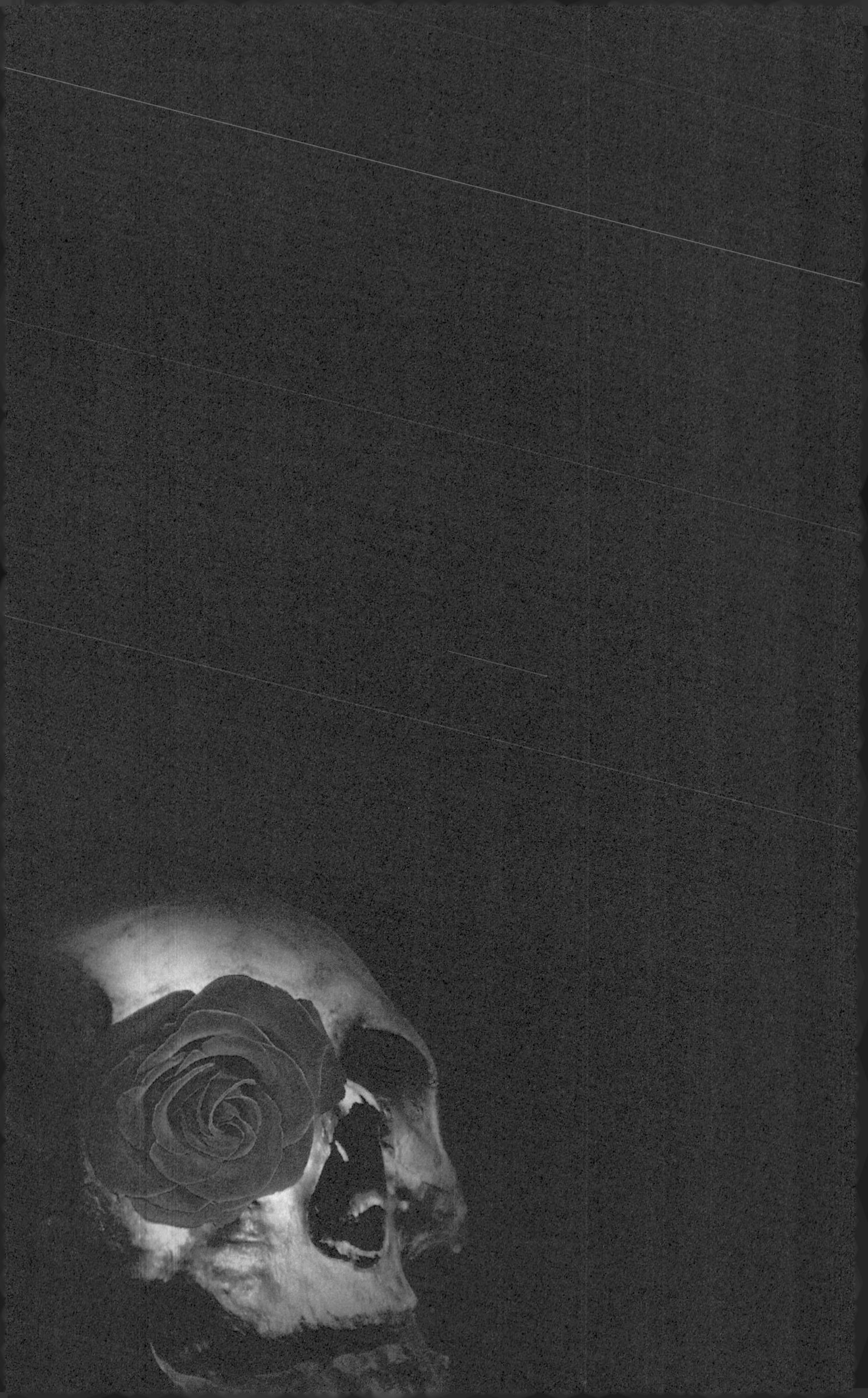

Twenty-Two

I slam the front door shut behind me, the sound echoing through the empty halls of the mansion. My school bag hits the floor with a thud, and I run a hand through my hair, trying to shake off the stress of today. Then my eyes fall on a brown envelope resting on the table in the foyer.

"Miss James." I turn to see Mrs. Louis standing on the other side of the table. "Shall I set you up with a snack in the sitting room?"

Smiling, I give her a nod. My eyes go back to the brown envelope. Curiosity piqued, I go over and pick it up. My name's written on the front in bold, black letters. With a mix of anticipation and apprehension, I tear it open and pull out a thick stack of papers. A movie script. My heart skips a beat.

Kelly told me that I would start receiving these if the finale of the show went as planned. I haven't had the heart to even begin watching the final season. While a lot of actors don't like watching themselves, I'm the opposite. I like seeing what I did wrong so I don't make that mistake in the future. But with this season, I don't know. It feels like something else besides the show is coming to an end.

I skim the cover page: "The Lost Girl" - Written by Jonathan Harris. My eyes widen. Jonathan Harris is a renowned director, known for his emotionally gripping films. I fumble for my phone and quickly dial my agent.

"Kelly, I just got a script in the mail," I tell her, trying to keep my voice steady, but there's no stopping the excitement. Starring in one of Jonathan Harris' films is life changing.

"Ah, Solaris! I was wondering when I'd hear from you," Kelly's voice chirps on the other end. "Yes, it's real. Jonathan Harris wants you in the leading role."

I squeal and then collect myself. "Are you serious? This could be huge!"

"It will be huge," Kelly assures me. "This role is going to make you an even bigger household name than you already are."

Her words cut through my excitement, and I still against the foyer table. More attention is the last thing I need right now. Not after what Silas and I did. But this role . . . it could change everything. I could be nominated for an Oscar.

"Kelly, I don't know," I say, biting my lip and making my way to the sitting area. "Do you think it's safe for me to take on something this high-profile right now? The public has been crazy since my mom's death. They're still speculating that I killed her."

"Solaris, listen," Kelly tells me, her tone becoming more serious. "This is the opportunity of a lifetime. Jonathan Harris doesn't just offer roles like this to anyone. He sees something in you, something special. And if he for once thought you did that, he wouldn't have picked you. You have to accept this role. If you don't, you might as well hang up your acting hat. You won't get this chance again."

I sigh, looking at the script in my hands. I know she's right. Declining would be essentially blackballing myself. "I get that, but I don't want to draw too much attention to myself. Things are . . . complicated right now."

"Complicated how?" Kelly asks, concern evident in her voice.

"It's just . . . personal stuff. I can't really get into it," I answer, regretting my recent decisions now. "I just . . . I don't know."

"Solaris, I know you've been through a lot, but this could be your chance to break away from TV and modeling. To show the world what you're truly capable of," Kelly's voice fills with conviction. "And let's be real, this role could open so many doors for you. You could have your pick of projects after this."

"I know, I know," frustration creeping into my voice. "But filming starts at the end of my senior year. I'll miss graduation and prom."

Kelly's silent for a moment, then she sighs. "Graduation is important, sure. But sometimes, you must make sacrifices for your career. This role could define your future, Solaris. *Our future.*"

"I just don't know if I'm ready for that kind of pressure," I admit, feeling torn between my dreams and my fears.

"You're stronger than you think, Kiddo," Kelly's voice gentles. "Look kid, you don't have to decide right now. Take some time and think about what you want from your life and where you want your career to go. If you're happy enough with the TV roles, then we'll stick with it. Just let me know so I can give Jonathan an answer."

"Okay, I'll think about it," I promise, feeling a bit more at ease.

"And Solaris?" Kelly adds, her voice softening. "Whatever you decide, I'm here for you. We'll get through this together."

"Thanks, Kelly," I say, a small smile tugging at my lips. "I appreciate it."

With a sign, I hang up and head to the sitting room. I sit on the edge of the couch, staring at the script in my hands. This role is everything I'd ever dreamed of. From the moment Mom got me an appointment with Kelly, I knew a Jonathan Harris film is what I wanted. I knew working towards that could change our lives forever. But Mom is gone now, and I have all of this, and the timing couldn't be worse.

I can't draw any more attention to myself, especially with Cruise and Loretta lurking around. And then there's the issue of missing graduation and prom. I've already missed so much this year due to obligations with the brand partnerships and the interviews. I didn't even get to go to homecoming. I can't miss graduation too. Those things might be irrelevant to most people, but they are important to me. Mom wanted me to experience what it was like to be normal. That's what she dreamed for me. And just because she's not here to see it fulfilled, doesn't mean I'm going to crap all over that dream.

A knock on the wall pulls me from my thoughts. I glance up to see Silas standing there with a tray in his hands.

"I told Mrs. Louis I'd bring this to you." He steps inside and places the tray on the coffee table before taking a seat next to me.

"Hey," he says, a grin spreading across his face and eyes landing on the script in my hands. "What's that?"

"A movie script," I reply. "My agent says it's a huge opportunity."

Silas takes the papers from my hand and looks over the cover. He lets out a long whistle at the sight of Jonathan Harris' name. "This is a big deal."

I drop my head to the back of the sofa and sigh. "Filming starts at the end of the school year. I'd miss graduation. On top of that, Jonathan Harris creates stars. A-list stars. Do you know how much media attention that would garner?"

He frowns. "We don't need media attention right now, Sol. And I kind of like the idea of kissing you in front of that prick principal of yours at graduation."

I roll my eyes at him. "You're just mad you got fired from Mountain Rose."

"I couldn't give two shits about getting fired from that school. I was there because you were there. No other reason. I just don't like that man. Didn't like him when I was a student there."

"Yeah," I say, my voice barely above a whisper. "But this role . . . it's something I've always wanted, Silas." I turn to face him on the couch, bringing my knees to my chin. "Do you know what I told Kelly at our first meeting? When I was just a kid?"

He shakes his head. "What?"

"I told her I wanted to be in a love story that defies time and generations. Jonathan Harris makes those movies. I won't get this chance again."

Silas takes my hand, his thumb brushing gently over my knuckles. "Solaris, I want to tell you to go for it. But I can't do that. We just killed someone. Media attention and fans digging into your life is the worst decision you can make after what we did. Maybe in time, once things have settled, you can go for it again. But right now, you need to just be Solaris James, heiress to the James' empire."

My shoulders drop at his words. He's telling me what I need to hear instead of what I want to hear right now. And I know it has to be said. I can't have everything and lose nothing. But . . . "What if there's not a next time?"

Silas lifts my chin, caressing my cheek with care. "There will be. You're an amazing actress. Jonathan Harris would be an idiot to reject you when the time is right. Preferably, after you have our four babies. I'm not getting any younger here."

I shove him in the arm. "Hypothetical conversation!"

Silas leans in, his lips finding mine in a tender kiss. The familiar warmth of his touch momentarily eases my worries, and I let myself fall into him. Lowering me back on the sofa, Silas brings my legs up around his waist and deepens the kiss. He settles between my thighs as if this is where he's belonged his entire life.

"Silas," I moan needing him to move, needing him to do something other than kiss me.

"Yes, baby girl?" he whispers.

"Please touch me," I beg him.

He chuckles and flips us around so that I'm straddling his hips. He rocks me back and forth against his hardened length.

"Ride me, Sol," he whispers.

I do as he say, grinding against him even more. Heat floods my core and I pick up speed. Silas' hands trail up the outside of my legs, leaving goosebumps in their wake, and under my school skirt. I don't know why I'm always surprised at just how good he feels, but I am.

Silas releases his hold on my hips and rises up, bringing us to a sitting position. He captures my mouth once, then twice, my breath coming in short pants. Then his mouth leaves mine and trails down my neck. The buttons on my crisp white button down snap, and I open my eyes to see Silas' heated gaze on me.

"You have on too many clothes," he groans into my skin.

He yanks my bra cup down, and I melt at the feel of his mouth sucking me. God, what did I do to deserve this? My hips move of their own accord now, and I pull Silas' head closer to me. We can't get any closer but that doesn't stop me from trying to defy nature.

When Silas' free hand reaches down and rubs against my damp underwear, stars burst behind my closed lids. A loud moan leaves me, and then there's another one. Another one that didn't come from me nor Silas.

Silas' hand stops, and my lids fly open. Our heads dart towards the entrance way at once. At the sight of Cruise standing there, stroking himself, Silas leaps up from the sofa and knocks me from his lap in the process. He reaches down and helps me up, only to shove me behind his back. I right my shirt and peek around him to Cruise.

"Don't stop on my account," he says, still stroking himself. "I was enjoying the show."

"What the hell?" Silas yells. "What are you even doing here?"

My brother puts himself away and steps fully into the room. "I live here. Unlike you."

"Leave." Silas' tone is more growl than words.

Cruise grins at Silas. "Are you threatening me? Again?"

Silas takes a menacing step in his direction, but I pull him back. The only reason I'm not going crazy right now is because Silas is here. I don't need him leaving my side right now.

"I won't say it again, Cruise," Silas tells my brother.

Cruise chuckles and comes over to us. He looks past Silas and right at me, eyes dropping to my thoroughly kissed lips. The tip of his tongue grazes his bottom lip and my stomach churns. An actual growl leaves Silas and he pushes me even farther away from Cruise.

My brother arches a brow at Silas. "We had a conversation a while back, where I told you exactly how this," he gestures between the three of us, "was going to play out."

"If you think I give two shits about your fucked up family dynamics and ancient traditions, you are crazier than I thought."

Cruise shrugs. "That doesn't change the fact that she's finally old enough to do what she was meant to do."

My eyes dart between Silas and my brother. There's something I clearly don't know, and I don't like being treated like I'm not here. Inhaling, I go to step around Silas, but he grabs hold of my forearm and pushes me against the sofa.

My eyes widen at his roughness. Not once in all the years I've known Silas has he shoved me aside like some little doll.

I stand from the couch, but Silas moves with me, making sure Cruise doesn't get another look.

"What are you talking about?" I finally ask neither of them in particular.

Silas ignores me. "You have no claim over her anymore." Claim?

"Gregory told me exactly how to keep her away from you."

"What?" I ask, confused more than ever. "When did you even talk to my dad?"

Silas continues to ignore me as he stares down Cruise. The easygoing expression my brother had moments ago is gone and he's snarling right back.

"You better not have—"

"Had sex with her?" Silas taunts him. "Multiple times. Without a condom. She even let me fill her with my seed and she. Loved. Every. Second. Of it."

I stare at the both of them, and then I turn to Silas, every time we've been together coming to the forefront of my mind. Not once did he ask about birth control. Not once did he suggest we slow down and use protection. Nothing. And then the baby conversation. Men don't talk about having babies. How stupid could I have been?

"Silas?" His name leaves my lips on a choke. "What are you talking about?"

"Yes, Silas," Cruise taunts him. "Maybe it's time we tell our dear Solaris about everything. This family. You and Loretta. The fact that Lena is our sister. Every. Little. Thing."

"What?" I shriek and my mouth literally falls open.

Lena is my sister?

But . . .

That would mean . . .

Oh, God . . .

I shake my head at the thoughts going on inside it. No, Cruise has to be lying. There's no way my dad would sleep with his own sister. Cheat on my mother. They were in love. I know that. I saw that.

"You . . ." Silas snarls and then punches Cruise.

I gasp. My brother charges Silas and they both flip over the stone coffee table. I step around, not quite sure if I should jump into this or not. While Cruise needs to go, this is not how I want it done. Here is not the place or time for Silas to be reckless.

"Stop!" I shout at them both, watching them each throw punch after punch. Neither of them listens. I step to intervene, catching Silas' attention for a single second. A single second is all it takes for Cruise to get the upper hand. He shoves Silas forward, and Silas' head clips the edge of the coffee table. I scream and rush forward. Cruise gets to his feet and grabs hold of my forearm, pulling me away from Silas.

"Silas!" I scream and try to break free from my brother.

Cruise slams me against a wall, knocking the air out of me. His hand wraps around my throat, cutting off my air and snarls at me.

"If you're so much as carrying that man's child, I will cut it out of you and make you watch as I shove it down his throat. Got it, sister?"

Tears stream down my cheeks at his harsh words. "I'm not pregnant."

He pats my cheeks. "Let's hope for your sake, you're not. There will be a doctor coming today."

My body trembles against him. "I'm not. I promise you I'm not."

"We'll find out soon enough." Cruise's hand drops from my throat and to my hand. He starts dragging me towards the sitting room's exit, but I pull away from him and dart to where Silas lay unconscious. I hear my brother's stomping first before he hauls me away from Silas by my hair.

"Let me go!" I scream at him, tossing in his hold.

Movement catches my attention and I glance up to see Silas stirring awake. Cruise hand tightens in my hair, as he continues to pull me out of the sitting room. Silas' eyes catch mine and I barely see him get to his feet, before Cruise pulls me around the corner.

"Cruise, please, you're hurting me!" I plead with my brother.

"You should have thought of that before spreading your legs for him." His hand tightens in my curls.

"How is that any different from you selling me to other men?" I shout through the pain.

Cruise pauses for a second, his hand not loosening. "So you remember?" His tone softens and lowers. "I chose them. They did nothing I didn't want you to experience. They were only meant to prepare you. Nothing more. Besides, they all. Wore. Fucking. Condoms."

"Please," I beg him again. "Let me go."

More movement catches my eye, and I sob at Silas slowly creeping up behind us. He places a finger to his lip, shushing me and I do. Within the next second, Cruise and Silas both crash into the foyer table.

I scamper to my feet just as Mrs. Louis makes her way down the stairs leading to my wing of the house. She has a broom in her hand as if she's going to do some damage. She lowers it though when she realizes it's Silas and Cruise fighting, and she can't really do anything to them.

"What is going on?" she shouts and the guys pull apart.

Silas marches over to me and takes me in his hold, my face resting against his chest as he massages the back of my head where Cruise was pulling. "Have someone escort him out of this house."

Mrs. Louis looks from Silas to Cruise and then to me. "Miss James?"

"Are you serious right now?" Cruise voice echoes throughout the foyer. "If anyone should be leaving, it is him. He's not even a James! He has no claim over any part of the James' estate!"

"Solaris?" I hear Mrs. Louis' motherly voice once again. "What do you want me to do?"

"I . . . I—"

"I'm gone!" Cruise yells. "But don't think this is over, Silas. I'm coming back for my sister."

The front door slams and I jerk in Silas' hold, more tears escaping.

"Shhh," Silas tries to soothe me. "I can handle your brother. Just go upstairs to your room."

I shake my head, not wanting to leave his side. Cruise literally just slammed his head into a stone coffee table. We should be calling the ambulance. Rushing to the doctor. He could have some internal bleeding. Or a concussion. Or anything. Cruise is gone now. We need to get him checked over.

"We need to call an ambu—"

"Go to your room," Silas commands, cutting me off, and I stiffen.

"You can't just—"

"Go to your fucking room!" his voice booms as he grabs hold of my nape. "And stay there until I come for you."

Words leave me, and even more tears prick at my eyes. Silas has never talked to me like this before. Never been this hostile before. I nod, and he places a gentle peck against my lips.

"Good girl." He releases his hold on me. "I'll be back. I promise."

I don't say anything to him as I dart past Mrs. Louis and flee upstairs to my room.

Twenty-Three

Solaris

I sit on my bed, staring at the door, waiting for Silas to return. The events of the day replay in my mind, and frustration churns inside me like a storm. I can't believe Silas sent me to my room like some petulant child that needed disciplining. I was only trying to make sure he was okay, and this is the thanks I get.

Like . . . seriously?

What the hell?

Glancing over at my clock, I huff out in even more frustration. Hours have passed, and my patience is wearing thin. Where could he be? Hopefully, not trying to find Cruise when he literally had blood matted to the side of his head. I roll my eyes and bring my knees up to my chest. This is truly ridiculous. This is my house. I'm not a child. I shouldn't have to stay in this room like one.

My stomach growls, breaking the silence, reminding me I haven't eaten since lunch at school. And the snack I was going to eat got destroyed.

"Ugh!" I cry out as I look at the clock again.

Either Silas is not coming back or he's going to wait until it's far too late for dinner. Either way, I'm not staying in this room another second. Hopping up from the bed, I storm over to my door, out my room, and head downstairs. The house is quiet, but I expect nothing less. Most days I forget I even have staff working here because literally no one makes a sound.

Once I make it downstairs and to the foyer, I notice the mess from earlier is gone and another vase of flowers adorns the table. I shake my head, bypass everything, and head towards the main kitchen. I really should tell Mrs. Louis not to bother with the main kitchen on this floor. Since it's literally just me here now, she doesn't need to bother herself with the main one. She can just use the kitchen in my wing, save her time and cleanup.

As I reach the kitchen, the comforting scent of home-cooked food hits me. Mrs. Louis and her staff are already bustling around, preparing dinner. I step inside the kitchen, and everything stops. Mrs. Louis turns to look at me, a wary expression on her face and everyone else scatters out another entrance, leaving just me and her. She pulls out a stool for me to perch on and I do, watching her return to whatever smells so divine.

"How you feeling, dear?" she asks as she brings over two bowls. She pulls out the stool across from me and sits.

I sigh again and take a bite of the soup. "Tired if I'm being honest. Everything's been so chaotic since my mom died. And then today, it feels like I don't really know anything."

"You know, your mom's the one who hired me on here all those years ago? I expected to be let go when she . . . left, but your brother kept me on," she tells me.

I don't bother responding to that. I'm not sure what there is for me to say. Instead, I take another slurp of the soup, the warmth of the food doing very little to soothe me.

"I don't understand what happened to Cruise," she continues, her voice tinged with sadness. "He was such a good boy when he was younger, despite the teachings of his grandfather. Then you were born, and he never left your side."

I scoff at her comment. If Cruise was around me, I'm sure it was for something nefarious. I don't even remember a time when Cruise and I were truly civil.

I nod along to her, not wanting to diminish her feelings towards my brother and push my food around in my bowl. "People change," I mutter.

She looks up from her bowl. "I know. I just don't understand how such a playful and charismatic boy became what I witnessed today. It breaks my heart to see him like this. So much like your grandfather. I truly thought that man's teachings wouldn't impact Cruise."

Guilt twists in my gut. I know Cruise's behavior is partly due to the family's dark secrets. Secrets everyone apparently felt like I don't need to know even though I'm quite sure some of them involve me. At the end of the day, though, this is Cruise. This is the man he let power and greed turn him into. If he was ever the boy Mrs. Louis knew, it was before my time.

I pat the woman on the arm, trying to console her. "I'm guessing you know more about these teachings and the secrets everyone seem to want to hide?"

She takes a bite of her soup. "The maids know everything that happens within these gates."

A throat clears behind us, and we turn around to see Silas standing in the doorway to the kitchen. The top three buttons of his shirt are undone, and his hair is a mess, like someone has been running their fingers through it. I frown at his appearance, taken aback. His shirt was not undone when he ordered me to my room.

Silas' eyes meet mine, his expression dark. He strides over to us and takes the seat next to me at the island.

"I told you to stay in your room until I got back," he says, his voice low and controlled.

Mrs. Louis glances between us, sensing the tension. "I'll leave you two to talk," she stands and excuses herself.

I bite down on the inside of my jaw, the frustration from earlier rearing its ugly head. Turning away from him, I go back to eating my soup in silence. How dare he show up like this? How dare he come to my house and look like he's been fucking someone else? How fucking dare he?

Silas yanks my bowl away from me, his patience snapping.

"You're acting like a child, Solaris," he says sharply.

My spoon clatters against the metal top of the island as I turn to face him, my eyes blazing. "A child? I'm acting like a child?" I repeat, my voice rising. "I'm tired of being kept in the dark, Silas. I want to know what's going on. I want to know about you and Loretta. I want to know what Cruise meant by claiming me. I want to know how Lena is my sister and not my cousin. I deserve to know the truth about my own life! And you . . ." I leap up from the stool, jabbing a finger into his chest, "were meant to be the one person that wasn't keeping secrets!"

Silas runs a hand through his hair, exasperated. "It's complicated."

"Then uncomplicate it!" I shout, shoving him. "I need to know. I need to understand what's happening. Why won't you just tell me?"

Silas sighs, his shoulders sagging. He looks up at me, his eyes filled with a mixture of frustration and resignation. "Alright," he says quietly. "You want to know everything? Fine. I'll tell you."

I cross my arms, glaring at him. "I'm listening."

Silas takes a deep breath, gathering his thoughts. "Your family has traditions. Traditions your father admitted to me when I walked in on him fucking your aunt."

My arms stiffen and my eyes go wide. "What?"

"Loretta and Gregory were fucking," he says again, slower this time.

I shake my head at him and take my seat again. "You didn't see it right. My dad wouldn't have—"

"They were having sex in the open for anyone to see, Solaris," he cuts me off and states it as plain as day. "I'm sorry to ruin who you precious perception of your father, but he wasn't as innocent as you think."

"But that's—"

"Yeah, I know." He doesn't allow me to speak the word. "Like I told Cruise, fucked up family traditions."

"But that was just them. That doesn't make it a tradition." I try to defend them, even though I know this family isn't even worth defending. I don't even like this family, but yet, Silas' statement about them is so horrid.

"Sol . . ." Silas grabs my hands and moves us back over to the island. "It wasn't just them. There is a tradition. Have you ever stopped and truly looked at the paintings on your own walls?" He talks to me like I'm a child. "Every daughter that is born belongs to the oldest male heir. And when I say belong, I mean that in the very biblical sense. Your father was never meant to have any children outside that didn't belong to Loretta. Cruise was his first mistake."

My eyes blink rapidly, attempting to understand this. It doesn't make any sense. My mom told me that my dad had a first wife before her. And she wasn't Cruise's mother. And I know Loretta isn't Cruise's mother.

"I'm confused," I admit.

"I told you this was complicated," he tells me. "Anyway, Gregory's first wife died. They say it was from natural causes, but I looked into her records. She was perfectly healthy. My beliefs, Loretta didn't like Gregory falling for the first wife. She was only meant to be a figure head for the public's sake. Just like the rest of the wives lining that wall."

I shake my head and get up from the stool, pacing across the kitchen. "Back up, please. I don't understand."

Silas gets up from the chair and comes over to me. He takes hold of my hand and guides me towards the exit of the kitchen. "Let's head up to your room. More private."

"I'm having dinner." I turn him down. Right now, I have no desire to be alone with him in my room. One, I'm still highly angry with him. Two, I am actually hungry. And three, he has yet to say why he came back to my house looking royally fucked.

"Solaris, please," Silas says to me. "I'm explaining all this like you wanted. Just grab the bowl and let's go."

"No," I tell him. "You don't get to leave and come back looking like that—" I gesture to him, "and expect me to go to my room with you. You think I don't know what's going to happen if you get me alone in there?"

"I don't care if you know or not. It's happening before the night is out anyway."

My brows jump at his words, and I pull my hand away from him. "Excuse me? I think not."

I take my bowl and another bite of my dinner. Silas spins me around on the stool, effectively cutting me off from my dinner yet again. I huff and cross my arms, glaring at him.

"You're ovulating right now," he states like it's a fact, and my eyes widen at his knowledge of my body.

"How do you even know that?"

He ignores my question. "It's the perfect time for us to try having a baby."

"Are you crazy?" I jerk back on the stool. "I am in high school. I am eighteen. My career is just taking off! And you're talking about a baby? That was a hypothetical conversation, Silas."

Silas grabs hold of my chin. "It's the only way I can break his claim on you. According to Gregory, you cannot be claimed if you have a child. For some reason, it's against your family fucked up traditions."

I shake my head at him. "You have to explain better."

Silas lets out a deep breath and drops my chin. He turns away from me and pace across the kitchen, running his hands through his already messed up hair. Then he turns back to me, his face as serious as ever.

"The daughters in your family can't procreate outside of the male heir. If they do, it is seen as an abomination. Cruise can't claim you if you have tainted yourself. A baby would spare you from this nightmare, and we wouldn't have to worry about your brother."

I hop off the stool, putting together the bare pieces of intel he's given me and storm across the kitchen to him. "So this entire time—from the first moment we had sex—you've been trying to breed me like some cow?"

He stares down at me. "It's not as bad as you're making it out to be. It's not like we can't care for a kid."

I shake my head at his flippancy. "That is not the point."

"Then what is?" he yells at me. "I am doing everything I can think of to save you. To protect you from your family. I came back for you. And you're upset?"

"Silas!" I cut him off, shaking my head at his words.

"Solaris!" he yells back.

"Your idea of protection is turning into the men you were so bent on protecting me from?"

Silas face hardens and he takes a step in my direction. "Don't compare me to them. Ever. I haven't raped you. I haven't taken anything you didn't happily give."

"You *did* try taking my choice. You didn't once ask me if that was something I was comfortable with or even wanted, which is exactly what they did to me. You just did what you thought was best."

Silas' eyes drop from mine, and I can see him working through my words. When his shoulders drop and he walks past me and over to the island, I follow. He drops his head into his hands and sighs into them.

"That's not how I wanted you to feel," he whispers. "I just thought . . . Your father thought it was a good idea. I thought it was a good idea." Silas looks up and meets my eyes, cupping my cheek. "I love you, Solaris. I have been in love with you since before it was appropriate and I hated myself for it. I wouldn't do anything to hurt you like that. I'm sorry."

I turn my face into his palm and kisses his hand gently. "I accept your apology, but Silas, I don't want a baby. I'm too young. I just got handed a role I've always wanted. And I don't think we're at a point to even consider your option. Maybe if I was twenty-one and graduating college. Or if you were thirty and retiring from music. We're not. And neither one of us is ready for a child."

"That's where you're wrong. I'm very much ready to start a family with you. But I understand that you are not." Silas sighs again. "This option means relying on Cruise's little black book to do a thorough job, and I don't know if it will be enough to ruin Cruise. He will still be a James. An angry James once we figure out how to leak that content of the book."

My head falls from his palm, and I pull away from him. I probably should have told him before now that I had Lena searching for the book and that we made a plan.

"Well . . ." I start and back away from him, grimacing a little. "I kind of already found the book. And I kind of, maybe . . . already have a plan."

Silas' brows dip and he cocks his head to the side, studying me. "What are you talking about?"

"Well, you suggested that we have Lena help, and she found the book. We came up with a plan at school to expose them with the help of Brandon Black."

"Brandon Black?" He questions me. "You hate that guy."

I shrug. He's not wrong. "Lena thinks his column is what we need to expose all the people at once. And if Brandon can do that, I'm willing to put my dislike of him aside for a moment. Besides, Lena likes him."

Silas quirks a brow at me. "When you say 'like,' what do you mean?"

I roll my eyes at him and grab my bowl of soup. "I think you know what I mean."

He shakes his head, not liking the idea at all. "No. He's too old for her, and he's into some fucked up shit."

"Like what?" I lean forward, curious. Lena mentioned something similar as the reason for them not going out again. I can't imagine it's that bad. I mean, he's Brandon Black. The man looks like he cosplays for fun on the weekends.

"Nothing you need to be concerned with. When are you meeting him?"

I shrug. "Whenever Lena tells me we are."

"Keep me updated," he says and snatches my bowl away, slurping down the soup.

"Hey!" I yell at him. "Get your own!"

"I just did."

Twenty-Four

Solaris

I sit on the edge of Lena's bed, watching Lena rummage through her closet. She's been at it for nearly an hour, trying to find the perfect dress. The sight of her pacing back and forth, tossing dresses over her shoulder, makes me smile. She's determined to make an impression on Brandon. I've already told her she can wear anything, and he'll be impressed. I mean, this is Lena. My cousin could make an old torn up bed sheet look amazing.

"This one?" Lena holds up a sleek black dress with a plunging neckline, glancing at me for approval.

I raise an eyebrow. "Are we meeting with a reporter or heading to a night club?"

Lena huffs, rolling her eyes. "I need to look perfect, Solaris. It's not just about the meeting. I want him to notice me." Her eyes drop for a second. "I want him to notice me and not be enamored by you like everyone else."

I chuckle, shaking my head at her silliness. "Trust me, he'll notice you. You could wear a potato sack and still look amazing. Besides, the only thing Brandon Black notices about me is my career and when I do something wrong."

She grins, finally settling on a deep red dress that hugs her curves in all the right places. "This is the one. What do you think?"

"Definitely seductive," I tease. "Brandon won't know what hit him."

She smirks, slipping into the dress and giving herself a once-over in the mirror. The dress clings to her like a second skin, accentuating her figure and highlighting her natural beauty. "Good. That's the plan."

Lena pulls on a pair of Louboutin's and then pulls her hair up into a ponytail. She gives herself another once-over in the mirror just to make sure she is perfection. Once she's done with herself, she turns to me, propping her hand on her hips. With an arch of the brow, she looks me over and frowns.

"Is that what you planning to wear?" She gestures to my outfit.

I glance down at the leggings I'm wearing and the T-shirt. "Umm, yes. I have to be seen in the brand's lounge wear."

"You know what, it's perfect. If you're not all dolled up, that means there's a less chance of Brandon noticing you."

I cross my arms and pout at her. "Hey! Silas hasn't complained about my leggings and T-shirts."

Lena rolls her eyes. "That's because my brother is helplessly in love with you."

I grab a pillow from the head of the bed and toss it at her head. "Whatever!"

She catches it and flings it aside. "If you mess up my hair, we're going to have problems."

"As if it didn't just take you two seconds to pull it up into a ponytail." I hop off the bed and grab my bag. "We should get going before we're late."

We make our way downstairs of my aunt's house. The faint scent of jasmine from the ever-present potpourri fills the air, mingling with the earthy aroma of the wooden floors. We head outside to where Lena's BMW has been pulled around front. I arch a brow at her and she shrugs.

"He's a reporter." She justifies the car. "I want to show him that I don't need a driver like some uppity brat."

"I have no problem with you driving." I raise my hands in defense. "It's just not you. Shouldn't he like you for you?"

She's rolls her eyes and gets in the car. The drive to the small café on the out skirts of Mountain Rose doesn't take long. Yet, the entire time we're in the car, I can't help but think about how Brandon is going to react to the information we are presenting. The public thinks this family is perfect. I'm about to shatter that illusion. And once Cruise catches wind of it all, he's going to be super pissed.

"Lena?" I call as we pull up to the café. "Do you think this is a mistake?"

She turns to me. "Solaris, I think this is brave. But I can understand if you are not ready. It's not me that lived it. What do you want to do?"

I clench my hands into the smooth leather. "I want Cruise to suffer. I want them all to suffer."

She nods in understanding. "Then we need to take them down. That starts with ruining their image."

"And what if it's not enough?"

"We can always hire a hitman," she jokes, opening the door to the car and getting out. "Now, come on. I have a man to win over."

I get out of the car and follow Lena inside. We stop just inside the door and search the cozy café for Brandon. I see him the moment his eyes land on us. We head to the last booth in the back of the café, away from listening ears and prying eyes. Brandon stands as we come to a stop in front of him.

"Wow, Lena, you look stunning," he says, his voice carrying a note of genuine admiration as he takes her in. His eyes drift to me. "You look good as well, Solaris, but that's nothing new for America's sweetheart."

I roll my eyes at him but stay quiet.

Lena blushes, a rare sight on my cousin. "Thank you. You clean up pretty well yourself."

He chuckles, running a hand through his tousled hair. "I try my best."

Lena and I slide into one side of the booth just as Brandon takes the other side. A waitress comes over, her eyes flickering between the three of us. She fumbles with her notepad as she tries not to stare too much.

"H-hi," she stammers. "Y-you're Solaris and Lena James. You're in my mom's café."

"Hi yourself," Lena greets the girl. "Can we get French vanilla lattes with sweet foam and a sprinkle of cinnamon on top?"

The girl is nodding before Lena has even finished giving the order. She turns to Brandon. "And you, sir?"

"Coffee. Black. No sugar."

She jots it all down and hesitates before backing away for a moment. We all watch her go, and I'm really hoping she's not going to be an issue. For a meeting such as this, meeting Brandon at the house would have been ideal. However, the topic with Cruise somewhere on the property wouldn't allow it. We didn't need my brother popping up and seeing us with Brandon and his book. And we certainly didn't need Loretta showing her face.

The girl is back with our order in no time. She places the lattes in front of Lena and me, and the coffee in front of

Brandon. She shifts from foot to foot as she stares from Lena to me.

"I . . ." she begins and then takes in a deep breath. "I really loved your show. That ending . . . wow! My friends and I created a group just to review it. Could I . . . would you mind . . . can I have your autograph?"

I give the girl a genuine smile and nod. While I don't normally like interacting with fans, mainly because they make me nervous, and I can never tell if one of them is going to be stalker crazy, this one seems cool. She squeals and tears off a piece of paper from her pad and hands it to me.

"No one is going to believe this!" she says as I sign the paper.

"Can you wait until after we leave to tell anyone? I'm kind of hiding from my family."

"Yes. Yes, of course," she squeals again and retreats.

Lena takes a sip of her coffee. "That was interesting."

"Your life always this exciting?" Brandon asks me.

I cross my arms and arch a brow at him. "Shouldn't you already know? You are the one who keep tabs on me."

"Sol!" Lena hisses at me and elbows me in the ribs.

"Ouch!" I hiss back at her.

Brandon leans back in the booth, his gaze flickering between us with a curious spark. "So," he begins, crossing his arms and grinning, "what's so important that you needed to see me in person?"

Lena leans forward on the table, resting her chin in her hands. "Maybe I wanted to see you again."

Brandon's grin widens. "You wouldn't need your cousin here if you did."

"We're always together. Don't you know that?" Lena counters.

Brandon's grin falls a bit. "In all seriousness, what do you two need?"

Lena glances at me and I nod, as ready as I'll ever be to actually let someone hear my story. Lena reaches into her bag and pulls out the little black book. She places it on the table in front of Brandon, her expression serious. He glances from the book to us and back to the book, confusion written all over his face.

"This book belongs to Cruise," she says, her voice steady. "It's filled with names, dates, and incriminating evidence. We need your help to leak the contents anonymously."

Brandon's eyebrows shoot up as he reaches for the book. Lena drops her hand from it and allows him to have it. I gulp and watch him. There's no turning back now. He's either going to help us on our terms or he's going to leak all of this regardless. He flips through the pages, his expression growing more serious with each passing second. The café seems to fall silent around us except for the soft rustle of pages and the pounding of my heart. My fingers begin tapping in rhythm to the sound against my thigh as his eyes move across the pages.

Maybe this was a bad idea.

You could have just killed Cruise.

I shake off the voice. No. This is better. I can't just go around killing people.

Of course you can. Or at least I can.

"This is . . . a lot," he murmurs, looking up at us. "What exactly do you want me to do with it?"

"We need you to expose these people and my brother," I say, my voice firm despite the nervous flutter in my stomach. "But it has to be done carefully. No one can know it came from us."

Brandon nods slowly, his gaze thoughtful as he continues to flip through the book. "I understand. But I'll need more than just this book. I need context, background information. Stories that will make this real for people. Can you provide that?"

Lena and I exchange a glance before nodding. "Yes, we can give you everything you need," Lena says. "But you have to promise us anonymity. No one can know it came from us."

"You have my word. This is career making stuff," Brandon assures us, closing the book with a decisive snap. "Now, let's talk details."

We spend the next hour discussing the contents of the book, pointing out key names and dates, and explaining the significance of each entry. Brandon takes diligent notes, his demeanor professional but intense. I do my best to not insinuate it was happening to me, but I can tell from the way he's looking at me that he knows. I'm not sure how I feel about him knowing this intimate detail of my life, but it really is the only way to get this out.

When Brandon's on his third cup of coffee and I have no more to tell him, he closes his laptop. He stares at me for a long time before sighing.

"Why do you want this to be anonymous? Your story—"

"It's not my story," I hurry to cut him off. "My brother did this to someone else. Those men did that to someone else."

My eyes blink too fast for me to even believe the lie, but I can't have people putting the pieces together. My entire life could be ruined. Silas' life could be ruined. I can't do it.

Brandon nods. "I promised you anonymity, and I'll keep my promise. But Solaris, sooner or later you'll have to talk about this. You can't keep something so vile bottled up inside of you. It will destroy you."

"You don't know what you're talking about," I mutter.

"Yes, I do. I had an older sister. While it's not my place to tell her story, just know that you aren't alone. An if she would've had someone like you to relate to, maybe she would still be alive today."

My eyes drop from his and I bite down on my lip, not saying a word to that. I don't want to be the face people see when they think of this unthinkable type of abuse. I don't want to see the pity on people's faces when they look at me. That might just be worse than people thinking I'm some pyro heiress.

"So," Lena says when the tension grows unbearable, and I have no words for him. "How long will it take for the story to drop?"

Brandon gives my cousin his attention. "Give me a day to craft the story and make all this digestible for the public."

I nod.

That gives me a day to prepare myself.

A day before the speculation starts.

Exhaustion and relief wash over me. "Thank you, Brandon," I say, my voice quieter now. "This means a lot to me."

"Anything for Solaris James," he states as he grabs his laptop and bag, standing from the booth.

Lena slides out of the booth, and I do the same. Brandon gives Lena a lingering look, and she takes a step in his direction, her hands intertwined behind her back as she twists back and forth in front of him.

Brandon clears his throat and tosses his bag over his shoulders. "So, would you like to grab a coffee again sometime? Or maybe dinner? Maybe have a conversation a little less . . . intense?"

Lena's cheeks flush, and she nods, a shy smile playing on her lips. "I'd like that very much."

Brandon brushes his hair out of his face and pushes the bridge of his glasses up. "Cool. I'll give you a call."

He steps aside Lena, and she turns to watch him go. I smile at the blush on my cousin's cheeks and the sparkle in her eyes. As much as reporters annoy me, I can tell she really likes him. She doesn't make a move until he's at the door and well out of here. When she finally does move, I pull out a fifty and place it on the table before following her. The waitress who served us gives me a wave on the way out.

Lena opens the doors to the car and get inside. I search the area and to my surprise, there's not one camera in sight. I slide inside and Lena pulls off, a small smile playing on her lips.

"You really like him, huh?" I ask, unable to suppress my curiosity.

She glances away from the road for a second, her smile widening. "Maybe. He's different. Smart. And the complete opposite of Taylor. I feel like I won't just be Solaris James' cousin with him. I feel like he'll actually see me."

I smile at the way she describes him. I wouldn't go that far, but I can see why she finds the reporter appealing.

"I guess Brandon Black is cute. If you're into the whole superman look-alike thing."

"Right?" Lena shrieks. "I'm not the only one who thinks that."

"Definitely with those glasses," I assure her, but then my tone turns serious. "Well, let's hope he listens to us and actually gets this story out there."

Lena nods, her expression mirroring my determination. "He will. I know he will. You just have to have faith."

I give her a weak smile.

My faith vanished a long time ago.

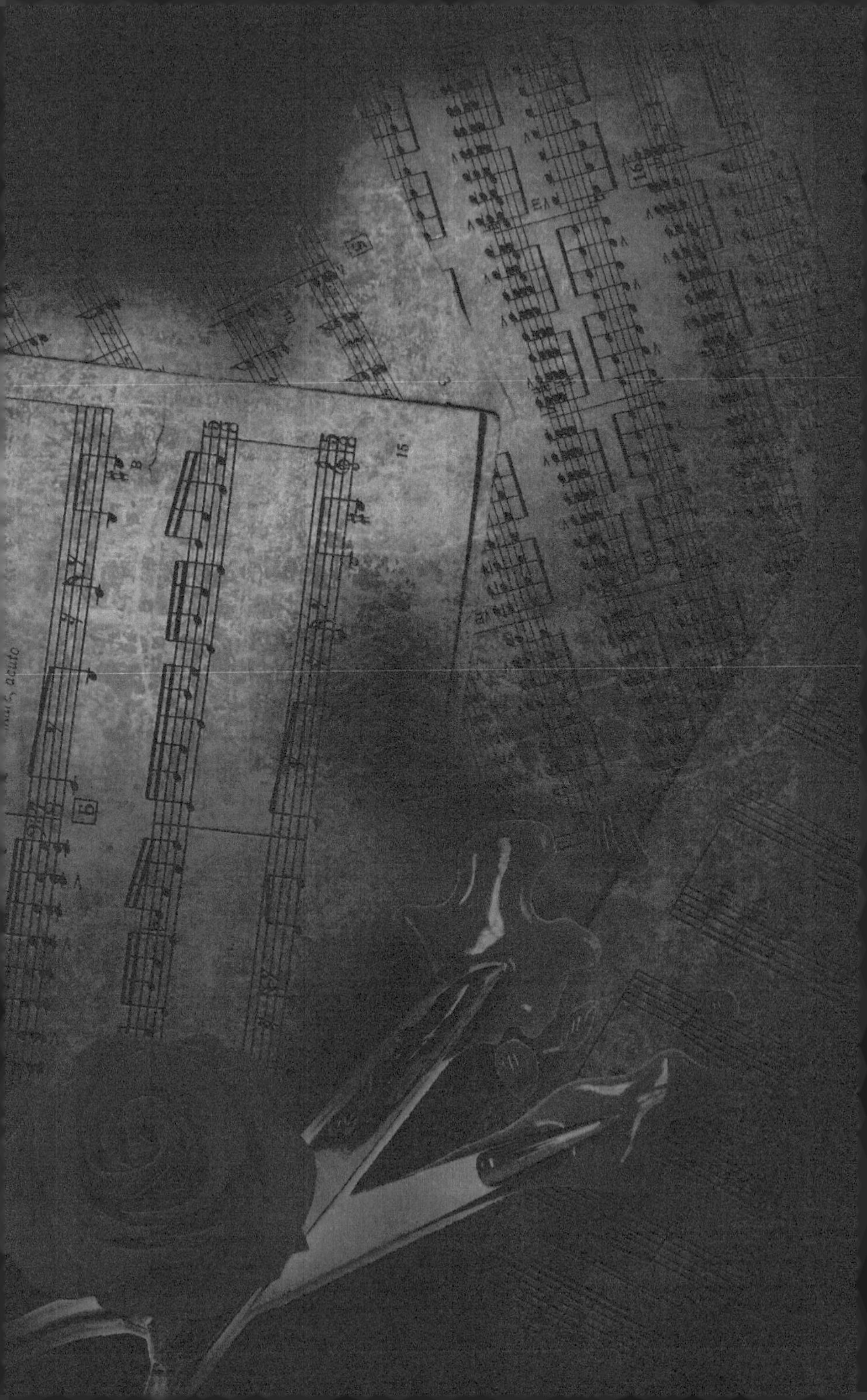

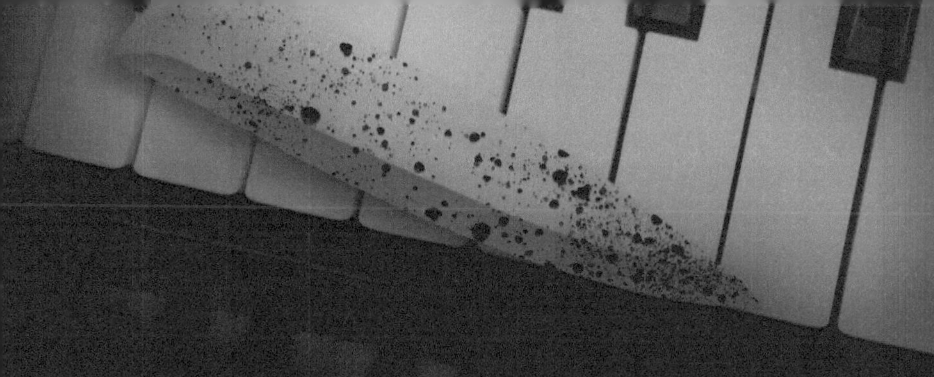

Twenty-Five

Silas

Six years ago

Blaring music sounds from inside Solaris' room, and I smile at the song she's playing. My song. Our song. I input the code to her door and slowly pushes it open. She spins around her room, belting out the lyrics, and it takes everything in me not to burst into laughter. She truly sucks when it comes to singing.

I close the door as quietly as I can and lean back against it. She continues to twirl around the floor, a pink dress in her hand and completely oblivious to my entrance. My grin falls at that fact. She needs to be more aware of her surroundings. I could be anyone entering her room and she's too focused on dancing with a dress. I'm going to have to talk to her about that later, but for right now, I simply cross my arms and wait for her to notice me.

After five minutes of waiting and listening to my voice on repeat without her even cracking an eye my way, I clear my throat. She doesn't hear me. I sneak over to her closet where she disappeared a moment ago and peek inside. Sol is flipping through rows of dresses, and my impatience gets the best of me. I step into her closet, and she turns, a scream leaving her as she steps over the hem of one of her dresses and fall backwards with a thud. I race over to her and bend down. I do nothing to hide the grin playing at my lips. Serves her right for her negligence. She should always be aware of her surroundings, especially with a brother like Cruise.

"What the hell Silas?" she yells at me. "You scared me!"

I hold out a hand for her to take and she does. "How did you not hear your room door beep when I entered?"

"Uh, I was dancing?" she says it more like a question as I haul her to her feet. "What are you doing here? It's late."

"Yeah, I know," I tell her and pull her out of her closet. "I just wanted to give you your Christmas present before I leave. What's with all the dancing with dresses?"

"There's going to be a New Year's ball at Mountain Rose Academy, and someone asked me to go," she states like it's nothing.

My stomach, on the other hand, knots at her words. I know it shouldn't, but . . . I can't really picture her going on a date with some pimply face kid. Actually, I can picture it. I just don't want to.

"Like a date?" I ask her.

She nods and a grin spread across her face, her cheeks pinkening. "Yeah. Um, Cruise introduced me to him the other day. He's a senior, which means I can go since he invited me."

"Cruise introduced you to this guy?" I question her, confused since I told her not to trust her brother.

"Don't get mad." She goes over to her bed and sits down. "It's not like I like him or anything. I just thought it'd be fun. Not a lot of junior high students get asked out by seniors. And Lena's going."

I follow her over to her bed and sit as well. Exhaling, I turn to her, "If you don't like him, you don't need to go with him."

Her eyes drop, and I can clearly see the sadness fluttering across her face. "But I can't go with the guy I like."

"Why?" I ask her.

Her face lifts and her eyes meet mine. I know before she even says anything that the guy she likes is unavailable. Off limits. Hell, he's not even in high school. I know all too well how wrong liking the guy she likes is, yet I still want her answer.

"Because he's not in high school and doesn't like me like that. And I want someone to like me like that."

"You're twelve. You don't even know what that means," I tell her trying to downplay her words. "When you're older, then you can date."

Solaris scoots closer to me on the bed. "I don't want to wait until I'm older. I want him to want me now."

I move off her bed and gulp, running a hand through my hair. This conversation needs to end. Now. She shouldn't be telling me any of this. I don't need to hear it. Turning back to her, I pull out the small box from my pocket, and thrust it at her. Solaris looks from me to the box and back to me before she takes it from my hold.

"What is this?" she asks, opening the box.

"Your Christmas gift," I tell her. "I want you to have it now before I leave."

She closes the box without glimpsing the contents inside. "Aren't you going to be back before Christmas?"

I nod. "Yeah, but Lena told me how you all open gifts on Christmas Eve and since I won't be back until late that night, I want you to have it now."

"What is it?" she asks, staring at the box.

"Open it and see," I urge her.

She shakes her head and hands it back to me. "No. Give it to me on Christmas Day. That way you have to be back in time."

"Sol, take the gift," I demand.

She shakes her head again and stands up on her bed, bringing her closer to my height. She places her hands on my shoulders to steady herself and sighs.

"You keep that one," she tells me. "I want something else tonight.

My eyes flicker across her face as I try to get a reading on her. For some reason, she's being awfully forward tonight. "And what do you want?"

Her eyes sparkle and her fingers dig into my shoulders, an attempt to keep me in place. Before I realize what she's doing, her lips are on mine and I taste her strawberry lip gloss. I shove her back, not thinking, and she loses her balance, falling over the footboard of her bed. She cries out, a thud reverberating around the room, and I race around to her.

"Sol!" I bend down to see tears trailing down her cheeks. "Are you okay?"

"Why don't you like me like that?" she asks as her fingers tap absent mindedly against her knee. "I thought—"

"You thought wrong, Sol," I tell her, voice softening so as not to offend her. "You're twelve years old. I'm a grown man. We can never be what you want."

More tears stream down her cheeks, and I hate that I'm telling her this. I hate that I'm breaking her heart. But then she starts shaking her head and swatting away her tears.

"No," she states and gets to her feet, hands on her waist. If she wasn't trying to look so intimidating, I would laugh at just how cute she is. "You're lying! I'm not blind, Silas. And just because I'm twelve doesn't mean I don't know things. I know a ton of things. A ton of things that you would like."

"Really?" I ask her, looking up at her from my perched position on her floor. "And those are things that no twelve-year-old should even be concerned with."

"You don't get to decide that. You're not my dad!"

I get to my feet at that. "Damn straight I'm not your dad! I actually give a fuck about you. I don't leave you here in a mansion with God knows who coming and going."

Her eyes widen at my tone, and it's a tone I've never taken with her before. But I don't know any other way to get her to change the subject. I can't have this conversation with her. I can't let her see that maybe, just maybe she's right, and I do have feelings for a twelve-year-old that I shouldn't have. None of that means I'm going to act on it, but she doesn't need to know my feelings. She doesn't need to even suspect or think there might be a chance with me. There isn't. I won't be another man that comes into her life just to abuse and use her. I won't turn into my father.

I hand her the gift again, but she shakes her head. "You should go."

My brows furrow at that. "Come on, Sol. Don't be like that."

More tears slide down her face and her eyes drop to the floor. Her fingers continues tapping against the side of her leg as she backs away from me, and I can't help the forward momentum of my own feet. I'm not leaving this room with her crying. I take hold of her cheek in my hand, and she yanks her face away. I grab her chin with a strong hold and tilt her face up to mine.

"You know I care about you. I'd do anything for you, Sol, but I can't be the person you want me to be," I tell her trying to convey just how much she does mean to me.

"Why?" her voice is shaky. "My dad is way older than my mom, and they work just fine. Besides, other older guys like me. Like Cruise's friend."

My fingers tighten on her chin at the mention of her brother and this so called friend. I know exactly what that friend likes, and it'll be a cold day in hell before I let him near her.

"And it's wrong. You're not going on a date with Cruise's friend. I forbid it."

Solaris jerks her chin out of my hold. "You can't forbid me from doing anything."

"If you go on a date with another boy, I won't come back."

Her eyes widen at my declaration. And while I know it's wrong for me to use her feelings for me against her, I don't care. If it will get her to stay away from anyone Cruise introduces to her, I will do what I must.

"But—"

"No buts," I interrupt her. "It's that boy or me. Choose now."

Her eyes narrow on me and she crosses her arms. "I hate you."

"No, you don't," I counter. "You love me. Now tell me what I want to hear."

Tears well in her eyes again and I ignore them. "I won't go out with him."

"And?"

"I won't go out with anyone Cruise introduces me to."

I pull her to me by the back of her neck, my fingers toying with the curls at her nape and kiss her forehead. "Good girl."

Her breath catches and I let her go, backing away from her and towards the door. If Cruise is introducing her to guys now, I can't hold off any longer. Gregory needs to know what's going on right underneath his nose. This can't happen anymore. With my tour starting after New Year's, I need to know she's going to be safe. I need to know that if I leave, she won't be hurt. I wouldn't be able to live with myself if I left and something worse happened to her.

"I have to go," I tell her. "You sure you don't want your Christmas gift?"

She shakes her head. "Bring it back to me on Christmas."

I nod and head out her door and down the flight of stairs that lead to her wing of the house. Without much thought, I tread to her father's wing. He and her mom are home tonight, but I know Gregory will probably be in his office. That seems to be where he's always at when he's not away on business.

I come to a stop at Gregory's door, the sound of him talking to someone stopping me from knocking.

"Can you draft it as soon as possible?" Gregory asks to whomever.

There's not a response, so I assume he's on the phone.

"They will get over it. I have every right to change it. It's mine after all," Gregory states, his tone firm and in control. "Yes. I'll fly out first thing in the morning to sign it."

When there's no more talking, I inhale and tap on his door, my mouth becoming dry. Movement from inside has me second guessing myself. While I know it's time to confront Solaris' father about what's been happening, a part of me gets that this man must already know what's going on underneath his roof. It's his home after all and his kids. He's the head of the family. And while he's told me some about the traditions in his family, he never once mentioned the type of abuse Cruise is inflicting on Solaris. Gregory has to put a stop to it. I need him to put a stop to it.

The door opens and Gregory steps into view dressed in sweats and a T-shirt. His normal clean-styled hair is in disarray, and he looks as if he hasn't slept in days. It's the first time I'm seeing the man not in a suit, looking immaculate. His brows furrow at the sight of me before he glances down the halls in either direction. Opening the door wider, he motions me inside.

"What are you doing here so late?" he asks, walking back over to his desk and taking a seat.

I go over to him and take a seat in one of the brown leather chairs facing his desk. "I came to give Solaris her Christmas gift before I leave in the morning."

"Right. You have a performance in New York," he remembers and turns around, taking a crystal canister filled with brown liquid from the buffet bar behind his desk. He pours himself a glass. "You want a glass? You must need it if you're coming to talk to me at midnight."

I nod. A little liquid courage won't hurt. Besides, he's right. We probably both need alcohol for this conversation.

"So, what is it?" Gregory finally questions after taking a gulp of his drink.

I take a sip and set it down. "Sir, it's about Solaris."

"I figured."

"I—"

"Are in love with my child," he states.

My eyes widen at his statement and then I'm shaking my head. "No!"

"No?"

"I mean, don't get me wrong, she's important to me. The most important person since my mom, but she's a kid. I wouldn't . . ."

He's nodding the entire time I'm trying to explain. "I know, Silas. I don't think you're that type of man, but that doesn't change the fact that I have eyes and so does my staff. We all clearly see that you more than care about Solaris."

"I . . . don't know what to say."

He throws back the contents of his glass and pours himself another. "Sometimes, there's nothing to be said. Sometimes, the heart wants what it wants and all you can do is wait."

I cringe at what he's saying. In no way, shape, or form should a father be telling a grown man to wait for his daughter. I would kill any man that even came near my child with the intent of something more. Yet, he's sitting here, drinking, and giving me the fucking green light. If that's his answer to what he thinks I feel for Solaris, then he's not going to take the situation with Cruise seriously.

"This involves Cruise as well. Not just Solaris," I state and Gregory's whole posture stiffens.

"I'm going to stop you there," he says and crosses his arms. "I know already."

"And you're doing nothing?" My voice rises a bit. Exhaling, I try to calm my temper. "Let me get this right. You're letting Cruise prostitute your twelve-year-old daughter, and you're doing nothing?"

Gregory sighs, his head falling into his open hands. "Cruise is very much a product of his environment. He's doing what my father taught him to do . . . what's expected of the heirs. We're meant to train them to be the perfect wife. It's a little complicated with Solaris. But it's part of the tradition."

Shaking my head, I rise from the chair. "The tradition where the male heirs in this family claim the female heirs. Where you breed them to . . . to do what? Keep up this image?"

Gregory points to the chair. "Sit down, Silas, and we will discuss this like men."

I chuckle. "Men? Men don't let their daughters get raped over and over and over. And here I thought you were the decent one in this family."

Gregory hands slam down on the desk. "I am! You don't think this eats me up inside? Why do you think I'm gone so often? I can't watch it!"

"Does her mother know? Is that why she's never here too?" I question.

"No. Elizabeth has no clue. That's why Cruise is doing this part the way he is. She would kill us all if she found out," Gregory says. "I've talked to Cruise about this. He told me her training would go in a different direction. That he would stop the . . . he said he found a guy for her that will make this more enjoyable for her. That there will be no more need for drugs."

I sit back down and down the remaining contents of my own glass. "The fact that you can sit here and say this shit is fucked up. She's your daughter."

"And he's my son. What do you expect?"

"I expect you to do what's right."

He shakes his head. "I wish I could. But as I told you before, Cruise has already claimed her. Solaris' faith is in his hands."

I stare at the man in front of me with wide eyes. "No. You have to do something!"

"I never said I wasn't doing anything!" Gregory shouts back at me. "Cruise can't touch her himself until she's eighteen. He can train her through whatever means he feels will accomplish what he needs from her, but he cannot physically claim her until then."

"Yeah, cause that makes it all the better." I lean across the desk, scowling at the man. "Either you do something about Cruise, or I will bring this family down. I will get whatever authorities I need involved."

"You will do no such thing, Silas." Gregory gets up from his desk and moves around front of it. He leans against it, legs crossed and staring at me. "And yet you say you're not in love with my daughter?"

"This has nothing to do with my feelings for Solaris!" I stand, meeting him eye to eye. "It's wrong."

He nods. "I agree, but if you go to the authorities, things will get much, much worse for her. I told you there were four families involved in this. If the James family go down, Solaris, Lena, Elizabeth, and Loretta will be shuffled to our successor. And from what I hear, the Bancrofts are much worse to their women than Cruise."

My eyes widen at that name. "The Bancrofts? As in the head of my record label, Bancroft?

"Yes."

"Shit."

"Exactly, which is why I just changed my will. As I told you, I can't watch this. And the only way I can think to stop it is if I'm no longer in the picture. I know my sister, and if something happens to me, she'll be the first to get rid of Elizabeth and Solaris. And Cruise, he's not going to follow."

I stare at him for a long moment. I must have heard him wrong. There's no way he could mean what I think he means. He wouldn't . . . I shake my head. There's plenty of reasons people change wills.

"What do you mean by 'no longer in the picture'?" I ask, not liking where this is headed. Sure, I want him to do something about this mess, but I don't want him to . . . Solaris would be heartbroken. She thinks the world of this man. A man that is allowing her to be assaulted over and over and over.

Gregory swats my question away. "Don't worry about that. I just need you to promise me something."

"What?"

"When she turns eighteen, find her and keep her away from Cruise and Loretta," he tells me.

I cross my arms. "Why?"

"Things are going to change. And you are the only one I trust not to harm her. Will you do that for me, Silas?"

My eyes flicker across his face, and I nod. I would do it even if he hadn't asked. There's no way Cruise is setting another finger on Sol. If I have to kill him with my bare hands to keep him from her, I will.

"Oh and Silas?"

"Yeah?"

"The only rule against a claiming is that the claimed not be with child. And since you're not in love with my daughter, you're the right person to know that."

"You're saying—"

"I'm not saying anything," Gregory cuts in, moving back around to his side of the desk. "I'm just telling you to love my daughter the way she deserves. Treat her like the ray of sun she is."

My mouth goes dry, but I nod. This is not how I thought this conversation was going to go. If anything, I saw this going horribly, horribly wrong for me. But this . . . I shake my head and stare at Gregory James.

"Please leave now. I have work to do." He points to the door behind me as he picks up his phone. "And don't mention this conversation to anyone."

I turn around and head out of the office, a little worried by what this man just revealed. He isn't really planning on offing himself, is he? I mean, he's Gregory James. He's the head of the richest family in the south. He could stop all of this without doing that, couldn't he?

Sighing, I run my fingers through my hair and head down the stairs towards the foyer. As long as whatever he has planned keeps Cruise and his 'friends' away from Solaris, I really don't care if the man offs himself.

Twenty-Six

T he chill of November nips at my skin as I step out of the Bentley and walk towards the grand entrance of Mountain Rose Academy. Today's the day. I got a text from Lena in the middle of the night saying that Brandon told her the article would go live this morning. It hadn't by the time I dressed and made it here, but I know it's coming.

Walking inside the school, I try to focus on the day ahead, pushing aside the lingering worry of Brandon Black's article. While the exposure might feel like a ticking time bomb, I still have school, and I still need to be present if I expect to graduate in the spring.

I go to my locker and pull out the books I'll need for my morning classes. I close it only to see Samantha standing with a smirk on her face, a piece of paper in her hand.

"Here you go," she tells me, still hanging on to the paper.

I reach for it and she reluctantly lets it go. I look over it with furrowed brows, a bit confused as to why she's handing me a check. "What's this for?"

She rolls her eyes but grins. "You won."

"Won?" I ask for clarification. "Won what?"

"The bet, silly. Remember, we all had a bet to see who would sleep with Silas O'Conner first."

I shake my head and hand the check back. "I didn't buy in to that bet."

She shrugs. "Yeah, well, we all knew you slept with him. It wouldn't really be fair for us to keep it."

"Okay then." I stuff the check in my blazer pocket.

"So . . ." Sam links her arms through mine. "What's it like dating Silas O'Conner?"

"I'm surprised you're just now asking," I mumble and let her walk me to our first class.

"Well, no one was really for certain you two were together, since you know . . . you're like cousins."

"Brandon Black published a picture of us kissing," I point out. "At my mother's funeral."

She waves away my comment as we enter homeroom. "That could have been like a familial thing. Anyways, are you coming to the festival tonight? Black Roses are performing, and I figured since your man is taking the stage, you would."

"Yeah," I tell her and take my normal seat in the center of the class. "I've already missed homecoming. I'm not missing the opening night of festival too. Besides, who else is going to support Lena in becoming Miss Mountain Rose?"

"You are aware that she could lose, right?" I roll my eyes at Samantha's ridiculous statement just as the bell rings, signaling the start of the day.

Classes proceed as usual. All my morning classes pass without the article dropping. A part of me is worried that Brandon changed his mind about helping us. That is until the last period. I sit in my physics class, attempting to concentrate on the lecture. My mind, however, keeps wandering back to the potential fallout from the article. I'm barely listening when, suddenly, a flurry of whispers spreads through the room like wildfire. Phones buzz and vibrate, the hum of urgent notifications filling the air. I pull my phone from my bag and click on the notification. My eyes widen and I quickly glance around the class just as everyone's eyes shoot up to meet mine. I fumble with my phone to actually read the article. Nowhere in it is my name mentioned, but Cruise's picture is plastered front and center.

More of my classmates glance from their phones to me. The room is a chorus of murmurs and hushed conversations. My heart pounds as I fumble with my own phone, hands trembling. Dozens of notifications start flooding my screen, all referencing the same thing: Brandon Black's article and my brother.

A text from Silas pops up on my scene.

Silas: Are you seeing this?

Another from an unknown number.

You're going to regret this.

I gulp at the clear threat.

"Is this true?" the guy from behind me questions, and I lift my head from the phone.

"Your brother runs a sex trafficking ring?" someone to my right asks.

"The senator buys little girls?" someone else yells.

I leap from my seat, heart pounding in my chest, and run from the room. I slam the door and lean against it, trying to calm the frantic pounding in my chest. At least no one is speculating that it's me.

Clicking heels catch my attention and I turn to see Lena rushing towards me, a bag slung over her shoulder and her blazer draped in her arms. She takes hold of my hand, pulling me down the hall.

"We need to go," she whispers urgently, her voice barely audible over the chattering being heard from inside all the classrooms.

I nod, my throat tight. We rush through the halls, my heart pounding louder with each step. As we step outside, I finally let out the breath I've been holding all day. People are talking.

The article is live. And Cruise and his "friends" aren't going to know what hit them. A grin stretches across my face as we make our way down the school steps.

The sleek, black Bentley is waiting at the curb, the driver already holding the door open for us. We slide into the back seat, and the car pulls away from the school, leaving behind a trail of whispers and speculation.

"This is good," Lena whispers. "People are talking. By this time tomorrow, every single last person Brandon named will be booted from their companies by the boards, and the FBI, Department of Justice, and whoever else are involved will be handling all of them. They're going down, Sol."

My grin falls and I turn to her. I didn't think all of those agencies would be getting involved in this. "Umm, do you really think they would care?"

"Of course!" she shouts then glances towards the front of the car, lowering her voice again. "This is big. And more than what they did to you. These are people of power abusing that power. Of course government agencies are going to step in. The senator paid Cruise," she lowers her voice even more until I'm barely able to hear her, "to rape you."

I shudder at that word. Not once since getting my memories back have I said that word out loud. I didn't want to, but that's exactly what Cruise did. He paid people to rape me.

The car pulls up to the gate and my window rolls down. I lean out and input the code. Slowly, the gates open to the property, and the car drives down the road and passes the stables to the manor. I reach for the door handle, but Lena grabs my hand to stop me.

Lena looks past me at the house, her eyes filled with worry. "Do you want me to stay with you? Just in case."

I shake my head, trying to keep my voice steady. "No, Lena. I can't risk you getting hurt if Cruise is here. I'll be fine."

Lena's face tightens with concern, but she doesn't argue. "Alright but promise you'll call if you need anything. Anything at all."

"I promise," I say, giving her a weak smile. "I'll be okay."

I step out of the car and watch as it continues driving down the path to Lena's house. I turn around and take in the imposing mansion. I make my way up the front steps, my mind racing and the pounding in my heart picking up once again. I half expect Cruise to be waiting for me, his face twisted in fury. The same rage I feel sometimes permeating off him in waves. But as I step inside, the house is eerily silent. No sign of him anywhere.

I let out a shaky breath, relief mingling with confusion. I head up to my room, the grandeur of the manor's décor doing very little to soothe me. Cruise could still be here. This is a massive mansion, and he does like to make an entrance. For all I know, my brother could be hiding in my room, waiting to ambush me. He could be anywhere in my wing of the house, just waiting for the opportune time to enact his revenge for me taking his little black book. Guess it's a good thing Lena still has it.

Opening the door, I search the room before stepping a foot inside. Everything's the way I left it this morning. Going inside, I shut the door and lean against it, letting out another breath. He's not here. I drop my bag at my desk and then go over to my closet. I change out of my school uniform.

I head back to my desk, sitting and spreading out my homework in front of me. Physics, usually a challenge, now feels like a welcome distraction. I dive into the chapter I didn't stay for, rereading over theories and problems, trying to lose myself in the equations and formulas. But my mind keeps wandering back to the article, to Cruise, to the unknown threats lurking in the shadows of my own home.

As the seconds turn into minutes and the minutes into hours, the tension slowly starts to ebb. My eyes grow heavy as I work through problem after problem, the numbers and diagrams blurring together until they're not even legible . I lay my head down for just a second.

A second is all I need.

When I wake, the room is dark, the only light coming from the dim glow of my crystal desk lamp. Across the room. On my desk. Where I'm sure I fell asleep. My body stiffens as I press down on the plush mattress and the down comforter beneath me. As I go to shift, I feel it—a presence beside me.

My heart stops, a cold dread washing over me. I turn my head slowly, my breath catching in my throat. Cruise is lying beside me in bed, his eyes open and fixed on mine. There's a cold, calculating look in them, a dangerous glint that sends a shiver down my spine.

"Hello, sister," he says, his voice low and menacing.

Panic grips me, and I go to scramble off the bed, but he reaches out, grabbing my wrist in a vise-like grip.

"Cruise, what are you doing here?" I ask, my voice trembling.

"Where is it?" he snarls and I flinch back.

"I don't have it," I tell him honestly.

He growls and the hand holding my wrist moves up to my throat. He squeezes and my hands shoot up to stop him.

"You think you can just ruin my life and get away with it?" he snarls. "You think you can expose me and walk away unscathed?How did you get Brandon Black to publish that article? How did you just so happen to leave yourself out of it? Hard to mention a victim without a victim."

Fear and panic swirl within me, but I know I have to stay calm, have to think clearly if I'm going to survive this. "Cruise, please," I plead, trying to keep my voice steady. "Let me go. We can talk about this."

"Talk?" he laughs, a harsh, bitter sound. "There's nothing to talk about. You've ruined everything, Solaris. Everything. The only thing you can do now is shut up and know your place."

His hand holding my throat squeezes tighter, his fingers pressing into my skin. His other hand clamps down over my nose, restricting my oxygen even more. I struggle, trying to pry his hands away, but he's too strong. The fear and panic threaten to overwhelm me, but I shove it aside. This is Cruise. He isn't really going to do anything to hurt me. At least not in away that means losing me.

"Let. Me. Go," I force out.

He leans closer to me, right next to my ear. "Silas isn't here to butt in now."

My eyes widen at the meaning behind his words. In the next second, his mouth is on mine, and I have no choice but to open or lose oxygen completely. I shove at him, but his weight is too much. I buck, but he still doesn't move. He chuckles at my attempts of defense, his lips finally leaving my skin.

"You have no idea how long I've waited for today. Did Silas finally explain our family to you?" he whispers and removes his hand from my nose to capture my hands in a single one of his. "You're so damn feisty. I can't wait to finally fuck you."

I suck in a large gulp of air. "I am not yours!"

"You are mine. Our father tried to change how our family has worked since before we settled here and made the U. S. home. But you can't change generations of traditions by merely killing yourself."

I freeze in his hold, his words sinking in. "Our father—"

"Killed himself trying to protect his little ray of sunshine."

I shake my head at him. No, my dad wouldn't do that. He wouldn't kill himself. "You're lying. He had a heart attack."

Cruise's mouth lowers to my neck. "Yeah. A heart attack caused by whatever drugs he used to try to save you. From me. From your destined fate."

I pull my arms trying to get free of him.

"You know what's funny, sister?" he asks me, eyes roaming my body like is the juiciest piece of meat. "Both of your parents are dead. One trying to save you. And the other as a warning for you to stay away."

My body stiffens in his hold at the thought of my mother. "Did you murder my mother?"

"Me?" He shakes his head. "Nah, I actually liked Elizabeth. She raised me like her own. But Aunt Loretta, on the other hand, would have had no problem paying her little hit man to send you a message. That sort of defeated my purpose."

I jerk against his hold. "And what exactly is your purpose? To rape me?"

His free hand runs over the swell of my breast and down my side. "Of course not, sister. This isn't rape."

"Then what do you call it?" I hiss at him.

"Doing our duty to our family. Producing the next heir. Making you obedient," he whispers in my ear at the same time his hand makes its way under my nightie.

"And that involved selling me?" I shout and his hand stills.

"Even with taking my book, you still are too ignorant to put it together. Everyone in that book is related somehow. They all belong to the four reigning families: the James, the Bancrofts, the Zhangs, and the Sokolovs. Since I was the James' bastard heir, I had trails to complete. But I didn't do them without keeping us all equal footing."

With his sudden distraction, I yank a hand free, not caring for a moment about his explanation, and grab the first thing my hand touches. A heavy crystal paperweight from my nightstand. I swing it with all my might. The base connects with Cruise's head with a sickening thump, and he lets go of me, rolling off the bed. I scramble away, gasping for breath, my hands shaking uncontrollably as he moans from the floor.

Finish it.

Finish it.

Finish it!

I stumble around the bed to where my brother sits on the floor, rubbing his head. Thick blood tints his blond hair and runs down the right side of his face. He glares up at me.

End this now!

Raising the paperweight, I aim to hit him again, but he holds up his hand.

"What are you going to do? Kill me like you did William?" he asks, and I flinch back at the question. "Yeah, that's right little sister. I know all about how you and your precious musician got rid of our step-uncle."

I tilt my head to the side and disregard his statement about William. He won't be here much longer to use that information against me or Silas. "What were you going to do? Fuck me against my will?"

He doesn't say a word, but his silence is answer enough for me. Red paints my vision and I swing again. Cruise grunts, but I pay him no mind. Just like he paid me no mind when he dragged me from the sitting room last week. I swing the crystal again and again and again, until I can no longer hear his pleading.

When Cruise finally stops moving and warm blood paints my fingers, I toss the paperweight aside. Blood seeps from the wound on his head. I stare at him, heaving out breaths. My eyes move to the blood coating my hands and I gulp back panic. What the heck did I just do?

I nudge his body with my foot, but he remains still.

He's dead. I've killed him.

The reality of it hits me like a freight train, and I feel my knees give way. I sink to the floor, my breath coming in ragged gasps. The luxurious surroundings of my room seem to close in on me, the opulence now feeling like a prison.

My eyes drift to the antique clock on the wall, its hands ticking away the seconds. My eyes drift back to the body, and I take a shaky breath, trying to steady myself. Finally, I stand.

What the hell do I do now?

Twenty-Seven

Solaris

A chill seeps through the thin fabric of my silk nightie as I stand in the center of my room, staring down at Cruise's lifeless body. Blood stains the carpet, dark and ominous, clear evidence of the life I have just taken. My breath comes in ragged gasps, my heart pounding wildly in my chest as I try to process what I have done. Yes, this was always the outcome I wanted. Yet a part of me figured Silas would handle Cruise when the time came. Just like he handled his father.

Silas isn't around though, and I couldn't let Cruise do what he wanted.

There was no choice but to handle him myself.

Now, he lies at my feet, blood still slowly seeping from his body. I run my hands through my hair, pulling at he strands. I don't know what to do. I don't have the contacts Silas' does. I step out of the blood coating my feet and race to my bathroom. Silas made me bathe the last time. I turn the water on, but then look back at the body. Bathing is pointless if the body is still there with no one cleaning this mess up. I really should have thought this through.

My mind races, searching for a solution, a way out of this nightmare. And then it hits me – Silas. Silas had cleaned up our last victim, had taken care of everything. He would know what to do. Racing over to my desk, I grab my bag and take out my phone. I dial Silas' number and it rings and rings and rings.

Where is he?

He's always gone when I need him.

Biting down on my lip, I make my mind up. I go to the bathroom, bathe, and change into something a little less bloody, before hurrying out of my room. No one knows the code for my door besides Silas and me. Cruise knew but he's no longer a problem.

My bare feet are silent against the cold, hardwood floors of the manor. The house is eerily quiet, the silence only amplifying the frantic beat of my heart. I make my way to the foyer and out the door. Each step on the cobblestone feels like an eternity, the distance between us a yawning chasm that I am desperate to cross.

As I near Silas' pool house, I let out a deep breath. There's a light on, which means he's here. Silas is probably just sleep.

That's the only reason he wouldn't answer my phone call. I slowly make my way through the house, turning off the light in the kitchen as I do, and head to his room. Muffled sound reaches my ears, and my body tenses. A low, rhythmic creaking grows louder with each step closer to Silas' bedroom door. My hand trembles as I reach for the door, pushing it open slowly. The sight that greets me is one that will be forever etched in my brain.

Loretta is on top of Silas, her movements slow and deliberate, her back arched in a way that makes my stomach churn. Silas' eyes are closed, his face a mask of reluctant submission. For a moment, the world around me fades, my vision narrowing to the obscene display before me.

Then, she moans.

The panic that had consumed me mere moments ago is replaced by a cold, burning rage. I slam the door shut, the echo vibrating off the walls like a song. Silas jerks up, eyes opening, and head jerking my way. His eyes widen and he shoves at Loretta, as if that can make me unwitness this. When she doesn't immediately fall off his cock, he yells at her.

"Loretta!" Silas exclaims and shoves her once more. "Get off me."

He shoves her to the floor, his movements abrupt and filled with disgust. Loretta lands in a heap, her eyes narrowing as she turns to glare at me. A slow, cruel smile spreads across her face, and she lets out a low, mocking laugh.

"Lookie here," she purrs, rising to her feet with a feline grace. "Looks like your little girlfriend wants to join in on the fun."

"Leave," Silas demands like he wasn't just allowing her to ride him with pleasure splayed all across his face.

Loretta walks over to where I stand and glances at me. "He really is quite good in bed."

I don't respond. Words feel inadequate, meaningless in the face of such betrayal. My eyes are locked on Silas, his expression one of shock and guilt. He opens his mouth to speak, to explain, but I cut him off with a look, my anger silencing him more effectively than any words could.

"Solaris, it's not what you think," he begins, his voice pleading, desperate as he climbs out of his bed. "She . . . she forced me. I didn't want this."

Loretta laughs again, a cold, harsh sound that cuts through the tension in the room. "Forced you?" she scoffs, adjusting her robe. "Oh, Silas, don't be so dramatic. You know you enjoyed every moment of it."

"Get out," I say, my voice low and deadly. "Now."

Loretta shrugs, a smirk playing on her lips as she saunters past me. "Careful, dear niece," she whispers, her breath hot against my ear. "Jealousy is such an unbecoming trait."

Her words ignite a fire within me, the rage I had been struggling to contain now boiling over. As Loretta leaves the room, her laughter echoing down the hall, I turn to Silas, my vision tinged with red.

"Solaris, please," he says, stepping towards me. "Let me explain."

But I am beyond listening. The betrayal is too deep, too raw. I move towards him, my hands shaking with the intensity of my emotions. Without thinking, I grab the first object my hand touches—a lamp—and throw it at him. He ducks, and I just continue grabbing whatever my hands land on and throwing it at him.

"Solaris, stop!" he shouts, racing towards me and trying to grab my arm, but I wrench it free.

"How could you?" I scream, my voice hoarse with emotion. "You . . . you let her . . . How could you?"

"I didn't let her," he pleads, his voice breaking. "I had no choice. She . . . she threatened you. She said she'd give you to Cruise if I didn't do what she wanted."

His words barely register. The pain and anger are too overwhelming. I don't care if she did threaten me, Silas still could have said no. He still could have fought for us instead of laying down and fucking that woman. I lunge at him, my hands finding purchase on his shirt, pulling him close. The room around us is a blur.

"Make it right," I whisper, my voice trembling. "Make it right, Silas."

In a twisted, desperate attempt to reclaim some semblance of control, I press my lips to his, the kiss fierce and demanding. Silas responds, his hands gripping my shoulders, his body tense with a mixture of guilt and need. The kiss deepens, fueled by the intensity of our emotions, a violent clash of anger and desperation.

I moan into his mouth, and a low rumble rolls through Silas. He grabs the underside of my thighs and haul me up his body. My legs wrap around him instinctively as he moves us back to the bed he was just fucking my aunt in. I shake my head. There's no way I'm getting in that bed. Silas' breaks the kiss and furrow his brows at me. I point behind him to the mirrored dresser.

He captures my lips again as he changes direction. Silas sets me roughly on the dresser, my back slamming against the glass. He breaks the kiss, looking me over with concern painting his features.

"You sure you want to be doing this?" he asks me.

I nod once and that is all it takes for him to grip my shirt, tearing it down the center, leaving me completely bare before him.

We move together, a tangled mess of limbs and emotions, the destruction around us forgotten in the heat of the moment. The anger, the pain, the betrayal – it all converges into a single, primal act. But even as our bodies come together, the rage within me remains, an unquenchable fire that no amount of physical release can extinguish.

Silas pounds into me over and over and over again, my back slamming into the glass. On his final thrust, it shatters around me, the shards of glass nicking my soft flesh like needles. Leaning back against the ruined mirror, our breaths come out in ragged gasps. I can feel the anger still simmering beneath the surface, the betrayal a constant, gnawing presence. Silas reaches out, his fingers brushing against my skin, but I pull away, the touch too painful to bear. I don't want his soft touches.

"Sol, please," Silas whispers as he pulls out of me. "You know I didn't mean to hurt you."

I shake my head at him, doing everything in my power to hold back my tears. He doesn't get them after this.

"I've asked you so many times about Loretta. Each time, you dodged the question. And now you want me to believe she forced you?" I shake my head again. "Make it make sense."

Silas doesn't say anything to that. I doubt he could even if he wanted to. My eyes move away from him and land on a piece of glass on the dresser top. I grab hold of it and turn it around in my hand. Silas' eyes widen in alarm, but he doesn't move, doesn't try to stop me. He knows better. With a steady hand, I press the glass to his chest, and begin carving my name into his flesh with deliberate precision. The blood wells up, dark and red.

Silas winces, his eyes closing as I finish the last letter. The sight of my name, etched into his chest, brings a twisted sense of satisfaction. But it is fleeting, the anger still burning within me, insatiable and relentless.

I drop the glass, my hands slick with his blood, and stand. The room is a disaster. Silas looks up at me, his eyes filled with a mixture of pain and regret, but I can't find it in myself to care.

"Did this," he gestures to his chest, "make you feel better?"

My eyes narrow on him. "No."

Silas nods, his gaze dropping to the floor. "I really am sorry, Sol. You were never meant to find out that she was doing that."

I scoff at his apology. It means nothing now. The bond we once shared is shattered, the trust irreparably broken. I go over to his closet and pull out one of his T-shirts, dragging it over my head. I turn to leave the room but stop when I remember the reason I came here in the first place.

"I need you to call your cleanup crew or whoever you called before." I don't look at him at all.

"What did you do?" he asks, coming up behind me and dropping his hands to my shoulders. "Tell me you didn't do something stupid."

I stiffen in front of him. "Cruise attacked me. And you were too busy fucking Loretta to care about anything."

Silas turns me around, his hands moving to cup my face. "Don't you dare say I don't care about you. I would slay a thousand of your family members if that made you happy."

I knock his hands away from my face. "Just clean the mess up."

I don't wait for him to say anything else. Instead, I leave his room and walk back to the mansion, rage still bubbling just below the surface.

The house is silent as I make my way back to my room. Cruise's body still on the floor. But there is no time to dwell on it now. There are bigger battles to fight, greater wrongs to right.

As I stand in the doorway, looking down at my brother's lifeless form, I feel a strange sense of clarity. The path ahead is dark and treacherous, but it is mine to walk. And I will do whatever it takes to ensure that those who have wronged me pay for their sins.

With a deep breath, I close the door behind me, and go sit next to my brother. The tears I was holding back finally fall, and this time, I don't hold them back. I love him. Loved. And I can't believe he would do this to me. That goes to show, I can't trust anyone. I should have known not to let him in. After all, Silas is the one who said we could never be.

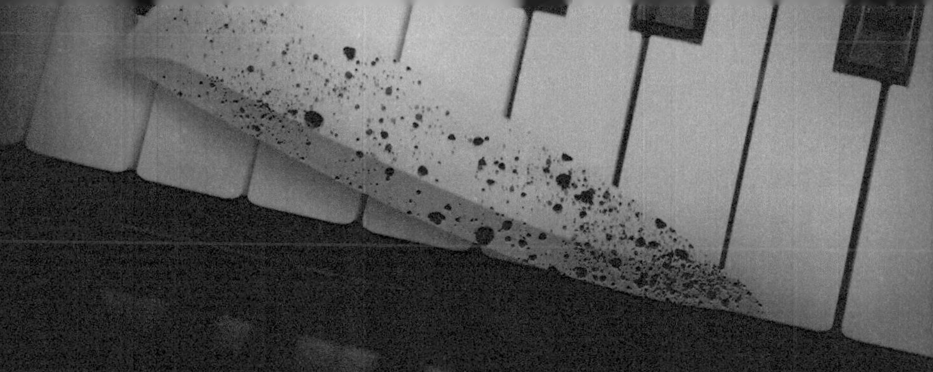

Twenty-Eight

Silas

Six years ago

I shove open the door to the pool house with a yawn and make my way to my room. Opening the door, my eyes immediately go to the clock on the wall, the ticking the only sound besides the shuffling of my feet and the wheel of my suitcase. It's 11:37 p.m. on Christmas Eve. At least I made it back intime to be home for Christmas like I promised Solaris.

Stomping over to the closet, I throw my suitcase inside without even unpacking it. It felt like today was never going to end. First, we had an interview. Then, the band had to be outfitted for the photo that's to be our first album cover. And finally, we opened for the main performance at the Rockefeller

Center, which is unheard of for a band with no album out yet. I could have chosen to stay in New York with the rest of my band, but I needed to get home. Besides, ever since our breakout single hit number one on the Billboard, my band-mates haven't known how to act. They've been partying more than normal. And fucking more than normal.

It's all been overwhelming. Still, it beats being here all the time and being Loretta's little fuck toy. A chill runs up my spine at the thought of that conniving woman. I'm sure she'll be coming for me as soon as she realizes I'm back home, but until then, I need some sleep.

Pulling my shirt off, I drop it on the floor and go over to my bed. I flop down and immediately drown my head under the pillow. My eyes droop closed as I let out yet another yawn.

Bang.

Bang.

Bang.

I jerk up in my bed and search the dark room.

Bang.

Bang.

Bang.

"Silas! Open up!" Shouting from outside my room has me clambering out of bed.

I glance at the clock again to find that I managed to get a few hours of sleep. Going over to the door, I open it, my heart stopping at the sight of a red faced Solaris standing there with tears running down her face in nothing but a tank top and underwear. Her hair is a frizzy mess, and her eyes are swollen from crying. She pushes past me and I close the door, turning on a light as I do.

Solaris sniffles as she paces back and forth across my room. I stand back and observe her, but the tears don't stop and neither does her pacing. When she finally looks at me, I go over to her and wrap my arms around her, pulling her to me. Her sobbing turns into wails as she burrows her face against my chest.

"He's gone," she cries and I try to rack my head for what she could be talking about.

Smoothing down her hair, I ask, "What do you mean? Who's gone?"

She pulls back enough to look up at me. The sight of her trembling lips and tear drenched lashes cause an ache in my chest, my arms tightening around her. Her throat bobs and she shakes her head at me.

"Come on, Sol. Talk to me," I urge her, picking her up and carrying her to my bed.

Her legs wrap around me, and she buries her face in my neck. She mumbles something but I can't make it out. Instead, I just rub her back and try my best to soothe her.

"I'm sure whatever is going on can be fixed. Just talk to me," I tell her.

She leans back, her eyes meeting mine for the first time since I opened the door. "My dad," she states, and I feel the shiver that runs through her body. "He's dead. Mom just found him."

"What?" I exclaim, my eyes searching her face for any deception. There isn't none. "No. Gregory was in perfect health when I left for my show."

My mind immediately goes back to the last conversation I had with him. He didn't . . . surely, he wouldn't actually kill himself.

"Mom said it looks like a heart attack. The ambulance is there right now."

I pull her close, closing my eyes and inhaling. "It's going to be okay. I promise."

Her body continues to shake against mine as I hold her. I can't believe this. I literally talked to him five days ago. If I honestly thought that was going to be his solution to this mess of a family, I would have at least mentioned my concerns to Loretta. I might not like the woman, but she would have made sure Gregory didn't do something this stupid.

"Silas?" Sol pulls away from my chest and looks up at me again. "Mom called Aunt Loretta over and she was angry."

"What did Loretta do?" I ask.

Solaris shrugs. "I don't know. I ran here. But they were arguing."

More knocking sounds at my door, and both Solaris and I stiffen. I shush her and she wipes at her tears. My eyes stay trained on the door as another knock comes. Harder this time. The only people that ever come to my room is Sol and Loretta.

And since Sol is already here and she said Loretta is with her mom, I have no clue who could be at my door.

"Son, I know she's in there," my father's voice booms throughout the room. "Let us in."

"Hide," I mouth to Solaris, and she scurries off my lap as quietly as possible. She crawls under my bed, and I wait until she's situated before going over to the door and opening it. My father stands in a suit and frowns at me. Who wears a suit at one in the morning? But that's not what has my attention. Behind my father are two other men. They are both at least a head taller than my father. The men push past my father and come into my room. They immediately go over to my closet, and I jerk around to my dad.

"What is the meaning of this?" I scowl at him. "Why are they going through my closet?"

My father sighs heavily, his foot tapping and his posture rigid. When he doesn't answer me, I stomp over to where one of the men is combing through the rows of my closet. I grab his shoulder and pull him to a stop. He shoves me and my back slams into the door. My nostrils flare and my hands clench at my side. I turn to my father once more.

"Why the hell are they going through my stuff? I just go there a few hours ago," I yell at him.

"We saw her come in here on the security cameras," the other guy states. "We just want the girl."

I shake my head. No way in hell are they taking her. "For what?"

"That's need to know information," the one behind me states.

"Need to know information?" I turn to him, looking him up and down. "And who might you be?"

"James' manor security. Now hand over the girl."

"Get out of my fucking room," I hiss at him.

"Silas, do as you're told," my father's voice deepens.

I step back, splaying my arms wide. "As you can see, she's not here. Continue your search somewhere else."

The two guards glance at each other before they head out my door. They stop behind my father who's frowning at me, but I don't care. My eyes remain on the security guards. I can still see them searching my room from their position at my father's side, but they're not going to find Solaris. My bed is too low for them to even suspect.

But then, one of the men's eyes stops on the bed. I turn-around to see what he could be looking at, but nothing under my bed can be seen. I give my full attention again and arch a brow at him. He motions for the other guard to go check out my bed, and I grab his arm to stop him.

"There's nothing there," I tell him.

"If that's the case, you wouldn't mind me searching." He pushes past me, bumping his shoulder into my chest.

My fists clench and I go to follow him, but my father grabs my forearm. "You can't stop this."

I jerk away from my father at the same time a piercing scream echoes off the walls of my room. I turn to see the guard dragging Solaris from underneath my bed, her fingers clawing at the rug to get away. She attempts to pull away from him, but his hold looks firm. I charge at the man, shoving him off her. He catches himself on my desk and glares at me.

"Touch her again, and you'll be losing that hand." My voice comes out a growl.

Solaris gets up from the floor and wraps her arms around me, the tears back again. I drape my arm over her shoulder, making sure to keep a good distance between us and the rest of them.

"Someone needs to tell me why you're in my room, trying to drag my guest out," I demand of the room. "Now!"

Solaris tenses at my side. Neither of the guards make a move to answer. Instead, it's my father who walks into my room and stand before me. He crosses his arms, and I can see the disappointment in his eyes. The fury he's attempting to hold back in order to look at least civil in front of the men. Can't have the good Mayor O'Conner looking unreasonable after all.

"Gregory is dead," my father states, and my eyes drop down to Solaris. "Loretta is in charge now, and she wants Solaris and her mother off the property."

"No!" Sol shrieks and holds on to me tighter.

"Actually, she can. Until there's a will reading, you are not allowed on the James' property," my father tells her and motions for the guards to take her.

Both guards advance on us and I step back, taking Solaris with me. They can't have her. I won't let them. My nostrils flare a little bit as I continue moving backwards. I will not fail her. Not again.

"Si?" she whispers into my bare back.

I don't say anything, just keep my eyes trained on the two men. I'll be damned if I let them hurt her. She has every right to remain on this property. It belonged to her father. Not Loretta and I'm not letting two beefed up wannabe jocks lay a finger on my girl.

"Back down, Silas," my father says, and my eyes cut to the bastard for a mere moment.

I notice my mistake right away as one of the guards grabs me and pulls me away from Sol. My fist fly at his face without thought, but the other guy already has a hold on Sol. She cries out and I whirl around to her. The guard at my back arm wraps around my neck and pulls me in the opposite direction of Solaris.

"Silas!" Solaris screams out as the guard in front of us hauls her up, her back to his front, his hold relentless.

I slam my head into the man's nose holding me, but his grip on my neck doesn't loosen. I throw the guard, and I back up against a wall, but he still doesn't let me go. Instead, I feel his free hand reach for something. Pain like no other shoots through my body, my muscles contracting as I go down. The guard tases me again, and I cry out at what feels like a ton of volts going through me.

"Silas!" Solaris screams again, but my body won't move. The security guard restraining me pulls my arms back and cool metal wraps around my wrists. I watch, a bit disoriented as Sol fights the other guards hold. She falls to the floor, and I guess the man is fed up with her fight because he grabs her by the ankle and drags her across the carpeted floor. The entire time she's trying to get loose.

I go to stand, to follow, but end up hunched over, vomiting nothing onto the carpet. Someone reaches for me, and I jerk out of their hold, my vision swimming in the process.

"You might want to see this, darling." My body tenses at the voice, and I try to focus enough to see Loretta.

She grabs hold of my arm, pulling me up right. I rub my eyes until my vision is clear again. Loretta is saying something, but all I can hear is the cries of Solaris. I rush over towards my bedroom door and just make out Solaris' hands as they disappear from the pool house's door. I rush towards it but am stopped my Loretta's claws digging into my forearm.

"Not so fast," she purrs at me. "If you make another move to stop what's about to happen, the little brat will pay. Do you hear me?"

I force my eyes away from the door the guard just dragged Solaris through and to Loretta. "Why are you doing this?"

Loretta shrugs. "I could always just have her mother removed and leave her with Cruise. Which do you prefer? I think I'm being generous."

I stare at Loretta for a long time. Gregory said she would do this the moment he was no longer in the picture. I guess he really did know his sister. That doesn't stop the ache blooming in my chest. And it doesn't mean I have to like the options at hand. I don't want Solaris going anywhere I can't follow, but I don't want her here either. The best thing to do is to let her go. To let her grow up and then go to her. I know that. I know that like I know Loretta is only out for herself.

"So what is it going to be: hand her to Cruise or watch as I toss her and her mother off my property?" Loretta questions.

My hands clench at my back and my lips curl into a grimace at Loretta. She's lucky that guard put cuffs on me. "You are a wicked woman."

"Choose her destiny," Loretta commands. "Set her free or keep her trapped."

I close my eyes and inhale, my eyes becoming heavy. I let out the breath and square my shoulders the best I can before meeting Loretta's gaze. She already knows what I'm going to choose. I can see in the smirk playing at her lips and the glee in her eyes. This woman really is the vilest person I have ever met, and I've met a ton of them since that record deal.

"Get her away from here," I choke out, a single tear escaping the confines of my eyes.

Loretta's smirk turns into a full-blown grin. "As you wish, darling. The family is waiting their exit."

We walk out of my pool house, and I immediately tense at the sounds of Solaris' cries in the distance. Loretta loops her arm through my elbow, and we walk all the way to the main manor, each wail from Sol a dagger to my already shredded soul. As we come to a stop in front of the manor, I take in everyone standing on the steps. All the maids, the butler, Lena, my father, and Cruise. Lena is the only one that looks thrown back by Solaris being dragged across the cobblestone path to a rusting car. When the door to the car opens, Elizabeth rushes out and over to her daughter.

"Let go of her!" she shouts at the man.

He listens and drops a shaking Sol next to her mother. Loretta lets go of my forearm and goes over to where the two of them stand.

Ice runs the length of my spine as Elizabeth scurries to her feet, hauling Solaris up with her. She shoves her daughter behind her back just as Loretta comes to a stop in front of them. My eyes take in the car at their backs, and I frown at the rust patches all over the car and the eroded hole on the bumper. I suppose Elizabeth must have owned it before Solaris' birth, meaning before Gregory. Since I've been here, every member of this family has always had plentiful. Neither one of them would be seen driving something so humble, but I suppose this is the life I'm destined to watch Solaris live now. It's still better than this life.

From my position on the steps, I can clearly see Loretta's lips turn up into a smile. Solaris steps in front of her mother, glaring at her aunt. Her hand taps the outside of her thigh in a constant pace, but I don't even think she knows she's doing it.

Loretta's smile looks like this is the best Christmas she's had in a long time, even with her brother just dying. Solaris' eyes move past her aunt and over to where we all stand. I can only imagine what's running through her head right now as she takes us all in. I know what this looks like. Like its us against them. Like I'm betraying her by doing nothing. I frown and go to step forward, but my father grabs my hand, keeping me in place. Lena grabs my other hand, and my watchful gaze pulls away from Solaris and to my sister.

She's looking up at me with tears in her eyes, and I can't believe that I didn't think to check on her. As much as Sol means to me, Lena means just as much.

"What's happening?" Lena whispers for only my ear. "Why are they leaving?"

I bend down to her. "We'll talk about this later, but don't make a scene, okay."

She nods and I stand, Solaris recapturing my attention at once.

Loretta clasps her hands in front of herself and stands a little taller. "We are sorry to see you go," she says to Elizabeth, and then looks back at us as if we're all in on this. "Please know that we all really do care about you."

I scoff at Loretta's false words and feel shuffling beside me. I squeeze Lena's hand, not taking my eyes off the situation.

Elizabeth takes a menacing step in Loretta's direction. "If that was the truth, you wouldn't be doing this. What would Gregory think about it all?"

Loretta smiles as if they're indulging in small talk. "Well, my dear brother, may he rest in peace, is no longer with us. And if he would have listened to me in the beginning and not broken tradition, no one would be in this atrocious situation."

"And your darling niece?" Elizabeth hisses at her. I can practically hear the venom in the woman's tone. And she has every right to be upset. Gregory hasn't even been cold a day and Loretta is doing this. And on Christmas no less. She could have at least waited until a memorial or something. Let them grieve their husband and father. Let them have the holiday with the only people they've been around for a while.

My hand roams down to the little box in my pocket. Shit, I still haven't given Solaris her Christmas gift. And now is not the time.

Loretta tilts her head to the side and says aloud for us all to here. "There is no proof this child belongs to my brother. You guys were only locked away in that cabin for a week, and you were pregnant so soon after. This child could be anyone's for all we know."

My eyes widen at her statement. After learning that Gregory is actually Lena's father and that the girls are sisters, I can't unsee just how similar they are. Anyone who can't see the family resemblance, even with Solaris being multiracial, is crazy. Loretta's whole statement is bullshit. We all know it.

Elizabeth's eyes narrow on Loretta and then they drop to her daughter. Her shoulders drop and I see the moment Elizabeth's resolve breaks. "Let's go."

Solaris jerks around to her mother. "What? This is our home!" she shrieks and I wince at the pain lacing her words.

God, I wish I could do something.

Hold her.

Hug her.

Comfort her.

Anything is better than watching this train wreck happen.

"No, it is not!" Loretta shouts, and Solaris looks over her shoulder at her aunt. "You two were simply borrowing time and space. Now, leave before I have my security drag you through the gates."

"It's the middle of the night! I have no clothes!" Solaris screams back at Loretta, and I'm just now noticing that she's still in her underwear and tank top.

"You don't have to tell us again," Elizabeth says and grabs hold of Solaris, pulling her away from Loretta.

Solaris fights her mother's hold, breaking away and racing over towards me. She stops and glances between Lena and me. "Do something."

My hand tightens around Lena, using her for strength. I shake my head at Sol. "Just go."

You'll be safer.

She stares up at me, eyes wide and mouth slightly ajar. She looks like I just crushed her, and I know I did. Solaris takes a hesitant step away from me and then another and another. I search the defeated look on her face, begging her with my own eyes to see that I'm saving her. That I'm doing this for her. But she can't see that. Her eyes drop from mine and she slides into the old car. Elizabeth closes the door and rushes over to the driver's side. The car pops to life, and I watch as they slowly drive off.

I bite down on the inside of my jaw and push back all emotions tied to Solaris. This is better. Not feeling is better. She won't be constantly abused anymore, and that thought alone is the only thing keeping me in place.

Besides, six years isn't long to wait.

And when these six years are over, these people will regret their actions.

Twenty-Nine

Solaris

The sun is just beginning its descent when I find myself standing at the edge of the vast, manicured lawn, staring blankly at the distant barn. A day has passed since I walked in on Loretta and Silas, the twisted scene replaying endlessly in my mind. The anger that surged through me then has only grown, festering and morphing into something darker and more consuming.

The chill of mid-November cuts through my jacket, but it does little to numb the pain in my chest. The crisp, cold air carries the scent of decaying leaves and distant wood smoke, mingling with the rage that gnaws at my insides. Carving my name into Silas' flesh was a futile attempt to purge the anger, but it did little to quell the storm raging within me. If anything, it only intensified my need for vengeance, my desire to make him suffer like he made me when I walked in on him fucking that woman.

I take a deep breath, the evening air filling my lungs with a sharp bite. My steps are measured, deliberate, as I make my way to the barn. Each step echoes with the weight of my decision, a decision that feels as inevitable as the setting sun.

The barn door creaks as I push it open, the interior cool and dim. The scent of hay and old wood greets me as I walk with purpose, my eyes scanning the shelves until they land on the metal canister tucked away in the corner. It's old, dented, and to my luck, filled with gasoline.

I grab the canister, its weight heavy in my hand, and turn to leave the barn. My heart pounds in my chest, a wild, erratic rhythm that matches the tumultuous thoughts swirling in my mind. The pool house is a short walk from the barn.

As I approach the pool house, the canister swinging at myside, a strange sense of calm settle over me. The decision has been made, the course set. There is no turning back now. I reach the pool house and pause, taking a moment to steady my breathing and collect my thoughts.

Memories of Silas flood my mind, each one a sharp, painful reminder of his betrayal. He deserves this and so much more. He didn't have to come back into my life and lie. He didn't have to pretend we were something we weren't when he was fucking Loretta this entire time. Although he has told me time and time again since yesterday that I'm reading the situation wrong, I don't see how I can be.

All I know is that his promises have been empty, his word shallow. And no matter how many times the tears leak from my eyes, I can't unsee Loretta and him, their bodies entwined in a grotesque display of lust and pleasure.

I open the canister, the pungent smell of gasoline filling the air as I begin to pour its contents around the pool house. The liquid soaks into the wooden exterior, spreading quickly and efficiently. I move with a mechanical precision, my mind numb to everything but the task at hand. When the canister is empty, I toss it aside and reach into my pocket, pulling out a box of matches.

My hands tremble slightly as I strike the match, the small flame flickering to life. I watch it dance for a moment, mesmerized by its simplicity, its power. Then, with a flick of my wrist, I toss the match onto the gasoline-soaked building. The flames erupt instantly, a fierce, hungry blaze that quickly engulfs the pool house.

I step back, the heat of the fire searing my skin, but I feel nothing. My eyes are fixed on the flames, their chaotic dance mirroring the turmoil within me. The pool house burns brightly, the fire consuming everything in its path, just as my anger consumes me.

A sudden noise snaps me out of my trance. I turn to see Silas running from the manor, his face a mask of shock and fear. He comes to a halt a few feet away, his eyes locking onto mine. For a moment, time seems to stand still. The world around us fades into the background, leaving only the two of us and the raging inferno between us.

I reach into my pocket, pulling out a sucker. Unwrapping it slowly, I place it in my mouth, the sweet taste full of flavor. I suck on the BlowPop, my gaze never leaving Silas'. His eyes are wide, a mix of disbelief and horror.

"Solaris, what have you done?" he shouts, his voice barely audible over the roar of the flames.

I don't respond. Words feel meaningless, empty. Instead, I simply stare at him, letting the fire speak for me. It roars and crackles, a testament to the destruction I am capable of, the lengths I am willing to go to exact my revenge.

Silas takes a step forward, then another, his eyes pleading. "Please, Solaris, don't do this. We can fix this. We can make things right."

I shake my head slowly, the sucker moving with the motion. There is no fixing this. There is no going back.

I lower the lollipop. "You lied to me. You fucked her!"

Silas closes the distance between us, grabbing hold of my free hand. "Sol, I'm sorry, but you know I had no choice."

I shove him away from me. "There's always a choice, Silas! And you made yours."

He shakes his head at me, but I step back. Away from the man that stole my heart as a child. Away from the guy who was my lover and best friend.

The flames continue to climb, the heat intensifying with each passing second. The pool house is a blazing inferno now, the fire reaching up towards the sky as if trying to escape its earthly confines. Silas stands helplessly, his eyes reflecting the flames as he watches his refuge burn to the ground.

A part of me wants to scream, to let out the rage and pain that threatens to consume me. But I hold it in, my resolve hardening with each passing second.

"Look what you made me do," I point to the engulfed building, my voice cold and detached. "You turned me into this. You're just like the rest of them."

Silas flinches as if I've struck him, his eyes widening with hurt and realization. He opens his mouth to speak, but no words come out. Instead, he takes hold of my hand again and pulls me close. I let him; there's nothing more he can do or say to hurt me. Nothing at all.

"If this is what you need, then you can burn it all down. I will still be here, Sol. Because you belong to me," he says with so much conviction in his voice that I almost believe him. "You are mine. And I am yours. We may be fucked up right now, but that truth is one thing you can't set fire to."

His mouth slams down on mine before I can respond, and my fingers tighten around the lollipop stick. I squeeze my eyes shut and try not to be affected by this. It's just a kiss. It doesn't matter. Nothing he does matters anymore.

When I don't make a move to kiss him back, Silas pulls back, hurt painting his features. "Sol, please. I love you."

My hands tremble at my side, my posture stiffening. My body turns feverish, but that could be from the flames. I shove Silas hard, but he stands his ground. I shove him again and again and again. He has no right to utter those words to me. No right at all.

"I hate you!" I scream at him, my chest heaving and ears ringing. "I hate you! I hate you! I-I hate you!"

My voice cracks on the last one.

He shakes his head and grips the back of my head, his fingers tangling in the curls at my nape. "No you don't. That's why this hurts so much. That's why I'm still here. Standing. Touching you. Because the one thing we both know, if you hated me, I wouldn't be capable of either of those things."

A tear slips from my eyes at his words and I wipe it away. Silas and I stare at each other for a long time, neither one of us seeming affected by the flames burning down his pool house. But when he goes to reach for me again, I turn away from him, bringing the lollipop back to my mouth.

"Sol!" he calls after me and I halt on instinct. "You can walk away all you want, baby, but trust me when I tell you, this isn't over."

The anger I've been feeling since catching him with my aunt, seems to fade a tiny bit at his words, more tears gliding down my cheeks. I don't turn back to him though. I don't acknowledge that his declaration has any influence on my heart. Instead, I walk back to the manor. Each step feels heavy, the weight of my actions settling on my shoulders. But there is also a strange sense of liberation, a freedom that comes from embracing the darkness within me.

Because we are one.

I ignore the voice, already coming to that same conclusion.

As I walk, the memories of the past day play in my mind, each one a painful reminder of the betrayal I have suffered. And while I know it's not healthy to keep focusing on that, it's the only thing keeping me from running back to him. The only thing keeping me from crumbling into a thousand pieces. And right now, I can't afford to break. There is still so much to do, so many wrongs to right.

I reach the manor and pause at the entrance, taking a deep breath. The house looms before me, a silent witness to the events that have unfolded. As I step inside, the scent of Mrs. Louis' potpourri greets me, mingling with the faint smell of smoke that clings to my clothes. The manor is quiet, the silence almost oppressive. I walk through the halls, my footsteps echoing softly.

I reach my room and close the door behind me, leaning against it for a moment. I wipe away the remnants of tears. The anger and hurt simmers within me, but now there is something else. A sense of clarity, a focus that I haven't felt in a long time.

Silas has betrayed me, and for that, he will pay. But he isn't the only one. It's time for Loretta to meet the same fate. For far too long, she's had a controlling presence over this family. Ever since my father died, everyone has cowered to her. Even Lena. It's time to finally put her in her place. And I will make sure she suffers just like me. Just like my mom did when her little hit man pulled the trigger.

I cross the room to my desk and pull out a piece of paper. Sitting down, I begin to write, my pen moving swiftly across the page. Each name, each action, each plan flows from my mind to the paper, a detailed blueprint of the revenge I will exact.

I am done being a victim. I am done being a pawn in someone else's game. I let Silas' distract me from the main reason I decided to come back here to the estate, but no more. I will be the one pulling the strings, the one orchestrating the downfall of the James' name.

And it will start with Silas. The flames of the pool house are only the beginning. He doesn't get to toy with me—tell me he loves me—and crush my heart like it's sand beneath his feet. No, there is so much more to come to him. He might had been he piper once upon a time, but now I have the flute. Now, he's going to be the puppet on the string, and he's going to dance until he breaks.

Just. Like. Me.

I finish writing and sit back, staring at the plans in front of me. Getting up from my desk, I walk out onto the balcony. Sirens in the background catch my attention, a grin stretching across my face as a sense of déjà vu encompasses me. The sun has set, the night shrouding the manor in darkness. But I can still see the faint glow of the flames in the distance. Memories of the night they said I set Loretta's house on fire flash through my mind, and I take a deep breath, the cool night air filling my lungs.

"We did it," I mumble to the ever present voice in my head. "We set that fire too."

It's about time you remembered who we are.

I wrap my arms around me and watch as the fire truck rushes down the path to what remains of Silas' house. There is no turning back now. The path I have chosen is dark, but it is mine. And I will walk it with my head held high, no matter the cost.

And as I stand here, looking out into the night, I know one thing for certain:

There's nothing sweeter than revenge.

Author's Note

If you are reading this, you made it to the end of the book! And in that case, I'm thrilled. *Nothing Sweeter* has been in the works for nearly a decade now. The character of Solaris was created back in 2015 after the passing of my father as a way to cope with the betrayal I felt from my own family. Originally, I was going to do nothing with her. But then 2019 hit and for reasons I am not going to state here, I was always angry and hurt. Solaris was my outlet. I wrote the first nine chapters of her story and then put her away again.

I struggled so much with what to do with this character. All I knew was that I wanted her to turn out to be the villain because I felt like my family had villainized my sister and me. But as a romance reader myself, I don't want to see my heroine as a villain. Heroines should be sweet, kind, and docile. We enjoy seeing them blossom into their own and take control of their lives.

And while Solaris is all those things, she was still hiding parts of herself. And those parts aren't usually favorable to the masses.

No one wants to read a romance about a teenage girl wanting to kill her family. Sounds more like a horror story. On top of that, people get touchy when mental health is involved. More particularly when there are negative connotations tied to mental health. Including that scared me the most. But what people don't realize is that mental health can't always be depicted with hearts and flowers or made to sound less severe. That's coming from someone who does suffer from mental health issues. While Solaris' issues are more fictitious, they are not out of the realm of possibility.

So, with all of that, I shelved Solaris' story again and didn't come back to it until May 2023. By then, I had let go of *most* of my hurt and anger so that I could look at this character more objectively.

And you know what? I FINISHED THE BOOOOOK!
Happy dance

I know this book isn't going to be everyone's cup of tea. In fact, I'm pretty sure many people are going to DNF it because of the triggering topics. However, I'm finally happy with this book. It has taught me so much about dealing with grief and hurt and betrayal, and while I haven't stabbed someone to death with a pair of scissors, it has been a great outlet. I hope that someone else who is struggling will also find solace in the fact that they are not alone and that it is perfectly fine to feel that way.

I mean, I'm not the only person whose family betrayed them after their father died, right?

Anyway, thank you for reading this book. I hope you were able to take something away from this first part. I am truly beside myself that this book has finally made its way into your hand.

T. Marie Alexander

Acknowledgements

Normally, this part is hard for me; I never know who to thank.

However, it's easy this time around. I only have a few people to thank for helping me.

The Heart Breathing Writing Community, you all are the best. This book wouldn't have been possible without all the encouragement and writing sessions.

Two, my beta readers, you know who you are. Thank you for all the feedback. Many of you made me think really hard about some elements of the story, and I tried my best to acknowledge your concerns and fix them. Some of you were invaluable. You even informed me of things I was unaware of and I deeply, deeply thank you.

Thirdly, I would like to thank my husband and Aunt Dorothy for pushing me to write out of my comfort zone. I normally don't write full-blown sex scenes, but they made me attempt it for this book and I'm happy with how they turned out. I can only get better.

Bloggers and ARC readers, you all are such an integral part of the process. Thank you for taking the time out of your schedule to mingle with these characters and spread the word.

And finally, to my readers, YOU THE BEST!!!!! You are the reason I return book after book and continue on this writing journey. You encourage me. You teach me. Thank you sooooo much for following me along this ride. I am honored that you chose to read my words and dive into my worlds. Thank you for allowing me to write what I feel. I will always give you 100 percent.

About the Author

Plagued with an overactive imagination, T. Marie Alexander spends her free time reading, writing, and critiquing movies. Her dream is to travel the world while building an empire. She loves writing stories with flawed characters going through realistic, everyday situations that most people feel more comfortable glossing over. Her hope is that her characters might help someone heal and feel seen.

Born and raised in Arkansas, she is married to a man who gets on her ever-flipping nerve but keeps her on her toes. She loves baking and sharing her treats with family and friends.

Website: tmariealexander.com
Facebook: authortmariealexander
Instagram: @authortmariealexander
TikTok: @authortmariealexander